I0785545

TRUTH WINS

Book Three of the Truth Series

By

LACEY DANCER

Letter from Lacey

Welcome back to Felicity's world, the everchanging landscape of danger, lies, betrayal and truth. Felicity's birth as a character occurred in, of all things, a romance. Felicity saved Lucy, the heroine and her lover, Alex. Then Felicity thwarted the villain who was involved in sex trafficking before he could implicate Lucy in his crimes.

True to Felicity's beginning, every character who has stepped into her world of the Farm and the Ranch of Skye/Sea, has arrived with a back story that just demands attention. Truth Wins is no exception.

In my world, better known as reality, Taranda was the most beautiful black woman I have ever met. We bonded over a Christmas jewelry sale. I do love real gem stones, the colors, the cuts and the designs. Taranda was manning the counter that day. I was hot on the trail of a tanzanite ring. Taranda's husky voice offering to help me and her smile got my full attention. Her name tag with the unusual name of Taranda was more interesting than even the ring in my size which I did buy.

One thing about writers, we are not shy about asking questions. I just had to know the origin of her name. Her mother was a major fan of Gone with the Wind. Tara from the movie became Taranda. I asked Taranda if she would mind if I used her name in a book. She visibly pleased and said I could. I'm not sure she really believed me about creating a story around her name, but here it is.

Like most of the group that Felicity has gathered, Taranda's background is deep, dark and painful. Taranda is not only a survivor but she has planted her feet, demanded that the world she knows take her on. She won't be overlooked or undervalued.

Been there! Done that!

"I am Taranda! Not 22!"

Interested to see what that means? You'll find the answers when you read Truth Wins. I hope you are as touched by Taranda's back story as I was. I hope you enjoy her strength and her grit as she stands with Felicity and company. If she knocks a certain snarky chef on his butt, well, he deserves it. Wait until you see how that turns out.

I hope you enjoy Felicity's latest mission. It was a challenge to write because this one is a maze filled with more questions than answers.

I love to hear from all of you. You can reach me on any one of the sites listed in the About the Author Section. All replies are created by me personally. If I am a little slow, know it is because some character is holding me hostage until I finish his or her scene. No matter how demanding they are, I always manage to surface sometime.

Lacey Dancer

TABLE OF CONTENTS

PROLOGUE

The Beginning

Felicity slid out of the limo, allowing the long length of her right thigh to show for the security cameras. Black was the color of the day. Blood spatter, if it came to that, didn't show. A breast displaying blouse with only two buttons fastened and a skin snug skirt with a right thigh slit meant that any observant eyes would be on her body and not looking for any security breaches.

Her driver stood respectfully beside her, his handle on the door, his eyes only on hers as he awaited his next order.

Today, she was Cat Moran. Brunette, six feet tall including six-inch heels. A man's walking wet dream with a cold heart. She preyed on children, any color, either gender and two age groups, the six to ten crowd and the eleven to fifteen group. Her known clientele with extreme perversions paid lavishly for the product she sold.

Her carefully constructed persona was much more diversified than the slice of rotten human meat who did business out of the heavily secured building in front of her. Mitchell was only interested in kiddies, starting at age five. Anything, his kiddie whores were things to him, was sold when it reached its shelf life of twelve. He had been in business one day too long.

Today was his last day of stealing children and handing them over to Roscoe to educate them in their new life. It had taken three months to build her persona and set these next two hours into motion.

Her mission was simple as her assignments rarely were. Mitchell was the target. His kiddie porn business which was getting set to go overseas was over. He had grown too bold, too visible to certain parties to be allowed to live.

No mention was made of the used up young girls she was here to buy. Their disposition was up to her. To the man behind the governmental desk, her current self-proclaimed boss, they were simply a way into Mitchell's office. An excuse at best. Collateral damage at worst.

He hadn't blinked an eye when he had said, "Kill the bastard. He dies and the organization he has built will collapse. Don't leave any witnesses."

Facts in hand, she had formed her strategy, set up her assets and her background. The final plan wasn't exactly what her boss wanted but there was nothing he could do to stop her. He would get what he had ordered. In the end, she knew damn well that was all that mattered to him.

Felicity knew she had a reputation for not following orders to the letter on occasion. Her boss hated her critical thinking but since she had always achieved his desired result, he confined his displeasure to words and hard eyed looks he probably practiced in front of a mirror since he had never set foot in the field.

She was too valuable an asset to fire. She could be anyone she chose. She worked alone and had eight years in a field where men and women were old, seasoned veterans at five. Most didn't live to see eight years of service. Those who did existed on the edge of burn out.

She wasn't near burn out but she was already on the road to walking away from the life and lives she had led. She had seen too many wasted deaths, too many lies, too many betrayals.

"Keep the motor running," she murmured to her driver. "I won't be long."

She stood in the row with four other girls. She was the oldest. Her name was Taranda, a fact that she repeated to herself daily. To them, her owner, her jailer she was number 22. The others in line with her were twelve years old to her fourteen.

She hated to the last cell in her body the man who sat at the desk as though he was a high-powered executive instead of the owner of a string of kiddie brothels. Soft voice, soft hands and words that dealt in pain and death. He raked in the money he made selling her body and others like her.

Such a polite word, brothel. It didn't begin to describe the hell and the horror of boys and girls ranging in ages from five to puberty. Once a girl got breasts, she was sold to the highest bidder. She didn't know when or by what standards the boys were measured as being too old for the filthy men and, sometimes, women who preyed on children.

She had been kidnapped, brought into the life of sex for hire just before her ninth birthday. She hadn't been a child since the night she had been thrust into the bowels of hell by the other man who was in the sound proofed room. That man wore a knife on his hip, the same knife that had given her the scar that marred the left side of her face from lip to cheek.

As much as she hated Jonathan Mitchell, the bastard who owned her, that emotion didn't come close to the feelings she had for Roscoe. If he had a last name, she didn't know it.

She wanted him dead in the most agonizing way possible.

The night he had repeatedly raped her had been the longest and most painful of her life. It had taken her a full month to heal enough to start earning her keep. Now, she waited to be sold.

She watched Mitchell without lifting her head or showing any sign she cared where she was or what was going on around her. She had developed that talent, that ability to divorce herself from anything or anyone to survive more than just the horror of her daily life.

She knew how to endure hideous pain without screaming. She knew how to pretend to be anyone or anything for those who paid money for the use of her body. She could make the sounds some bastard ramming into her needed, the groans of pleasure, the cries of pain at the first strike of a hand, belt or whip so that the beatings some needed to get off were not as intense as what she could have and had suffered before she had learned to take herself somewhere else.

She was Taranda. She was not number 22. She would find a way to escape. Her new owner might just be the way. She had to be alert, ready.

One chance that was all she needed. One chance. And if that bastard Roscoe turned his back for one second, gave her one opening, she would gut him from hip to hip and stand in his blood.

She had dreamed of his death, felt in that dream his blood flowing over her black skin, scarlet rivers of death. She felt the rage rise in her and fought to control it. Those girls who fought, who whined, who did anything to call attention to themselves were drugged. She had learned that before she reached her tenth birthday. Some were even given to Roscoe for taming. Those girls were never seen again.

Just one chance she promised herself as she won the battle with her rage.

The door opened across the room and a woman strolled in. Taranda watched her every move. The newcomer hadn't so much as glanced at her or the other girls. She moved silently to the desk, stopping a foot from the chair in front of it.

She didn't take a seat. She could have been a model, with her glossy dark brown hair, every strand in place. The bitch. Her scarlet nails were polished to match the toenails that peeked out of her needle-sharp black heels. Everything about her black clad figure spoke of money and power. There was no expression on her face as she looked at Mitchell.

"You're early." Mitchell frowned at her empty hands. "I don't see my money."

"I haven't inspected the merchandise."

Taranda could hear the temper in Mitchell's voice. She could hear no emotion in the woman's, no reaction at all on her face. Taranda controlled a shiver. The room felt colder somehow. The buyer didn't seem to know how dangerous her owner was when he was angry.

"Do it."

The woman nodded once and turned toward them. Taranda was at the end of the line so she had time to watch the way that the buyer looked at each them. When she stopped in front of the second girl, she turned her around to look at her back. The welts on the white skin were clearly visible, some of the marks with dried blood on them.

The fools hadn't bothered to even clean her after her last client Taranda thought with a silent internal sneer.

She stopped in front of the next and did the same. When it was her turn, Taranda wanted to move so that the woman didn't touch her but she didn't dare. She would betray how much attention she was paying. The woman's hands on her shoulders were light, almost gentle as she positioned her as she had the other four.

Taranda knew she would see the old and new scars that the excuse of the cotton slip she wore did little to hide. Wasn't the slash on her face enough?

When she obeyed the pressure on her shoulder to face front again, she didn't look down fast enough. For a split second she was staring into eyes so cold and calm she almost shivered in spite of her control.

The buyer turned from her and strolled back to the

desk. "We have a deal."

Taranda found she couldn't stop watching the woman as she reached casually into her handbag. Her hand came out in a blur of motion.

Suddenly, Mitchell made a wet sounding groan. Blood spurted from his throat as his hands came up as though to stop the flow.

Taranda barely had time to blink as the woman pivoted and made another move. Her hand was no longer empty. A flash of silver sliced through the air as Roscoe reached for his gun.

Taranda stared as a knife buried itself to the hilt in his gut. She watched him fold into himself as he hit the floor. Red spilled onto the wood, pooling around his body.

She stepped forward, drawn by the guttural sounds that Roscoe was making, the sounds she had heard in her dreams for years. His fingers clutched at the knife as though he was trying to holding it in place.

She started to reach down for the hilt. He was dying. She wanted her hand on the weapon when he did. She had seen her fingers gripping the knife. She needed to feel him die in pain. His harsh breathing was the music she had longed to hear. His face contorted in agony pleasing her in ways she had never known not even in her dreams of vengeance.

Suddenly, the woman was in front of her. She caught

her wrist before she could touch the knife she wanted to hold so badly.

"You can't. If you have blood on you, I won't be able to get you past the guards." The words were soft but clear and brooked no argument. Her hold was like a chain.

Taranda angled her head enough to still watch Roscoe out of the corner of her eye. She couldn't bear to miss a second of his pain. She looked at the woman who had gutted him. The knowledge in the calm eyes holding hers caught her attention as nothing else could have.

This stranger knew what Roscoe had done to her. She didn't know how she knew but this woman understood what she wanted, needed so badly.

"You're getting us out of here?"

Was it possible? Could it be true?

How could she believe this stranger? How much she wanted to believe. Anywhere, even another brothel had to be better than here.

Felicity caught the flicker of hope in her eyes. This girl wasn't drugged as the others. There was intelligence and strength in her cat amber eyes. Rage. For the moment, a desperate need to kill.

She was a complication. The four other girls in the line with her hadn't even changed expression with the bloody scene in front of them. Only this child had seen, understood, wanted, needed to feel the pain and touch the blood of Mitchell's enforcer. That kind of hate had been burned into her in hell.

"Yes. We're escaping."

"Who are you?"

"No time now. We have to go. I've completed the deal and we are walking out of here. I need you to keep on pretending you're like the others so that we can get past the guards. Can you do that?"

Felicity didn't want to leave her but she would if she couldn't get the girl's co-operation. Live or die were the stakes for all of them.

Taranda nodded. She was getting her chance to escape. Mitchell was dead. She studied Roscoe. His face was white, his eyes closed, his breathing harsh in the almost silent room.

"He'll die? You promise."

"Yes. The guards won't check for a while. He'll bleed out before we get out of the building."

Taranda looked into those calm eyes. The voice told her nothing. It held no emotion. She didn't trust, had lost the ability to believe in anything or anyone. Something about the woman was demanding she believe.

Could freedom be this close? All she needed was one chance. This was the first step out of hell.

"I'll help," Taranda offered slowly.

Felicity nodded. She turned to urge the girls to the door, lining them up so that the guards outside would not be able to see in the room. She gave simple commands and got exactly what she asked for from each drugged child. The black girl seemed to understand what she was doing and helped get everyone ready to leave.

"We have to move fast without looking like we are in a hurry."

"They'll do what you want," Taranda said.

If this woman was going to get them out of hell, she was going to do everything she could to make it happen. When the woman nodded, she caught the hand of the girl in front. Taranda knew her a little. The others would follow.

Felicity reached past her and opened the door then spoke behind her as though she was responding to something that Mitchell said.

Taranda stepped through the door, pulling the girl with her. She made sure she didn't make eye contact with the guard. The others followed with their rescuer bringing up the rear.

Taranda counted every step down the long hall with no doors. Then they were outside, stepping into the sunlight. A limo pulled up and a man in a uniform got out to open the rear door.

"Get in."

Taranda obeyed the snap in the command from the man and the press of the girls behind her. In seconds, the door shut and the man was in the front seat sliding the limo into traffic.

"We are going to be changing vehicles in a few minutes. We need to move fast."

"You're not the police."

The woman shook her head. "What's your name?"

"Taranda."

"Theirs?"

"I don't know. We had numbers."

"Yours?"

"Twenty-two."

"How old are you?"

"Fourteen, I think. I'm old. He tried to sell me twice but no one wanted me with this scar."

She didn't touch the mark that Roscoe had made that night when she had nearly bitten his damn dick off. She hadn't meant to but the bastard had shoved it in her mouth and she had almost choked on it. She was in agony from the reflexive action. She still remembered the taste of his blood on her tongue.

Felicity studied the mark for a minute. The girl was beautiful, a real stunner even with the scar. Without it, she could have been sold singly for considerably more than she had been priced in a group of hard used girls.

"The others?"

"I'm not sure." Taranda shrugged. "Usually anyone over twelve is sold. The pervs want kiddies not girls and boys." The bitter contempt in her voice was clear.

"That part of your life and theirs is over."

"Lady, you don't know shit. It ain't never over for us. You think we will forget?"

Felicity leaned forward just slightly. "You won't forget, not completely. You know that. You're a fighter. You figured out how to avoid being drugged into submission. You helped me get out of that hole with all five of you."

"I wanted to kill him. Instead, you got to gut him. I dreamed about watching a knife slide into him, watching the red gush out. I wanted it. I needed it and you got to do it." Anger she had been banking for years drove every word.

"He gave you that, didn't he?" Felicity gestured to her own unmarred cheek.

"Yes," Taranda hissed, rage was a lava flow of emotion in the single word. "That bastard raped me so many times in one night that I lost count. I begged to die and he laughed.

I bled and he laughed. He ripped me apart. When he couldn't get it up anymore, he used stuff on me. He tore me up inside. I don't ever have to worry about having children."

Tears stood in her eyes but they didn't fall. "Gutting

him wasn't enough."

"Nothing would have been enough."

Taranda stared into those calm eyes and read the truth in the quiet words. Suddenly, the anger, the pain and the bitterness hurt as much as what had happened to her that night and all the nights and days that followed.

"I am tired of hurting. Dying sounds better."

Felicity reached out and took her hand. "Dying isn't better. Living is. If you will let me, I'll help you see that."

Her hand was warm and strong. She couldn't remember a time, even before she had been taken when someone had touched her in just this way. Here was strength, here was honesty, here was caring.

"Why?"

"Because you matter."

"How can I? You don't know me."

"I know more than you think. You were brave back there. Look at them. You have been in that hell the longest and you are still fighting. They gave up. You didn't."

"Who are you?"

Felicity ignored the question. "Does my name really matter right now?"

Taranda frowned. But before she could answer, the limo pulled to a stop. In a few short minutes they were in a van and heading back the way they had come. The limo and driver continued in the direction they had been going. Now, the woman drove for hours, sometimes on highways, some on small roads.

Then there was a plane sitting on a narrow strip of black in the dark. The moon was shadowed by low lying clouds as the plane lifted into the night.

The woman asked no questions and even allowed her to sit in the front as the stars filled the windows. It was the most amazing feeling to see the sky spread out with nothing to stop the plane from going anywhere.

Freedom had a taste. It was clean air and the smell of leather so soft she had to stroke it. Freedom had a sound. The high-powered thrust of the engines of the jet taking her far away from pain without end and terror with no one to hear her screams.

"I want to learn to fly."

Felicity glanced at Taranda. There was the beginning of a smile on her face and a bright light in her dark eyes. She had a place for the four girls sitting listlessly in the rear of the plane.

She could send Taranda with them. Marie knew how to handle the victims, what they would need to recover, if recovery could be achieved, and to build a new life.

Taranda's will to survive, even her blood thirsty need for justice, appealed to Felicity. Here was intelligence.

Strength. Courage and vision in a girl barely a teen.

"Finish college. If you still want to learn to fly, you can train to be a pilot."

Taranda snorted out a sound that held mockery too old for one so young.

"I ain't got the money for college. That's just a dream."

Taranda knew what freedom felt like. It was the open sky in front of her. She didn't know how much money it would take but she would do anything, even work on her back, to fly.

"It's not a dream, Taranda. You helped me when I needed it. We might not have made it out of there without your help. I'll help you with college. Consider it payback."

Taranda turned her head sharply, looking away from the open sky to the face of the woman whose name she didn't know.

"Do you mean it?"

Could it be that simple? Was she lying? Could she trust her?

"I mean it."

Felicity had a place for this damaged girl. The two men who managed it for her would not be pleased with her new acquisition. Jonah especially would not appreciate Taranda. They would all have to live with her decision.

"I mean it. You have to study. You'll have chores and rules. I can promise you that you will never have to suffer rape again. No man or woman will lay hands like that on you again."

Taranda looked at her for a long moment, judging truth from lie. She wanted to believe. For the second time, in a long time, she needed to believe.

"I still don't know your name."

Felicity smiled faintly. She had had so many names that it made no difference to her what anyone called her. But it mattered to this child. Because it did, Felicity used the information as a goal and a promise to a girl who had nothing but the thought of revenge to help her survive.

"Does my name really matter right now?" she asked for the second time.

"I'll make you a deal. When you're eighteen and when you have a high school diploma in your hand, I'll tell you."

CHAPTER ONE

Present day

"I know you pick this damn goat trail just to aggravate me," Ace said as he eyed the beginning of the climb. It led to the top of the small mountain that was a mile from the back of Felicity's home.

She laughed softly. Ace might hate the trail but he also enjoyed pitting himself against the demands of the upward trek in the dark, especially when there was no moon like tonight. The man had a competitive streak as wide as he was tall.

"You lost the poker game."

Ace matched his stride to Felicity's. The woman had legs that began at her ears and ate up the ground as though they were crossing level terrain with not even a hint of an obstacle in sight. She also was as competitive as he was, in everything.

She was intelligent, canny, sneaky and one of the most creative lovers he had ever known. A spine of steel and a fighter who could kill as easily as disable.

"Only because you cheated better than I did."

"You started it."

He cursed when he heard the faintest snap of a twig beneath his boot. "I sound like an elephant plowing through brush."

He was less than a foot away from Felicity and he could barely tell she was breathing, then only because he was concentrating on catching her making the smallest sound. The woman moved like a ghost.

"You're not as noisy as you used to be," she murmured as she cocked her head. She caught a scent on her trail, a smell that was human not animal. She signaled her three dogs to form a perimeter. Alpha took the lead.

Ace didn't speak as he went to alert when the Dobermans fanned out. The trail should have been empty. No one, as far as he knew, in the compound used it but the two of them.

He checked his arm unit as Felicity scanned hers. The technology was worn by everyone at the Farm. The lightweight construction had a small screen, a navigation system, a map of the area as well as sensors to deactivate the various security fields that protected the compound.

To forget to slip the unit on in the morning was a big mistake. The security around the Farm was tight and every barrier, when tripped, was set to drop an intruder into unconsciousness.

Right now, the two tiny dots on the map display with the ID readouts were a surprise. Taranda was waiting in the darkness.

To have Jonah with her was even more curious. The older man communicated very little with anyone and then only in grunts if he was forced to converse. He hated people. His constant companion was his weapon. It was either in his hands sending death down its site or slung by a strap on his muscular shoulder.

Ace stopped beside Felicity. He cocked a brow in a silent question.

"It must be important," she said so quietly that her words barely reached him.

He nodded. That tone meant Felicity wanted to talk to the younger woman.

"I'll wait for you at the waterfall. I'll take the dogs."

She signaled the trio to obey Ace. She waited until the four shadows slipped into the trees, vanishing with very little sound. She took the faint trail on the right, the one that led back to the compound.

Ten years ago, on Taranda's official graduation from high school, she had given Taranda permission to train on her trail. The area was dangerous and only the best of the best was allowed to pit themselves against the trail. The trails were private and no one on the teams but Taranda had the right to use them without her permission.

The girl she had rescued had more guts and determination than anyone so young she had ever met. She set goals, often seemingly impossible ones and met them. One of those goals had been to work for Felicity.

The job, as she saw it and described it to Felicity when she asked for a chance to stay at the Ranch after she finished college, required maximum physical development and endurance. Skills in hand combat and weapons were critical.

But most of all, the long legged, stunner with the scar on her cheek was determined to learn to fly. She had stood in front of Felicity that day, fiercely intent on succeeding no matter how tough the training would be.

Felicity had watched her for four years while she had learned with home schooling, going from an almost illiterate kid to a poised and focused young woman. Felicity had watched Taranda drive herself to build a life out of the hellfire of her childhood.

Not once had Taranda taken the easy way, the safe way. So, she had given the girl a chance with a simple but demanding task. Make it to the top of her mountain in an hour and she could train with those who were the small crew of men and woman she was grooming for her own dream. The hike should have taken a reasonably skilled trekker a little under ninety minutes.

Taranda had managed the path in fifty-eight minutes. She had been winded and had clearly fallen more than once. She'd had scratches and cuts on her arms and hands. The fierce light of success in her dark amber eyes had demanded her reward.

Felicity had given Taranda the right to use her trail. Taranda had never intruded on Felicity's time on the path. Until tonight. This time, she wasn't alone.

She wondered at the inclusion of Jonah. He and Nelson had handled much of Taranda's initial training. In the early years of the creation of her dream of the Farm, she had still been actively involved with government work. She had often been away from the Ranch and mountain that eventually became the Farm for months. Only between assignments was she in residence.

Jonah and Nelson had houses on the Ranch. When they weren't on assignments, they managed her properties in her absence. She had met the two men when they were on the same operation. Both were ready to leave government work behind. Neither wanted the civilian life.

In the three weeks they had sloughed through a South American jungle together, she had discovered they were men like her father, patriots who had given their best to their country only to discover their training made returning to civilian life impossible.

She had just bought the three mountains and the ranch in the valley between. She had offered them a job. They had taken it on a temporary trial for both sides. They had been together for a year when Felicity had deposited Taranda on them and headed off on her next mission.

The advent of Taranda in all their lives had been a trial, an adventure and challenge for all of them. Jonah had once said, in a rare moment of word usage, that living with Taranda, trying to teach her anything was like tromping through a minefield in the dark and blindfolded with fools firing cannons aimed at their heads.

Felicity stopped in the shadows, close enough to hear their conversation.

"You're not my trainer any more, Jonah. My behavior is my responsibility."

"Your behavior is crap. If you don't think Felicity is aware of the way you and Benny are going at each other, you are brain dead. She knows why too. Hell, most of us do."

Felicity could hear the exasperation in Jonah's deep growl. She knew he was scowling and pacing. To her knowledge, Taranda was the only person but Nelson, his spotter and expert marksman in his own right, who could stir Jonah out of his hermit mode and into a conversation, of a sort.

"Tell him about it."

"What makes you think he doesn't know?" he demanded as he swung around to stalk back to stand in front of her.

"Maybe he is trying to tell you that, just because you seem to get every man you want, he doesn't have to follow the same path."

Taranda looked him over. Jonah was forty-seven to her twenty-eight. The man was still ripped in all the right places and he was a great lover. He was the first man she had willingly chosen to have in her bed.

He had taught her what it could be like being with a real man. She had learned everything she had ever known about pleasure in sex from him. He had shown her how to give pleasure as well as how to respond to the needs of her body.

"I got you," she pointed out with a knowing look she knew would piss him off. If she couldn't fight with Ben, Jonah was the next best target. He didn't back down. If she won, she would feel it.

Jonah growled one of his favorite obscenities, his blue eyes flashing with temper. "I was your tutor. That is what you asked of me and what I agreed to. I've lived more in the nineteen years between us, little girl, than you can even imagine. Benny has his own hell. He isn't safe for any woman and he knows it. Why do you think I have never taken a woman for my own?"

He turned from her to stare into the darkness. He couldn't see her or hear her but he could feel Felicity watching. He would have cursed the damn wrist units if it would have done any good.

"I told you this was crazy place to have this talk. We've got company and now I can dump the problem in her lap."

He glared at the woman who stepped out of the shadows. He respected her as he did no other female, including the smart ass sitting behind him.

"Why did you agree to it?" Felicity asked as she strolled into the tiny clearing that held three boulders and not much else.

Jonah wanted to ignore the question he was still asking himself. "Because I was stupid enough to let you dump her on me for a week. That damn week lasted a month that turned into years. Do something about her. She is giving me indigestion."

Rifle in hand, he stalked off, making no attempt to

mask his progress down the short trail to the compound.

Felicity sighed. Jonah's moods were legendary. She hoped he didn't run into anyone with a problem, at least for another day or two. Six foot one pissed off Jonah was not a safe opponent.

"What happened this time? Specifically?"

"I hadn't intended to intrude. I needed to be away from everyone for a while. I know you and Ace like to trek up here at night. That's why I stopped here, off the main trail. I wasn't paying attention. I didn't realize that Jonah had followed me."

Felicity studied Taranda for a long moment. "Even here, you know better than to lose your sense of awareness." When Taranda only nodded, she added, "I'm waiting for an answer."

"I acted like an ass. Benny and I got into it again." Taranda sighed roughly.

"The only good thing about this fight is that most of what I was thinking didn't come out of my mouth. I left the dining room before I said too much. You don't need to tell me that this thing with Benny and me needs to end."

"If you know that, why hasn't it?"

She did not like getting involved in any of her people's private lives. By the very nature of their work, the risks they took individually and as team members meant there was an inherent closeness that was critical for success and survival.

Situations that stirred up trouble no matter how small had to be resolved.

"I backed off twice. You know I did. Hell, I know when a man looks at a woman a certain way. He wants me but he hates the feeling. I thought it was my skin color versus his at first.

This is the twenty-first century. Black and white coming together shouldn't matter. But that isn't it. Then I figured, maybe it's the age thing. It's only thirteen damn years. It's not like it's fifty years or something that big. What is it about age between people in bed? What difference does that make?"

She could feel Taranda's frustration not just hear it. Benny wasn't a sunny personality on a good day but Taranda had a talent for lighting the fuse to the streak of nitro in him that she hadn't known he possessed.

"Taranda, you're asking the wrong person. Talk to Benny. More than that, stop fighting at meals. I'm with Jonah. You two are giving us all indigestion."

"Lately, I haven't started anything. I know what this place and the work you do means. I would never do anything to mess that up. I probably started the war but he has taken it over.

Jonah is trying to tell me he isn't interested. A man who isn't interested doesn't keep reconnecting even if it is over my 'picky eating'. I'm not a picky eater.

Right now, I can't think why I've been wanting to jump his bones for a damn year. Tried another man. Thought, hey sex. I needed to scratch an itch with someone I like. It should have worked. It didn't work worth a damn. I had to fake it."

She snapped to her feet and took a sharp turn around the small area. "I don't do fake sex anymore."

She stopped in front of Felicity. "It's not sex, or least not only sex. What do I do, Felicity? I can't talk to him about it because he won't let me close enough to try."

Felicity stared at the face she had known for fourteen years. She had seen it first when the look in her eyes was banked rage and a fierce determination to kill.

She had seen it elated when Taranda had gotten her college degree. She had seen it ecstatic when she had gotten her first pilot's license, then the helicopter she treated like the child she would never have. What Felicity had never seen was frustration and confusion.

"I don't know the answer, Taranda."

"You must. You and Ace are together. A team. Bonded. You don't wear rings but you are more married than anyone I have ever seen."

Felicity didn't remember a time when she could be surprised. She discovered she was surprised now. She had never examined what she and Ace had. Didn't need to. It worked in more ways than she had ever thought it would. That didn't mean her situation applied to Taranda and Benny.

"I don't have an answer. No two of us are the same even if I did have an answer. What I can do is arrange a meeting between you. Jonah has a point. Indigestion should not be on the menu at every meal.

That won't fix the feeling aspect, yours or his. That will be up to both of you. Whatever the answer, get it out of the dining room. The dojo at ten tomorrow. Find an answer that doesn't involve the rest of us in your verbal matches."

Taranda nodded. She was not happy with the answer but at least she would get a face to face in private. If Ben didn't want her, he would have to have the guts to tell her. Then it would be his loss. And hers, damn him.

"You want me to do what? Are you out of your mind? You pay their salaries. Hell, you pay mine. You talk to him." Ace sent waves splashing around them when he sat up with a jerk.

Felicity leaned back against the rock, lightly moving her hands in the water that still retained the heat of the sun.

The pool was only about six feet deep, surrounded by rocks and small boulders. There was a tiny waterfall feeding the pond, sending ripples above and below the surface. The night was a dark cloak around them. Her dogs were on guard and they were alone.

"Mad looks good on you, lover," she purred, enjoying his reaction.

There were distinct advantages to having a man she could trust in her life. Without him, she would have had to deal with Benny and Taranda. This way she could share the load.

"No, it doesn't." He eyed her suspiciously. "You were planning on talking to both of them tomorrow anyway. How did I get roped into this?"

"I could remind you I pay your salary." She ignored his expletive. "You brought it up."

"Yeah, like either one of us cares about that." He frowned.

"I agree with Taranda. Benny is interested and she certainly isn't hiding the fact that she is interested. Put them in a crisis situation and they work together like they are two bodies with one mind.

What's his problem? It isn't racial. If there is any of that here, I haven't seen any signs of it. We've got more colors and nationalities than the UN. Age? There's what, ten years between them? That's nothing."

Felicity stretched her legs out. "Benny's story is his own. It's about as bad as it gets."

Ace hadn't expected her to tell him Benny's background. She kept everyone's secrets including his own. That didn't mean he couldn't collect information himself.

"I know he spent five years living on the streets. He's clearly educated and he certainly knows what he is doing with almost any kind of weapon, including knives. I know combat training when I see it. I've heard him tirade in three different languages. He knows a lot more than a few handy curses."

Felicity studied him as he relaxed back on the boulder behind him, his legs brushing hers. Neither of them wore a stitch. There was sexual heat simmering in the silence but there was no demand.

The limited light suited him. The sharply chiseled lines of his face spoke more of strength than handsomeness. His eyes were evergreen dark, secretive more often than not. His black hair was straight, no hint of curl to soften anything about him.

"He does. He could head one of the teams and I would be glad of it."

They could discuss problems, plan missions, work out strategy and still know that they could turn to each other for that fire, that intimacy that locked out the world that was so often filled with pain and death. Moments like these were a gift she had never thought to have.

"Instead, he stays in his kitchen, when he isn't sniping

at Taranda, and steps into the breach when there is a crisis."

She nodded.

"He doesn't practice on the field."

Ace had seen Benny in action. The man didn't miss and he was as sharp as anyone on the teams. That meant he not only had skills but he kept them honed to a critical degree.

"He has his own range, just south of the training course. He and Jonah have competitions occasionally."

She tipped her head back to look up into the heart of the darkness.

"The situation between him and Taranda has to be settled one way or another. No more sparring at meals. The two of them will sit down and act like the adults they are and talk. The dojo will be free at ten tomorrow. I expect him to be there."

Ace knew he wasn't going to get out of talking to Benny. What the hell did he know about relationships and dating? The closest he had come to the first had almost gotten Mia killed and he hadn't really dated anyone in years. The rules had changed and he didn't know them anymore. He didn't want to learn them either.

"I'll deliver the message."

He didn't want to think about the mess any longer. Benny should deal with his own sex life and he was definitely letting him know he didn't intend for Benny's problems to interfere again with his own pleasures.

Ace leaned forward enough to grasp Felicity's ankle and tug her to him. "Do we have any more problems to sort out?"

She eased through the water, sliding up his body, fitting her length to his. He was as hard as the rocks around them but much more inviting. She positioned herself on him, joining their bodies as she watched his face. His hands settled on her hips, tightening possessively.

"Just one."

He laughed roughly as she clenched around him, tightening her muscles with a skill that few women in his experience possessed.

"Yours or mine?'

"Does it matter?" she asked as she brushed his lips with teasing bites.

He slid his fingers into her wet hair to hold her close. "No, not even a little bit."

"How do you feel about a nightcap?" Ace asked as he shed his briefs.

"I feel very friendly about it. Make it two fingers of bourbon for me."

Felicity walked naked to the closet. She rarely slept in

anything but her skin. Occasionally, she felt the need to indulge herself with something different in night wear. The added benefit of her whim was the interest a certain man had in her choices. He did like the feel her wrapped in silk.

She was in the mood to indulge them both. She had a small section of her closet filled with decadent lingerie. Tonight's selection was emerald green with splashes of peacock blue. The deep cut of the bodice showed off her breasts and the hip high cut to the slender length showcased the legs. The almost transparent fabric was a tease with every movement, a silent bit of foreplay guaranteed to please him as much as her.

Ace leaned against the door of her closet, a glass in each hand. Like Felicity, he preferred skin to cloth when he slept. He watched the silk slither down her lithe body, caressing and skimming over the elegant curves that made his palms itch.

She was in a mood. The sultry look in her eyes said she was imagining what the next hour would hold. The way she subtly licked her lips was a calculated move that matched the dare of her cocked brow.

"That smile is lethal."

Felicity knew how to use her eyes to reply. Her amusement deepened when she watched his body respond.

"You can handle it."

He offered her one of the tumblers then toasted her

before he took his first sip.

"I can," he agreed. "I haven't seen this one before."

He reached out to slide a finger down the edge of the silk that barely covered her right breast. Her nipple tightened, pushing against the fabric. His lips curved in satisfaction at the rapid response.

When she slithered into silk, satin or lace, he knew she was holding nothing in her thoughts but him. No Skye/Sea, no Farm, no Ranch, no problems. Only them. The two of them together. Nothing was more seductive to him than that concentration.

"It just arrived this morning when you were working out with Cam."

She moved past him, making sure the silk touched his skin. For convenience and security, she did most of her shopping online. In the past, it had been a necessary chore only. Since Ace, she had discovered she enjoyed certain elements of retail. Seductive lingerie had become a personal favorite.

"I'm going to check the system before we turn in. Coming?" She glanced over her shoulder, laughing at his appreciative grin.

Since only one step separated them, it was easy to slide his fingers through her hair, holding her in place. He bent to nip lightly at her bare shoulder.

"I'm coming now and I'll be coming later too."

Her smoky laugh went straight to his loins. The woman was a deadly mix of temptation and challenge, in bed or out. Ever changing, she offered him trust. She allowed him to see her as his lover, not just as Felicity, a woman of many faces, many names and many skills that few could match.

For now, in the quiet and the security of the home she had built, the world was locked away. They could forget everything but each other and the pleasure they could share.

No missions, no cruelty to be exposed and destroyed. No danger. No death. Only Felicity. Only life.

CHAPTER TWO

Senator Gordon stared at the monitor, frozen in place, chills racing down her bare arms. She had been playing with computers since she was old enough to spell the word.

First, as an amusement then later as a way to ferret out information that was to her benefit. It was amazing what a person would put on the internet and that didn't count all the public data.

She had gotten boyfriends that she wanted that another girl had. A little whisper in the right ear was so easy. Later, so profitable when she needed extra money.

She had discovered a world of secrets with just a few keystrokes. This unit had one IP address under a name that no one would ever connect with her. She knew how to protect her secrets. Necessity had made her an expert.

Now that she was the new woman in the senatorial offices, she needed every edge she could get. Her backers, one in particular, had spent lavishly to get her elected. He had asked nothing of her yet but she knew his money had an IOU attached to every dollar. She had to be able to deliver when he began to call the debt due.

For that, she needed information on the people with whom she would be dealing. Being new, meant she wasn't yet buried in upcoming work. She had the time and privacy to dig into files that weren't supposed to be easily accessed.

Who had a mistress and where? Sometimes, who or what gender. So many people on the Hill were such hypocrites, espousing all sorts of socially popular opinions while playing their dirty little games behind the scenes. Family members were a great source of leverage.

Misspelling a name by two letters took her down a road she had not even known existed. Curious, dodging trips and fake cyber trails she found files with names that didn't match or have any connection to the information inside the folders.

In her experience, no one went to this much trouble unless the data was not just valuable but potentially dangerous. She looked at one of the files generated by one of the major behind-the-scenes power players.

His name was spoken in whispers because his

department was well known for its ability and the resources to investigate and find answers. Careers had been destroyed by his work. Scandals were made glaringly obvious for public consumption or buried so deeply that they would never see the light of day.

Seeing the names of two dead men she recognized captured her full attention. Idle curiosity escalated to intense concentration. The sentences filling her screen shocked her when she had thought herself immune to surprise.

A heart attack for a popular Senator that wasn't natural as it had been reported in the news. Then a few days later an automobile accident that was carefully staged for a man serving in the House of Representatives.

The two had been suspected of doing business with members of a foreign power. A single man had made the decision to end the duo's activities without due process. All it had taken was a phone call to some company.

"How can this be?" she whispered to the empty room as she skimmed the data in front of her. She was not naïve but she had not envisioned this. Being run out of office was one thing. Being murdered was a whole new game.

Both had been suspected of aiding foreigners, unspecified by name, in creating legislation that generated revenue in questionable enterprises also unnamed. The head of the department hadn't worked through official government channels.

Why?

Instead, he had brought in an outside contractor, Skye/Sea Security Consultants. If what she was reading was true, that person had found the men guilty and had engineered their deaths in such a way that no scandal would touch Congress or the administration at the time.

There was no indication that the file had ever seen the light of day except in front of the man who had compiled it. This kind of leverage was invaluable if applied properly. She would have used it without a qualm if the words on the page hadn't created chaos in her own mind.

The dead Senator had inhabited the office that now had her name on the door. Granted he had been assassinated five years ago as had the member of the House who was just as guilty if the data in front of her was true.

The dead Senator's term had been finished by a man who was known to be so black and white in his thinking that he was like a rock on many issues. He had run for re-election and won. He was the man that her backers had helped her defeat when he had tried for a second full term.

She did not believe in coincidences. Or luck. Or men throwing money her way out of the goodness of their hearts. More worried than she had ever been in her life, she searched the campaigns of both officials. At first, she found no cross with anyone that she knew was involved with her own run for Congress.

Finally, when she had thought she was clear, she stumbled over a single name, a charity she knew too damn well..

"No. No."

She shut her eyes as she cursed graphically, using words she had carefully edited from her language the moment she had decided to become a public figure.

She had just begun to attain her dreams. She could not afford to be looking over her shoulder for some privately hired assassin to kill her. She wasn't that damn brave. Anger pushed out fear. The bastard who had put her in office had to have known about the deaths.

The man knew everything. He knew her dream and had dangled it in front of her, making her see things could move faster than she had ever dreamed.

She reached in her handbag for one of the burner phones she kept for calls she didn't want traced. The man, she wasn't allowed to even speak his name except at public functions he attended, knew of the burners. He had even approved her foresight.

The voice that answered wasn't his. He had given her a word that would connect her to him. She waited for a full minute before he responded.

"I need to see you." Silence. He always seemed to weigh her every word. She waited.

"You sound upset."

She thought quickly. She wanted a meeting in the open, in a place where she could be sure that she would be safe. The man was well known in Washington. He could and did go everywhere, often present at political venues and parties.

"That is not nearly a strong enough word for what I'm feeling," she admitted bluntly. "I need to see you. Tonight. Three hours. The offices will be empty by then."

Another silence, longer this time and conveying his displeasure at her attitude. She didn't give a damn. Right now, he had no hold over her. She had done nothing wrong. His money had been donated legally and appropriately.

"I give orders not take them."

The cold tone and the soft delivery held a threat. She had a threat of her own.

"Baldwin and Rogers," she said then waited. If she had found that file, someone else could. She was taking a risk in pushing him but death was final. And she wasn't ready to die when she was just starting to live her dream.

"Someone will call you with arrangements. This line, in an hour."

She heard no emotion in his voice, nothing to give her a clue as to how involved, if at all, he had been. She was scared enough, angry enough to refuse.

"No. Here, where I am safe or not at all."

Silence, this time was thick with suspicion and menace.

Finally, the voice agreed. "Be very sure that we will be alone. You will not like it if I find out differently."

"I'll check the offices to be sure no one is on this floor but me. I'll let Hank at the security desk know to let you through without the usual check. He won't be any trouble."

"If he is, you will not like the result."

Sharon hated that purr in his voice. She ended the call and slumped in her chair. She was taking a terrible risk but she couldn't see any other way to go. Flight was out of the question for so many reasons. Going to the government was just as likely to get her a box next to her predecessor as it was to get her protection.

The man wanted something from her. Until he got a return on his huge investment, she had to believe he would want to keep her alive. She looked at the information that she wished she had never seen.

Printing it out was too risky and she didn't want the man to know how good she was at hacking. She found the data by accident. That, at least, was the truth.

She got to her feet and moved to the heavy masculine designed bookcase. She had found an area on one of the shelves where the backing had separated from the shelf. Her laptop fit in the tiny space between the wood pieces.

She slid it into place and returned the books in front of it to their proper positions. She stepped back to survey the shelves. Nothing showed that she had moved anything. Now, all she had to do was wait.

The man studied the woman in front of him. Sharon Gordon was not his first choice for a power figure on the Hill. They had needed a replacement that was hungry and willing to do whatever it took to achieve her own ends. Sharon Gordon fit that description.

So much of their plan was already in place and working. Losing the two men she had named had put a temporary halt to new acquisitions.

His partner had not liked the delay and had demanded the first of two replacements. Gordon had been selected and elected. They were ready for the next phase. Every step had been calculated and tested. The stakes were high, potentially in the billions of dollars. It wasn't just the money that drove him. It was the power, the kind that built countries and men.

He had a partner. Many would have questioned his choice of co-conspirator. Perez was a criminal in the worst possible way. A man way below him in standing but a man who had the spine and the money to be an asset to his plan.

A man who understood the game, who more than matched him in power and financial resources. One day, he would control all. His partner was two decades older. He would use him, then take over when the time was right. For now, he let the older man lead.

His partner had pointed out they needed a Senator, not a specific Senator and since his share of the buy was double his own investment, he had agreed to own this Anglo woman with a sprinter's body and a hard ass attitude. He didn't like her. He preferred working with men, less emotional, much more predictable.

Nothing about her appealed but her price tag. Even that was not enough to please him as he stood in her private office with a locked door behind him. He was very aware of the empty outer office and the silent hall beyond.

The meeting was too unsecured to suit him but he was armed. His bodyguard stood alertly in the shadows of the bookcases. At least, the guard downstairs had waved them through as promised, no security scans. He hadn't bothered to give them more than a cursory glance.

Although Gordon's lack of conscience was useful, he didn't like anyone who lacked loyalty and honor, man or woman. In his business both were critical if one was working in the shadows.

Some might call her beautiful but he found her cold.

And demanding. She had dared to insist on this meeting. Only the edge of fear in her voice had decided him to agree.

Sharon stayed seated behind the desk when they entered as quietly as smoke curling out of a fire. She had used the time she had waited to decide on her approach. Showing any more weakness than she had already betrayed wasn't smart. She needed answers and reassurance.

She gestured to the chair in front of the desk. When he only stood, watching her with dark eyes filled with endless patience, she leaned back as though his refusal didn't matter.

"I have found a file that outlines an investigation on two congressmen, one being the Senator who died in this office from a supposed heart attack. The two were suspected of dealing with foreign interests.

Oddly enough, the investigation wasn't handled by the government but was hired out to a private firm, Skye/Sea Security Consultants."

She waited for a reaction and got nothing but silence. Even the bodyguard showed no response.

"Once the men were found guilty, an order was given to terminate them in such a way as to keep the investigation under wraps. In short, no scandal."

"Why would you think this concerns either of us?"

"I don't believe in coincidences," she replied, measuring her words out slowly. "The name of the charity you represent is on both men's list of donors.

You want something from me. You've got a hefty investment in my career. I want what you are giving me. I know I am going to pay for your help. I am prepared to keep my part of the bargain.

What I won't do is keep looking over my shoulder waiting for Skye/Sea Security to decide I'm guilty of whatever you're planning so I have to die."

She wanted to stay calm but she could hear the sharp anger rising in her own voice. She hoped he didn't hear the fear.

His gaze flicked over her and the clear desktop in front of her. "You have proof of this?"

"I saw the file."

"How? When?"

She shrugged, trying to act as calm as he was. "I wanted to know the people around me. The more I know, the more I can deliver on what I owe you. The file was a product of my research."

A lie? Why? Truth? Possibly? The guard downstairs knew they were in the building. His public disguise was flawless. The same with his bodyguard.

He was a wealthy businessman who possessed dual nationality. He was often at public events for charities and political gatherings. He was very comfortable being in the company of the movers and shakers in the States.

He could force the information out of her if he had time and privacy. He had neither here. To take her with him was to risk the loss of the anonymity his public persona gave him. Too much depended on his ability to move freely about the halls of government.

When two of their congressional plants had died so inconveniently, he and his partner had had suspicions. They had put their best people on the ground to check out the circumstances of each death.

They had found nothing that indicated any move or investigation by the government through official channels. Even their search through the known unofficial ways had yielded nothing.

Now, this woman who was barely controlling her fear and anger dared to suggest a different interpretation. It was almost impossible to believe Gordon had managed to do what his people hadn't.

His computer experts would have one more chance. If they failed again, they died. Gordon thought herself safe. She was wrong. He would pluck her out of her home and have his answers. She would then beg to tell him everything she knew. A day or two at most either way. He could afford the time.

"They are not important. Neither is in the picture now," he pointed out. "I will consider your situation. Skye/Sea

Security is not a problem that can't be handled. No one, no company is so secure that it can't be removed if necessary."

At least she had given him a name. He had some knowledge of this company but, so far, their paths had not crossed. He preferred to keep that circumstance as it was. He needed more information before a decision could be made.

What she had found, his people could find. She thought herself a hacker. Those he had set to watch her had heard her remark once to a very close friend on her interest in such things. He owned better.

For the moment, calming her was necessary. He and his partner were poised to reap the benefits of the money they had spent on her.

"You have the seat you coveted. You have the money you needed for your campaign as Governor of your state. We planned and executed your election well.

The house, the car, the staff, the programs you implemented we financed so that you became the people's choice for the next term. When we lost the man before you, you were positioned by us to win his seat. You did. We have kept our part of the bargain. If Skye/Sea Security becomes a problem, we will handle it."

"I didn't know I was putting myself in a position where I could get killed," she shot back, still trying to come to grips with the situation in which she now stood, figuratively and literally.

Having a department that held such power to order death and then cover it up was terrifying. She hadn't wanted to have a meeting with this man. He scared her more than her worst nightmare.

"If they did an investigation as you say, they found nothing they could legally use to remove them from office. I only have your word that this department ordered their deaths. Their positions have nothing to do with you. Or with us. They are dead. Old men die. Heart attack or accident, death is death. You are jumping at shadows."

He laughed softly, genuinely amazed at her naivete. "I had not thought you a fool with a child's imagination. Cold blooded, greedy, yes. Naïve? Impossible to believe. Why would we pay so much if there was no danger?"

His tone changed to soft velvet, lightly flavored with his south-of-the-border accent. He felt his guard shift. The man knew him well. He was not pleased. The woman would learn that failure or fear always had consequences.

"I own you. I can keep you in luxury or hold you screaming in agony for days without end. You will keep the bargain we made or die."

Chills raced down her spine. Only the data she had discovered kept her in place. She feared the man in front of her almost much as she feared the information she had found through a mischance.

A private organization, funded by black ops dollars. One call, one mistake and a private firm could dig into her background, her campaign, report their findings to another department that would then decide her fate. Death, made to look like an accident. Two that she had found. How far back did this group go?

Despite her efforts of control, her voice rose in anger. "So, I am supposed to forget about Skye/Sea Security Consultants? You can't leave them to kill me."

"If you are careful, why should anyone look at you? You will find a way. Or have you forgotten who you are and, more importantly, who put you in this office?"

His dark eyes were as cold as black ice as he shrugged. "If you can't get the job done then I will go shopping again. You are so easily replaced."

She opened her lips to reply, but a slight sound caught her attention. From one heartbeat to another, the man and his bodyguard pivoted toward the door. When the bodyguard started to draw his weapon, the man shook his head and signaled him into the hall.

Gordon froze in place. She barely heard the lock disengage or the guard leave. She had been so sure that she was alone on this floor.

A few short minutes later, the bodyguard returned with

no more sound than he had made leaving. Then her donor was looming in front of her with a look of controlled rage on his face. She cringed in her chair.

"You fool," the man said softly. "Were you so arrogant that you lied about checking to see that we would be alone? He could have heard every word you said."

"Of course, I checked," she snapped then gasped as the guard reached out and caught her hair, jerking her out of her chair. He said nothing, simply waited for orders.

"Let me go," she demanded. "I checked. I am not stupid. The last meeting on this floor ended hours ago. I told you that."

She moaned as the fingers in her hair twisted painfully, tightening so that she was almost sprawled across her own desk.

"Who was in this meeting?"

The soft question was more frightening than a shout. "I don't know. How could I ask without suspicion? I had no need to know."

"You need to know now. Deal with it."

"We don't even know if whoever it was heard anything."

"Punta," he purred roughly. "He would not have run if he had not heard something. You were shouting. You have more to lose than I. Your name is on the door. Mine is not.

There are more ways to die than by an accident that is no accident. Would you like me to show you?"

The pain in her head increased with the cruel grip of the guard's fingers. She tried to stifle another moan but didn't succeed.

"Do you like the taste you are getting?" Suddenly the shine of a lethally sharp blade filled her vision. "Would you like to taste your own blood?"

She stared at the knife poised a breath away from her face. "No," she whispered.

"Then find the man who 'might not have heard anything'." He turned to head for the door.

The pressure on her scalp was gone in a heartbeat. Tears of pain and fury filled her eyes as she watched the panel shut silently behind the two men. She managed to collapse in her chair.

For long moments, she just breathed, more terrified than she had ever been. She needed to think. Impossible when her mind was filled with that soft voice and the image of that sharp knife.

Slowly, feeling as though she could barely lift her hand, she reached for her phone to call the security desk on the first floor. She was taking a risk but she didn't see any other way to find out who had been in the hall to overhear her conversation.

"Hank, Senator Gordon. I thought you said I was the only one still working tonight. My people were getting ready to leave and I heard footsteps in the hall."

She managed a little nervous laugh. She might end up looking like a foolish female but she was covering all bases with the truth if not the reason for it.

"I'm afraid I got a little uneasy. One of my guests went out into the hall to check for me but he didn't see anyone. Was there someone up here or was I just imagining things?"

"No, Senator. When you came down to tell me about your visitors, I forgot about Mr. LaPlante still being in the building. You don't have to worry about him. He's with a private security company. That's probably who you heard. Want me to check?"

She almost asked the name of the company before sanity prevailed. She didn't dare show that much interest. There were other ways to get the data she needed.

She managed a second laugh. "Absolutely not. I feel foolish enough as it is. I'm not used to a city as big as Washington or halls with marble floors and chandeliers in working offices."

She sounded like a nervous idiot. Hank had told her all the senators on her floor had left, Walton being the last one. LaPlante had to have been visiting him. She wanted to confirm that but decided that was too risky.

Hank chuckled as she hoped he would. "It takes a while to get used to it. If you want, I'll escort you to your car when you're ready to leave."

"Thanks for the offer, I really mean it but I need to toughen up. I know there are security cameras everywhere. I'll be fine."

"Just let me know if you change your mind."

She barely heard his offer as she realized that LaPlante must have left the building by some way that didn't involve going by Hank's desk. That was worrying. How? As far as she knew, at this time of night, it was the only way in or out.

She went to the book shelves to retrieve her computer. Calling on every skill she had, she searched for who LaPlante was. She had a starting place with Walton and the fact that LaPlante was employed by a private security company.

Each of the senators headed certain committees. She was very aware of the topics currently being discussed. She made it her business to remember names and faces. It was critically important to know all the players and those who reported to them. Gossip was a great source of information

Walton, a Senator from a west coast state, had recently had a security problem with his daughter. The girl had almost been taken off the street despite having a bodyguard. The incident had been the talk of the chambers for the last week.

Using the information and her own skills at cyber

sleuthing, she connected the names. Walton had been looking for and apparently found a private firm to handle his security. Since he could afford the price tag, he was getting his way as long as the bodyguards, two in this case passed government security. LaPlante was the man setting up the detail.

That gave her what she needed to trace LaPlante's background. A new wife, no kids. A house on the west coast. His travel arrangements were set for departure tomorrow. That didn't give her much time.

At least she had a name and leverage for LaPlante's silence. She made herself reach for her handbag and the last of her burner cells she kept for emergencies. She inhaled deeply as she tapped in a number that was written nowhere but in her brain. Everyone had skeletons, she reminded herself. For once, hers might be a tool to save her life.

No voice answered the ring.

"Hello?"

Another hesitation filled with silence.

"I don't believe it. Change your mind about never speaking to me again?"

The harsh voice and the sarcasm in it were memories she had hoped to never revisit. She kept her voice low. Being overheard once was a harsh lesson with this kind of consequence.

"Obviously. I have a job for you."

"Why would I do anything for you?"

"I can give you fifty thousand reasons."

The silence on the other end of the line was deep with suspicion.

"Who do you want dead?"

She closed her eyes against the words she hoped to the God she didn't believe in weren't the truth. That kind of outcome would give him a way to ruin her.

"That won't be necessary if you are smart. I need leverage. A dead body only complicates things. Just pick up one woman. It has to be tonight."

"I'm listening," he said slowly. "You can take tonight off the table. A kidnapping takes time to set up. Not to mention a place to hold the hostage."

"It has to be tonight," she snapped.

"Then find yourself another man. I don't have a death wish."

She was losing him. Her fingers tightened on the cell.

"One hundred thousand. I'm sending you a picture of her and an address. It has to be tonight. You're less than a hundred miles from her. That's a thousand a mile in case you can't do the math."

His silence meant he was considering accepting. She hadn't been sure that even the large sum of money would gain his cooperation. Maybe it wasn't large enough.

"Two hundred and you have yourself a deal. Up front."

She sagged in her chair, so relieved she was lightheaded.

"Hell no. Half now, the other half when you have her and I'll want video proof." She heard his curse. She had heard worse.

"Alright." He rattled off a string of numbers on a bank they both knew.

"Make the transfer first. I'm not driving one inch until I see the money in my account."

"Twenty minutes."

It would take her that long to leave the building. She definitely didn't want to make the transfer from her office, burner phone or not. She needed her laptop and a building with internet access that wouldn't ping to her addresses so she could do a cyber transfer.

"I won't wait longer. Twenty minutes or no deal. Unlike you I don't go back on my word."

She dropped the burner in her bag and leaned her head on the desk. She just needed a minute. Her scalp felt raw. Her nerves were in knots and she had to go downstairs, make nice with Hank as she left for the night.

"What a mess!"

She lifted her head and took a deep breath. She could do it. She had to do it. Failure was not an option.

CHAPTER THREE

Felicity studied the screens in front of her. The check was a nightly ritual that was critically important. Every one of her programs for security were registering all systems up and running. No alerts. No unexpected activities and no problems with any of the teams on current assignments.

She sighed deeply as she leaned back and moved to one of her newer programs. So far, she had found it to be very informative, especially internationally. The areas where she had teams were relatively quiet. Certainly, no threats were currently looming on Skye's horizon.

She glanced at Ace. He looked as relaxed as she felt. A nightcap with lazy tangle of lovemaking was a great way to end a day. When they finished this last check, they could take up where they had left off. She had some ideas on that.

Before she could speak, the computer signaled an incoming call on a line that was only used in emergencies. She initiated a trace then allowed the call to go to message.

"Safe line. Critical contact. Immediate threat. Trace and return."

The line stayed open just long enough for Felicity to complete the trace. Even as the system gave the information she was getting as much visual as she could with her satellite feeds. One heat signature and nothing else around the caller. No buildings, just space. A male voice with a French accent. An accent she recognized.

"That sounds like Andre," Ace said, studying the screens as intently as she did.

Felicity keyed in commands. She never took anything at face value. Too many lives depended on her vigilance. "Or someone who knows he trained here and managed to get or make a usable voice print."

She never believed the unexpected. She manually engaged her system to check the authenticity of the message. The computer detected no signs of manipulation. There was enough change in pitch and delivery to indicate what she was hearing wasn't an artificially created voice.

Felicity commanded a trace of the number. The voice

answered on the first ring. It was Andre. Her life had too often depended on her ability to recognize vocal identities.

"Not much time. On assignment in D.C. Just leaving the building. Overheard an argument, one man, one woman. Shouting. Her not him. S.S.C. is a major problem. Tried recording, jamming somehow. Name on the office door was Gordon. Whole building is Senate offices."

She could think of only one connection in Washington regarding the Senate and that was not good. Skye/Sea Security Consultants did covert jobs for one man and there should have been no leaks to Andre's location. There should have been no record at all.

"Where?"

Andre relayed the address for the building then the floor and office number.

"Were you seen?"

"Yes. One man at least. Not close enough to immediately identify. Can't be sure. Not here undercover. If I'm made, they can get to my wife."

"Travel arrangements?"

"Not using. Get home on my own."

"No. Sending pick up. I'll arrange to have your luggage picked up at the hotel before you fly out."

She gave quick directions. She added another contact number for Andre.

"Disable the GPS on your vehicle."

"Done before I left the parking lot. Burner cell. Have one more. Destroying this one when we're done. My wife?"

"We'll cover. Change vehicles. How long ago?"

"About ninety minutes. Had to get clear and make sure I wasn't followed. I couldn't get her." The fear in Andre's voice echoed in every word.

Too long. The thought went no farther than Felicity's mind. If Andre had been seen, if the plan was important enough, the people involved concerned enough, someone could already be moving to eliminate the threat he represented. One way was taking his wife hostage. A loved one made superb leverage in the right hands.

"You'll know the pilot. Be there."

Felicity severed the connection then made sure that the line for the incoming was purged from her system. She wanted no trails leading to the Farm. She put the Farm on 'blue', the silent signal going out to everyone in the compound and at the Ranch.

She contacted Taranda using the wrist unit. "Taranda, I need you. Control ASAP."

She didn't wait for confirmation. She made a second call. "Benny, ready ASAP. Control meeting."

One more contact to the hangar crew with instructions took only a few seconds.

Again, no confirmation was required. She knew her people and they knew the meaning of 'blue'. Or thought they did. They hadn't dealt with this kind of 'blue'.

She stripped the emerald silk from her body as she strode out of the secure room and headed for her closet. Ace changed with the same speed and efficiency as she did. Black jeans, tee and boots. They and the dogs entered the elevator together. They exited the house at a jog.

Taranda flowed out of the shadows from the left. The black woman was barely visible in the limited light. She asked no questions as she followed them to the command center. Benny came out of the night without a word. Dressed in head to toe black he was more visible than Taranda but no less lethal.

As soon as Felicity checked the status of the lockdown, she nodded and engaged the satellites to monitor the Farm and the Ranch as well as the extraction point to which Taranda was going.

"We have an emergency extraction, one man, Andre LaPlante. Taranda, you have the jet. Time and stealth. Full scan going in. Touch and go. We will be monitoring. I call it, you abort and cover your tail. If I go dark, the computer will have instructions. Follow them."

She saw the questions in Taranda's tiger eyes but Taranda answered only with a nod.

"Benny, on the ground, whatever it takes, you are sanctioned. Weapons and ammo on board already."

Benny touched the strap of his favorite weapon. If he needed anything else, hell was coming and Felicity needed everything he could give. "Got it. Jonah?"

She shook her head. "Back in three hours."

"If he can be got, we'll bring Andre in."

"He can be got," Taranda said grimly. "I'll run if I have to but I don't like it. Let's get in the air."

She spun on her heel and headed for the door. Benny was there before her. Normally, she hated the way the man could surprise her. Tonight, she was glad for his speed and his skill with his 'honey', the weapon slung over his shoulder.

He didn't miss. He had no nerves she had ever seen. And he didn't quit. Like her, the Farm was his home and there was something happening that was putting the compound at risk. She didn't know the details of the teams that were out but she did know there shouldn't be any threat from any of them. Andre was a strange addition and she didn't trust strange at all.

Felicity keyed in a number. The cell was answered on the first ring. Fortunately, she had four of her people on the ground on another assignment in the same city where Andre lived. Two men, two women for a high-profile couple visiting for a low-profile international summit. Their assignment would be over by noon tomorrow. Good timing if she needed everyone home. One pair was off watch and available.

"Boss?"

"Both of you. Incoming address and details. Immediate extraction. No cell response. Risk high. Report situation ASAP." Even as she gave the instructions, her fingers raced over the keyboard, gathering intel on Andre's wife, home and cars with tags.

"On it."

Ace read the information on Anhe LaPlante. He knew enough Chinese to translate the lady's name. Calm and peaceful was the first half and water lily the second. He hoped her name was true but he had an itch at the back of his neck that said it wasn't.

"What happens to the teams that are out?" He glanced at her as she continued to key in information, much of which was not showing up on any of the screens in the room.

Felicity engaged fail safe programs, contingency information and the final way out before the destruction of the Farm and the Ranch. None of what she was doing would show for long. If the Farm was attacked and overrun or destroyed, the most important failsafe would erase even the slender link that she was currently using.

Only someone getting possession of her computer would have a chance of finding her instructions and those they guarded. Once the program was activated, it went to self-destruct mode to protect it from any kind of tampering. The clock started ticking. If the home system was compromised, the link was severed.

"The 'blue program' is set up to not only lockdown the Farm and the Ranch but to send out instructions if returning here isn't safe or possible. Everyone will be given an untraceable new identity, a safe bank account with five million and a house in his or her new name in different places in the world. Tracing any of our people will be a lot like looking for invisible needles in an infinite number of haystacks. Included in the packages are instructions for possible choices. If I survive, they have an option of contacting me when a certain number goes active."

Ace had always known that Felicity didn't expect to live to retire but he hadn't realized how completely she had protected each of her people if the Farm was overrun.

"What name did you give me?" If she died, he would be laying close by her. He had signed on until the end.

She smiled faintly. "Is this where you intend to tell me that we win together or lose it all together?"

"Yeah. Something like that."

He slid a hand to the back of her neck and pulled her close. "I wouldn't know what to do with five mil. Keep the money and stay alive."

"Planning on it. I am damn hard to kill and I sure don't intend to buy it with a sneak attack."

She kissed him hard then pulled back. "Let's find the SOB who may be putting this mess together."

He laughed roughly. "Let's do that little thing. I mean really, we have so much information to chase. We might even be jumping the gun."

She flashed him a grin without taking her eyes from the information scrolling across the screens. "Better that than dying from one we didn't prepare for. Are you up deep diving into Gordon's life? I want everything you can find from her last gyn exam to every dollar she has ever made and where it came from."

"With the programs you have, I can probably find out how many hairs she has on her head."

"Good. Make it happen. I'm going to hack into the security of her office. I love security cameras. I want at least one picture with enough detail for a facial recognition search."

Taranda settled into place on the flightdeck. The low throb of the jet was a purr that would soon turn into a hungry growl for freedom and speed. After checking her instrumentation, she eased the aircraft free of the boarding area and onto the landing strip.

She was aware of Benny sliding into place beside her, strapping in for the lift off. In seconds, she started the run down the tarmac. Her senses were keyed to the craft she loved. The lady could race the sun, maneuver as though there was no obstacle in her way. Speed and stealth were the goals this night.

The jet lifted eagerly into the sky, no longer chained to the ground by gravity and separation from her pilot. Flying low, using the most rural routes possible, Taranda demanded all of the speed and agility the craft possessed.

Benny watched Taranda guide them through the moonless night, her eyes on the screens that clearly depicted the mountains around them, the elevations and the airspeed. The low altitude slowed the jet somewhat but Taranda and her aircraft were rapidly eating up the miles between safety and danger for the man they were meeting.

"Want coffee?"

"Yes. Thanks."

He released his seatbelt and eased past her to head for the gallery. The jet was always stocked with Taranda's favorite coffee which happened to be his own. They had a lot in common, not that she had ever admitted that. It only took a few minutes to have two mugs ready. He sipped the rich brew as he returned to the flightdeck to fit her mug into the holder on her left.

For a moment, he was close enough to feel her heat and catch the faint exotic scent of her skin. A hell of a time to remind himself how much she appealed to him. He shook off his response and concentrated on the mental wall he wouldn't cross. He was too damn old for her, not so much in years as experience.

Taranda lifted the mug as Benny took his place beside her. "I need this. I don't mind flying anytime but it is nice to have a little notice so I can get my coffee on the way out the door."

"I'm with you on that. I've never lost the need for a fix before I start working. I'm told it helps my mood."

Taranda glanced at him then grinned. "Honey, nothing helps your mood when you are in the kitchen. I don't think there is enough coffee for that."

Benny shrugged. He knew he could be moody. Once he hadn't been. The things he had seen and done had destroyed the life he'd had before he had gone to war.

"The only time you aren't moody is when we are working like this."

"We can't afford my moods here. People die when someone forgets to pay attention."

Taranda made a course adjustment. They hadn't ever been alone like this she realized. Always, there had been other members of the team when they were on a mission or people around them when they were on the Farm.

"It has never been just the two of us before."

He was too aware of that. "So?"

She had a question that had been bugging her for years. She reached out to set their comm units on mute so that their words went no farther than the jet's cabin. Now she had the time and the privacy, she would get an answer.

"Why do you snipe at me every chance you get? You don't do it when we are working like this." She was tired of wondering and if it took the whole trip, he was going to give her a reason.

He wasn't going near that answer. "You snipe at me too."

"You started it."

Benny lowered his mug to stare at her. "I did not."

She looked at him, her eyes like gold lasers drilling into his words. She had given the situation a lot of thought. Generally, she could get along with anyone. She didn't have to like anyone to work with him or her. Respect skill, yes. That was a critical need. Liking, not so much.

"I don't think it's because you don't like me. We do fine in this kind of setting. I have guarded your back and you have done the same for me. That's trust and I don't think either of us trusts that much, that often."

She was right about that. He did trust her as he did the

men and women who worked on the teams. He had to. His life and other lives depended on that trust in her skill to do her job. She had never failed any of them.

"Working together is enough goodwill, don't you think?"

"That's an evasion. There is no one here but us. What is the problem? My personality?"

She waited a beat and got no answer. "My skin color?" She didn't want to think that was the reason.

Benny carefully set his mug aside and angled his body so that he was facing her. "I damn well don't deserve that last question no matter what we have said to each other. I have never in my life judged anyone on skin color, religion, culture or gender. I have more faults than I care to count but prejudice is not one of them."

"What is it then? Because it sure is hell is something."

She wasn't going to let the subject alone. "This isn't the time."

"We have a little over two hours of privacy and I can multitask."

"I don't want to multitask."

"Make an exception."

He could hear the dare in her reply. Damn her for forcing the issue. He didn't want this discussion. If she was any other woman, if he hadn't guarded her back or she guarded his, he might have been able to construct a polite, fictional answer. Trust was a very inconvenient and demanding emotion. Trust would only be satisfied with truth.

"Alright. You want an answer. Here it is. I'm a man who hasn't been with a woman in months, too damn many months. You're a living, breathing challenge and I'm hungry. You are also too damn young for a man like me."

He bit off every word with a temper he never took into battle with him. He didn't want the emotion, didn't need the emotion right now and he damn well couldn't stop the fury that her challenge lit.

Taranda was stunned at the lengthy blast. He was not a man who used an extra word if he could avoid it. He was furious and, unless she had suddenly lost her survival skill of reading the male of the species, he was frustrated down to the bone.

"My age is the problem," she said slowly. She kept most of her attention on the instruments which were tracking their flight path. She could answer this nonsense blindfolded.

"I will be forty-one my next birthday. You're in your mid-twenties."

"I'm not. I'll be twenty-nine on my next one. Even if I was younger what does age have to do with sex?"

He flicked that answer away with a swift slice of his hand.

"It's not the number of years so much as the experience. At the end of my first tour in the Mideast I came home carrying baggage that my wife couldn't handle and neither could I. I had nightmares. Loud noises threw me back into battle mode.

I tried to return to the civilian world, the home we had, the friends but I couldn't hold a job. Even the everyday concerns, the jokes, the discussions were irritating. The people around me had no idea how other cultures treated the weak, the young, and the women.

Drugs would have been a fix but it was also an ugly road to travel if I got stupid. Alcohol helped for a while but not enough.

I didn't belong anymore. I had skills that mattered, that saved lives. I signed up for a second tour. I left my wife pregnant without either of us knowing. I got an email with the announcement that she wanted a divorce and that she was pregnant."

He paused to remember, the regret he had felt that he wouldn't be there for the baby's birth. Their divorce was just one more loss. Then relief that he would not be there to show her and their baby the ugly side of his moods. Rage and grief ate through the memories. He wouldn't revisit them, not now, not ever.

He had told her the truth but not all of it. He had

slammed the door on that part of his past, that dark hell that still lived in his nightmares.

"I got out of the service. I tried counseling. It didn't help. I couldn't live in the civilized world. I didn't even understand it anymore. One day I walked out with a back pack and the clothes I was wearing. No one depending on me anymore. On the streets, I found a lot of men and some women just like me."

He looked into the darkness that surrounded the jet, for a moment, lost in the memories of long days and nights where all he heard was the sounds of battles raging, men dying, screaming. Women brutalized and children slaughtered by high powered weapons. Body parts littering the ground from landmines and bombs. It was easier to think of the war and the damage that bullets and bombs could do than the empty home he had left behind.

He hated the color of blood. He had seen too much of it and yet, on the Farm, he had found a home, doing what he had been trained to do. The people he saw every day, worked with, trained with carried their own baggage.

Like him, they had found a place where their skills weren't wasted but used in a way that made sleeping through nightmares possible. This time, innocents, old or young, were saved not killed or brutalized.

His story was like so many of the ones she had been

trusted with by a few of the members of the teams. All of them were scarred one way or another. Some showed and some didn't.

She lightly traced the pale arc across her cheekbone. She could have covered the disfigurement with make-up. Felicity had even offered her the funds to do cosmetic surgery. She chose neither.

"You aren't the only one with an ugly history."

"I know that. Most of the people around us come out of some kind of government work."

"I didn't."

"I figured that out on my own."

"So, because I didn't fight a war in some country not my own, I can't handle what happened to you?"

She glanced at him, one black brow raised in challenge.

"I didn't say that."

"There are wars where you know your enemy and your friends. There are also wars where you are the only one fighting. That was my war and it started when I was almost nine years old. A kid raised by a drugged-out grandmother whose daughter had overdosed."

Benny watched her face, heard the soft words cut through the hum of the jet's engines. He had never considered what her reasons for being on the Farm might be. He should have. He knew that she was not from any military or government background.

"The state paid her monthly so I would have a home. Great home. I cooked, cleaned, got myself to school and home again until the day I didn't. I doubt anyone even noticed I was missing when I got snatched off the street less than a block from where I lived.

I was a good-looking kid, long legs, shiny black skin, big eyes and not filled out yet. A perfect black doll for rich pedophiles. I had a name but they gave me a number, 22.

My owner handed me over to Roscoe for breaking in. He was hung like a bull and he liked giving pain. I screamed, begged and cried until I lost my voice. I fought while he raped me and when I managed to scratch him, to bite him he repaid me with this."

She touched the scar she had hardly felt in her last moments of consciousness.

Benny felt rage build, responding to what had been done to the child, to the woman with those hellish memories. If her rapist had stood in front of him, he would have gutted him and watched him die in great pain.

"I was dying, lying in a pool of my own blood, feeling as though I had been ripped apart. I passed out. I don't remember much of the days after that.

But one morning, I finally woke up enough to know I was in hell. It took a month for me to be well enough to earn the food I was eating. I earned it on my back or on my knees. I learned that some men needed pain to get off and others wanted to give it. If there was a depraved way to have sex, I learned it or risked another round with Roscoe.

That was my life for five years. Then I was too old for the kiddie brothel. I and four other girls were to be sold. We were brought to the owner's office with Roscoe standing guard.

Every minute of every day, every second that a man pounded into me, I promised myself that one day I would use Roscoe's knife to kill him. I would slide my hands through his blood and I would be free. That day, I watched him. I kept my head down but I watched him. I didn't care if I died as long as I killed Roscoe first."

He hoped she didn't carry that image with her. He would have done it for her. What was one more body, one more death to him?

"Then Felicity came into the room. She was the buyer. She looked us over, one by one and then moved to the desk to finish the deal. Only she didn't buy us. She freed us by killing the owner and then Roscoe in two moves so quick that it took a minute for me to realize what she had done.

Roscoe dropped to the floor, blood pouring out of him. I had to touch it. I knew he was dying but I had to get his knife. I had survived my time in hell so that I could kill him. Just that one thing.

I reached for Felicity's knife sticking in his gut. Felicity has such a soft voice sometimes. I heard it then. Gentle words when I had never known kindness nor gentleness.

She said no. She needed my help to get the girls with me away. They were drugged. I wasn't. I had learned how to separate my mind from my body so that they wouldn't turn the whore they had made me into an addict.

She didn't try to touch me or them. She asked for my help. I looked into her eyes and somehow, I believed her when she said she had come to get us out."

She stared at the instruments in front of her. Her freedom began the moment she had listened and given up need to kill Roscoe. Felicity had done it for her.

"I went with her. She gave me a life. The first taste of freedom I had was sitting beside her in her plane on a night like this. The girls in the back, all but me drugged by Roscoe. He hadn't bothered with me for years because I never fought again, never said no.

Felicity explained that she had a place for all of us, where we could stay, go to school, even college if we wanted. We would have all the help we needed for as long as we needed so that we could build a new life. I said no. I didn't want that. What I didn't say then was I trusted her. I didn't trust anyone else. She had gotten me out. I would go with her anywhere. Do anything."

She smiled faintly at the memory. "Felicity has a way of looking into you sometimes. She sees what others don't. She could have forced me. I was only a kid. I had no weapon. No skills. She asked what I wanted. I told her I wanted to work for her and I wanted to learn to fly."

"You did both and damn well too."

His quiet words startled her. He had said nothing from the moment she had begun her tale. He had listened.

"You are the third person I have ever told," she said quietly. "Only four people including you know it."

"Besides Felicity, who are the other two?"

"Jonah and Nelson. Felicity had to tell them. She told me about the Ranch and the two men who managed it for her. I should have been scared of being handed over to anyone, especially men. She told me that she owned three mountains, the ranch and the valley around it. She said she had a house on one of the mountains but that her work kept her traveling too much to leave me there.

I needed to go to school, get an education if I really wanted to learn to fly. That meant I needed supervision. She took me to the Ranch and I met Jonah and Nelson."

She grinned at the memory. "You should have seen their faces when they got a look at me. I was all attitude and defiance. Jonah grunted his opinion in Farsi but I didn't know that then. Nelson sat down like someone had knocked him over the head.

Felicity ignored their reactions as though they were both ready to take me on. I figured I could get them mad enough to refuse and then she would have to keep me with her. It didn't occur to me that she could just dump me somewhere to keep me out of the way."

She shook her head over her own blindness.

"Thirty minutes later, I was installed in a room with nice furniture and even a TV and a lock on the door. I didn't know then that either of them could have picked it in seconds. To me, it was the first security I had ever known. I had a lock and door, privacy, a bathroom of my own. So, what if the two in house with me weren't any happier than I was about having me stay. I would stick it out. Felicity had promised I could learn enough to become a pilot."

Benny could imagine the scene the way she was telling it. He could also imagine what Jonah and Nelson had to say when she wasn't present.

"It's a wonder the three of you survived."

Taranda chuckled at the memories. "Don't ever get either of them started on those years. The three of us had a hell of a learning curve.

There was no way I could attend conventional school. So, I was home schooled. Nelson and a couple of the ranch wives handled that.

Jonah taught me to ride and, because I bugged the life out of him, to track. When I turned fifteen, Felicity came home from her work. She stayed for a month after my birthday. I begged her to let me learn martial arts. Jonah got that assignment too."

Benny laughed at the images of Jonah with his language of grunts being a teacher of anything for the girl Taranda described.

"I wish I had been there. It's a wonder either of you managed any of that. Jonah isn't known for his patience."

She laughed with him. "Believe me, he said that more than once. I was a hellion. I had never known discipline with caring. I had never had chores or rules like do your homework, clean your room.

Neither Jonah nor Nelson were the huggy-bear types. They knew as little about handling a teenager as I did about being one. I stopped counting how many times Jonah threatened to quit. At least three times, every trip Felicity made back to the mountain.

Nelson wasn't as vocal but he kept pointing out to Felicity that they were men and knew nothing about a girl growing into a woman. Felicity got that part of my training and neither man gave ground on that aspect. Make-up, high heels, dress code and feminine products never entered any conversation with them present."

"With your history, how did you handle dating?" he asked quietly. The strength, character and courage of her story was clear. That she could see humor in her new life was a testament to her resilience and determination.

"I cornered Jonah one night. Nelson was away on a job for Felicity. That was a first since I had been brought to the Ranch. By then I knew I either had to be chained to the past or I had to write myself a new future. I needed to know I could respond to a man."

The muted sound of an incoming communication from Felicity interrupted her story. Benny watched her face and voice change. Taranda answered, her tone all business, not a sign of emotion. The past had no place here.

"Showing you are about an hour out?"

"On the money. Retrieval." Taranda used verbal shorthand for information on the safety of Andre's wife.

"Five minutes away."

"We'll make it two for two," she promised before signing off.

Benny rose, his empty mug in hand. "More coffee?"

She nodded as she made a minute course adjustment. "We're starting to enter populated areas. Beginning scan now."

CHAPTER FOUR

"I'm twenty minutes from touchdown."

Cam's check-in was right on time. With Taranda collecting Andre and 'blue' in place, he had been the only pilot left to handle the extraction for Andre's wife. Felicity had to be on site to handle security and the co-ordination of teams incoming and redirecting if necessary.

The pair picking up Anhe were parked across and down the street from Anhe's house. If everything went according to plan, Anhe would be in the air and on her way to the Farm in a little over an hour.

"Good. The team has just arrived at the pick-up," she replied.

Using the shoulder cameras each wore, Felicity watched her people split up at Anhe's house, one to the front door, one to the back. The neighborhood was quiet. The lights on in the house looked normal. There were faint sounds from inside that could have been a television or a movie playing.

Joe and Lucy had been partners for three years and were very good in tight situations. She hoped this turned out to be an easy assignment.

Lucy knocked on the front door. No one answered. "She could have fallen asleep in front of the tube." She reached out to try the knob.

When it turned easily in Lucy's hand, Ace cursed quietly. Felicity said nothing. Her people didn't need her voice distracting them as Lucy drew her gun and relayed the situation to Joe.

"Hold. My door is locked. Need a second."

Felicity glanced at the monitor that showed Joe picking the lock. In seconds, there was a barely audible click as the lock disengaged.

"On two."

Felicity watched both enter together, silently clearing each area until they reached the family room. The scene was as orderly as the rest of the interior except for the body of the slender woman lying in a boneless sprawl on the bamboo floor. The open eyes staring at nothing living and the odd angle of her neck told her story.

"Scan the room for me, Lucy."

Felicity saw nothing obviously out of place. If there had been a fight or an attack, there was no sign of it. Someone had cleaned up the scene. She watched Joe bend over the body, checking for bruises or any indication about what had happened.

"Joe?"

"Guessing, here. Looks like she has some skin under her nails on her left hand. Calluses on her hands consistent with someone who knows how to fight back, maybe martial arts."

"My file on her says she is trained. Not competitive. She's a southpaw."

"A couple of dark spots on her knuckles too. I'd say she managed to land a couple of hits."

He eased his hand gently under her head. "She's got a bump on the side here but no blood. As close as she is to this end table, I'd say she went down here, cracking her head on the way. Could have broken her neck then or someone broke it for her when she was down."

He inspected the table, using a penlight to check under the corner and under the edges. "I don't see anything, not even a hair."

Felicity considered her options. Leaving the body to be

found by someone would start a law enforcement trail and a hunt for Andre as a person of interest. He certainly had an alibi but having him in the open and vulnerable was simply not on the table.

Equally, he was one of hers now. He had risked a lot to warn her. That meant that the umbrella of protection she gave all of her people and those they loved extended to him from the moment he had called. His wife would not be left behind nor in the care of strangers.

"Lucy, pack a bag for Anhe. A suitcase with just a few essentials, things a woman might need for an overnight in the hospital. Joe, set the scene. You are both wearing gloves so we don't have to worry about prints. I want it to look as though Andre took her to the hospital.

Joe, I need a little disarray on the couch cushions. Anhe was laying there, hurting. Maybe a glass with water and a little ice on the end table. Leave the TV on low. They were in a hurry and forgot to turn it off.

You'll also need something that won't be missed to wrap around her. I don't want to leave any forensics in the rental car."

"I'll check the garage. Her car is there. I saw it through the window when I used the back gate. There's a side door across from the back porch. We'll be able to get her out without anyone seeing us if the house is dark. I'll get her loaded then lock up after Lucy."

Felicity muted the vocal to her team. "Ace, see if you can find them a route out of town that keeps them off the main streets as much as possible. I don't want any camera shots if we can help it. If you can't route them around the cams, blind them."

"On it."

She reengaged the verbal link to Joe and Lucy. "Set a speed record. I don't know how much time you have. Lucy, you take the car. In the dark with your black hair, anyone seeing you will see Anhe. Ace is looking for a route now to ditch the car and get Anhe into your vehicle. Joe, I don't want that car found."

She glanced at Ace. He nodded as he keyed in the directions to their com units. "Co-ordinates are on the way."

In less than fifteen minutes, the house was locked. One lamp still burned and the TV was playing to the empty room where the scene had been set if anyone came looking for Anhe or Andre.

Her team's exit was smooth and silent. As soon as they were on the road, Felicity updated Cam on the situation. His curse matched her feelings.

"We're monitoring. So far nothing is heating up. As soon as the switch and disposal are made, they will be heading your way. I'll advise."

"Something better go right tonight. Tell me T. has her man," Cam replied.

"Not yet. She's minutes away." Felicity disengaged with Cam and concentrated on Taranda and the pick-up in progress on the monitors in front of her.

"Descending. Strap in."

Benny clicked his seat belt in place. A dark touch and go was not his favorite thing. How Taranda could see in the black around him he didn't know. But she could. It wasn't the first landing with no lights he had survived.

"I hate dents in my baby so I won't hit anything," she murmured as she eased the jet down lightly, feeling the land meet the wheels. Flaps and throttle with a light touch, the bird settled gracefully on the private runway. Benny was out of his seat before the jet stopped completely. Weapon in hand, he moved to the door.

"I see him. He's alone," Taranda said quietly as the scanners gave her a clear picture of the area around them. She felt the cabin depressurize as the hatch opened.

A moment later, Andre was on board. She turned the jet around as Benny secured the door.

"Any word on my wife?" Andre asked as he settled into the closest seat to the flightdeck.

"Communications are as light as possible. I know she has been picked up and is on the way to the Farm," Taranda answered as she increased speed for take-off. "You'll see her in a few hours."

"Andre on board," Taranda reported to Felicity as she reached her cruising altitude with a wide swing west. "Heading home."

"Let me talk to Andre." She only had to wait a few seconds before Andre spoke.

"You have Anhe?"

"She is with one of my teams and on the way to Cam. He will be flying her to The Farm."

She needed him to stay focused on providing a background for his and Anhe's temporary disappearance.

"The two of you need a cover if anyone is checking on you. Call your boss and tell him that Anhe is very unwell and you're really worried because she sounds so bad. Since you have completed your work in Washington, you are flying home earlier than anticipated. You might need some time off to take care of her depending on what the problem is.

Ace is taking care of getting you a ticket and putting you on the plane. I have someone picking up your luggage from the hotel. Luckily, we found a really full boarding list, so if anyone starts asking questions and no one really remembers you, there is a believable explanation."

Andre nodded. "I can do that. Maybe I have to take her to the hospital. That would explain an empty house," he added, thinking quickly.

She had thought the man sharp when he had trained with them on the Farm. He was proving that impression yet again.

"Exactly. She will be with us by the time you get here." Felicity ended the call before he could ask any questions.

She leaned back in her chair. The situation was loaded with problems but at least Andre was out of harm's way. Anhe was not being left in a house with no one to know that she had died. Andre was not facing his grief alone.

"You didn't tell him she was dead. Smart and kind."

"Easier on them until Andre gets here. Nothing can change what happened. Telling him while he sitting on plane where he can't see her and give in to his feelings isn't going to help any of us."

"Like I said, smart and kind."

"He risked his life to warn us. He's one of us, at least for now. We don't leave our people behind and we don't leave their loved ones either."

Cam adjusted his final approach for landing. Piloting wasn't his favorite thing which was why he was back-up only.

He wouldn't have been that if Felicity hadn't needed him to get his license. Having Taranda as his instructor had not been fun even if she was a damn good teacher.

Tonight's flight was critical for so many reasons. He wished he wasn't carrying home the dead wife of a man he liked once he got past thinking that Andre was interested in Mia.

He wouldn't wish on anyone what Andre would be facing when Felicity told him his Anhe was dead. He got a hole in his gut just thinking about what he would feel if it was Mia who was lying lifeless behind him.

"Touching down," Cam said, knowing that Felicity was tracking him.

"On my way." Felicity stood and stretched, easing the strain of muscles held in a single position for hours.

She had two images of the men meeting with Gordon. Both had passed through security without the guard using the metal detecting equipment. That told her that the duo was expected and not considered a threat. She saw the pair enter Gordon's office. Beyond that, the cameras did not go.

She saw Andre walking down the hall, stopping, a frown on his face. She watched him retrace his steps and move into the open doorway of the outer office. He stood still for a moment, clearly listening. Then he was running.

A man shot out of the doorway and gave chase but

Andre had too much of a lead. If the man saw anything at all, it was Andre's back. Someone would have to ask questions to discover Andre's name. That bought them some time but not much.

Andre would have checked through with the guard. All Gordon had to do was ask the right question.

But would she?

Ace glanced at her then returned his attention to the information slowly emerging in front of him. Senator Gordon was losing any illusion of privacy. Her personal and political life were emerging in the data on the monitors.

None of the facts, so far, provided a reason why a woman had died. What was Gordon protecting? A woman was dead by accident or design because someone was covering her ass and the asses of whoever had bought her.

"We're getting a lot of data but nothing solid enough to explain the response that Gordon put into play. Following the money for her campaigns is definitely illuminating for a newly elected Washington official. She has some big money behind her, but I don't see anything irregular yet."

"Neither do I. Let's hope the facial recognition gives us the connection."

"I'll keep on this or do you need help with Anhe?"

"I've got it. The dorms are empty right now since we don't have any trainees this month. We have a room ready for

Andre when he gets here. That won't matter to him. He'll want to see Anhe first."

She headed for the coffee pot. The next hour was going to be difficult and that was just the beginning. It would get a lot worse when Andre landed.

"If you are getting one for me, I'd rather have cold caffeine for a while."

Felicity replaced the pot without pouring another cup for herself or Ace. "Actually, that does sound better."

She got out two cans and handed one to him. "Call me if you get to a final layer before I get back. I'll be about an hour. I want to make sure Anhe will be ready for Andre when he gets here."

Ace nodded without stopping what he was doing until he heard the door close behind him. Only then did he program the system to auto and lean back in his chair. He popped the top on his drink and took a sip.

He thought of all the layers of activity both physical and mental going on tonight. Felicity had staged and managed every detail, overlapping and coordinating people on different coasts. Designing and implementing a cover story on the fly. Making sure that any loose ends were tied.

Now, she was meeting a plane carrying a body, personally escorting it to a place where Andre's wife could be laid to rest to wait for her husband to grieve over her death.

He had no doubt Cam could have handled the details, but Felicity hadn't left him with the unpleasant task.

He should have known she had a place for the dead. She lived with life and with death. She understood that any of them could die. She cared enough to make sure that she had a place for her people, for those left behind. Because Andre had warned her, risked danger to do it as soon as possible, he had become one of them. Anhe's death was now a death of one of their own.

Felicity stood in the shadow of the hangar as Cam brought the plane to a halt. The soft sound of footsteps behind her made her turn. Mia came toward her.

"Cam let me know he was landing. Let me help. I knew her a little through calls and text."

"Are you sure? This isn't going to be easy."

"I know. I can't promise not to cry but I won't walk away. This is important, for her and for Andre."

She heard the door on the plane open. She watched as Cam eased down the steps, cradling Anhe's body in his arms. Felicity could have brought a cart to the strip but she hadn't. Carrying her home seemed right.

She and Mia walked beside them, neither saying a word. The door to the small chapel was open and the lights inside bright enough for sight but soft enough for reverence. Cam carried Anhe to the room in the back.

The three of them worked in silence to prepare Anhe for Andre. When she was ready, they stepped back to judge the scene they had created.

Anhe lay on a raised platform beneath a white sheet draped from shoulder to toes. Mia had brushed her long black hair until it lay smooth and shiny against her pale skin. Her black lashes were silky fans on her cheeks. Everything about her was delicate and finely made.

With Cam's help, Felicity had bathed Anhe and dressed her from the wardrobe she kept for various disguises. Mia's choices were perfect.

Mia had stayed as close as possible to the style and colors of Anhe's own clothes which were stained and creased from death and traveling.

They couldn't give Anhe life but they could give her dignity, peace and caring in death. Andre would not see her the way her people had found her, left on the floor where she had fallen surrounded by the smell of death when the body purged itself.

"At least there are no marks on her. No signs that she suffered," Mia said softly, tears stinging her eyes. Felicity had saved her the painful task of bathing Anhe by sending her to wardrobe for clothes for her.

"I hope it helps him," Felicity murmured as she collected the small container holding the skin fragments that she had cleaned from Anhe's nails.

Anhe's defense against her attacker might just help catch the person responsible for her death. Maybe that would help Andre. Maybe he would feel more deeply the strength and courage of the woman he had married.

"Me too. They weren't even married a year." Cam dragged his hand through his hair. The cool, quiet of the room was peaceful yet he couldn't feel anything but anger.

Felicity touched his arm. "She was always going to die, Cam. Better tonight than later. They would have hurt her badly to force him into the open. Whether he obeyed or not they would have killed her. As fast as we moved, they were faster."

"I know." He cursed roughly. "I don't have to like it."

"No. When we find them, we will give her justice. That's all we can do."

She turned from death and headed for the door. "Pass the word about Anhe. Whatever Andre needs, we'll be there for him."

"If it helps, I think you're right not to tell him what happened until he gets here."

Right or not, it was the choice she had made. "I hope he sees it that way."

Cam watched her head across the compound to the control room. He had helped her care for a woman she didn't know and he had seen no emotion on her face nor did he hear it in the few words spoken between them.

He pulled Mia close to him, needing her warmth, the feel her alive in his arms. He had seen her tears, the gentle way she had helped Felicity and her relief at not having to stay for the cleansing.

The task the three of them had completed had been difficult on so many levels. Someone else might have just laid Anhe out and covered her with a sheet.

Felicity had a crisis in the making and she could have delegated the chore and no one in the compound would have hesitated to do what she asked. One and all were intimately acquainted with death and what it did to the human body.

Yet she had taken the ritual on herself. Her hands had been gentle, as tender as a mother handling a well-loved child. She hadn't just cleaned Anhe's body. She had thought of clothes, sending Mia to hunt for just the right colors and design.

Andre might not even notice what had been done for his wife. Grief blinded in so many ways.

But when Andre saw his Anhe, he wouldn't see what they had. He would see her beauty and her peace. Cam hoped it would give him some peace to temper the grief.

"I wish you hadn't had to face this tonight and yet I am glad you were here. It helped."

"I wanted to be here for Anhe and for you. We are together in all of this. I won't break and I won't turn away from things that hurt."

She leaned into him. "Let's go home."

Cam shut the door to the cool, silent room. No matter what, Felicity had done everything she could for a woman she had never met and a man she had only known for a few short weeks of training. He and Mia had done it for the man they knew and the woman he loved.

CHAPTER FIVE

"What have you got on Senator Gordon?" Felicity asked as she took the chair beside Ace. The screens in front of her held the long version. She would get to that later. Right now, she wanted Ace's summation.

"A bought and paid for politician. What I don't see yet is any actions of hers as a return on the investment that was made. Eight years ago, she was a county official finishing her first term in a southern border state. With no more than four years of public service, she ran for governor. I am still compiling a list of donor names.

She didn't spend lavishly on the campaign trail. Her staff made every dollar count and managed to garner more private donations than anyone with her limited political history should have been able to get. She beat out the popular incumbent by a healthy margin.

She spent four years in the state capitol. Then Senator Baldwin dies from a heart attack with no history of heart trouble just before running for re-election. Another man was elected to finish out his term.

The senator taking over for Baldwin had been known as a traditionalist with a rock-hard view of right and wrong. He had been popular with the voters and served had successfully for the year and a half remaining of Baldwin's time. His record should have been an asset when he came up for re-election.

However, when he sought the full term seat, he lost badly. No one believed the newcomer to the political scene had a chance against him. The odds makers had been wrong. Gordon had won.

"There's our first link."

When Ace leaned back in his chair, his green eyes fixed on her face, she filled him in on the details of Baldwin's demise and the investigation Skye/Sea Security had conducted. The information she had been given had checked out. She had taken the assignment and meted out the verdict that had been rendered by those higher up in the food chain.

The result, no scandal on or off the Hill.

Ace cursed fluently in two languages perfectly suited

for his feelings.

"Well said. I would like to have the fool in front of me who put our name in a record somewhere. The whole point of putting us on Baldwin's trail was to not leave any paper behind to bite anyone in the butt. No scandal, no blowback was one of the major focuses of the mission."

"Andre said Gordon mentioned two deaths. There was another politician?"

"Not in the Senate. The House. Same problem. Same owner."

"Finish your summary of Gordon while I pull up my notes on Baldwin and Rogers. We may get lucky and find some crosses with Gordon."

Felicity keyed in the search information. In seconds, the screen split to show each politician's information. Then she set the system on background to search for any matches, events, people or organizations, between Gordon, Baldwin and Rogers.

Ace laughed without humor. "Right and I have some Nevada oceanfront property to sell you. He or she could be hiding under a trust or a charity or an alias. Having those names will probably be just the first layer. We'll need the to do a secondary search on every little donation if that is what we find."

"Agreed. I love auto searches. The computers do the

work on stuff like this and I can concentrate on other areas. I doubt the first layers are going to give us the name or names we need. Whatever this plan is, it is well thought out. We'll find the cross if it exists."

Ace inclined his head. None of them would quit until they did.

"Back to our newbie senator's story. With very little real prep, Gordon flings her hat into the Senatorial race. Money comes in a steady stream. Same campaign manager. Same tactics."

Her whole pitch was based on what she could do in Washington. She didn't do any smear campaigning and she didn't go the divisive route either. She was photogenic and articulate. The media's golden girl who ran on issues not bashing her opponents."

"Same big donors?"

"A lot of them but not all. I have been running them individually. So far, everything looks good."

"How good?"

Ace shrugged slightly, feeling the tightness in his shoulders from sitting in front of the computer for hours. He had always preferred action to inactivity.

"I'm a cynic. I don't know anyone in politics this clean. As governor, she didn't make promises on the campaign trail that she didn't keep in office.

Improved low-cost housing. Attention to the homeless situation and three new shelters paid for by private donations in the first year of her term. Those are only the highlights.

She tackled the illegal immigrant issue, reduced the numbers by increasing the patrols and the budget to pay them. Instead of keeping the illegals on our side of the border when they were caught, the patrols turned them back with an armed escort that included guard dogs.

Very few people, even desperate ones, want to go up against a dog trained to attack, especially if there are kids involved. At a guess, I would say the ones who wanted in badly enough moved east or west to a state not so heavily patrolled."

"That had to help her Senate run."

"It did. Big time."

Ace rose and stretched tiredly. "Taranda should be landing in less than thirty. We could use a short break if for no other reason than to walk out the kinks. Meeting Andre with the news of his wife's death is going to be tough."

Felicity stood, accepting the idea of a break. Before Ace, she wouldn't have considered the thought. The responsibility she carried had been hers alone. Having him in her life had changed her thinking as he shared more and more of the day-to-day operations of the Farm's expanding reach.

"I wouldn't mind twenty minutes in the hot tub."

Ace groaned. "I was going to settle for a walk in the

woods. No screens to scroll facts and figures until my eyes feel like they are bleeding sounded like heaven until you mentioned the hot tub. If I wasn't so stiff, I would race you."

She laughed softly as she took the hand he offered. "You aren't that stiff. And I usually beat you."

"Not always."

He pulled her close and kissed her hard. For a few moments, Felicity was his woman not just the boss of everyone on three mountains, the various arms of Skye/Sea spanning untold miles across too many borders to count. She held lives in her hands, ones to be taken and many to be saved.

The electronics around them hummed, shifting through data at mega speeds. Powered by many programs of her design, the information was filtered and collated into facts specifically aimed in preset directions. With the power of technology behind them, Felicity more often than not found the answers she sought.

For now, they could have their moment before she had to tell a good man his wife had died because he had chosen to do what was right. Ace didn't envy her the coming task.

"Do you want me with you when you meet Andre?" he asked as they crossed the compound to her house. Her three Dobermans came out of the shadows of the trees, their eyes alert for any command.

Felicity took a second to greet each dog. "I thought

about it but I think it would be easier on him if it is just me."

As she straightened, she looked at him, one brow cocked as if to ask his opinion.

As little as six months ago, she wouldn't have made the gesture. They had been lovers for almost a year. She had slowly opened her life and her world to him. Rarely in a way that required verbalization. Little things, a gesture, a look or a hand held out.

"I think just you would be better for him. Is Cam alright?"

"He will be. I hope he is taking a few minutes with Mia. He knew Andre better than either of us. He had more training classes with him. Plus, it hasn't been that many months since he almost died himself. Before that, worrying about Mia while she fought to survive the beating she took and their new relationship added a number of layers."

They entered her home together.

"You know I think I would like a couple of hard laps in the pool instead of the hot tub. I need the exercise."

As an answer, Felicity pulled off her tee and reached for the button at her waist.

"Me too." She shed her jeans and panties with a few wiggles.

Ace grinned as he stripped just as fast as she. Naked, her hand in his they stepped through the open sliders to the patio. They dove into the water together, surfacing and pacing each other in a series of laps and speed turns.

The warmth of the pool, the lack of anyone else but them and the sound of the water rippling around them was better than a stiff drink at the end of a bad day.

Ace surfaced, felling relaxed and limber. He draped an arm over the edge of the coping and slicked his black hair back. "I needed that."

Felicity dipped her head so the water could take care of the hair dipping in her eyes. She lay on her back, lightly moving her hands to hold herself in place.

"There was a time when I wouldn't have thought of this. I'm glad I don't live like that anymore."

Ace slid a hand up her bare leg, not in a bid for sex but for affection. "I didn't do much more than work either. Sex occasionally was the closest I got to taking a break. I didn't even notice how empty my life was."

"Being alone was safer. No one to worry about me and no one I had to worry about."

He shook his head. "You worried. Everyone who works for you is important to you. You cover their backs every day. That worry is as much a part of you as your hazel eyes and your unbelievable laser intelligence.

No one here is just an employee. Not blood kin but definitely brother, sister, friend. You don't show anyone how much you worry but they know you care. That's why no one ever hesitates to step into the next mission, take the next chance."

She dropped her feet to the pool bottom. "You give me too much credit. I couldn't do what I do without everyone here. The teams, the support staff who never pick up a weapon. I need them all."

"You do. Expanding as you are, you built this compound, bought three mountains and a valley with a ranch to provide a home for disenfranchised people who simply can't function easily in the outside world.

The skills they have been taught, the memories they have in countries that most people only know as sound bites on the news have irrevocably changed them, destroyed their ability to return to the world that they sought to protect. You have given them a way to protect and to live with the unlivable."

He framed her face with his hands. "You gave me a place. I was getting ready to walk away from government work but I couldn't see myself with a nine to five job. I had lived on the edge too long to settle for suburbia. I'd had a gun somewhere on my body for most of my adult life. I don't know how anyone trained like that can go back to what is called normal."

"Don't turn me into some kind of saint or savior. I'm

not. I can't live out there either. I don't want to. I am doing what I was trained to do."

"We all are and we are doing a damn good job of it."

"We don't always win."

"No but we don't quit." He pulled her to him, content to hold her, to feel her heart beating against his.

His heat was a comfort and a gift. "Our break is over," she said quietly. She raised her head to kiss him lightly.

"I know." He lifted her to the edge of the pool then levered himself up to sit beside her. She got to her feet and offered him her hand. He took it.

"I hope Benny is in the mood to cook when he gets back. Nobody in the kitchen makes an omelet as good as he does."

Felicity laughed as they walked indoors to dress. "You know very well the first place he heads whenever he returns from a run is the kitchen. You'll get your omelet."

Taranda adjusted her course. Almost home. It had been a long night and she needed fuel just like her jet.

"Buckle up, Andre. Landing in five."

She didn't have to tell Benny. He knew the route almost as well as she did. Besides, dawn had painted the land below in shades of rose and gold, highlighting the landscape like a picture. The weather was clear. The land was easy to read.

"Is there a steak in my future?" she asked as she initiated the descent.

"Since I'm making one for myself, I can easily make two."

She flashed him a grin. "The way I like it?"

He chuckled. "Are you planning on picking at my cooking, woman?"

Before the flight, she would have snapped back a reply that would have started her down a path they had taken too many times. Now, she didn't want to fight. She didn't need it. Telling him about her past wasn't the way she would have thought would clear the air between them but somehow it had.

"I have been a bit of a bitch about it," she admitted as she felt the tires touch the ground. Flaps and throttle slowed the sleek bird.

"Well, I've been a prick."

She laughed as she eased to a stop. After she cut the engines, she looked at him. "Are we done sniping at each other?"

"Looks like it."

"Felicity will be pleased."

"At least you didn't get the talk like I did."

Benny grimaced. He didn't want to think of that in any reality. "Just make sure that you tell her the war is over."

Taranda laughed at the command in his voice and his pained expression. For a moment she tried to imagine the scene of Felicity discussing their version of verbal foreplay with Benny. She almost wished she could have been a fly on the wall to that conversation. She unbuckled her seat belt and stood in the confined space.

"We deserved it. We know better." She moved off the flightdeck so he could have room to stand.

"Sometimes, knowing better doesn't get the job done."

Andre was at the door, waiting. "Thanks for picking me up."

"All in a day's work," Taranda said as she unlatched the hatch. The steps deployed. Felicity was waiting on the tarmac.

Andre glanced around, expecting to see Anhe. He frowned when he realized no one but Felicity was present.

"We're on alert status. Anhe is in the compound. I'll show you."

Felicity glanced at Taranda and Benny. "You'll need another cart."

"We'll walk. I want to stretch my legs. Okay with you?" Taranda asked with a glance over her shoulder for Benny's answer. His nod was quick.

Felicity inclined her head before walking away.

"Something's wrong," Taranda murmured as she watched the pair leave. "Felicity could have brought Anhe here." She started down the path with Benny beside her.

"I have been thinking the same thing since we picked up Andre and his wife wasn't on the com. Our jammers are secure enough that Felicity could have allowed a short call."

"She wouldn't have lied to him about her being here." She frowned, realizing her reply was a knee jerk rather than truth.

"I take that back. She would have if it meant success of a mission. But I don't see how that would have mattered in this case."

"She's here all right. The question is in what condition?"

"Beat up like Mia, hanging on by a thread?"

"Or dead."

"Shit."

Benny took her hand, something he wouldn't have attempted hours before, something she wouldn't have allowed. It felt good when her fingers curled around his.

"I second that."

"What aren't you telling me? Is Anhe hurt?"

Andre couldn't see anyone in the compound as Felicity drove across the center yard that usually had a few people moving from one place to another.

She pulled to a stop in front of a building he hadn't noticed during his training. It was set away from the others. Small, it was almost hidden by the trees around it. A narrow path curled to the right under the shade of the heavy branches.

"I promise you she isn't hurting, Andre. As fast as we moved, as quickly as you called us when you got clear, we weren't fast enough. Someone got to your house before us. She fought back."

Pain stole the air from his next breath. He focused on Felicity's face, her calm voice soft, kind.

"As near as we can determine, she fell or was shoved. Her neck was broken in the fall. We brought her home for you. We took care of her."

Andre stared at the small structure in front of him. Of all things he had imagined, this outcome was not one of them. He didn't want to walk through that door, see his Anhe. Even as the thought formed, he made himself slide out of the golf cart. When Felicity joined him, he couldn't think of a single word to say.

Felicity opened the door. There was a small room, dimly lit, with benches like a chapel between him and where Anhe lay.

The light was a soft glow around her. She lay beneath a white sheet. Closing the door behind them, Felicity stayed just inside the room.

Andre walked slowly down the short aisle toward his wife. He stopped a few inches from touching her. So beautiful, her dark hair a soft rain against her pale skin. Her dark lashes hid her golden eyes. He would never see them open again. Never see her smile again. She had died alone.

With a low groan he went down on his knees beside her body. He curled an arm around her and laid his head on her shoulder. The exotic scent of her skin was gone. Her bones were so very fragile now. He couldn't hear her heart beat, wouldn't hear it ever again.

Turning from them, Felicity gave Andre privacy for his grief. Ace was waiting for her when she stepped out into the sunrise. He slipped an arm around her and walked with her to the small bench under the trees.

"Are you okay?"

Felicity leaned her head on his shoulder. There had been so many times in her life when she'd had to face horrors and tragedies alone. In moments like these, she was very glad those days were over.

"Yes. Thanks for being here."

"Always. We are in this together. Heaven or Hell."

"It makes a difference." She watched the door.

Wanting to give her mind another path, Ace said, "Cam and I raided the wardrobe since Andre didn't have any clothes with him."

"I missed that one. When did you have time?"

"You had more important things on your mind. I called Cam while you were making us coffee. When you went to meet Andre, we raided the clothes racks. We found enough stuff to outfit him, assuming we guessed the sizes right. We put it in one of the rooms in the men's housing.

Mia made sure there were some snacks and drinks in the mini frig in case he wants to eat without people around him. She put the number for the kitchen in plain sight on the desk. She talked to the kitchen and they said that food delivery for a day or two wouldn't be a problem. She promised to mention it to Benny."

"Good ideas on all of it. The kitchen arrangement is fine as long as we are only on 'blue'. If we have to escalate the risk, that's off the table."

"Understood." Ace heard the door open. He released Felicity and rose to stand beside her as Andre joined them.

He held out his hand to Felicity. He didn't want to leave but he couldn't stay in that room that held only death. He couldn't think. He needed a place to be alone.

"I won't ever forget what you did for Anhe, for me. You're sure she didn't suffer?"

"I'm positive. I checked when I was taking care of her. There were only two marks on her, small bruises on her left knuckles."

She held his hand firmly, watching his expression, hoping she was using the right words, the words she would have wanted to hear.

"She fought back, Andre. Anhe fought for you and herself. She had skin under her nails. She did her best to tell us who tried to hurt her and was trying to use her against you."

She watched the tears form in his eyes. She wished she had more to give him.

"We are looking for the person or persons who hurt her. I promise you we will not stop until we find them."

"You mean that?"

"I know that. I never met her until this morning. Being with her, caring for her, I saw that. The team who found her saw that too. Cam flew her home for you, carried her here to wait for you."

Andre broke then. A harsh sound and a bowed head. Grief came in a rigid stance for a man trying to stand when he needed to go to his knees.

Ace draped an arm around his shoulders and guided him to the golf cart. Felicity watched the two head for the men's quarters. She exhaled deeply, wishing this morning was over. She would rather be unarmed facing a rifle pointed at her heart than to relive the last half hour.

Death always left pain in its wake. She had seen so much. It never got easier.

CHAPTER SIX

"What do you mean she broke her own neck? How?"

Sharon dropped into the chair behind her desk. Midmorning and she felt like she had been waiting for hours for a call that told her that she had control of the situation. Only she didn't have control. The fool had bungled the job.

"All you had to do was snatch one stupid woman. And you screwed it up. You owe me one hundred thousand dollars, you bastard."

"I owe you nothing, bitch. You didn't mention the woman was into martial arts and she was good."

He fingered the scratch on his cheek. If she hadn't broken her own neck, he would have done it for her for the three gouges on his face and the two punches in his ribs that still hurt.

"I paid you to do a job and you didn't. Her husband is gone. He didn't check out of his hotel. His luggage was still there when I had it checked right after I talked to you."

"Not my problem."

"You haven't earned that hundred thousand yet. Find him."

"Wrong. I am not chasing that bitch's husband. No telling what he knows about fighting and I'm not in the mood for your half ass intel. You want him so bad, find some fool to hunt him for you. I won't forget you screwed with me on this."

"How was I supposed to know what she could do?"

"You think you are so good as a hacker? You missed that little detail and it cost you. Not...My...Problem," he added, spacing the last words for emphasis.

He jabbed the red dot on his cell. He was done talking to Senator Gordon. He had done more than enough of her dirty work over the years. The only good thing about this night was that he had a hundred K in his bank account and she had shit.

He laughed harshly enough that his ribs hurt. His fists clenched. He really wished he had broken that woman's neck himself.

Sharon sat still, looking blankly at the far wall. She didn't see the expensively framed portrait sized photo of her taking the oath of office as a new Senator.

She had come too far, had too much to lose to stop now. She had to think. She had her investor demanding she deal with LaPlante on one side and LaPlante aware of her cyber dive into well-hidden government records she had no business knowing existed on the other.

Since she didn't have the government knocking on her door yet, she had to assume LaPlante went to the other group involved in the reports she accessed. Skye/Sea Security Consultants.

The minute she realized what she had uncovered they had become a problem. She wasn't about to suffer a convenient heart attack or an accident like her two predecessors.

If Skye/Sea Security had been assigned once, they could be again. She didn't dare risk trying to discredit them. That might end up shining a light on her and her backer. She wasn't fool enough to believe she could hire enough muscle to take them on and have any guarantee of success.

Failure was not an option. The man had made that clear. He wouldn't wait forever. He had told her to handle the situation. The wife's death was unexpected and rendered her useless as leverage.

She now had LaPlante's name. She had no other resources except her backer. He had to know that. All it would take was one phone call. She had a new supply of burner phones.

Maybe she had been stupid not to think of that to begin with, before she had sent Mickey after LaPlante's wife. She wouldn't have lost that hundred K.

She laid the cell down on her desk beside her computer. She stroked the keys. Maybe LaPlante's name and a copy of the report would cover her ass for not getting the wife as leverage for his silence.

She had firewalls and alerts on her system, the one she used for hacking. None of them had been triggered. She had spent hours honing her skills. She knew she was good but finding that report had been sheer luck. However, it was on her system now.

She could give the man something he had to want. She could give him the name of the head of the department who had ordered the off the book's investigation of two of their congressmen and ultimately ordered their deaths.

LaPlante, Everly and Skye/Sea Security Consultants.

All three were threats to whatever the plans were in the works. She had no proof but the file and two deaths.

Whatever was planned had years of implementation involved. To invest that kind of money, time and preparation meant that the reward had to be epic.

How she fit into the plan she didn't know and that terrified her. She had thought she was simply exchanging donations for political favors. That kind of deal happened all the time. It was almost business as usual in the game of politics.

By finding that damn file, she had put herself in jeopardy. If only she hadn't demanded that meeting. She pushed away from the desk to pace the room. She had to think. One stupid, emotionally driven impulse had gotten her in this mess. A critical mistake. She could not afford another.

On the third return trip, she eyed the phone. She had no other choice. It was a risk, a huge risk. But she could see no other way to cover her ass short of going to the government herself.

What could she tell them? Yes, she had major money behind her but she had done no favors as governor nor in the Senate.

No matter how deep anyone dug, they would find nothing questionable. Her backers were as clean as she was as far as she knew but did she want risk imprisonment if she was wrong. She didn't dare produce the file. That was a crime, hacking secure governmental links.

That left Arturo as her only option. She was right back where she started. The file had gotten her into this mess. It might be the way out. She reached for the burner cell. She had no choice. She had to make it work.

The man had only one name. She could give him two more. Everly could very well save her life. His position gave him the power to investigate the donors and dispose of them with no one the wiser. The two congressmen were proof of that.

If she couldn't make this work, she was a walking dead woman. She had no doubt that Arturo Santiago could make that happen with a simple call or a single word.

As he had pointed out, she could be replaced. She was living proof of that. She was a replacement herself.

She made the call, went through the single word verification then waited a full five minutes for the man to speak.

"You have the situation contained?" The smooth voice held an edge of danger that warned her to waste no words.

The last thing she wanted to do was admit the failure of her plan to control LaPlante. She was out of options. She had no other choice.

"I have the name of the man who overheard our meeting. It is Andre LaPlante. He has not returned to his home. He did not make his scheduled return flight."

"You do not have him?"

"No."

"It has been hours and you have information I could have gotten in minutes and you think this is enough?"

She shut her eyes for one second. She should have known better than to think that this man would not demand an explanation.

"No. When I found he had not returned to his hotel nor made his return flight, I sent someone to his house to kidnap his new wife. She was killed in the attempt. With her as a hostage, I would have had bait for him to come out of hiding and a hostage for his silence."

Her delivery gained her not a word of response. Her hand wanted to shake. Death was closing in if she didn't give him something to offset her failure. Damn Mickey!

"The man who ordered the investigation of my predecessor is Harry Everly."

If this name didn't work, she was dead. Simple and unstoppable.

Everly. He had attended too many parties, too many political events not to recognize the name. The man had great power and a career that spanned decades. He would not have thought him to have been in the position to order the death of anyone.

This woman had found what his people could not? What else did she know?

"You think this is important to me?"

She took a deep breath as silently as possible. She had one shot. She hoped it wasn't her last.

"Your knowledge of our government is extensive. You must have heard the name. He is very highly placed and very powerful. Not a good enemy for either of us.

I left an alert on the file I found. It has not been tripped. I can give you a copy of the file. You have LaPlante, Everly and Skye/Sea Security."

Marco stared at the names he had written. He did indeed want the names. Skye/Sea Security was only a problem if the company was hired again. It was not a regular contractor.

LaPlante, as long as he hadn't contacted anyone about what he had heard, needed only to be found and eliminated.

Everly was a different matter. He was a problem. Until this stupid woman had found a file that his best people hadn't been able to locate, he'd had no idea who had disposed of his assets in Congress.

Gordon had a use he had not anticipated.

"You will send me nothing. You will tell me exactly how and where you found this file. If you have lied to me...."

"I have not," she hurried to assure him. Verbal was better. This way there was no trail from his system to hers. She quickly explained how she had accessed the file. She added the code to the trip she had attached.

He said nothing when she finished. Her hand tightened on the cell. She mentally reviewed everything she had told him. She had left nothing out. He now knew everything she did.

"You have omitted one name on your list."

Sharon frowned. "I gave you every name in the file." Silence was his answer. Then she understood. He wanted Mickey.

"He knows nothing. Only LaPlante's name and his address."

His lack of response was chilling. The danger was not over yet. Mickey's failure had put her in this position and himself in the crosshairs. His fault not hers.

"Mickey Grainger." No answer. She added Mickey's address.

"Pray."

The tiny disconnect sound of the cell was a relief. She set it carefully on the desk and just stared at the small rectangle. She had done many things in her life but never had she ordered someone's death.

Yet, Mickey's failure had led to this. All he had to do was get the woman. Not her fault, his.

Marco settled behind the desk that his father had

bought at an auction. Over a hundred years old, it represented the heritage that a determined man could create with his own sweat and blood. He glanced out the window to the vast stretch of land that he had added to his father's holdings.

His father had given him an enviable life, money, education, travel, the best of everything money could buy. He wanted that and more for his children and his children's children. The Stud that had been the source of his father's income was no longer the main pipeline.

He had developed other financial streams that were rivers of wealth and power in a number of countries around the world. He worked in the gray area between legal and criminal. Unlike his partner, he avoided violence except in defense. He had no interest in weapons, whores or drugs.

He turned from the view to reach for the landline phone on the corner of his desk. He punched in a number that existed only in his memory. Finally, he had an answer for the problem that had been a worry and a shadow over his very lucrative dealings north of the border.

"Marco. It is good to hear from you, my friend."

For a man who had clawed his way out of the worst of the streets, his partner had a quiet, almost accent-less, educated voice.

"Business has kept me very busy. I have a report on our joint venture that I think may be of interest."

"You know I am always interested in news of our mutual dealings. Shall we say lunch today?"

"Excellent. I would be delighted."

"Eleven?"

"Excellent."

"I will look forward to it."

Marco hung up the phone then pressed a small button under the edge of his desk. His office door opened. His bodyguard waited silently.

"Bring the programmer."

The man nodded, leaving as soundlessly as he had entered, shutting the door behind him.

Now, he would see if the Senator had given him valid information.

CHAPTER SEVEN

Felicity entered the dining hall with Ace at her side. She had sent out the message to everyone in the compound to gather for a meeting.

The dining hall was a dual-purpose area. It was big enough to hold the twenty-seven people who represented the total of the Farm's workers. Trainers, support staff such as kitchen help, cleaners, electricians/plumbers, mechanics, building and yard maintenance. The Farm was completely self-sufficient.

The Ranch was present virtually via a closed circuit, heavily cloaked and encrypted signal. The attendance there was just as diverse and as important as those on the Farm. The Ranch provided the bulk of the food needed for the human and animal population of both locations. It was also the home base for those of the Farm who had families. Lifetime housing was provided at no cost to every employee.

More importantly to Skye/Sea Security, Felicity provided security for her people. In the possible escalation of any situation they faced, she had the ability to move the innocents out of harm's way which was one of the points she would be discussing.

Ace stopped at the edge of the small circle open at the front of the room. Felicity stood before them. The Ranch gathering was on the screen on the back wall facing her. She looked at every face, taking a second to make eye contact with each of her people.

"We have been through 'blues' before. We all know the drill. Lockdown, alert and guard until the threat is eliminated. Days or hours, it doesn't matter. We don't return to green until I am sure the threat to us is over.

Right now, I am looking at two possible threats. One, I suspect will be relatively easy to neutralize without having any impact here. The other is potentially much more complicated and considerably riskier for all of us.

For those of you with families, we will protect your loved ones if the second threat becomes a certainty. As of an hour ago, a chartered cruise ship is enroute to a port in Louisiana. Our transport chopper is fueled and on standby.

There are twenty on the Ranch who will be transported out of harm's way.

An airlift will happen well before any direct threat to us. The helo will land at a private airstrip. A luxury bus will take all passengers to the port. The bus will have an invisible escort for the entire trip.

Your families will board the vacation ship. The crew are specially trained bodyguards. Your wives, husbands and children will have no idea that they are being heavily protected.

The ship will sail to an island that has no connection to Skye/Sea Security Consultants or Skye/Sea. As far as your families are concerned, this is an all-expense paid holiday for them, a bonus from Skye/Sea Security Consultants."

Felicity was aware of every change of expression. The worry of what could happen to the relief that those with families found in her arrangements for their loved ones.

"Those of you here who are not armed or trained will be included in the trip. That will add another eight people to the flight. Cam will have your names.

This is for your protection, not because you aren't as important to our operation. You simply are not trained for what may come. Also, by going, you help legitimize the story surrounding the trip.

I'm counting on every one of you to support the evac

and the trip as I have described it. We may not need the evac. I hope we don't. We have to be mentally and physically prepared if we do."

Again, she looked at every face, made eye contact with each person, even those on virtual. "I am counting on everyone to do his or her part, no matter what it is."

"I'm in," a gruff voice in the live audience in front of her said clearly as he looked at those around him.

"Me too," a woman added virtually. "My kids will love it. And if sitting on a beach somewhere helps, I can sit with the best of them."

Other voices spoke up, until everyone agreed aloud. Some with just a word, others with gratitude and determination.

"Thank you all. For now, 'blue' holds. I am tracking the threats down. When I know more, you will too. No mention of the trip until I give you the go."

The screen in the back went dark. Those closest to Felicity moved nearer. No questions were voiced but a lot of offers were given for any kind of help she might need. Felicity accepted the thanks and promised to call on anyone needed for more.

Ace watched the group slowly disperse until nothing but a few feet of space was between them. These months with her had given him an appreciation of the organization she had built single handedly.

The commitment of those in the compound was clear. He had seen it every day. He had seen it the few times he had been to the Ranch. He had not, until this meeting, realized how completely Felicity had considered all possibilities. To the best of her ability, the woman left nothing to chance.

There were so many things he wanted to say, but this wasn't the time or the place. They had work to do.

"Can we have our omelets now? I thought I was hungry before, but if I am going to gear up for a possible war, I want a really big breakfast first."

"I heard that," Benny came out of the kitchen carrying four plates. "I can listen and cook at the same time," he added in case anyone thought he wasn't paying attention to Felicity's meeting.

Taranda followed him, carrying four filled mugs of coffee. "I can multitask too," she said as she set the drinks beside each plate.

Cam walked toward them with Mia at his side. "Where's ours?"

"Not cooked. You didn't order." Benny sat with a scowl. "I am not a mind reader."

Felicity shook her head as she took a chair. The coffee was hot and the food was just what she needed. Cam signaled to one of Benny's crew. In seconds, he rattled off his order and

Mia's favorite French Toast with ham. Two mugs and a glass of tomato juice were delivered.

Cam eyed his lover. Mia grinned at him and pointed to the glass. "Liquid vitamins."

"I don't like drinking something that looks like blood, especially early in the morning."

"I don't like seeing you shot and as pale as a ghost with IVs poked in more places than I want to remember."

Tiny in height and weight, delicately built, her dark eyes gleamed with determination. It didn't matter that Cam was six two to her five feet. That he outweighed her by one hundred and twenty-five pounds. Her lotus blossom delicacy hid the heart of a warrior. She had survived a beating by four men when a certain corrupt agent had wanted to teach Ace a lesson.

"Drink the damn juice, Cam," Ace said with a grin. "She won't shut up about it if you refuse. Coffee makes a great chaser."

"Beer would make a better one."

"You are not having beer for breakfast."

Taranda glanced at Felicity who was eating as though everyone was silent. "Are they going to get the 'talk'. I don't think Ben and I were ever this bad."

"I don't waste my time herding cats. Mia, what have you found on the name I gave you?"

Cam was good with computers and so was Ace. Mia was better than both. Give Mia the smallest cyber clue and she wouldn't stop until she found every hidden byte involved.

"Everly has a big cyber mouth. You were right. He did make records, very detailed, including photos. I couldn't find anything that shows that he sent them to anyone or any place. It reads more like personal notes. A good bit of it seems speculative.

He named names. The stuff I accessed was encrypted, buried in a mess of reports that were a couple of years old. It took me three hours to dig it out and that was knowing that there was something to find and the person most likely to have generated it."

That spelled accident to Felicity. "Someone stumbled over it?"

Mia shrugged lightly. "That's what it looks like to me without more information. I can track the hacker. If he or she is any good, it could take a while. I didn't because you said not to."

Felicity could hear the eagerness in Mia's voice. She thrived on the challenge of hacking another hacker. She was skilled in martial arts and very good with weapons but her real value was in her weapon of choice, her computer.

"Can you poof the information?"

Felicity used Mia's personal word for obliterating data,

wiping out every visible trace, corrupting the drives of where it had once been so that current retrievable methods wouldn't work.

"I can. It takes time and I need to know who found the information or there is still a copy out there, maybe more than one by now. Don't forget there may be hard copies as well which I can't do anything about. How short a clock are we on?"

"It's already ticking."

Felicity pushed her plate aside. She had eaten without really tasting her food. It wasn't the first time. Mia was a full member of the Skye/Sea Security Consultants but she wasn't privy to certain covert aspects of her operation.

The work Skye had done for Everly's department had occurred before Felicity had clearly defined the tasks that the two separate arms of operations of Skye/Sea Security did.

Allowing Mia to track the information to Gordon was opening the door to the very intelligent younger woman's speculation. She had to stop Everly's account from spreading. That leakage was critical for so many reasons. She could do it but, as Mia pointed out, removing cyber data took hours to destroy beyond hope of recovery.

Ace had only found one name in common with the two men she had been ordered to remove. The donor was a heavy backer for both Gordon's election to Governor and to the Senate.

The amount of money that had been poured into Gordon's campaigns as well as some state programs for which Gordon had been lauded was interesting. Ace hadn't been able to find any evidence of where those contributions had been repaid by Gordon.

Felicity didn't trust the visible charitable view of the heavy donor. Millions spent with no obvious return. It didn't play for her, not at all.

"Poof the information that you have. Let me know when it's gone."

Felicity clearly saw Mia's disappointment but she didn't question the order before she left the table with Cam at her side.

"Taranda, I may need you for a short trip tonight. We'll be using the jet. Get some rest."

"I'll be ready."

A 'short trip' was Felicity's verbal code for a touch and go, in and out. Taranda knew the drill. It wasn't the first mission carried out with little warning and maximum speed. The only question was where and that one was never answered until they were in the air.

Ace walked with Felicity to the house. He had lived with her long enough to know she was arranging information, known and unknown, lining up resources, human and equipment. Covering all the contingencies she could see and running a mental gauntlet of possible problems.

"You are really good at letting me think without staring at me," Felicity murmured as they entered the elevator together with the dogs.

"I have an idea about what you are planning next. Could be wrong."

"What do you think I am planning?"

She would bet he did know what she had in mind. In so many ways, they thought alike. She hadn't expected that bonus when she had opened her life to him.

"A little B and E with your truth drug in your back pocket. It's the fastest and safest way to find out about Gordon's backer and just where she may have sent or to whom she may have given the information she has on Skye/Sea Security. There is always the possibility that she generated a hard copy and just handed it over for someone to take care of us."

"The question really is, would he? What I did years ago only took out two politicians. Everly never gave me a list of the contributors to either of my targets. I found that on my own. There was no need for me to know that information. What you have found so far may be a sanitized version of the original lists of donors. That's going to take time to verify before we can compare the donor lineup to see if there are any crosses with Gordon.

Skye/Sea Security is a legitimate business. Also, what is the gain to the donor if that is who we are dealing with? Everly still exists. He's the one who hired us. Taking us out doesn't eliminate Everly or his power to hire someone else."

"I agree. I don't see her backer coming after Skye. At least not in the short term."

"What I want to do is dry up the leak. Then we will find out who the backer is and what he is intending to do with Gordon? If he is connected with the two men I took out, why wait so long to put another person in place? If he did wait?"

"Neither of us think he did wait."

Felicity entered her secure room and locked down the house. "No, I don't think he waited. I think someone is already in place and powerful enough to make whatever he needs to happen a fact. He or she may have been working up in the ranks even then.

The question that is teasing me is what is Gordon's role in this plot? She's too new in the Senate to be of much use. She has no real power base as yet. Having lost two men, was she brought in as a Trojan Horse to protect the real power figure?"

Ace slid into the chair beside hers as he turned the idea over in his mind.

"Now, I see why you have kept the 'blue' status. I

wondered. It seemed like overkill. You don't believe she is the problem."

"Right now, she's an irritant, a diversion. Maybe for Everly. Maybe for someone like us. Maybe for the person or persons who backed our two congressmen.

Mia couldn't find any information that said the data had been accessed by anyone but Gordon. Accidents do happen. She might just have given her backer information that he has been hunting for years."

"Definitely stay on 'blue'. If the stakes are high enough that he bought two congressmen and now possibly more, we are definitely at risk. Like you said, Everly still exists."

"I wonder for how long?"

"Grab him. Torture him for information. What he might know but hasn't acted on or been allowed to act on as yet. Drug cartels like to make statements with bodies. Leaving their handiwork on public display is a favorite, often too effective tactic."

Felicity engaged her systems. "You and I are going hunting. What we don't know could destroy us. I am not ready to die yet."

"I plan on retiring from the field when I get too old to be any good on that end. I am not dying in the near future."

He wrapped a hand around her neck and drew her to him for a hard kiss.

"I'm in for the long haul. Whatever he has planned isn't going to work," he promised her when he let her go. "Give me an assignment."

"Everly. I want everything you can find down to his first tooth."

Ace nodded and focused on the screen in front of him. He knew how to do a deep background search and Felicity's software made the task a lot easier.

Felicity concentrated on the man Andre had heard with Gordon. She checked her facial recognition program first. Satisfaction gleamed in her eyes when she found both images identified.

Arturo Santiago and his bodyguard. EnviroWorld again. She did not believe in coincidence. She studied the information on the two. Both men were the same age. She pulled up the images of them entering the office building and being admitted with little more than an absent nod from the guard on duty.

If the guard had been one of hers, he would have been fired on the spot. No one, vetted nor expected should have passed his station that easily. She flagged the guard's name for further study as she concentrated on the two men.

Their smooth, balanced way of moving, spoke of training in fighting, probably martial arts given the flow of their steps. No swagger, no need to posture or pose. There was a slight imperfection in the fit of each jacket. Armed. Placement indicated both were right-handed, at least for shooting purposes.

The lazy guard had just let two armed men into a secure building. She would not only have fired the door guard but made sure that he never worked in any security field ever again.

The visitors had to know the cameras existed yet they acted as though being recognized didn't matter. Her life in the shadows had been an unending slide from disguise to disguise. Lifts in shoes, appliances in the mouth to change the shape of the face. Wigs, padding, makeup, dyes, contacts. She would bet that the men in front of her bore little resemblance to themselves in reality.

Handsome and sleek but no features in common beyond the dark eyes that the camera and lighting in the elevator caught clearly. The bodyguard had entered last and exited first, the move so smooth that she knew it had been repeated many times, probably for years.

She focused on the shoes as they walked down the hall to Gordon's office. Her program had both men one inch over six feet. The back of each shoe was higher by an inch than it should have been. Inserts to change the height on both? Also, a heel that was higher on the bodyguard. The computer calculated another half inch.

Feature by feature, the program analyzed the faces, projecting what the removal of oral appliances would do to each man's look. Probability of accuracy was calculated with each virtual sketch. The system scanned the bodies with the same details and possible results.

Felicity added a passport search on both men to the list of computer tasks. The passport images popped, showing the same faces that she had on the security cams. Minutes turned into hours as she worked. Only the sounds of fingers moving over keys broke the silence.

"When you have a stopping place, you'll want to have a look at this," Ace said as he leaned back in his chair. He keyed in a command to transfer his findings to the screen on the wall in front of them.

Felicity paused her program before she glanced up. Harry Everly had a pristine reputation on the surface. A career man who had systematically moved up in the ranks.

She had dealt with his various departments in his rise to the position he now held. While she didn't fully trust those she worked for and with, she would have said he was more honest than most and certainly, in her personal experience, more forthcoming when the job required adequate intel.

Ace knew when she finished the first screen. A few key strokes brought up a second version of Harry Everly. This picture was a man who had made large irregular deposits in various off shore accounts under different names. Houses in other countries. Even a small island off a European coast that boasted a pool, a dock and a yacht including full time staff.

"It looks like he started taking about twelve years ago," Ace said. "About four years before he tapped you for the investigation on the congressmen."

"I was still working for the government then. I had started Skye/Sea Security. Jonah and Nelson were already here, taking care of the Ranch, riding herd on Taranda and overseeing what I had begun building here. They did most of the first few security operations I had then. I took Everly's assignment when I was supposedly on vacation. It wasn't the kind of work Jonah or Nelson did.

He could have fed this information through his own department. I asked him why at the time. He said he didn't know how deep the corruption went. He wanted the head, if I could deliver it. What he didn't want was a scandal if he went through channels. Washington often has more leaks than a sieve. I agreed as long as the information he gave me checked out. He swore it would and it did."

She got to her feet, needing action for a moment while she reevaluated the past. She paced closer to the screen. Harry had used Skye/Sea Security and made three million on the deal. The money trail ended there. Who had paid him and why? More questions.

She remembered how carefully she had checked the information she had been given on the two congressmen. That had been real enough, damaging enough to warrant the investigation that had ended in a cyber block she wasn't equipped to cross then. The sanction was real too.

The facts did little to mitigate the realization that Skye had been used.

"He admitted that part of the reason he was using my fledgling company was because it was so new. No ties to anyone. Easier for him to keep a lid on the situation. I had great references as a single consultant but nothing straight out of Washington."

"References?"

She shrugged. "I only gave him four names and contact numbers. The numbers were easy to route here. Nelson is very good with voices and accents. It was simple enough to create fictitious businesses and identities to match my needs."

He grinned. Felicity had a devious mind. He really liked that about her.

"You built this place and its rep on a bunch of carefully edited excerpts from your government days?"

"Of course. The situations were real enough. All I had to do was give them the proper background."

He shook his head. She made it sound so simple when he knew damn well it wasn't.

"I'm working on following the money. The transactions are bouncing all over hell and back. I found one that ended with a closed account. Dead end there."

She returned to her chair. "Good work. We will definitely have some questions for Harry tonight."

"So, two B and Es? At least they are in the same city."

"Taranda wouldn't care either way. She would rather be in the sky than on the ground no matter what the reason."

Anyone who knew Taranda knew that to be true. He hadn't been considering the younger woman, only the one standing in front of him. Two interrogations including getting through tight security in both cases was demanding and tiring. Felicity could handle it. They had dealt with worse situations.

"I am glad the drug works fast. It saves time on an operation like this," he commented as he got back to tracking the money through cyberspace.

The chemical mixture that Felicity had created was good at getting to the truth. It could kill in larger doses, leaving the victim looking as though he or she had had a heart attack. With the regular dose, a person would answer any question and have no memory of the interrogation.

He could personally attest to the last, since Felicity had used it on him when she had come to Mia's rescue. He hadn't even been left with a headache the next morning.

"It's the best way to get to the truth."

"What are you going to do about Everly?"

"It depends on what he tells us. Leaving him in place for the short term for sure. I don't want to alert anyone that we are digging deep. The money trails in this situation are coming from really deep, well-hidden pockets.

Whether those pockets have anything to do with whoever has bought Gordon is the question. I can think of a number of reasons to eliminate the two targets that may have nothing to do with Gordon. They hadn't performed as ordered or needed? They skimmed funds? Shot their mouths off to the wrong people?

Or he may have taken them out for some reason that has nothing to do with what Gordon may be being positioned to do. We need answers. Not more questions."

She turned from the screens to look at Ace. "We have the EnviroWorld cross now but that doesn't mean it is the right one or the only one. I didn't find anything in Baldwin's and Roger's finances back then that linked to corruption. We don't see anything in Gordon right now either."

Felicity looked at the handsome face filling one of the wall monitors.

"Arturo Santiago is the common link but there still isn't a damn bit of evidence of anything more than money spent with nothing asked in return.

Even his and his bodyguard's reaction to Andre's

eavesdropping could be explained away legally. The guard didn't get close enough to do anything but give chase.

We don't have anything to tie him to Anhe's death either," she reminded him as she turned to face him.

Ace nodded, his face grim with the knowledge of the various ways a guilty man could escape justice. "We'll get the answers. I don't like the filth we are wading through, the damage that could be still occurring that we haven't uncovered as yet."

"Someone has infiltrated our government, not just once but at least three times, now with Gordon's potential. We need hard evidence. We are going to find him or her. We are also going to know why and how, before we're done."

CHAPTER EIGHT

Ace stepped out of the shower, took a towel for himself and handed one to Felicity. "Which one of them do you want to take first? There isn't much to choose between them on the basis of security."

"We'll start with Everly. He has been in the field. If we are dealing with the same people that we caught on camera with Gordon, the two of them clearly aren't worried about being seen or identified by whatever name they are using in the U.S.

Whatever Everly has done, he is part of our world. I want to know his role in this, how far it reaches, his connection to the two men with Gordon if there is a connection. There is an outside chance that my targets were removed so that Gordon could be groomed and brought into an operation that is still ongoing."

Felicity dried her body as she continued her summary.

"Gordon hasn't been in town long enough to do much damage. The computer is sifting through her work in the Senate. So far, it hasn't popped anything more unusual than funding for a program to study the mating habits of some bug I can't even pronounce."

Ace draped his damp towel over the rack.

"You couldn't pay me to run for that office. Some of those proposed bills are a thousand or more pages. There are too many tacked on addendums that have nothing to do with the main focus to suit me."

Naked, Felicity left the bathroom. She glanced out the undraped windows. The sun was setting in a silent show of fiery red and bronze. She didn't have time to enjoy the finish of the day. Hers was ending with a race to the east coast and some drug induced truths from professional liars.

"Neither one of us would do well in that environment. For one thing, we aren't trusting enough not to read every page of anything put in front of us," she pointed out as she pulled on black silk panties and a black sports bra.

A black long-sleeved tee, cargo pants, socks and boots made moving through the shadows easier. She strapped her com unit on her forearm.

She was aware of Ace matching her selections. She moved to the special locked cabinet in the secure room to remove four vials of her truth drug. She should only need two doses but she never left home without a back-up supply.

As she reentered the bedroom, an incoming vibrated on the com unit. "Taranda."

"Ben and I are on board."

"In ten," Felicity acknowledged as she headed for the elevator. Ace punched the button as she stepped through the doors.

Another vibration. "We're in place, boss. Mia's on com. I'm ready with the satellite feeds. We're a go here."

"Moving," she replied as they left the house. Her dogs fanned out to roam the compound. Another line of defense. They could have taken a cart, but she wanted to stretch her legs with a light jog. Ace had the same need.

They moved together along the side path to the landing strip. With each barrier between the main yard and the open field of the strip, the com units deactivated the perimeter security long enough for them to pass.

The jet was rumbling gently when they boarded. Benny secured the hatch as Taranda began the taxi to the strip.

Felicity moved to the flight deck.

Taranda glanced at her. "Pilot?"

She shook her head. "No."

Grinning, Taranda eased the throttle forward, sending her baby smoothly down the tarmac, gaining speed with every foot. She had never lost the thrill of feeling the craft begin to lift as the air collected under its wings. The nose coming up, the land falling away and the sky wrapping around the jet like a lover was a sensation that had no clone.

Felicity watched Taranda's face. The younger woman lived to fly. She could so easily bring to mind that too thin face of the sexual slave she had rescued fourteen years before. So much ugly knowledge, so much need to kill the man who had hurt her so badly by stealing her innocence and her ability to give birth had lived in her eyes.

Until that moment, when the jet she had owned then had lifted into a dark night carrying Taranda and the four girls with her into a new future.

Taranda had asked for two things, to learn to fly and to work for her. Because the girl had helped her rescue herself as well as the four being sold with her, Felicity had changed her plan for Taranda's future. The four had been placed in a school, educated and counseled. Eventually, when each was ready, each had gone on to a new life, with a new name.

Taranda had chosen the toughest course. She had also been the most difficult to handle. In the end, she had attained her two dreams. Felicity had never regretted that change of plans. Equally, she had made a solemn promise to Jonah and

Nelson that she was never bringing another Taranda into their lives. They had barely survived her change from a driven, raging girl to a barely tamed woman by using a lifetime supply of luck.

"Too bad I don't have to push it," Taranda said when she leveled out at their cruising altitude.

"I don't want to get there any earlier than we have to."

"How long are you thinking?"

"Three hours. Ace is driving."

Taranda looked back to see him watching them as he took the mug that Ben handed him. "I hope Cam and Mia are looking for speed traps for you."

He saluted her with his coffee. "They are. The faster we do our job the quicker we can go home."

"I vote for that." Benny passed Felicity a mug and put Taranda's in the holder on her left. "I don't like hanging out on the strip. It is a bit difficult to explain we're waiting for the boss to do a little B & E on a Senator and a governmental department head."

"Ben, you know you live for risk taking."

Benny shrugged off Taranda's teasing. A day ago, he wouldn't have been able to resist hitting back. He liked the new way they had. He didn't know where it was going, but he liked hearing her laugh. He even liked her teasing, a little.

"I live to cook. I'm taking my coffee and going to the

back. I'm working on a new recipe."

Ace cocked a brow at Felicity as Taranda made a slight course adjustment. She shrugged.

Apparently, Felicity had managed to end the verbal duel between Benny and Taranda without him having to talk to Benny about the situation that had been making the dining hall so uncomfortable. 'Blue' had saved him from that very awkward discussion with Benny.

He'd had no idea how many hats he would have to wear in his new life. Hunting down spies and traitors was more in his skill set. Relationship counseling was definitely not.

"How is it possible that you were unable to find the records when I gave you a place to start? You have been out hacked by a woman?"

Marco watched the young face in front of him. He could almost smell the sweat of the resident hacker's fear. The emotion was often a better motivator than greed. He waited a moment, letting the silence emphasize his displeasure.

"I do not pay for failure."

The hacker gulped audibly. "I cannot find the files. I have followed every operation the woman has generated from her three known IP addresses. There is nothing. Only work and very little personal contacts. Perhaps she generated them herself," he dared to suggest. "I can continue looking."

The man leaned back in his chair, relaxed in his position. There were other ways to get the information. This way provided the most privacy, the least paper trail. He might enjoy watching his partner deal with the arrogant, cold-blooded Gordon himself, if his hacker couldn't find the answers they sought. Right now, that was not an option. They had other plans for her.

They had lost so much time, replacing the men who had died. They had been assured that the deaths were nothing more than truth. Their plot had escaped discovery. Inconvenient but reparable.

Their plan was still working, even without the two so helpful greed-driven government officials. Even with only one of the original three in place, the plan was still producing even better than anticipated.

However, they'd had to find and replace one of the men. Grooming an American politician took time and proper placement in a seat of power. Gordon was so sure that her importance to them gave her some leverage. Fool!

"You will find the information. Otherwise, you will not have a job." Or a life. Failure was not an option.

"I understand."

Marco disagreed silently. As he had told Gordon, there was always someone to fill a vacancy. Money was a great incentive. Removal of an unsatisfactory employee was done with a word. Simple and immediate. His partner was more than skilled in that fine art. Plus, he enjoyed his work.

The plans for Gordon's future were in place. She had an important purpose to serve but not the one she expected. He smiled as the door closed behind the hacker who might very well precede the cold-blooded Senator Gordon in death. Time would tell.

He reached for his phone. For this call, he preferred a landline. Cells were open to other ears. Some things did not improve with progress.

CHAPTER NINE

Felicity left the flightdeck to move to the rear of the jet. Benny moved by her to take the seat beside Taranda. They would be landing soon.

She and Ace would leave the plane. Benny would be onboard to stand guard. Both he and Taranda were armed. Felicity didn't expect any trouble but she preferred to be prepared for any contingency.

Right now, she wanted to stretch out the kinks of sitting for so long. When she turned, Ace was on his feet doing the same thing. Muscles rippled beneath his black tee and snug cargo pants as he bent and shifted.

The woman in her appreciated the view. The partner in her knew Ace could more than hold his own in any situation.

Stealth or fight, he was a match she had never thought to find. She could have and had done this kind of night maneuver alone. The task was easier with two.

"I didn't think to do this when I was twenty," she said with a faint smile.

"I didn't think to do a lot of things when I was that young. I wasn't in the business then anyway. A good thing. I had a temper back in those days."

She cocked her head as she bent and stretched in front of him, copying some of his moves and adding others. She could feel her muscles warming, energizing.

"Really?"

"I needed to learn control." He shrugged as he finished stretching.

"I had an instructor who taught me a damn good lesson. Busted my butt for me when I mouthed off once too often. We were working one-on-one after class. I didn't see it then but I figured it out later, he set me up. Best damn instructor I ever had. Told him so a couple years later just before he retired."

She chuckled. "Did it hurt?"

He shook his head. "Not even a little. By then I had seen what the lack of control meant in life and death situations. He helped me learn how to stay alive."

Felicity knew exactly what he meant. She, too, had seen

the loss of control in tight situations take lives, good and bad. She couldn't remember a time when she had lost control simply because her father had taught her patience and stillness before she had understood what the lessons meant.

"Staying alive is the real name of the game."

"Touchdown in ten," Taranda announced as she positioned the jet for landing.

Felicity dropped into the seat beside Ace and strapped in. There was barely a bump as the plane settled on the runway. She and Ace unbelted together and moved to the door. The second the jet stopped in the shadows near the hangars, they exited together.

Taranda had the interior of the jet dark within seconds of them shutting the hatch. The night was cool enough that she and Ben wouldn't be sweating in the silent aircraft as it pretended to be as empty as the other planes around them.

As promised, a black car waited on the grass. Low slung, built for speed, it looked like many that were used in the area. Ace drove while Felicity contacted Cam. Satellite connections made a much more secure link, especially since the communications arm of Skye/Sea owned two.

"How does the first destination look?"

"A go. He's home and alone. Only one heat signature," Cam responded.

He glanced at Mia and got a nod. "Mia is ready when

you are."

Mia had already hacked into Everly's security. She was ready to shut down the system at each point when Felicity and Ace needed a dark window.

"Twenty minutes."

Felicity cut the connection and muted their end of the conversation. "We are blurring the lines a bit on this one."

"You mean the drug?"

"Yes. Cam knows about it. I've had to use it a couple of times when the clock was at zero. That was before Mia joined us."

"She'll handle it. In the months she has been in operations, she has seen a lot of what we do. She knows the risk to all of us, maybe not as graphically as we do but enough to know getting the truth is critical."

"She's at a disadvantage since she hasn't had any real field work. This situation is a maze that has so many twists and turns that we still don't know the way out."

Felicity glanced out the side window as the streets flowed into upper class neighborhoods with larger statement houses.

"Do you think she would handle it better, if we went in and beat the answers out of him? We are capable of it. I know I have done it a few times.

Damn hard on the hands and I hate beating on

someone even if they deserve every blow. When death happens because of information you don't have, you learn to do what has to be done.

Your way is a hell of lot more humane than hammering on someone who can't fight back. Besides, people can lie even when they are dying. All it takes is commitment to an idea, a person or a cause. You know that as well as I do."

"All good points and all true. She hasn't sat through an interrogation."

"She is getting her seasoning. The green is rubbing off. She didn't break when Cam was shot and still held his ground so that the rest of us could get that kidnapped family to safety.

She kept giving accurate information. If she was shaky or scared to death, I sure didn't hear it as she was calling out enemy positions and extraction points while you were arranging for a doctor and flying yourself and him to meet us halfway.

Cam is alive because she didn't break. Because you got the medic to us in half the time, the time Cam didn't have in spite of blood transfusions and Ricky's trauma care."

"All true. I wasn't thinking of her breaking so much as the questions she might have later. And what she could use to find her answers."

He glanced at her. "Warn her off."

"I already have."

"If she agreed, you can trust her word."

Felicity stared into the night. "She wouldn't be sitting beside Cam right now if I didn't believe that."

She also knew Mia's sharp mind and her love of puzzles. The more complex the better.

When Ace made the turn off the main road into their destination neighborhood, Felicity connected to Cam. He would direct them now rather than use the onboard navigation system which had been disconnected for this trip as had the GPS for the vehicle.

Her pick-up man would reconnect both after he retrieved the car. No trail would be left with the onboard computer system to be traced back to this night's work.

"I have you on the screen, Ace. Take the next right."

Ace turned as directed. They passed homes that were showplaces behind ornate gates and, in some cases, guards at the entrances. Everly's home was one of those.

Ace kept his speed even, while Felicity gave the appearance of a woman with her lover, returning home for the evening. The darkness was great camouflage but it wasn't perfect.

Everly's gate house was tucked into a high, manicured hedge. The gates might look ornamental but on closer inspection, if one knew what to look for, the barriers were heavier than most, the vertical rods thicker and the room between, too thin for anything but a hamster to slip through.

Lights illuminated the grounds, eliminating any shadows on the open lawn between the perimeter hedges and the flower beds spread out like skirts around the white brick two story house. The windows were dark. Two in the morning meant most, if not all, of the neighbors would be asleep. Less possible witnesses.

"At least he doesn't live in a gated community," Ace said when they cleared the house.

"Take the next turn on the right, two intersections then a right onto Baylor," Cam directed.

"Third driveway on your right. Sharp turn into the drive. Big ass oak blocks the view of every house but the one on the left. It's empty. Owners are in Spain for the next month. Software security only."

"What about the one in front of me?" Ace demanded. He pulled close to the house. The garage in front of him opened with a soft rumble that was barely audible. "Tell me you are controlling the parking."

"I am," Mia answered. "You can't leave the car in the open. There are roving police cruisers every hour. The next one is a half hour out."

"Answering your question. Messy divorce. No one has occupancy until the court rules. Neither partner has paid the last three months of security so the company has stopped their services. Mia found the data. The firm hasn't actually turned anything off so Mia did, boss. Made it look as though the stoppage was generated from their systems. You're clear on security. Where you are actually shares a property line with Everly."

Ace's brows rose at the information. Mia and Cam had still been refining the details of the residences of both targets when they left the compound. The streets were long and curvy. It was possible with all the right turns.

"Handy."

"Good work," Felicity said. "We're silent."

She eased out of the car, knowing that Mia and Cam had eyes on them from the satellite as well as from the body cams she and Ace wore. Every inch of their progress was monitored

Mia relayed information on their location. The car was hidden. One fence to cross, an open backyard, locks on the outer doors, sliders. Then they would be in. They had broken into tighter security. Time was the problem tonight. They had very little of it so every second counted.

Mia was the time keeper.

In minutes, they silently entered Everly's house. Cam's quiet directions were succinct and accurate. Ace closed the bedroom door then moved to one side of the bed as Felicity took the other.

Ace wrapped his hand around Everly's wrist at the same moment he applied pressure to Everly's carotid artery. Felicity held the other wrist.

Both of them were careful not to apply enough pressure to leave bruises. Everly barely had time to register the pressure on his neck with more than a startled jerk of wakefulness. Ace and Felicity easily controlled his movements.

In seconds, Everly lay still. Ace used a tiny penlight to reveal the small patch of his skin for the injection. Felicity applied a tourniquet then administered the drug. Ace moved the small circle of light to a spot close enough to Everly's face to highlight every expression. Cam and Mia would be see what they were seeing.

"Ready?"

"When you are," Cam acknowledged.

"Police cruiser just passed your location. No alarm. Tracking and timing," Mia reported.

Felicity monitored Everly's pulse as she watched his face. The movement of his lashes and a slight grimace warned he was waking.

"Harry?" She kept her voice soft and low, sliding into that space between sleep and waking. The distorter would take are of disguising her voice. "Can you hear me?"

"Yes."

She asked two basic questions to which she knew the answers. His monotone responses and immediate replies confirmed the drug's effectiveness.

"Do you know of a company called Skye/Sea Security Consultants?"

"Yes."

"Have you ever used them for any reason?"

"Yes."

"When?"

Everly answered, giving the day, month and year.

"What was their assignment?"

"To investigate Congressman Warren Rogers and Senator Andrew Baldwin."

"Why?"

"My director had been told there was suspicion of favors being granted, legislation being passed that favored foreign parties, possible drug cartel involvement."

"Told by whom?"

"Unknown. CI is all I know."

"If evidence was found, what was the rest of the assignment?"

"Termination made to look natural."

"Why?"

"No one wanted a scandal for the media to turn into a frenzy. Or retaliation if it was a drug cartel infiltration."

"Why didn't you use your own people for the assignment?"

"Too many people have access to my files. Director wanted no paper trail. Hire outside, private contractor."

"Why Skye/Sea Security?"

"New company. Good reputation. Never worked with them before. No tie to us was essential."

Felicity considered the last the only reason that rang a bell. "Why was never working with you before important?"

"None of my money was involved. Any scandal stopped with Skye if anything went wrong."

My money? The two words were significant. Felicity looked across Everly's prone body. Even in the muted light she could see and feel the alertness in Ace's stance. He had caught the same significance of the wording she had.

"You were involved in the corruption?"

"No. I'm a patriot. I hunt traitors. I don't help them."

Her drug smoothed out most emotion. The faint ring of indignation in his words meant his feelings ran deep.

"What do you mean by your money?"

"Budgets are made by men who don't know what my positions needed. Traitors always have hidden accounts. I take what I need for my people. They risk their lives for their country. They deserve more. So do I."

"Cutting it close, boss. Ten minutes max to exit," Cam

warned.

Felicity was as aware of the time as he was. "Is Gordon a traitor?"

"Don't know. Haven't been given any orders on her."

"Are you watching her?"

"From a distance for now. Too new on the Hill to be a problem."

"Were you ordered to look for any connection between the congressmen and Gordon who replaced one of them?"

"No."

Felicity frowned slightly. She would have checked that possibility.

"Did you look yourself?"

"No. Director said watch only. The new replacement seems clear, so far."

"Do you know anything about EnviroWorld?"

"Charity. Big contributor."

"Do you know anything about Arturo Santiago?"

"Their rep. Born in the U.S. Lives in South America."

"Have you met him?"

"Yes, at parties, fund raisers."

"Have you investigated him?"

"No, no reason to."

Two more question, then she would make a quick dive into Everly's computer.

"Harry, why did you make a file on the disposition of the Congressmen?"

"Personal use. Protection. Information is always valuable when you climb a ladder."

One last question. "What are the ID and password for where the file is stored?"

Everly answered.

"Got it," Cam murmured.

"Do you have any back up?"

"No. Too risky"

"Are there any trips?"

"Two."

"How are they deactivated?"

Everly recited the sequence needed to bypass the trip.

"You're cutting it too close, boss," Cam warned. "Two minutes, forty."

"We need to move," Ace murmured as he continued to monitor Everly while Felicity moved to the desk on which the computer rested.

He divided his attention between Felicity and Everly. In seconds, her fingers were racing over the keys, searching for the file, every reference to any activity that might have included the file being sent to another location or duplicated in another folder.

He watched her deleting the information, then the

history. When she was certain every trace had been removed, Felicity inserted the flash drive she had brought with her.

In seconds, she uploaded a virus that would activate the moment that Everly went online again. The bug would destroy everything stored on the unit, including the hard drive. The infection had been crafted to look like a major glitch rather than sabotage.

"Boss, twenty seconds. Move it or jab him again."

Felicity stood as the screen went black. It was time to leave. One of the advantages of the drug she had concocted was the amnesia like effects it had.

Without her voice and questions disturbing him, Everly would slide into sleep. When he awoke in the morning, he would have no memory of her visit or the information he had given them.

When he booted up his computer, the virus would infect everything online. It would be a swift strike with no time for Everly to stop the chain reaction. In minutes, the unit would be useless, the drive corrupted so badly that no current program would be able to recover one tiny byte.

CHAPTER TEN

"I need a bath," Ace said when he eased the car out of the garage and onto the street.

"He's a patriot. Bullshit. Over twenty million in various accounts under other names. Four houses in different areas of the world. A couple of really expensive cars, a yacht, an island and a boxcar load of taxes that patriot hasn't paid to his government. Too bad he didn't have a reaction to the drug."

"Not necessary. We found his hidey holes. It won't be hard to leak the information to the right people. He'll go to prison without any reactions to the drug. Right now, he is better left where he is."

"I wish we could have bugged his house while we were in."

She had the same wish, one they had explored and discarded before leaving the Farm.

"Too much of a risk. As good as our tech is, there is still a chance of detection. Then the questions start. The system gets a good look and they find the blips when we got in."

She reminded them both of what they had decided. Ace's answering curse held the same level of frustration he had expressed then.

"I'm satisfied that I got rid of that file."

"Same here. You cut our timeline to the bone."

"No choice. Besides, with you monitoring, if he started to come around enough you would have put him out with the carotid and I would have jabbed him again," she reminded him.

He shook his head. Her cool response, words and actions were typical of her. They had succeeded. Subject closed.

"So, we are not only looking for the man or men behind Gordon but dodging the government keeping a watchful eye on Gordon at the same time."

Felicity's lips curved at the anticipation in Ace's voice. A much better reaction than frustration.

"Feeling up for the challenge, are you?"

He shot her a look that was equal parts anger and determination.

"As long as this cat and mouse game that greedy jackass thought up doesn't get one of us killed, yes. If it does, the game is over."

Felicity agreed with his reasoning. She didn't feel the emotions that he did. Logic worked much better for her until the situation was resolved. Later, she would match his anger, bite for bite. Now, purpose and a plan were what she wanted, what she had.

"Gordon is next."

"It had better be a fast next. Three thirty and counting." Cam's reminder was to the point.

"Five miles," Mia relayed. "One heat source inside. Two patrolling outside."

Felicity nodded once. "At least we don't have to swim across the river. Wet tracks in her house wouldn't be explainable."

"As long as the boat is where it's supposed to be."

"It will be. The same guy who handled the car did the boat. He hasn't failed me yet."

Ace had discovered early on that Felicity seemed to have odd contacts in all sorts of places. Equipment popped up on time, exactly when needed. Paperwork got passed with very little attention. Victims, people in need, were dropped off by aircraft on country roads where other contacts waited to transport them to safety and a new life.

Need to cross a shark infested stretch of ocean during a storm? Easy. Use a personal submarine, refuel from a fishing trawler waiting to exchange designer clothes for scuba equipment and wet suits.

"I thought my life was one challenge after another. I was wrong. You give a whole new meaning to clandestine missions."

"The only way to catch the people I hunt is to outthink and outplay them. That takes contacts of all kinds," she said quietly, understanding him.

"There is too much at stake to lose."

Mia studied the screen in front of her. She had heard every word that Ace had said. She had thought the work that Skye/Sea Security did was complex and worldwide. Even the kidnapping rescue that had almost gotten Cam killed had been well within those parameters.

Tonight, she was seeing something different in the operation spread across the wall screens. Ace and Felicity moved like a unit. Two bodies, one mind set. There was a grimness to Ace that she had never seen.

Felicity looked and sounded as calm as though she was instructing her in some new martial arts move. She had injected the drug with a practiced ease that said she had done the same thing many times before. Her questions had evolved with a smooth speed that emphasized that conclusion.

Neither Ace nor Felicity had been shocked by what Everly had betrayed about his own behavior. Ace was angry. His comment about the drug reaction disturbed her.

Everly was a traitor, no question. But in those moments, he had been defenseless. Ace had clearly been comfortable with him dying from a drug reaction.

She knew Ace killed. All of them killed. But there was a great deal of difference between killing when someone was trying to kill you than when a person was defenseless like Everly had been.

"I can hear you thinking," Cam said quietly, his eyes on Mia's face. "Everly won't get away with what he is doing."

"Ace was ready to kill him tonight. The man was drugged. Ace would have been happy for him to die from that drug."

"So would I. Maybe Everly believes all that shit he is spouting. But a patriot doesn't need a bunch of property in another country or two. He doesn't need citizenship papers for another country either. What good does that twenty mil he has do for the men and women who he feels deserve more? Notice he added himself to the list."

"Yes, he deserves prison but death because Ace or Felicity don't approve? The legal system will sentence him on the evidence we've collected."

"Maybe. Maybe not. All he has to do is offer some names that no one has, and he could walk. Go live off one of his protected accounts in another country."

He waited a moment for the truth of that possible outcome to set in.

"Mia, this is the forest fire burning out of control that most people think is only a story plot in some book or movie or on TV. If you can't take the heat, you need to get out of the kitchen."

"What about us?"

"I am a part of this. I believe in what we do. The people we help. Remember Amanda and what her future was going to be. Remember her mother being raped by her kidnapper in front of her daughter and her husband.

A good man died, his wife with him. Someone was paid off on the security team sent to take them to safety. If Felicity hadn't protected Amanda from the person who had placed a traitor in the detail sent to Amanda's family, Amanda would be just as dead as her parents. Instead, she is in one of the most prestigious, expensive boarding schools in the world. A new name. A new life.

The fire we tend is hot but it burns clean. New lives, new choices out of the flames, every time."

"You almost died."

Mia couldn't forget the moment she had seen him, when Ricky and the doctor had been running beside his stretcher as they pushed through the doors of the small surgery in the medical building.

His golden skin had been leeched of its color. She had been barely able to tell he was breathing. His eyes had been closed, blood on his body, the smell of it in the air. The urgent orders from the doctor. The worry on Ace's face as he had watched the door to the operating room close.

"I did," Cam agreed. "Felicity risked her life to redline her jet to get me the medical help I needed when the helo couldn't go fast enough to get me home.

Taranda did everything but turn the chopper carrying us into a rocket. Benny said she pointed it north and slammed the throttle to full and didn't let up until we landed at the designated point to meet the jet. Ace gave me blood when he was bleeding himself.

Right isn't always delivered by the rules. Sometimes, breaking the rules is the only way to save lives. You said you were in. I'm not the one questioning my choice. You are."

Mia stood up and stalked to the mini frig for a cold soda she didn't really want. "I am not like you, Ace and Felicity. I have never seen as much blood, injury and death as I have over these last months. I'm trying to adjust, damn it."

The uncharacteristic curse was just one more thing she

had to adjust to. "I am on a steep vertical learning curve." She turned sharply to face him.

Cam closed the distance between them. He took the soft drink from her, popped the tab and handed it back. He wanted to touch, to pull her close and tell her everything would be all right.

But he didn't make promises he might not be able to keep. Reality could be and often was a kick in the teeth. Mia had to accept that and find a way to live with it.

If she couldn't, he didn't know how their relationship could survive. He had tried living in the normal world. It didn't work for him. Even for her, he knew he could not go back to that world. The Farm and all it entailed was his life.

"I know that. We all know that. You can't go back. Even if you could, you would still remember everything, including the reason you are here and not still living your previous life.

You almost died. But for the skill of the surgeon Ace knew, the way he and Felicity got you away from his house and to help, you would have died. Everyone who matters to you thinks you are dead. For their sake and for your own.

Do you regret that? Do you regret that Ace and Felicity stood for you, lied for you, pulled in favors for you? Risked their lives for you?"

She stared at him, the words hitting hard, dragging up her past and the memories of physical pain beyond speaking, beyond screaming. Knowing she was going to die alone and in agony.

Then there was the fear when she awoke after the surgery, barely able to move, one hand immobilized. The question of whether she would ever use it again a nightmare for weeks. The pain of physical therapy.

She looked down at the fingers that still worked, still found answers for desperate questions. Without Ace, without Felicity she would be dead at worst or damaged beyond repair at best.

"No," she said quietly as she looked up at him. She saw the compassion in his eyes.

"None of us can go back but we can make a difference, put our skills and talents to use in ways we couldn't do in the outside world."

She leaned her head against his chest, inhaling the scent of him as his arms came around her. "I'm trying to catch up."

"You're doing fine." He stroked her silky hair, his eyes on the clock ticking away the minutes remaining of their window of opportunity. He would rather hold her but they had work to do. "We...."

Mia stepped back before he could finish. She still had the emotions, the doubts, the fears. She had made her choice. If she had to see things she wished she had never known, too bad. She lived because of Ace, Felicity and a doctor who worked to save any who needed him.

".... have work to do," she finished for him. "People in the field. I won't break again." She would learn. She had too much to lose if she didn't.

He touched her cheek. "You bent a little. You didn't break."

Mia didn't agree but she wouldn't say so. Instead, she took a sip of the cola in her hand and headed for her desk.

"Three minutes away," she murmured when she reengaged communications.

She barely spoke above a whisper. Sound carried over open water, where not even a ripple or a bird call disturbed the night. Ace's slight nod conveyed her message was received.

"No change in heat signatures."

The satellite gave her a clear picture via the body cameras. The darkness around them was lit with an eerie green light. Ace and Felicity were paddling silently on a diagonal line across river.

The boat was black so that it almost disappeared on the water. There was only an occasional golden glow in the few houses on either shore. Certainly, no outdoor activity but for the two guards around their target.

She watched the rear patrol quarter the lawn leading

down to the dock. "Hold. Patrol checking the water."

Three swift strokes took the boat closer to the shadows of the shoreline. She watched Ace pull a gun with a suppressor and aim it at the guard. She might have wanted to look away but she made herself wait, stay alert as Ace and Felicity waited.

Mia focused on the man as he checked right then left. A second later he turned to continue his patrol.

"Leaving the dock. No sign of alarm. Moving to the south side of the building. Go."

Felicity nodded as she slid her paddle into the water. They had five minutes and forty seconds to make it to shore, cross the lawn, get through the locked sliders and into the relative safety of the house. Mia would take care of the security for the few seconds they needed for entry.

They made the deadline with forty seconds to spare. A narrow margin that didn't allow them time to linger for more than few seconds in the room rimmed with undraped glass. Standing to the side of one window, Ace watched the patrol round the corner of the patio to check the sliders. The faint rattle of his hand on the doors was barely audible. Felicity held a similar position across from him.

Finally, satisfied, the guard moved on, his back to them as he crossed the grass and headed for the dock.

CHAPTER ELEVEN

Felicity led the way upstairs, following Mia's whispered directions on the house's layout. She had hacked the information from the security company. Two minutes and counting when they entered the Senator's bedroom.

Using the same procedure that they had with Everly, Felicity injected Gordon with her drug then engaged the voice distorter before she spoke.

"Can you hear me, Sharon?"

"Yes."

Felicity voiced her test questions. Sharon's answers confirmed its effectiveness.

"Did you research Senator Baldwin?"

"Yes."

"Why?"

"I needed to see how he worked, who he was."

"What did you find?"

"He had a heart attack. No history of heart trouble. His last physical said he was in good health, taking no medications."

"Did you search for more?"

"Yes. I stumbled over a weird file."

"How?

"I screwed up the search word but, the title of the file wasn't about him but it had Baldwin's name in it."

"Anything else?"

"A House member had a car accident later."

She shook her head a little, a frown creasing her brow. "Weird file. Shouldn't have been where it was."

"Did you print out the file?"

"No."

They had dodged one bullet. No paper copy existed. With an erasure of all references to the file history and the hard drive on Everly's and Sharon's computer, Sharon wouldn't be able to provide any file because the information would have effectively ceased to exist. The thoughts went no farther than Felicity's mind.

"Did you tell anyone about the file?"

Felicity didn't need to ask if she had mentioned

Skye/Sea Security Consultants. She already had the answer to that.

"Yes."

Felicity glanced at Ace. Another thread to pull. "Who did you tell?"

"Not supposed to use his name unless we meet at a public gathering."

"We are at a gathering. What is his name?"

"Arturo Santiago."

"Who is he to you?"

"Connection to one of my largest supporters."

"EnviroWorld?"

"Do you know where he lives in the U.S.?"

"Visits here. I think he lives in Venezuela, maybe Colombia."

"Near any city?"

"Don't know."

It was time to get creative. The reasoning was swift, instincts honed through years of experience.

"Did he speak of his life in Venezuela? Maybe to someone at a party or a meeting?"

She was aware of Ace's increased interest at the change in the line of questioning.

Sharon hesitated, then answered slowly. "A few times."

"Where?"

"At parties."

"What did he say?"

"He enjoyed the rural life very much. He raises horses." Her brow wrinkled. "Pass something."

"Paso Fino horses?"

"Yes."

"Does he breed them?"

"Yes. Champions."

"Anything else?"

"Not horses. Flying. Owns a plane."

"He's a pilot?"

"Yes."

"What kind of plane?"

Sharon shook her head slightly. "Didn't hear."

Too aware of the seconds ticking into minutes, Felicity moved to the financing. She still had to deal with the file on Sharon's computer.

"What does Santiago want you to do for him?"

Sharon fretted, her head turning in agitation. "Nothing yet. Scared. The two men he helped, died. Someone heard us. Knife. Shut up. Find him."

"Pushing it," Cam murmured in her ear.

She had to risk a few more seconds. The Senator's slow pulse told her the drug was holding.

"Did you find out who overheard you and the man

talking?"

"Yes."

"Who was it?"

"Andre LaPlante."

"Did you tell the man?"

"Yes. Later."

"Who did you tell first?"

"Mickey. Fool. He killed her."

One important question answered. Now, they could move to get justice for Anhe's death.

"What is Mickey's last name."

"Grainger."

"Where does he live?"

As Sharon gave his address, Felicity monitored Sharon's pulse.

"Did you tell the man, Arturo about Mickey?"

"Yes."

She had the answers she needed. Now for the clean-up part of the evening. She asked for and got Sharon's passwords. Fortunately, Sharon had her system in her bedroom.

Felicity signaled Ace to continue monitoring then asked Sharon one last question about her protection on the file. She moved swiftly to the computer on the desk across the room. The Senator recited the information including the data on her trips to secure the file.

Felicity knew she was in the red zone of the drug's influence. She had less than three minutes to complete her cyber invasion.

Ace watched Felicity work, mentally counting down the seconds. When she stood and nodded to him, he released Sharon's wrist and stepped back from the bed.

They left the room as silently as they had come. With Mia's directions, they were out of the house and back in the boat within ten minutes. They completed the river crossing in silence.

"We'll leave the boat where we found it."

Felicity's whisper barely reached Ace as she slipped her paddle out of the water. She laid it in the bottom of the boat. Ace matched her movements.

He stepped out first and held the craft while Felicity used the bow rope to tie it to the small tree that overhung the river. The shadow of the branches overhead was a very effective camouflage and its limbs provided the mooring.

She joined Ace for the short hike to the car. The boat would be gone by morning, before anyone could see it.

Ace started the car and eased onto the street. "Gordon is really spooked and pissed. I got that much in spite of the drug. At least we have a place to start on finding Anhe's murderer. And another name to follow."

"I think terrified is more accurate. Her fear was strong

enough to partially override my drug. As far as Mickey is concerned, let's hope we don't run into any more aliases."

"I'm hoping the address is not fiction and he isn't in the wind because Anhe died."

The traffic was light for the trip back to the strip. Ace was tired and he would be very glad to see this night over.

"Sounds like Santiago threatened her with a knife."

"It also sounds like Arturo told the Senator to handle Andre. A break for us. Arturo clearly has deep pockets and, as yet, a hidden agenda. He would have been able to hire any kind of talent. Expensive, skilled personnel who wouldn't kill the leverage that would control Andre. Arturo made a mistake there."

Felicity studied the darkness in front of them. The occasional street light barely lit the almost silent roads.

"If EnviroWorld and Santiago are dirty, we are talking years here. What kind of plan takes this kind of time frame? Most corruption has a much faster time line. This charity has invested heavily in the three we are sure of and I didn't see one connection to him or his charity in the corruption I did verify."

"If Santiago is getting any favors out of the good Senator, it sure as hell hasn't shown up yet. Not on anything we have found so far. That confirms what she told us."

"At least we have some strings to pull that we didn't have. Also, we can give Andre some closure if we can find

Grainger."

"Santiago's mistake gave us a lead to follow. He probably figured if anything went wrong, she would be the one at risk. He's in the clear."

"He thinks," Ace said.

"The Senator knows she has been bought and she has no idea what she is going to be asked to do."

"I would say with two dead congressmen before her, recipients of Arturo's generosity, she should be shaking in her designer heels," Ace responded. "Nothing in her background said she was naïve nor incredibly stupid."

"There is a reason why the phrase 'blind ambition' exists. Greed is incredibly short sighted in my experience."

Felicity leaned her head against the rest as Ace maneuvered the car through the light traffic.

"Now, I want a bath. Baldwin's name in a file hidden by a man who should have known better. All it takes is a mistake in spelling doing a cyber search. Anhe died over that mistake. As simple as that. Everly was worse than stupid to have created the file at all."

"At least it is wiped out of existence now."

"Two people knowing are two too many. With Arturo and his bodyguard knowing, that makes three and four. Who did they tell?"

"No evidence. No file. No tracks," he reminded her.

"Everly will keep his mouth shut. Even if he doesn't, he has nothing to show anyone."

"He's got enough friends in the business, people who owe him. We both know how it goes. Even if he gets caught for his money handling, the government might just let him go with a verbal slap and an early retirement. Less scandal.

Besides, look at his record. He has finished every assignment with a minimal loss of life and definite convictions or removals. I doubt an open trial and conviction will serve anyone well. As far as the government is concerned, he didn't steal from them only the bad guys."

Ace didn't disagree. "Your cynical side is showing."

"My cynical side is always showing. Reality and survival are harsh teachers."

He could agree with that too. He had seen too many deals with men who deserved multiple lifetimes in prison. If the victims in the world had been alive to have a voice, their screams would have blotted out all other sounds. He had made deals himself to get the bigger fish. Every time he felt as though he was swallowing acid just outlining the terms of a shady deal for the greater good.

"We have seen too much," he said harshly.

"The world has seen too much. Life continues. Wars still happen. Advanced civilizations fall so that humankind retreats back into simpler times. Man starts over, again and again, making the same mistakes. We haven't learned much since we walked out of the caves."

"You're tired."

"So are you. Cam. Mia. Benny. Taranda. Every one of us could write books on what humanity is doing to itself. I wonder if we will ever learn?"

There was no answer to her question. "We can only do what we can."

"I know. For every one I rescue, there are thousands I can't reach."

Ace glanced at her before he made the last turn. Her head was back, her eyes closed. The airstrip was quiet except for the whine of the jet engines warming up.

"Taranda is ready to fly."

"So am I," Felicity agreed as she opened her eyes. She reached into one of the deep pockets on her right thigh. She took out a thick envelop and put it in the glove compartment.

Ace locked the car and pocketed the key fob. It was impossible to leave it in the car as the vehicle would not engage the locks with the keys inside. Tomorrow the car with have its own tag back and the small boat would be returned to its place at the holiday rental kiosk for weekend vacationers.

Felicity entered the plane first. Ace followed, shutting the hatch. Within seconds, Taranda eased the jet down the runway. The cabin was scented with the fragrance of breakfast and coffee. She discovered she was ready for both. Having Taranda and Benny on board had produced an unexpected bonus.

The moment Taranda leveled out at her chosen cruising altitude, she announced, "Belts off, breakfast on. Ben was bored and I was hungry. We figured you two would be too."

Benny moved to the small galley at the rear. "I have mushroom and cheese omelets, bacon, ham, toast and potatoes. Coffee and juice, orange or tomato. Give me your choices and I'll plate it."

He stared at Felicity, daring her to refuse his food. "Don't tell me you aren't hungry, boss. If you aren't, you should be."

Felicity knew a hint when it verbally hit her in the head. Her body needed fuel. Except for a short nap, she had been up almost twenty-four hours straight. With the mouth-watering aromas filling the cabin, she could definitely handle the menu Benny was offering.

"I'll have ham, an omelet, potatoes and orange juice. I'm way over my quota of coffee, mother." Felicity sighed deeply, relaxing for the first time in hours.

Benny chuckled. "I've been called worse. Ace?"

"Add another slice of ham to mine and toast. No coffee for me either. Wouldn't mind some iced tea if you have it."

"I do. Two plates coming up."

"What about me?" Taranda demanded.

Benny laughed. "Don't you remember who made up the menu? You get one of everything. So, do I. Only hot chocolate instead of coffee."

Felicity's head came up. That got her attention. She didn't have much of a sweet tooth but she did like chocolate in almost any form.

"You have hot chocolate?"

Benny replaced the small carton of juice he had been ready to pour. "Two chocolates and two iced teas, boys and girls. We've earned out kibble tonight."

CHAPTER TWELVE

"We need some sleep. Not just a nap." Ace pushed the elevator button to the third floor. "After a hot shower, at least five hours."

"Are you channeling mother Benny?"

Felicity stepped out of the elevator and stripped her tee shirt and sports bra off. She slung them over her shoulder and unfastened her belt as she headed for the bathroom. Boots then pants and panties. She nudged the boots out of the way and tossed the dirty clothes in the corner basket.

"I have no desire to be your mother. I'm thinking of me. I am beat and I know damn well we are going to be cyber searching for hours if not days," he replied.

He stripped with the same single-minded efficiency

that she had. His boots joined hers in the corner beside the hamper.

Stepping into the heat and the steam of the shower, Felicity moaned as the massage shower head did its thing. Muscles quivered with the aquatic pummeling. Her eyes closed, she let the water wash her clean, mind and body.

Ace's hands on her shoulders were a benefit of having a lover who knew her body as well as she knew his. He found every kink that the shower had missed. She relaxed against his chest; her head dipped forward to give him complete access to the knots of fatigue in her neck.

"Going to sleep on me?"

"No. Just wallowing in the pampering." His husky question was an invitation.

The feel of her wet curves sliding against him was stirring parts of him that should have been ready to bed down for the night. The need was building slowly, not a race to the finish line. Rather, it was an easy slide into the world that held only the two of them.

No death, no betrayal, no lies, no deceptions.

She turned in his arms and slid hers around his waist. His kiss was comfort and affection, two emotions she never thought to find with any man. With Ace, it was easy to give and receive both. All roads didn't always lead to a climax.

"My turn," she murmured when he lifted his head.

"You don't have to tell me twice."

He changed positions with her. Her hands were strong, smooth in some places, callused in others. The rough and the smooth felt good as she forced the knots from his shoulders and neck.

"Too bad you didn't think to put a bed in here. It's big enough."

"After a day like this, I'd bar the door and drop into it for a week's vacation. I wouldn't get any work done."

She stepped out of the shower to dry. She handed him a towel when he joined her.

"I can't see that happening." He scrubbed his hair dry then started on his chest. "Have you ever had a vacation?"

"Oddly enough, I am not the workaholic you think I am. This house, the trails behind it, that pool in the clearing are my favorite vacation spots. I don't have to guard my back or look for a flash in the sun that shouldn't be there. I go naked in the woods if the weather is right and I don't have to worry about being armed.

You have no idea how much I enjoy that. In the spring and the summer, I have my horse brought up from the Ranch. I use the other mountain for trail riding. He likes it as much as I do."

She walked naked past the bed to the door of her secure room.

Ace followed quickly. "You are not working. You set the auto searches in Venezuela and Colombia from the jet. We need sleep."

"I want to do a quick check on the results. We're still hitting a brick wall finding Santiago involved in the money aspect of EnviroWorld. He isn't on the board. Only an employee. There are a couple of South Americans and the rest are U.S. citizens. The charity has its headquarters in Washington. Santiago appears to be the wine and dine guy only. Ten minutes, tops.

Depending on the numbers, I can refine the filters. At least we aren't having to search the whole continent. Only two countries, maybe." Standing she keyed the data to display on the wall screens.

"You know that Santiago is one of the most popular last names in South America."

"The list proves that. I can't realistically use a filter based on his possible income extrapolated from the size of the political donations to Gordon since the charity was the source of the funds. That would have been a big help.

The names within range of a public air strip reduced the number a little. But what if he has a private field? I do. It would be much easier to come and go without anyone even realizing he is using a disguise here."

She stroked in the new parameters. "I didn't think of

that on the plane."

"We got no sleep the night before last. It is three hours short of dawn now. That means a few hours short of forty-eight since either of us has been horizontal for more than a nap. If that is all that got missed, we are doing damn good."

She nodded, knowing he was right. The computers could continue the search while they recharged. "Let's go to bed."

"I thought you would never ask." He headed for the door with her following.

She turned off the only light in the room. There was no moonlight. They didn't need it.

"I didn't ask. You did."

"Semantics."

He slid between the sheets and waited for her to settle beside him.

"I'm too tired to argue and win."

"Good. Turn off your computer brain so I can turn off mine."

He pulled her close until her head rested on his shoulder. His favorite position. He felt her relax as her hand slid across his chest to lay against his heart. Now, he could sleep.

The light knock on his door was a surprise. No one bothered him once he called it a night. The kitchen was shut down until morning. The compound was dark. Wearing only his black briefs, he picked up his nine mil and moved silently to the door.

"Open up, Ben. I promise not to attack you."

"Taranda?" He released the lock and opened the door.

"In the flesh, Ben." Her grin flashed with wicked amusement. "I see you are in the flesh too." She cocked a black brow at his near naked state and his semi arousal. "Nice abs."

"I didn't expect a visitor."

The reaction of his body to her smooth black skin barely covered by a pair of snug shorts and a very brief bra top, the color of his favorite tea, was definitely visible. He wanted to reach for his pants, but he would be damned if he would, with her almost daring him to cover up.

She stepped forward since he hadn't moved aside to invite her in. "We didn't finish our conversation."

In the second it took for him to make the connection, she was past him and sitting on his couch and crossing her long bare legs. He shut the door. Short of throwing her out, not going to happen, he wasn't going to sleep any time soon.

"You should be tired. The rest of us are."

"I had a three-hour nap. Needing sleep then flying is a good way to crash." She shrugged, the light playing tag with her skin with every movement. "Besides, I wanted to get this behind me."

Setting his gun aside, Benny sat in the chair across from her. "You don't have to tell me any more, Taranda. We all have our secrets. I do."

He thought of his young wife and their baby, barely three months old. Dead from a drunk driver who never stood trial. He relived his nightmare almost every time he closed his eyes. Sleep was never his friend, only a sadist lying in ambush the minute he allowed himself to sleep.

Knowing what she did about him, she couldn't not tell him. He wasn't the only one who had lost too much to believe that right always won and the bad guys always paid.

"No, you don't. I have to level the playing field," she replied quietly. "It's only fair."

Benny saw the knowledge of his past in the dark sympathy in her eyes. He stiffened. The last thing he wanted to do was discuss his murdered child and wife. His fist clenched against the rage that was still as incendiary as it had been when he had seen the site of the hit and run massacre.

"Felicity wouldn't have told you and she is the only one who knows. How did you find out?"

The pain in his voice matched the look in his eyes. She knew the feeling, intimately. She wanted to touch. She knew what she would have done if anyone had tried when she felt the kind of pain she could feel coming off him in waves.

"I hate questions without answers. Home schooling means virtual learning too. That means computers. Felicity was the only female role model I had. She knows computers and she taught me stuff. You can find out anything if you know how to look. I looked, Ben."

A soldier coming home on compassionate leave so he could bury his tiny baby girl and her beautiful dark-haired mother. The pictures of the mangled stroller, the tiny sheet covered spot twenty or more feet from a larger cloth cover and the long smears of blood on the road told a grim story.

The smaller white square was as flat as the road. Both caskets were closed for the church services.

"Sorry is just a word that doesn't cover a damn thing."

"Leave it alone, Taranda." He rose and walked to the open window. The dark night felt like looking into his own soul. If he even had one left.

"The best part of me died with them. She was divorcing me. She couldn't live with the man I had become. I couldn't either. That was why I signed up for another tour. She sent me a letter about a month before the baby was born, told me she was filing the papers. I wasn't there for our child's birth. I never got to see my baby."

Taranda felt the sting of tears she never shed. The bone deep guilt in his voice hurt like nothing had hurt in a long time.

"I know about the kind of pain that cuts so deep you feel like your heart is gone. It never really goes away. Maybe it shouldn't," she said softly.

"Are you trying to kill me? Use the gun. It would be easier. The son of a bitch got away with killing my wife, my baby. I never saw them again. I wasn't there for either of them. I never got to hold her. Susan named her Emily. That's all I have of our baby."

Taranda rose and went to him. She slid her arms around him, holding on when he tried to shrug her off. Every muscle in his body felt as stiff as a board.

"He paid. Ben."

"Leave it." Pain and rejection filled the harsh growl.

She couldn't leave him alone in the hell of his memories. She had to try to reach him. She couldn't make his past better any more than she could erase her own. But she could remind him he was not alone. That someone cared. That she cared.

"Burning to death, trapped in his own car is worse than prison ever would have been," she said quickly as he ripped her hands from him and turned. The fury on his face changed to shock.

"What?" He grabbed her arms, his eyes trained on her face. "Where did you get that?" he demanded harshly.

"I found the information on the web." She stared at him, barely feeling the pain of his fingers digging into her arms. The shock on his face was clear.

"Are you sure?"

Stunned, she realized he hadn't known. She cursed herself silently. She had been sure he did. She wished she had never gone digging into his past. She couldn't take it back. He needed facts. Not emotion, not her guilt for invading his privacy, searching through his secrets.

"No one else was involved. The police were chasing him. He had almost hit another pedestrian. He crashed into a guardrail at a high rate of speed, flipped a couple of times. The car burst into flames according to the report. It was too hot for the officers to get to him although they tried. The fire truck didn't get to the scene in time to get him out. He died screaming, beating on the windows trying to escape."

Ben felt as though the life and breath had been sucked right out of him. All this time, he had thought the bastard had escaped prosecution. His nightmare hadn't just been his baby's death, his wife's murder. It had been the acid of believing their killer still lived, still breathed, still felt the sun on his skin.

Taranda was aware of his fingers digging into her arms. She risked sliding her arms around him. When he didn't try to shake her off, she stepped closer until her body touched his.

"I didn't know. No one told me." He could barely get the words out.

"I was in another country when it happened. It wasn't a big story as far as the media was concerned. No headlines or anything. Just a visit from the chaplain. A compassionate leave. I claimed what was left of their bodies but I never got to see either of them again."

She felt the pain of his grip lessen. His hold changed, drawing her closer. This wasn't the way she had thought the first time of being in his arms would be. She knew too much about pain that couldn't be healed. She remembered well the first touch of comfort and compassion she had ever been given. She had fought it because that caring touch was like a hammer blow on the rawness of her emotions.

"You didn't try to find out what happened to him?"

"I was told he was out on bail. That the police were investigating. His parents were prominent people in town, not just in wealth but influence. He had a history of drunk driving. I couldn't face knowing he was living in his rich daddy's lap while my wife and my baby were dead. I never got to see either of their faces," he repeated. It was his recurring nightmare. "The damage was too great."

He leaned his head on her shoulder, the tears he had never shed, slipping beneath his lashes. Their murderer was dead. All these years, the man he hated with every breath he drew was dead. He had died screaming in agony.

Taranda felt the moisture on her bare skin. No one had ever cried for her. After the night with Roscoe, she had never again shed a tear for herself or anyone else. Feeling the trickle of moisture leaking from her eyes now was a shock. She wanted to pull away. She had to stay.

This man drew her as no one ever had. She had learned to enjoy her own body, to enjoy the touch of a lover. But her heart, her emotions beyond sexual pleasure had been dead. Murdered in the long hours of pain and degradation meted out by a sexual sadist.

To discover that she could feel Ben's devastation was like a door opening to what she had lost. She had a choice to step through or run.

Her arms tightened around him. She was no runner. Life hadn't destroyed her so far because she didn't quit. She wasn't changing tactics now. So, she held on, her tears gliding down her cheeks, across the scar that she looked at every day.

She leaned her scarred cheek against his head and let herself feel all her emotions. She saw again Roscoe lying at her feet, blood pouring from the slice in his gut, his hands red with the life draining out of him. She understood Ben's need to know his family's killer had not died easily.

As they stood together, Ben began to talk, his voice rough with the emotions pouring through him. He spoke of the funeral, his need to dull the pain with a bottle. His refusal to listen to anyone trying to console him or explain the horror of what had happened.

"I spent days in a drunken haze. I only sobered up enough to go back to the Middle East to finish my tour." He sighed deeply then raised his head to look at her.

Taranda slid her hand down his arm to slide her fingers through his. "You need sleep. We both do." She expected resistance. Instead, he walked with her to his bed. He held her hand as he laid down.

For a long moment, she looked at him then eased to the edge of the bed. He moved over without releasing her hand.

"Just sleep."

She nodded. "Just sleep."

"I smell coffee."

Ace opened his eyes to the dawn lighting the sky outside the windows and a naked Felicity carrying two mugs toward him. He could see the steam rising over the rims. If there was a better way to start the morning, it could only be having his woman in bed beneath him or her on top of him, smiling as they came together.

"How long have you been up?"

"Five minutes. A computer alert and the smell of fresh

caffeine woke me. The auto searches are complete. We've got a manageable list to work with."

She sat beside him on his side of the bed as she passed him a cup.

"Did we manage three hours?"

She laughed. "Almost four."

"We slept in."

She shook her head. "I could probably risk taking us off 'blue'. I can't see the logic in attacking the compound. As far as anyone is concerned, Andre is in the wind. No one is aware he is here."

"Or his wife is dead, also here. What are we going to do about that?"

"I'm going to talk to Andre today. Get his feelings on what he wants."

"I can keep on the list unless you want me in on the discussion."

"I'm not sure. Neither of us know him that well. I am hoping he will be at breakfast this morning so I can get an idea of how he is doing."

He nodded. "As far as the 'blue' is concerned, if you are asking an opinion, I would say leave it on until we know exactly who we are dealing with.

Arturo Santiago is a South American citizen but he was born here. He has gotten to three Congressmen. To do what?

There are more questions than answers."

"Agreed. Whatever concerns us directly has to be cleared. The situation in Congress is a priority too. I don't like possible foreign interests manipulating our legislature."

"Hopefully, solve one, solve the other."

Benny rolled over and found himself nose to nose with a beautiful black face and dark serious eyes. He blinked then frowned. He could feel her long body stretched beside his. Her heat, the exotic scent that was hers alone stirred parts of him he thought as dead as his family. His body damn well needed to cool down.

"That is not the way to wake up with a naked woman in your bed," Taranda informed him.

Oh, yea, she was naked alright and his body was telling him painfully how interested it was. He was sliding on the edge of control, his brain barely engaging enough to remind him he was a grown man and in command of his own libido.

To divert his thoughts, he dragged up the memory of what had been left of the night. The pain that had been his constant companion for too long was muted, a shadow of what it had been. Taranda had opened a door he hadn't known existed.

The man who had murdered his wife and child was

dead. He died screaming as fire ate away his life. Taranda had given him that knowledge. There was nothing he could give her that would ever repay that debt.

"You stayed," he said slowly. The image of her sliding into bed, of her fitting her body to his was clear. The feel of her in his arms had muted the pain just enough to allow him to close his eyes without seeing his dead child in his sleep.

"I can't thank…"

Taranda touched a finger to his lips. "Don't say that. Not between us. You don't look at me and see 22. Should I thank you for that?"

"No." The answer was rough with emotion barely held in check. He hated the thought of what she had survived.

"We can't change the past. Neither can we live there. We have today."

He searched her face, the tiger eyes burning with life, challenging him to take the day and her.

Taranda could see none of the agony that had contorted his face only a few hours before. She felt his arousal and yet he wasn't reaching for her, ready to use her to slake his need. His restraint intrigued her.

In her experience with her chosen bed partners, they thought with their dick most often when they first awoke. Here was a man who didn't. She had only known one other who had such restraint. He had been the first to show her how pleasurable sex could be.

She knew her body well enough to know it wanted what lay beside her. Snarky Benny, Ben the man who cried in her arms, the warrior who never showed fear when bullets flew. Benny who cooked like an international chef and cursed with the fluency of a drunken sailor.

"I'm glad you didn't leave after I fell asleep."

"I started to then I changed my mind. This bed is big enough for two."

She didn't want to remind him of his pain but she couldn't pretend she hadn't cared that he was hurting.

"I know what it's like to be alone in the dark with the past beating on you."

He thought that over. He realized that he had felt her beside him for the few hours of sleep he had gotten. Her heat, her scent had been a comfort. The sound of her breathing drove out the aloneness he had felt for so long.

"That explains you in bed but it doesn't explain you in bed naked with me."

He cupped her scarred cheek. The pale arc might have been disfiguring to some. He saw only the strength and the courage of the woman who refused to hide the mark or use it to vent her bitterness on others. Taranda did neither. She simply was Taranda, scar and all.

"I always sleep naked. I can't sleep clothed. I might

have to fly today, depending on what Felicity and Ace find. I had to sleep so I stripped. You were too out of it to notice."

"I'm not out of it now."

She laughed softly as she slid her hand down his chest straight to his groin.

"Tell me about it," she invited as she stroked his length.

Benny rolled onto his back, using the arm under her to bring her with him. Taranda flipped a leg over his hips so that she straddled him.

"I like the way you move. You flow when you walk, black silk in motion."

She cocked her head, surprised at the description. "I've been called a lot of things in my life, but black silk isn't one of them."

"I'm glad. I want to be different."

Taranda touched his face, the soft fur on his jawline. Lately, he had taken to wearing a short well-groomed beard and mustache. She liked it.

"You are, Ben. You always have been even when you have been Benny snapping at me like a pit bull."

She was beautiful. Long limbs. Black satin skin and tiger eyes. Her voice was husky even when she was furious. If she had any nerves, he had yet to see them. Give her a job that most would see as a death mission, and she would fly straight into the heart of hell with fire in her eyes and steady hands on the controls of whatever aircraft she commanded.

"You don't call me Benny anymore."

She leaned down to kiss him, their first. Gentle, no demand. Not yet.

"In my head, you've always been Ben," she said softly when she drew back.

Then she grinned, a flash of devilment in her eyes and a wicked look. "Benny is the cranky chef."

He chuckled. He knew a dare when he heard one. Two could play that game. The differences in their ages didn't seem so important any more. Maybe she was right. Her history was as ravaged with pain and loss as his own.

"You need a little target practice. You aren't sitting in the right place."

He spanned her waist with both hands then lifted her just enough to position her over his shaft. "How good are you at riding?"

Taranda settled on him, using her inner muscles to wrap him snugly within her body. "How good are you at being ridden?"

"Let's find out."

CHAPTER THIRTEEN

Felicity and Ace entered the dining hall to find half the tables full. Felicity's favored spot was empty. Taranda came out of the kitchen, an apron pretending to be a skirt wrapped around her waist. She balanced four plates with the skill of a veteran waitress. Felicity knew for a fact she had never waited tables in her life.

Taranda deposited the food in front of her and Ace. She set the two remaining plates across the table then took a seat.

"Ben is bringing the coffee."

"Ben?" Ace said, one brow raised.

"I prefer it to Benny." She shrugged, her minute bra top moving a little with the gesture. "Hope it's all right to share your table. We are hungry."

Felicity studied Taranda and her half smile. It wasn't hard to read Taranda's mood. She had the look of a woman very pleased with herself and the world around her. Felicity shook her head.

"You're bragging without saying a word. You started that at seventeen."

"I had something to brag about then. It was the first time. First times deserve bragging."

"Not if you are trying to be discreet."

"Discreet? Me?"

Benny joined them, handing out mugs of coffee. "She isn't discreet. Doesn't have a discreet bone in her body."

Taranda cut her eyes his way, grinning. "Why should I? I like my life and I believe in having fun. Been to hell and I am never going back."

The ring of truth in her words didn't overshadow the laughter in her amber eyes.

Ben nodded at her plate. "You bugged me to make Eggs Benedict. If it gets cold, I don't want to hear about it."

She used her fork to poke a hole into one of his egg yolks. It drooled yellow over the muffin under it.

Ben looked at his plate then at her. "What are you? Twelve?"

Ignoring him, Taranda took her first bite. "How are the programs doing on generating a list of possible Arturos?"

"You're wasting your time, Benny. When she is in this mood, it's easier to just let her have her way," Felicity advised him then switched her attention to Taranda. "We've got a list of nineteen."

"I needed fuel even if Felicity was ready to dig into the search manually the minute she saw the list."

"And some exercise that didn't involve B and E," Felicity reminded him.

Ace grinned. "I didn't notice you complaining."

"I only agreed to walking over because this was faster than cooking and cleaning up after." Felicity pointed a fork at his plate. "Eat or you will be sitting here alone while I work."

"Do I need to salute?"

"Do you know how? I don't remember military service in your file."

"See, I told you they wouldn't mind if they knew," Taranda said to her lover.

Benny sighed and reached for his coffee. "I didn't think you were intending to make a statement for the whole compound."

"Easier to get it done this way. Everyone can deal with his or her surprise, get it out of the way and go on to the next interesting development."

"At least, neither of us will have to fumble our way through another talk," Ace pointed out between bites.

Benny grimaced. "Don't remind me. Really, don't remind me. I had no idea how close I was to that little scene."

Felicity ignored the byplay. The Taranda/Benny feud was over, not in the way she had thought but the result was a peaceful dining hall.

"Taranda, I might need the jet. The guys are checking her out this morning."

"I'll head to the hangar as soon as I finish. I'll work on restocking the galley if they haven't gotten to it."

Benny set his fork aside for a moment. "Boss, I thought about something last night while we were waiting for you. Taranda and I batted the idea around a bit. It might not be possible all the time, but I can set up precooked meals for on board use. Nuke and eat. Salads. We do it occasionally but not as a regular thing."

"Storage?" Felicity asked with a look at Taranda.

"If we minimize some of the galley storage, we should have enough room to put in extra refrigeration. I can talk to the guys this morning while we are checking her out. Wouldn't be a bad idea for something similar in the chopper."

"Let me know on both. Great idea if it works space wise." Felicity pushed aside her plate. Another situation had to be addressed.

"Have either of you seen Andre?" Twin head shakes matched her expectation.

"Has he ordered any food from the kitchen?" she asked Benny.

"No, I checked when I came in this morning."

The room Andre had been given came equipped with a mini frig with drinks, a coffeemaker with essentials and a few snacks. He had been with them for about thirty-six hours without any contact. His wrist unit was showing normal vitals which was reassuring but his absence was not.

"I'll start the next search if you want to talk to him," Ace offered.

She sighed. She had never found a fool proof way to be in two places at once. "I need to set up whatever he wants done with Anhe."

"Give me five minutes and I can have a tray ready for you to take with you. With you shoving food under his nose he might eat. He won't taste much but he'll have something in his stomach."

There was nothing in Ben's quiet voice to hint at the hell he had survived with his wife's and child's death. Now that she knew, Taranda felt his pain. Under the cover of the table, Taranda laid her hand on Ben's thigh. When his fingers wrapped around hers and squeezed, she was glad she had reached out.

Benny rose and started to pick up the dirty dishes. Taranda was faster.

"You cooked. I'll clear then head for the hangar."

Ace watched the two split the work. He said nothing until both were out of earshot.

"Six months of sniping and all it took was them going to bed together," he muttered quietly enough that only Felicity could hear. "Why didn't we just lock them in a room with a bed?"

Felicity had seen Taranda's face when Benny had made the comment about food having no taste. She had a feeling that the two had discovered just how much they had in common.

"More than sex went on in the wee hours of this morning."

She wondered how much Benny had confided in Taranda. Based on what she had seen, not only in Taranda but Benny too, she would bet Taranda knew the whole story. She had never seen Benny so relaxed.

He had teased Taranda and allowed her to tease him. The Benny before today wouldn't have done either.

"It's easier planning a mission than dealing with people and all the messes they make with emotions," she commented as she set her empty cup aside.

"I don't know how long I will be. Run the last two filters first. Maybe we will get lucky."

"I'll contact you if I have a hit." Ace got to his feet as

Taranda came out with a tray.

"I'll walk with you, boss. We are heading in the same direction."

"I have to tell you, this new you takes some getting used to," Felicity said as they left the hall.

Alone on the path, Taranda slowed. She had one question that had been burning a hole in her brain since she had seen Ben's reaction to the information she had given him.

"Why the hell didn't you tell Ben about how that son of a bitch who murdered his wife and child died?"

The attack came with no warning. Felicity's eyes narrowed at the fury in Taranda's voice.

"Watch your tone. I don't take that from anyone even you."

Taranda wasn't in the mood to back down. She couldn't believe the Felicity she knew would leave anyone hurting the way Ben had been hurting.

"I have never seen you cruel but withholding that was monstrous."

"I didn't withhold a damn thing. Are you telling me, he had no idea that that drunk had died in a fiery car crash? I thought he knew. What little he said about the man was centered on his father getting his son out on bail. He had to have known that there was no trial simply because the bastard had finally managed to kill himself instead of someone else."

Taranda saw the truth on Felicity's face, heard it in her voice. They had known each other too long, in many ways too well for Felicity to lie to her.

"How could he not know?" Felicity demanded. "It was in the news. Surely someone in her family told him."

Taranda cursed roughly as she shook her head. "He crawled into a bottle to escape the pain. He said he stopped listening to anything anyone said once he knew the murderer was out on bail.

He said he stayed drunk even for the funeral. He couldn't bare knowing he wasn't allowed to see his wife or child. Understanding what that meant is the last memory he has. He can't even remember being at the church or the burial."

The memory of the disjointed words and phrases that had poured out of him with his tears was something she would never forget.

"Dear God," Felicity breathed then she frowned. "How did you find out?"

"I searched for anything I could discover about him. Hacked into everything when normal searching left holes in the story. I knew if we ever got in bed, it wouldn't be just a little fun with a likeable male.

Not just because we live and work together but something else. I can trust up to a point. Sex for pleasure is that point. Sex with something extra raised the issues of trust. I haven't seen him date and he rarely leaves the compound, so he wasn't enjoying strange every now and then. It made me curious."

"You didn't leave any tracks?" Felicity started moving again.

"No and I didn't try to hack you even though I knew you would have everything I wanted to know. My ears are still stinging from the one and only time I tried.

I used mostly public records. It wasn't that hard to collect the data. The police report was the only snag. I did that little dive when I was in Canada last month. Since I was Terri Mitchell on vacation it seemed like a good opportunity. Worked off the hotel Wi-Fi."

"I think I taught you too much about computers."

Taranda shrugged, a glint of self-directed amusement in her eyes. "I love learning. Computers offer a challenge and a goal. What more could I want?" She stopped at the entrance to the men's dorm.

Felicity took the tray. "Whatever you said and did, helped him," she said quietly.

Taranda looked beyond Felicity for a moment then back. "I remember years ago, when I didn't think I could live with the memories that made sleep torture. All those nights in hell, I hadn't dreamed. The minute I got to the Ranch, all I did was wake up screaming."

She reached out to Felicity, her hand on her arm. "You remember that night you stayed overnight. I had a nightmare. You were the first one in my room. Jonah was right behind you and Nelson.

I was screaming. I had my hands in my hair. You pulled my hands away from where I been yanking hunks out by the roots while I screamed. When I couldn't yell any more, you were still holding onto me. Do you remember what you said?"

Felicity nodded. The night was forever etched in her memory. No child, no human should have had to feel the agony she had seen carved into Taranda's face.

"You survived hell because you are stronger than those bastards knew. They are dead. You are alive. You have a choice. Die in the hell they forced on 22 or make Taranda a heaven that has no end. Your choice, Taranda, always your choice. You want to fly. Now do it. You are not 22. You are Taranda. Spread your wings, Taranda. Spread your wings."

Taranda had heard and, in some small, still part of her, felt the power of the words then, the truth, the fury and the determination of the woman who had opened the gates of hell and offered her the first freedom she had ever known.

Felicity had looked at her and seen Taranda not 22. She had believed in Taranda.

"Every time I fly, just before the wheels leave the earth,

I say '*fly, Taranda, fly*'. Because of you I can."

She nodded toward the door. "He may not know how to fly now. I know you'll find the words he needs." She released Felicity and walked away without looking back.

Felicity watched her long-legged strides that radiated confidence and strength. Despite the hell she had been through, Taranda hadn't broken.

She hoped Andre didn't either. She entered the building and walked down the hall. Every year, the Farm was closed for training for a month. It wasn't always the same month. Patterns were not smart for anyone in her business.

The barracks were empty now except for Andre. She heard no sound as she tapped lightly on the door.

"Whoever you are, not now."

The rough words vibrated with pain. Felicity inhaled deeply then turned the knob, half expecting it to be locked. It wasn't. The room was dark, the curtains on the single window covered by a blanket.

"Go away."

"Not an option. You aren't eating."

Her ability to see well in the dark got her across the floor to the desk beside the bed. She set the tray on the bare surface then yanked the blanket off the curtains then opened them to the sun.

Andre blinked as he lay on the rumpled bed, fully

clothed except for bare feet.

"I know you're trying to help." He threw an arm over his eyes. The light hurt. The darkness was a cave of isolation. He didn't want anyone.

Felicity stood over him, reading the pain eating into him. The guilt. Hiding from it, burying himself in darkness wouldn't change one damn thing. Anhe was dead. Acceptance was hell but it was also the beginning of living again.

"Because you called us first, taking the time to get to a secure area, you believe you failed Anhe."

He groaned as though she had gutted him. What little she could see of his face contorted in agony.

"Yes."

Softness wouldn't get through to him. Only truth, hard facts that no amount of shading would change the result.

"If you had not called us, the team wouldn't have arrived as quickly as they did. Anhe fought, Andre. However, it happened, accident or design, she was not taken, tortured, possibly raped before they killed her. Her only use to them would have been to get to you. She did not die screaming your name. It was quick."

He shoved upright, glaring at her. He swung his feet to the floor.

"She is still dead."

Fury blazed in his eyes. He wasn't hiding now.

"Yes, but not because you didn't move fast enough. Not because you didn't get the fastest help possible to her. The guilt is theirs. Not yours. Not hers. You love her. Would she blame you? The truth, not what you feel but what she would feel," she demanded of him.

His dark eyes stayed on her face, his hands laying limply on his knees. For a moment he felt the energy of his anger flow through him. As quickly as the strength came, it ebbed into a dull kind of mist. He sighed deeply, wishing she would just go away, leave him to his search for peace, if only for a second.

"No, she would not blame me." H could barely speak the words he knew to be true.

"Would she have chosen to be taken as a weapon against you if she had known how the fight would end?"

"No," he admitted slowly. He looked surprised as though the question had offered a new thought, a new feeling. "She knew there was danger in what I do."

Felicity heard the beginning of acceptance sliding into his tone. She pulled his desk chair out and sat in front of him. She could see a glimmer of life in his eyes.

"We have a few leads and the name of the man who may be involved with her death. Every free member of the Farm is on it. Cam, Mia, Benny, Taranda, Ace and me. We won't stop looking for those who took her life. Not vengeance, Andre.

Justice. Do you want to be with us on the hunt? Or is the darkness what you want? What she would want for you?"

"You know who did this?" He latched onto the most important fact. He searched her face, seeing nothing but cold purpose in her eyes.

"I believe we do. We have a possible location. We got the information early this morning."

His hands clenched into fists. He wanted his hands around the throat of the man who had killed his Anhe. "I want in on the hunt."

"Then eat, shower and dress. We will be in the control room in an hour."

"Anhe," he managed the name. "I need to make arrangements." He sighed deeply. It hurt to think of what he had yet to do, to think of doing.

Felicity breathed a mental sigh of relief. Andre was starting to take back control of his life.

"You are one of us now, if you want to be. Anhe is one of us because she was with you. We have a place here when we lose one of our own. She is welcome to be here with us if you wish."

Andre dipped his head, the tears standing in his eyes. "I had not thought...."

Felicity interrupted, wanting to keep his thoughts moving in a forward motion. "Ricky is our medic and also our chaplain. He can perform the service for you."

He reached for her hand, squeezing it hard. "We both wanted cremation."

"Then that is what it will be. I have a number of dresses in the wardrobe room. You may choose one or I can do it for you."

"I can not thank you…"

"No thanks for this ever, not between us or anyone here. Cam brought her home. Ricky tended to her spirit. I to her body. We take care of our own. It is an honor."

She stood. "Eat before the food gets cold. We have a lot to do. You're needed."

"I wish you could have met her."

"I did when I saw the marks on her hands and the way that one room looked. She fought, Andre. For you and herself. Courage and determination. She is a delicately built woman with the heart of a warrior."

"Would you choose for her and me?"

She inclined her head. "It would be my honor."

Felicity left the barracks and headed for the wardrobe room. On the way, she contacted Ace.

"Tell me some good news."

"Down to three possibles using facial probabilities, the horse breeding and a private landing strip. Are you on the way?"

"No, I have to make a couple of stops. I'll be about an hour or so. I'll meet you in control. Andre is coming on board."

"How is he?"

"Was wrecked with guilt."

Ace cursed. He knew that route too damn well. "Did you pull him out of it?"

"I think so. I'm picking out a dress for Anhe. They had decided on cremation."

"We have facilities for that?"

"Yes. Used once. I'm here. I'll see you in an hour."

She entered the building and locked the door behind her. She didn't want any interruptions. Or to be overheard. She engaged video capability as she made a call.

"Taranda, I need you to make a quick hop for me. Denver is best. I need a blanket of white roses and two vases of long-stemmed whites as well."

"For Anhe?"

"Yes, I need them for tonight. Make it happen."

"You'll have them."

"Call me when you are close. I want them to go straight to Anhe. Can you handle arranging everything?"

Taranda nodded. The fact that Felicity was trusting her to care for the woman none of them had met made her task important.

"There's a white sheet over her. Leave it but make sure

it doesn't show. I only want to see the flowers. The tall vases at her head. We can't risk giving her a memorial with all her family present but we can give her this."

"She will be surrounded by white flowers. I'll make it right."

Felicity nodded. "I know it."

Ace looked up when he heard the door open behind him. The lack of the sound of footsteps told him who had entered control. He concentrated on the screen in front of him. It was duplicated on one of the large units mounted on the wall.

"Using the computer-generated facials after you removed the possible disguise appliances, I've narrowed it to these two. I hope Blanco is the man we want rather than Perez."

Perez was an ugly piece of humanity who had managed to slide out of every law enforcement officer's hands, since he was birthed. Illegals, sex trade, human trafficking, weapons. The man was a snake in bespoke suits who rubbed elbows with celebrities and politicians even as he turned the next bloody deal.

Side by side the two facials could have been brothers although they did not appear to be related. Marco Santiago

Manuel Blanco and Ricardo Perez, no middle name. If they had been siblings, Perez would have been the older brother by almost two decades.

"Perez has Paso Finos but doesn't breed them. Marco is my pick. His mother was a professional singer and actress in Mexico. His father, Mateo Arturo Blanco started as a small horse breeder then struck gold with a colt that no one thought was worth the price of feed. He was the foundation of the Blanco Stud for Paso Finos. Also, check his middle name. Santiago. Daddy's middle name is Arturo. The man wasn't very smart to use either."

Felicity shifted her shoulders, her eyes trained on the images in front of her. "Arrogance can be incredibly blind. Why would anyone connect him to his alias? His disguise is very good. The names are some of the most common in his country. Convenient. Easy for him to remember, to respond to."

He keyed once and the screen changed. "This is his spread, near the border of Colombia. The landing strip is long enough to handle almost everything except a commercial air bus. The hangar isn't for just one plane.

He is the registered owner of four aircraft. One chopper. Two private jets and one cargo carrier that is set up for transporting his horses to new owners as a special benefit or to competitions. His Pasos are highly regarded, both for showing and breeding."

Felicity quickly scanned the summary of his personal life. His wife was beautiful, his sons as handsome as the father. The daughter was pretty but not nearly as eye catching as the rest of the family.

"One wife, fifteen years and three children, two sons, one daughter. Mistresses?"

"Not so far. He appears to be a devoted family man. He certainly lives well but not extravagantly. He donates quite a bit to various charities in his own country.

I've been digging into his finances. I'm not finding anything unusual. He travels with and without his wife. If he travels alone or with his family, he always takes his bodyguard with him."

Ace brought up Diego Cortez's picture, profile and full face, as well as a compilation of his personal background and his financial status.

"Remind you of anyone?"

When she nodded without comment, he continued, "They went to school together. Their fathers were about the same financially at the time. When the Stud took off, the money gap widened. The friendship stayed.

Diego has his pilot's license, prop and jet. No helo on record. Diego does the flying when Marco is alone. Marco also has a pilot's license, jet only. When they were younger, both did competitive shooting. If one didn't win, the other did."

"Very convenient. Long standing friendship, that means a lot of loyalty and trust. His salary is nearly double what his listed position should command."

Felicity walked closer to the screen, studying Marco's face. She could see exactly what appliances and makeup tricks he could have used to become Arturo.

"You didn't find any crossover between Arturo and Marco?"

"Not a damn thing. Nothing except that name Santiago and Arturo. Could be a coincidence. I am never a fan of those." Ace leaned back in his chair, scowling at the screen.

"Neither am I."

Felicity turned to face him as the door opened and Andre entered. She watched his eyes track to the images behind her. He stopped, studying the monitors. After a long moment, he walked toward her.

"I did not get much of a look at the one chasing me but I don't think this is the man."

He spread his hands, wishing he could say the opposite. "The face was fuller here." He touched his cheekbones then traced an arc beneath his chin."

Felicity turned back to the enlarged image. "All right. Let's have a look at the second possibility. Then I want to run the hall security footage."

She moved to the station she usually manned and keyed in a new search. "Let's see if we can find some footage, preferably in motion of the body guard. He can disguise his face and even alter his body shape. Let's see if he thought to change the way he moves, his mannerisms, his tells, the way he smiles, that kind of thing."

"I'll set up a second search for public footage on Ricardo. Good call. Your experience is showing."

She glanced at him, a faint smile on her face. "Once in a while I let it," she murmured just quietly enough so only he could hear.

CHAPTER FOURTEEN

Felicity's arm unit signaled an incoming. She glanced at the ID. Taranda's timing was on the money as usual.

"Landing in ten, boss. Fully loaded as ordered."

The flowers had arrived. Ricky was on alert that the service for Anhe would be happening tonight, the time depending on Taranda's return with the floral arrangements. Benny had texted that everyone, including Jonah and Nelson at the Ranch, who knew that Anhe was dead, wanted tom attend the service.

"You know what to do. Time?"

"The weather is perfect. The outdoor setting will be too. Ninety minutes tops. I'll contact you."

Felicity ended the connection. Neither Andre nor Ace

looked up from the various recordings and stills they were using for comparisons on the two possibilities.

With both engaged, she texted Ricky to let him know Taranda's arrival time. He texted back that he would be going over to give her a hand with the flowers. Mia had volunteered to help as well. If Taranda needed ninety minutes, she, Ace and Andre had more than enough to keep them busy.

"There it is again," Ace muttered as he zoomed in on the Marco then added a side-by-side image of Arturo as he and his bodyguard were walking into Gordon's office.

"The man's right-handed but he reaches for the door knob with his left. Here's Marco, look at him getting into his car. Left hand opening the door again. I've got two images of Arturo doing that and four of Marco."

Andre focused on the monitors on the wall. "I have found nothing in common between Arturo and Ricardo. In every image I have, Ricardo uses his right hand as he too is right-handed. Also, Ricardo's bodyguard is quite different in body type than the man I saw with Arturo. Unlike Marco, he does not always use the same one."

Felicity studied the pictures. "His stride is the same too. Watch the angle of his head when Marco is listening to the man at the desk and then the woman here."

She walked to the large screen, studying the two images. "Do you see it? The lighting is different and in this one the woman is shorter so he is leaning down just a bit."

She tapped the image of Marco at a party then turned from the monitors. "He is good with the mechanics of his disguise but not with the changing of his habits.

"It's not much to go on but I agree that these two are the same man," Ace summarized grimly.

Andre's eyes narrowed as he studied the handsome man who looked as though he could have been a CEO of a major corporation. "He killed my Anhe. Why?"

Felicity turned to Andre. She had expected his questions. He needed truth not platitudes.

"The information we have gathered is that he didn't directly have anything to do with her death. He told the Senator to handle the problem before either of them knew your name. The Senator found out who you were from the security guard. The man had your name. That's all he told Gordon when she asked. She found your employer on her own.

The senator is very good with computers and she was able to obtain your home address. She contacted someone named Mickey Grainger and gave him the information about Anhe. She ordered him to kidnap your wife in case you proved to be a problem with what you overheard.

I have Cam and Mia searching for him. The Senator gave us his address and that is bogus. He has a sheet so that gives us another avenue to search. We won't stop until we find him."

Ace watched Andre absorb the data they had discovered. In his place, Ace would have wanted every detail. He understood Andre's anger, his need to have a hand in finding his wife's killer. The man radiated restrained fury and total concentration. His clenched fists spoke of his need for action.

"We won't stop looking, Andre," he said quietly, seconding Felicity's promise.

Andre studied them for a long moment. "There is more than my Anhe at stake, isn't there?"

He rubbed the back of his tight neck without taking his eyes from Felicity's face. She gave nothing away except the facts she wanted him to know. In some ways, he wished he could read her. In others, he was glad that he could not.

Ace stood at her side. His expression told him nothing more than Felicity's. He had trained with both. He knew each was deadly both physically and mentally. If Anhe's killer could be found, he believed they would find him.

"Yes. If Blanco is in this so deep that he had to create an alter ego that allows him free access to too many powerful people in Washington, he is a major problem. Gordon told us she recognized the name of the charity he uses to shield his identity on the list of the two dead congressmen.

There are other common donors in the two congressmen but only one large scale contributor for Gordon which appears on their lists. The charity goes all the way back to when she was elected governor. The congressmen's donor list is even farther back."

He frowned. "So whatever is happening has been going on for a long time?"

Felicity nodded. "I think this plan has been working for at least six years based on the donations on record. Marco/Arturo may not be the only person involved. Gordon has accepted over six million before she was elected to the Senate. Three million just to get her elected as governor of her state. Whoever handled the funds, knew how to work the system and the limits on contributions. It took us a while to find a lot of it."

Felicity leaned against the corner of the desk as she watched him assimilate the information.

"So far, we haven't found anything questionable enough in her state leadership to even hint as to why so much was spent with no special favors granted in return. At least not on her side. The donor certainly continued to lay out money for two very needed and very popular issues. Those successes played heavily in her campaign for the Senate.

The situation is very similar to the way one of the men who died got elected to his post. The other had been a Senator for three terms."

"This makes no sense. No one gets someone elected without getting something in return."

"It makes sense if the goal is not one or two small favors but some very large ones. Drilling rights for off shore oil deposits or drilling on national lands, environmentally protected lands. Easier border restrictions. Embargos on certain countries to force the use of other countries products. Redirecting focus off drug traffic or sex traffic.

Pick one. Any of them could mean billions of dollars to the man or group with a strong Congressional foothold. Legislation is constantly being passed. Often, there are hundreds of pages in one bill with so many little paragraphs that hide a study for this, a grant for that.

Who reads those pages, word for word or even completely understands all the legal information? Aides, secretaries, assistants? You can bet it isn't the elected official who is using his or her time to speak to the media or give speeches at luncheons and dinners where he or she is paid to appear."

Felicity paused long enough for him to understand the range of possibilities. Anhe had not died because of some minor plan or crime.

"Then there is campaigning for re-election. Time consuming when one is on the Hill. Flying to this rally, this town meeting. How many pieces of legislation don't get enough scrutiny? An insider would know who shortchanges his or her work. That same insider would know how to bury important data in this study, that grant being added to a bill."

Andre stared, wishing he could deny the picture she painted and knowing he couldn't.

"Searching for something like that sounds impossible. How do we find what is being hidden in that way? We don't even know what the unknown party is trying to achieve."

Felicity turned to study the faces on the monitors. They had found connections. They had names. The likenesses were there. The motive was money. The means were clear. Every step, every piece of information, no matter how small, was making the picture clearer.

"Not impossible, just difficult. It looks as though we have found the link that Gordon saw. The names, Santiago and Arturo have a definite connection to Marco Blanco. Marco would have been smarter not to use a name that was closely associated with himself."

She shrugged. She had seen intelligent people do incredibly stupid things. "I have the computer compiling lists on all three congressmen, living and dead. We cross check the bills they worked, if there are any. Then we start reading."

Andre stared around the control room, the state-of-the-art equipment. "I had no idea of the scope of what you do here? This area was not covered during my training. The weapons and tactical course is just a small part, isn't it?"

"A vital part. Less training or no training means death or capture to those in the field, on the front lines which can be the same thing."

She came to him and sat down facing him. They had a direction to investigate. Technology was working constantly behind the scenes. Right now, there was a more immediate need.

"I sent Taranda to Denver for something for Anhe."

She watched Andre's face change. For a while, he had set his grief aside to help find his wife's killer.

"If you are ready, Ricky is prepared to give Anhe's service tonight. The stars are out and the night is clear. Everyone knows she is with us. With your permission, they all would like to attend. Jonah and Nelson too. It is unsafe to involve her family, but we can give her this if you will allow it."

He was stunned at the offer and the number of people who wanted to be with him when he said good-bye. He had not expected anything like what she was offering.

"Everyone?"

Felicity nodded. The emotions she saw on his face was relief and raw grief barely held in check.

"I will walk you over so that you can be alone with Anhe for a while. You can see what we have done for her, see if you wish any changes."

He caught her hand, squeezing tightly. He looked beyond her to Ace who watched silently. "Will you come with us?"

Ace nodded. He had seen death too many times not to understand that some needed people around them when this moment came. Some needed only solitude.

"I will. We'll stay if you need us."

"I can sit with her first?"

Felicity got up with him, still holding her hand. "For as long as you want. There is no rush."

He glanced at the huge screens filled with information. "With so much…"

Felicity interrupted before he could finish. "The computers are working. We have something to do that is more important to all of us. One of us, needs all of us."

"There are not enough words." His voice was thick with emotion as he looked at her. He had not thought beyond this moment and Anhe's death.

She shook her head. "You have already said them. We are with you."

They walked out of the control room. The path leading to the small building tucked under the trees was softly lit. It branched to the right, curving through the shadows to a tiny clearing at the back.

Anhe lay bathed in a soft golden glow of the lights surrounding her. White ribbons were draped from the branches above her like a delicate canopy. The streamers rippled slightly in the light breeze creating flickering shadows over her still face.

She lay beneath a blanket of white roses and ferns with an arc of white vases filled with white roses at her head. Lush ferns with lacy frons curved around the base of her last bed.

Her left hand, her wedding band gleaming softly in the light, lay on her flower covered breast. She had one white rose bud tucked in her fingers.

"Dear God," Andre whispered, his eyes on the woman he loved.

With a harsh sound of grief, he released Felicity's hand to walk toward his wife. She was so beautiful, so still.

Taranda with Mia beside her stepped out of the shadows to join Ace and Felicity.

"I hope Mia and I didn't do too much. They were barely home from their honeymoon. We thought having her wedding ring show would matter to him."

"I don't think you could have done better."

Felicity watched as Andre laid his hand over Anhe's. She could feel the first sting of tears she hadn't shed since her father had died. She had stood in the trees like Andre would tonight. Only then, she had held the torch for her father's funeral pyre.

She would spare Andre that devastating memory with Anhe. He would have instead the beauty of his wife resting under the stars, the soft breeze rippling in the leaves curving above her. Nature provided the setting and the music for her service.

This flower filled night, the white ribbon canopy, the golden glow of the lights around her created beauty around a beautiful woman. When the rawness of grief softened, he would know a woman he barely knew as more than a pilot had cared enough to orchestrate the setting under the trees.

Another woman, a friend, a woman who shared the same heritage as his wife had helped give him these moments. These same women, like the rest of those who would attend the service, would fight beside him, if it became necessary, to get justice for Anhe.

He hadn't expected the support, the simple kindness, the wonder of strangers and people he barely knew offering him so much, giving so much to his wife, a person none of them had met. He would never forget this night and those who had given him these memories, these moments.

Felicity knew that none of what they had done would give Andre back the life he had lost with his Anhe. She hoped it would give him comfort.

Ace put his arm around her shoulders. He could see the

sadness on Mia's face and the sympathy on Taranda's.

"He may not know or feel it yet, but you three have made this night something that he will bear easier than he would have with a more conventional service."

Felicity sighed silently. "I hope so. I am going to hand him off to you. I doubt he wants to attend the service in his slacks and a shirt he has worn all day. He's going to need a suit."

"I know where wardrobe is. I'll take care of it."

Felicity turned into him. "I'm glad you're here."

He leaned his head against her hair. "I am glad you took me on," he murmured to her. He kissed her lightly then let her go.

"I'll lay out your clothes for you," she offered as she stepped out of his hold. "Let's get ready, Taranda."

Mia laid a hand on Felicity's arm. "Cam and I are still digging. With Grainger having a record, we have strings to pull. We got some rest as ordered. Ate too. Benny was adamant. We're fresh. We can get back to work after the service. Do you want us to work in control or should we keep using Cam's place?"

Felicity would have preferred they were all in control. Andre's grief was so raw that having the search for Grainger with all of its possible dead ends before they finally found him would just add to Andre's pain.

"Cam's place. Andre has enough on his plate right now. Let me know the second you find anything."

When Mia nodded, she added, "I am calling it by one a.m. You and Cam need to be as fresh as possible. Ace and I may have more B and E to do soon and we will need you in control. Unless you are on a hot trail, shut it down by one."

"If we are hot...."

"I hear about it."

"One. I have to change. Cam and I will be back in thirty."

She looked at Andre, standing beside his wife, his hand covering hers. "You did a good thing, bringing her here, Felicity." Mia walked away without waiting for a reply.

She had come to know Felicity better. She cared for those who worked for and with her. She stood for them when they needed her and back when they didn't. Mia had never known anyone like her. So cool, so controlled and so aware.

As much as she admired her, she couldn't imagine the price she paid every day to be who she was, doing what she did.

"How is Andre?" Felicity asked as she watched Ace wrap a towel around his waist and head toward the bed where his clothes lay spread for a quick change.

"Holding on. He said he didn't know how you had the time to do what you did for Anhe. I told him that it was your idea. Taranda and Mia did the work with a few touches of their own. It mattered."

Briefs, shirt, pants, belt already threaded through the loops. A deep blue tie. He hated the things but this occasion called for the effort. When he finished, he turned to find Felicity holding his jacket ready. He slid his arms in, settled it on his shoulders and fastened one button.

"You look really good, woman."

She wore a black sheath that was without any ornamentation. She could have been born for the color. The dark fabric against her soft golden skin highlighted the strength and the power of her cut muscles and lean body.

"You look as dangerous in a suit as you do in assault gear," she said, returning the compliment.

"I was thinking the same about you." Her arm unit, barely visible against the fabric of her dress, vibrated. She glanced at the information on the display.

"Ricky says the crowd is gathering. Andre just arrived."

She engaged vocal. "We are on our way."

"You do good work, Taranda," Ben said quietly. The setting was reverent, calming even beautiful. "It will matter that you made everything so perfect. Not being able to see someone you love one last time isn't something you ever forget."

Taranda slid her arm through his, joining them. She leaned against his side, wishing his past could be undone. It would have meant that they would never have met. More importantly, it would have given him his family, alive, well and growing. Maybe the divorce wouldn't have happened. She had no doubt he would have been a good father either way.

"His last vision is her in death. Yours is your wife alive. Think of that, Ben. From what you told me of your Susan, she would have been a loving mother. Your baby knew love. If I were Susan, I would want the man I once loved enough to marry even though I filed for divorce to know that I still carried his child when I could have ended the pregnancy. I would want him to remember that. Not grieve for what you couldn't change, couldn't prevent."

Benny turned his head, looking into her dark eyes, eyes that had seen as much of hell as his own. He hadn't thought of that picture before. In all the useless words that people had yapped at him, nothing had meant a thing.

Andre's wife and what Taranda had done for her. What she was saying now mattered more, made more sense, opened a door that he had slammed shut.

"I couldn't think of the future I lost," he said slowly. "I

couldn't face it."

"That was then, Ben. This is now. You can face it now. You're strong enough. You've always been strong enough. You just had to take the time to heal."

"Voice of experience?"

Taranda saw Felicity with Ace beside her join the group spread among the trees. She saw her give a nod to Ricky.

"No. Voice of Felicity. I think she has lost much more than any of us know. She shows no one, except maybe Ace, any visible emotion. But she has an uncanny ability to take a verbal scalpel to a poisonous wound and let it bleed freely. I wouldn't have survived my past without her."

She nodded to Andre as he turned from his wife to face the crowd.

"He will heal too. In his own time, he will find his peace. I think he has already started. It looks like he is going to speak."

Andre looked out on those gathered around him and Anhe. Felicity and Ace, Cam who had brought Anhe to him. Cam's Mia, so much in common with his Anhe, her heritage, her belief in life. Taranda. He would never be able to thank her enough for what she had done to make this night something he could keep close to his heart.

Even Benny, sending food to him when he did not feel like eating. Ace helping him settle on the right tie.

Finally, Felicity. She had brought his Anhe to him. Sent one of her own, in a jet to bring his Anhe home. And now to give her a final resting place.

"Thank you all for coming here for my Anhe. None of you had ever met her but you have come. I will never forget what you have done, for her and for me. There are not enough words. Just know that I honor all of you as I have never honored any others, even my own family."

CHAPTER FIFTEEN

"I hate ties. What fool thought tying something that could probably suspend five hundred pounds without tearing around a man's neck makes a bit of sense."

Felicity slipped her feet out of the six-inch platform heels that were an adventure to walk in on a gravel path.

"He was probably the same fool who invented heels for women," she suggested as she stripped to the skin.

She still needed an hour to check the searches she had running. The long day wasn't over yet. They were closing in, but not fast enough to suit her.

"It might be a woman."

"Might be on stringing up a man. Your species does give mine a lot of reasons for that idea. However," she continued before he could interrupt. "She sure didn't invent heels. Your kind is fixated on legs, among all the other various female body parts. The taller the heel makes the woman the more the males in sight drool."

He came to her as naked as she. He wrapped his arms around her. He reminded himself that, despite the chances that Felicity took, she knew very well how to defend herself. She was tough, smart and canny. But she wasn't indestructible.

"Don't include me in that group. Your legs look best in sleek black pants with those ground covering boots that lace half way up your calf. I can't tell you what they do to your tight little ass when I am following you up a wall or down a tunnel."

She tipped back her head, laughing at the description. She expected amusement in his eyes and found only hard truth. Her amusement died as she reached out to touch his face.

She wanted to tell him not to worry about her but knew she was wasting her time. Just as she would be wasting her time if she told herself the same thing.

"You're supposed to be paying attention to the mission not my butt."

She traced the line of his jaw. Emotion she had never thought to feel filled her for only this one man. He was hard, tough and dangerous. Most women might take him for a temporary lover but not forever, not for a husband who would come home to her every night.

He saw her for the woman she was. Still, he wanted her. More, he stood with her in danger and in peace. He was a gift she had never thought to have. Because her life came with no promises that she would survive beyond the next moment, she understood the importance of every breath, every thought.

Andre, in his grief, would remember every second wasted, every word not said, every touch not given. She would not leave that legacy behind, not for herself or for Ace.

"I love you. Admiring my ass or drooling over my boots, I love you. For your information, I like your ass too. I'm never going to admit to drooling but I definitely have a few fantasies about you in your cargos minus the black tee."

She cocked her head as she slid her hand down his chest. "We need to check the computers. I think I can wait to play out a few of those fantasies if you can avoid drowning in drool."

He caught her hand before she could reach her target. The woman had a sneaky streak of a sexual tease that he really loved.

"I love you too but if you touch that, the only thing either of us will be checking is the nearest horizontal surface. We can't. Too much at risk."

"Once in a while I wish neither of us was so

committed."

He tugged her short hair just hard enough to make her wince. "Liar. We are together because of who we are. I wouldn't change a thing."

"Neither would I," she agreed as she released him and walked with him to the secure room and the work that was waiting. "Coffee or cold caffeine?"

"You tell me. I think it's my turn to stock us."

"Cold for me." She tapped the keys in front of her as she took her seat. Before sharing this room with Ace, she would have brought the systems online verbally. With two, manual worked better. Less noise and distraction.

Ace set her soda on her left. She had a habit of continuing to type while she drank, hence the straw sticking out of the can. For a moment, he admired the view. Felicity naked and focused on her computer pets was a sight. A damn arousing sight. He glanced done at his body. A woman could hide her response. A man wore his like a flag.

He cursed. She laughed without taking her eyes from the screen. She was very aware of him standing beside her.

"If I had pants on this wouldn't be so damn obvious."

"I'm not stopping you. Besides you don't have pants big enough to hide that." She nodded to the shaft right at her shoulder height.

He cursed again and eased carefully into his chair.

"Now, that I have gotten used to your strange affection for nudity when you're in the house, I don't want to wear anything either."

"Wearing snug fitting clothes, boots and being armed is heavy. Sometimes, the gear feels like a cage. No freedom. Shedding it is like stepping into an open space, no weight, no constriction, nothing between me and the air around me. I love feeling the movement of air against my skin, not just my hands and face. I like the feel of the wood floors beneath my bare feet."

She leaned back in her chair and took a sip of soda. "You asked me about a vacation a day ago. This is a mini vacation for me every day. I peel off my clothes and leave the job, the people who live and work here and the business outside. Even when I am working like this, hunting for people or information."

"You keep this room here. Not on the second floor with the work-related disguises and the workout room. It's work."

"It is."

She turned her chair to face the open door behind them. The bedroom wall beyond the door was mostly windows of bullet proof glass. The forest was a deep green canvas with moonlight filtering through the branches of the trees.

"I can be alone with my computers. Until I was fourteen, I had little contact with the outside world. It was just my father and me. I had to learn to live in a heavily populated world to do what I was born and trained to do. I don't really like it. I prefer solitude. It is why I built this house the way I did. It's why no one but the builders and I have seen the inside when it was finished."

She turned to face him. "Until you came."

"You let me in."

"You aren't a man to deny."

His look was a challenge, daring her to believe that he had forced his way into her life.

"I wanted to keep you out."

She barely remembered her reasons why now.

"Something in you called to something in me. You taught me what loneliness was. I didn't like it. Being alone isn't being lonely. I figured the wanting was all there was. I was wrong."

"I thought wanting was all there was, too. I was just as wrong. I didn't grow up in isolation like you did. I am well acquainted with loneliness as an adult.

You know the risk of having someone in our kind of life. Not just the time away from home but the secrecy, the calls in the middle of the night to be transported to some hell that could get you killed. If I needed a woman, I usually dealt in one-night stands which is much better than self-service.

The one time I risked something more almost got Mia

killed because that idiot Monk thought he could get to me through her. I didn't expect to find a new way of living at my age. I sure didn't expect to become your lover and then to discover I love you. We were both wrong."

She laughed softly and tapped her can to his. "I'm a carbon copy, except I never found a male like Mia even for a little while. I'm glad we were both wrong."

"Let's get this done for tonight. We need a little target practice and then sleep."

"Deal."

"With luck, Cam and Mia will come up with Grainger's location so we can move on him. One thing has been bothering me. Even with the two dead congressmen, Marco or Arturo didn't make any visible attempt to change what he was doing when he donated money to get Gordon elected."

"Arrogance possibly. Besides, Everly had specific instructions for me. There was to be no record of any kind of investigation. The government is divisive enough without another scandal. He didn't just want the men stopped. He wanted the situation obliterated without anyone knowing that anything had been wrong to begin with. With that kind of secrecy Marco/Arturo might not have been able to find out the real fates of his two plants. He would have no reason to change his mode of operation."

"Yet, Everly took a chance, doing the one thing he said

he didn't want."

She nodded. "Leverage if he ever needed it, probably. I don't work with people I don't know. I researched him. He was and still is a power player. He didn't rise to the top as fast as he did on his work alone. He knew secrets and he knew how to apply pressure without crossing the line."

"Against you?"

She shrugged. "Maybe but I doubt it. Skye/Sea Security just wasn't big enough then to be a problem. More likely against the man who ordered the takedown. With what we know about him now, Everly had a secret agenda besides being his version of a rabid patriot. He was sure he had buried his report. He was not just a fool but he was wrong."

Ace frowned. "Nothing is hack proof for more than five seconds after it goes on line if we were only contending with our citizens. When China and Russia are added into the mix the number probably tops out around three seconds."

Felicity sighed, remembering the dealings of the two congressmen she had killed on Everly's orders. What Everly had presented for information on their corruption had proven accurate, but it had nothing to do with Arturo/Marco. At least not on anything she had been able to find at the time.

The plot that Rogers and Baldwin were involved in was relatively simple. A word in the right ears is worth gold in many circles, especially concerning new technologies. Rogers got three million tax free in an offshore account for sharing information with interested parties. Baldwin received four. Thanks to the anonymous tip to Everly, I got to them before they could spend much of the payoff."

"Did you use the drug on them?"

She shook her head. "I hadn't finished perfecting the formula. The timing of it was the hardest part. I had to have a consistent window of minutes for interrogation."

"So, you didn't find out who was behind the scenes?"

"That wasn't the mission. Everly said that he had a team on the ground handling that end. I wanted to believe him. His answers were plausible. His information was accurate but something felt off about the situation.

He had never lied to me before but I felt like he was then. I double checked everything he gave me. It all checked out. I did the job. He was adamant that I didn't leave any kind of trail to follow. The same was happening on his end. Every time I worked with him, I found him secretive to the point of obsession. Making that file is completely out of character."

"He didn't know your work very well."

"As Skye/Sea Security, no he didn't. He only had my references. I had seen him when I was in other guises involving other operations. Normally, he was controlled and barely communicative. He produced intel, answered questions with as little information as possible to get the job done.

This time he seemed edgy. He hid it well. I might have missed the change if I hadn't had prior dealings with him. His behavior read like he was being pressured by someone. It could have been his boss. We now know it wasn't. He was ass deep in the game.

I'm damn glad I didn't take his word for Baldwin's and Rogers' guilt. I tracked the payoffs as far as I could with the programs I had at the time. Both led me overseas bouncing all over hell and back."

"Our targets are South American. Your target, if they had let you off the leash, would have been in a totally different direction. Were Rogers and Baldwin used as distractions from something bigger, something that took longer to set up?

Or a test run for another project, something totally unrelated? I'm not saying politicians can't be bought but it isn't that easy."

"The bottom line is the investigation I did had nothing to do with Arturo Santiago. His name never came up except on the donor list that I generated for Rogers' and Baldwin's campaign and then only under EnviroWorld, the charity he represented at the time. Then he appeared to work for them officially as a consultant."

He looked at the information on the screens in front of him. Technology had come a long way. Felicity's equipment, her operation itself was more sophisticated than any he had seen.

She had billions at her disposal. She could siphon off money in and out of every offshore account ever created if she was so inclined. He wasn't fool enough to believe that hers was the only system out there capable of some version of that kind of power.

"Whatever is going down has cost a lot of money with no visible as yet return."

"You're as cynical as I am," she said as she put her remaining searches on auto then got to her feet. She only had one more task.

She engaged vocal only, then contacted Cam. The wrist unit indicated both were working. Her clock said five minutes to one.

"We are calling it as we speak," Cam answered before she said a word. "I think we are getting close to Grainger but nothing hot yet. Mia and I will hit it first thing in the morning unless you want us to tackle something else."

"No. Stay on him until you've nailed him down. He's a loose end. I would rather we find him than someone else. Dead men are not good sources of information."

"Will do."

Felicity cut the connection. "Now, we've used our hour. We need sleep."

He grinned as he stood. He caught her close and lifted her into his arms. Her surprised expression was a memory he would carry for a long time.

"Bet you didn't see that coming."

She curled her arm around his neck then leaned in to nip his ear with just enough pressure to issue a warning. She tipped her head back, laughing at his muttered curse. She liked his tricky side. Until he had come into her life, laughter had been in short supply.

"Is that the thanks I get for being romantic?"

She nuzzled his throat, using her tongue to glide down his jugular. His arms tightened in reaction to the light caress.

"No. The gratitude part comes when I find the target." She used her free hand to stroke his length. His response rippled through the muscles holding her.

"Keep that up and I may drop you on your ass," he warned, meaning every word. What he didn't add was he would be right on top of her, thrusting into her heat.

She had learned to be a very creative lover. It was almost a job requirement. She knew moves she hadn't shown him yet.

"Want to bet?"

His eyes alight with challenge, he answered without words. He released his hold on her over their bed.

Using her arm around his neck and a quick twist of her

body, she scissored her legs around his waist.

"You want to play?"

He caught her butt in both hands. "Oh yeah. I do like to play games with you." Still standing beside the bed, he slid into her with one smooth stroke.

"I really like the way you find your target."

CHAPTER SIXTEEN

Felicity climbed silently, very aware of Ace beside her and her Dobermans keeping pace with them. The morning was so crisp and clear that every breath felt pristine. No sound of civilization disturbed the trees or the stream rippling and bubbling beside the path they had chosen for their warm-up.

"How many of these trails do you have?" Ace asked.

He had jogged for fitness in the city but he had never enjoyed it. It had been a chore he used to keep in peak condition. Now it was a pleasure to start the day with Felicity matching him stride for stride.

"As many as I want. That's one of the benefits of being the boss." She turned her head to grin at him. "I thought you might like a change up."

He trusted that look in her eyes about as far as he could throw the mountain on which they were running.

"How long is this one?"

"Nine point three miles. The last mile is an almost vertical climb."

"Am I going to see any goats on this new hike?"

"I don't know. I haven't tried this one before. We'll find out together."

She laughed at his expression. "You know you would rather be doing this than sitting in front of the computer all day. Which is what we will probably be doing. I am going on the theory of *eat dessert first*."

Ace could feel the incline increasing. His muscles were warming nicely, his heart rate was as it should be. He liked the feel of his body moving fluidly over the rough path.

"This is not, by anyone's standards, dessert."

"It is to me," Felicity replied as she upped her speed.

He matched the increase. Neither of them was breathing heavily but, having seen the topographic map of the land, she knew it would be a good physical test for them.

"You're very quiet this morning."

Cam watched Mia stare out the undraped window of their bedroom. His house was small, perfect for a single man who spent more time at work than lounging at home in front of a screen of some sort.

He hadn't been sure that Mia would like the compact structure that he had designed. It had everything he needed from the king-sized bed to an oversized soaker tub and a huge shower. He was a big man and he hated bumping his elbows in confined spaces.

The kitchen was eat-in only. He hadn't bothered with a dining room. He never had guests. Only Mia had been inside his home.

"Talk to me, honey. I can't help if I don't know what's bothering you."

Mia turned from the window. "Anhe has a family. They don't even know she's dead. They didn't get to see her like we did. None of us had met her but we were there last night to be with her one last time. The people who love her weren't.

I understand why. Felicity made Anhe's service beautiful and Andre will have that memory. The situation is the fault of the people who are hunting Andre and who killed Anhe. I get all of that."

Cam wrapped his arms around her and pulled her close. "You're thinking of your family. The similarities."

She laid her head on his chest. "Yes. I had to die so that they would be safe. Monk might not be the only enemy Ace has out there. Some fool might decide if he couldn't get to me, he might make do with someone in my family.

I don't regret my choice, not really. But my family didn't have a body either. No place to go to mourn, to remember."

She lifted her head to look at him. "What we are doing has a high price tag. What Ace did then and now. What Felicity does every day. What they do every day."

"What has been done to us is the price tag. You didn't get a choice in becoming a pawn in a game of corruption and betrayal with one of Ace's bosses using his power against Ace. No matter what Ace did then, you would have died.

Anhe didn't choose to be a hostage for Andre's silence. No matter what Andre chose, his wife would have died. Looking at Grainger's record, it would have been an ugly, painful death. He likes brutalizing women.

Most of us in the compound chose to fight for our country and what we believe in. No one mentioned that many of us would find it impossible to return to the life we had known, before we discovered what man could and did do to those weaker than the strongest.

The hyper alert states we brought home with us had no place in society. We became a danger to ourselves, to others. The mood swings some of us have make it impossible to even keep a job much less raise a family, be a husband a woman needs and wants at her side, in her bed or be a wife a man needs in his life."

Mia touched his face. "I'm in your bed. You've never hurt me or even scared me except when you got shot. You aren't a danger."

"I could be. The Farm gives me a place to be who I am now. A place to use my skills in a positive way. It helps with the moods, the need to do something. I don't regret my choices. None of us do. Our families, if they still exist, are safe from us because Felicity has given us a life where we can be the people we have become.

Our children don't grow up with a mother or father with nightmares of blood, bombs, and brutality. They don't deal daily with quick tempers and mood swings that no amount of counseling or medications can really relieve."

His eyes held memories she wished she could erase.

"I don't regret my choices either. It gave me you and a new life. I do hate that I had to hurt my family to protect them," Mia said firmly. "It's just that I think of them sometimes. I an miss them and not regret the choices I made to keep them safe."

"You are safe too. Alive. Doing work you love with people who care about you. Do you think that your family would regret your choice if they knew?"

She thought a moment, realizing that she had never considered that idea.

"No," she admitted slowly. She sighed deeply as she leaned into him. "I hadn't thought of what we did that way. It does make a difference."

He lifted her in his arms and carried her back to their bed. They needed to be working. Being together for just a little while mattered more. The future came with no guarantees. Andre's loss was proof of that.

Right here, right now, he had someone who loved him, someone who worked at his side while they tried to help others in untenable situations. Mia's heart had shown him more of himself than he had known existed. He wanted every minute he could beg, borrow or steal with her.

Felicity studied her table by the windows. The usual two chairs and one table had become two tables fitted together and seven chairs. How had that become a regular occurrence?

Taranda arrived with four mugs of coffee before she and Ace had a chance to sit.

"Ben is coming with our plates," she said as she slid into the chair with its back to the window.

"That accounts for four seats. Who are the other three and since when do I have a conference breakfast on my schedule?" Felicity asked with a raised brow.

"It's easier to get Andre to eat if he knows you're here.

That's one place. Cam called over to order for him and Mia. That's the other two. Group chow, easy to give us all our assignments. Saves time."

Ace hid a grin as he sampled the caffeine starter. The cut of Felicity's eyes in his direction made him chuckle. His woman was too aware to miss his enjoyment of Taranda's quick reply.

"Are you under the mistaken impression I need you to lighten my load?" she asked Taranda softly.

Taranda shrugged, the light sliding over her bare shoulders, tracing the smooth, black skin against the red silk halter blouse. The vibrant color fit her mood this morning.

"I wasn't thinking of that. Why would I? I was thinking I want to help with more than just flying to and from wherever. I am definitely not as good on the tech stuff as the rest of you but I can monitor searches and set them up. I can hack a bit too as you well know. Put me to work."

Benny arrived with four plates. One of his helpers followed him carrying a basket of pastries and a pot of coffee for refills.

"Four steak and egg specials. Looks like we had the same idea. Cam and Mia better get their asses in gear. Their omelets will be ready in a minute."

He settled beside Taranda as his helper set the basket and pot on a trivet in the middle of the table. Satisfied with the presentation of his skill, he thanked the woman and waved her back to the kitchen.

"I went over the plane and the helo with Taranda yesterday. I am working up menus for you to approve or change. With everything going on do you want to wait?"

"No, the prepared food on board is a good idea. The kitchen is your domain. I don't need to check the menu. You know the nutritional needs our kind of work demands. Better, that memory of yours keeps everyone's likes and dislikes on a list."

Benny stared at her for a moment then grinned. "Now, that is a nice way to start the morning. Makes me brave enough to suggest a new freezer for storing the meals. We are close to capacity now. I don't have enough storage for what I have in mind. I want to be able to make a number of meals ahead with everyone's specific tastes.

All I will need are the names of whoever is going to be onboard and I can just load the aircraft from the main freezer. Sealed and labeled, the meals should be good for up to six months, although I doubt any of them will last that long at the rate we are using the helo and the jet. I'll add a few generic dinners for any guests."

Felicity cut into her steak as she considered Benny's suggestions. "Good thinking. Taranda, you want extra work? Here it is. I need you to make a trip to Denver for the freezer."

"Boss, I'd like to go along. I know what I want. I've got the measurements for the space we have. Kevin can handle lunch. He already has the menus in hand and prep is up and running for desserts and breads.

Also, I want to see what is available for the trays for the meals. I checked out possible accessories online. I'd rather see what's available in person. I don't think we want disposables. Too flimsy. That means a space saving tote for the dirty trays and utensils to outfit the helo and the jet."

All good suggestions and now that the idea had been advanced, Felicity could see the possibilities, especially over long hauls.

"All right. Both of you take off as soon as you finish breakfast. Taranda, if we find Grainger, I want to move fast. It looks like he's in the wind and he may not light for very long."

"I'll be less than an hour away. We'll be monitoring. You call and we'll be back ASAP."

"Looks like Andre met Cam and Mia on the way over," Ace said with a nod at the main door of the dining hall.

Kevin arrived with two plates and two filled mugs and one empty. He glanced at Andre as the trio reached the table.

"Your breakfast will be out in a minute. Is coffee alright or do you want something else?"

Andre took a chair. "Coffee will be perfect."

Felicity watched Andre as Kevin filled his cup, set it in

front of Andre then left. The man looked much better than he had the day before. The dark circles of exhaustion and grief beneath his eyes were lighter today. He moved with more energy, more awareness of those around him. He was still grieving but now he had a purpose and a goal.

Find Anhe's killer.

Felicity, with Ace beside her, sat in front of the computer keyboards and studied the wall monitors displaying the plans of Marco's estate. The man owned a little over nineteen hundred acres of prime pasture and agricultural land. Not only did Marco breed, sell and show Paso Fino horses but he also had a dairy of Carora cattle that was gaining a reputation for its quality milk and cheeses.

The main house was a sprawling family home in the center of a cluster of slightly smaller buildings including barns, stables and housing for the estate workers. The compound was surrounded by lush grounds and a man-made lake complete with a waterfall. Colorful gardens spread like exotically colored skirts around the walls of the home. A free form pool, a jewel of design and creativity, dominated the back lawn and gardens.

"Marco obviously likes to live well."

Ace highlighted the clearing with a long landing strip

north of the house. The larger of the buildings beside it had the dimensions of a hangar for aircraft.

"No neighbors within sight or sound," Felicity observed. "The closest is miles away. We should be able to get in and out without detection. Only minimal security, a couple of night guards and dogs. Some cameras. We can tap into those as well as any alarms."

"I do not understand what you intend to do." Andre frowned at the screen on the wall. "Are you planning to kidnap him? To break in looking for something specific? Surely, hacking into his computer would produce valuable information."

Felicity looked away from the estate. "We need answers Andre. Gordon doesn't have them. It is very possible that two men may have died because of a scheme about which we know nothing. Their involvement might have been more than what Skye/Sea had found back then.

If the corruption died with them, it makes no sense to worry about the file now. Plus, there is the question of millions of dollars in donations for which no benefit has been sought or received. Most important of all, Anhe died to protect whatever is going on."

Andre realized he was getting a crash course in how the Farm could work when the need arose. Felicity and her teams had put together an incredible amount of data. Using what could be documented, she and Ace had extrapolated possibilities that demanded explanation.

"I do not like dealing with bodies while someone gets away with killing," she said quietly.

She watched him pale at the blunt assessment. "To move forward, we have to have answers. This is the only way."

"How? By torture with his family in the house? Are they to be hostages?"

Felicity got to her feet without taking her eyes from his. She was aware of Ace's barely controlled anger at Andre's challenge.

This was why she hated questions. She didn't want robots who simply obeyed without thinking but she did want trust. Right now, she didn't have time to build that trust between Andre and herself.

"You haven't seen us in action so I will cut you some slack this one time. There is a reason why I don't encourage questions. They waste time and emotion."

She watched him silently for a moment to let her rule take root.

"I will explain this one time. I do not use innocents. Not man, woman or child. Nor do I use torture. It's damn unreliable for one thing. Time consuming and messy. It also involves a controlled location and usually others to provide security.

The information can also be unreliable. Given certain mind sets, a person can die being tortured and still not reveal information. He or she could even lie. There are far better ways."

Andre spread his hands. "I meant no disrespect. I just don't see what you intend."

"A drug. Easily administered. Very fast working and reliable. Best of all no memory of the interrogation. Usually, the most difficult part is getting to the target, circumventing security both in and out."

"You can do this?"

"We have done it," Felicity confirmed.

"Multiple times," Ace added. "In and out like ghosts."

Andre started to ask a question then rethought the idea. "It appears that you plan to move soon," he stated rather than queried.

Felicity noted his change in wording but before she could reply, her unit vibrated. She glanced at the read out then engaged vocal.

"What have you got?"

"We've found Grainger," Mia announced. "Naples, Florida. He got a speeding ticket on his California license. His listed address on the ticket checks out as of today. He's renting a place."

In seconds, Mia transferred the data so that it scrolled

onto the wall screen. The ticket, the address highlighted, an aerial of the house where Grainger was supposed to be.

Felicity moved closer to the enlarged view and studied the layout. "Taking him out there is not on the table. The surrounding houses are too close. I see a lot of kiddie equipment in the yards, front and back. That means too much activity almost around the clock, especially now that it's summer. It won't be really dark there until almost ten.

There is no way to get him out, either conscious or unconscious. He's not a small man so he's going to fight unless we can get in when he's sleeping. There is a dog in this house on the right."

She pointed to the miniature house for the pet. She tapped another yard on the left. "Those look like holes that no one has bothered to fill. That says dog too."

Ace nodded. "I bet they bark every time a leaf blows across the street. Smarter to lure him to a location we can control."

"You are not going to kill him?"

Andre wanted his life. Grainger had taken Anhe's future. He did not deserve to live when Anhe was now ashes in a pretty jar.

"Justice, Andre. Not vengeance. As much as you might want it right now, you won't want to live with that resolution for the rest of your life. Anhe would not want it for you."

"The world does not know my Anhe is dead. He cannot be tried for killing her. How can she have justice?"

"There are many ways to that goal. He has a sheet of women he has brutalized. One of the last ones was savagely attacked. She almost died and she is permanently paralyzed from the rapes and beating he gave her.

She tried to press charges. The legal process got him as far as an appearance for a bail hearing. Bail was set and he paid it when he had no money. Three days later, the woman's younger sister was raped and beaten.

Grainger, under a different name, is in the wind. He left behind DNA so the two rapes have a clear connection. We can return him to California and he can stand trial. This time there will be no bail."

"He deserves to die."

Felicity agreed. "Yes, but we are not the judge and the jury. Skye/Sea Security does not override the legal community. That would make us no better than those we hunt. Think, rapists did not do well in prison. Death is quick. Incarceration is not. He has a temper and he likes using his fists."

Ace unfolded from his chair. He understood exactly what Andre felt even though Mia had not died from her injuries. She could have.

"We go in, lure him to a controlled location and take

him back to California to face his trial. Two women will stand for what he has done to them and to others. They deserve their chance to tell their stories," Ace pointed out. "When they stand for themselves, they will be standing for Anhe too."

Andre looked at the face of the man on the screen who had killed his wife. He thought of Anhe. She had not suffered. She had not been raped, brutally beaten. Paralyzed. Two sisters suffering the same fate because one had been brave enough to press charges.

His Anhe would have admired the woman's courage. The courage of her sister. They, too, deserved their justice. He exhaled deeply then looked at Ace then Felicity.

"Selfishly, I wish he would die at my hands. I want that very much. But you are right. The sisters should have their justice. I know my Anhe would want that for them.

I ask one thing. I need to be with you when you take him. The world does not know my Anhe is gone. Only I and the people here know. And the Senator who sent this man to take my wife. I need to see him caught. I hope I see fear in his eyes."

He spread his hands. "As much as I want his blood on my hands, I will not touch him. I give you my word. He will be left to justice in the courts, before the jury and the judge. I will be able to sleep easier if I can do this. Will you let me?"

Felicity read the truth in his eyes. He would keep his

word. Physically, she could easily deny him what he asked. Emotionally was another matter entirely. He understood. His need, his wife's wishes. Justice would be served.

"You will be with us." She saw his relief and his commitment. Both mattered.

CHAPTER SEVENTEEN

"All buckled in?" Taranda asked the question without glancing away from the instrumentation in front of her.

"We're ready," Ace answered for everyone.

Taranda would have preferred the jet. Nothing beat Baby's speed. But in this case, the helo was a better option. The jet required a landing strip of reasonably level ground. The chopper could drop down almost anywhere. No strip required.

There was a preserve area about three miles from their destination. An easy jog for the three-person team going after Grainger.

She reached cruising altitude and pointed the chopper south and east. She had three refueling stops to make, all touch-and-go which added to the trip length. They had roughly five hours before reaching their destination.

"What if you can not get Grainger to follow you out of the bar?" Andre asked curiously. He hoped that was not a question that would get him another of Felicity's reprimands.

Ace laughed. He'd had a preview of Felicity's disguise for this mission. Only a dead man wouldn't respond to the hip high side slit in the electric blue leather skirt. No man with blood in his veins would be able to resist trying to find out if she had a stitch on under the second skin skirt.

The blouse, curtesy of a squash in and push up bra, outlined every curve as though Felicity was wearing a wet tissue. Add just-got-out-of-bed tousled hair and fire red lips resulted in an instant hard-on with the corresponding loss of male IQ.

"Believe me, getting him to follow her isn't going to be the problem. You haven't seen her in character yet."

Cam snickered, the sound carrying clearly through the earbuds each was wearing. He was control and Mia was data search and monitoring.

"Felicity, Taranda, I think this is op is turning into a boys' locker room," Mia commented as she tracked the helo southeast.

"Hey, I didn't say a word," Benny objected. "Besides, I have seen the boss in character. I wouldn't know her unless she introduced herself."

Andre frowned. "You use disguises that much?"

"I use whatever tools the job needs. If we were trying to draw a woman out, Ace or Cam would be the bait. You wouldn't recognize either of them."

"Not Benny?" He looked at the older man and wondered.

"Not me, ever. Not Jonah or Nelson either. Any of us would make crap bait. Bad attitudes. Ace and Cam can fake it. We can't."

Andre frowned. "Mia? Taranda?"

"Not me. Computers are my strength. Not face to face pretense," Mia replied before Felicity could.

Taranda touched her scar without turning around. "Disguising this is tricky. One slip and I would blow the op. Besides, like Mia, I have other skills."

She made a minute course adjustment. It took precision and attention to handle the helicopter.

"You are pretty enough to make bait but that accent, slight though it is, would need to go unless Felicity wanted a French veneer. Again, one tiny slip and we risk screwing an op. One or more of ours could die. Not a good trade off," Taranda continued without looking at him.

Felicity studied the layout of the bar that they had discovered that Grainger seemed to frequent. Mia had found that gem with the help of two charge slips on Grainger's credit card under one of his aliases.

Fortunately, it was a neighborhood establishment that believed in security cams. Mia had assessed the feeds for the last seven days which was all the management kept on hand before erasure.

Grainger was a man of habit. A damn fool habit. Every night between six and seven he got in his car and drove the three blocks to the bar. Pool was his sport and he was damn good.

The owner didn't allow betting on the outcome but it was common for the loser to buy the winner drinks. The number varied according to the game.

Grainger rarely bought his beers. Felicity suspected he wouldn't have bought any if he had played to win every game. He lost just enough to keep other men interested in trying to beat him.

He occasionally played women. Even let one win. She had been good but not as good as he was. Felicity had watched him watching his opponent. She had seen the second he had decided to throw the game. His target had been bent over the table, her shorts riding high on her cheeks, outlining every curve and indention.

The front view of her lush, braless breasts wiggling with every positioning of every shot had apparently been the deal clincher. She won. He bought her drinks and twenty minutes later walked out of the bar with his hand on her barely covered butt.

The plan of action was easy after that scene played out. She was the bait. She knew how to play pool and had played for higher stakes than drinks. She might not beat him but she wouldn't lose by much. Either way, she would get his attention.

Taranda started the descent to the first refueling. No one was exiting the helo except Taranda. The rest of them would keep their heads turned away from the windows as though they were conversing.

The sun on the tinted windows of the chopper made getting a clear look at any of them inside difficult if not impossible. Felicity had used this stop before. The private strip was family owned and the son handled the fuel pump during the day, a cousin handled any refueling after hours.

When they were in the air again, Felicity went over the plan one final time.

"Benny, you are cover for the helo and Taranda. Cam and Mia are in control. Andre, Ace and I, once I am Kitty Kane..."

"Minus the heels," Taranda interrupted. "There is no way you can jog three miles over dirt paths for most of it in those shoes."

"Taranda, shut up. When we get back, I'll show you that those heels can do it and so can I. I won't do it now because they do slow me a little."

Cam chuckled. "I want to watch."

Ace grinned. "I'm going to watch."

"I'm going to be in the kitchen," Benny stated.

Felicity laughed softly. "Finally, a smart man."

She tapped the screen on her laptop. "Pay attention. We'll arrive at the bar by six. We'll wait here until we see him park."

She pointed to the small group of trees and scrub bushes that took up a corner of the land at the back of the bar. The parking lot was a rough patch of dirt and clumps of grass occasionally showing green. Everyone parked in a ragged line determined by whoever got there first. From their vantage point, they could see anyone leaving or arriving.

"I'll give him twenty minutes to get a game started. I'll lose the first game and win the second. If he sticks to the way he played the other woman we saw him pick up, he'll buy me a drink and talk a little. You'll know when we are getting ready to come out."

She looked at Andre. "Move fast and don't talk from that point on, even if you think it's safe. You and Ace will get in the trunk of the car. It should be big enough since he has a full sized, older model.

We don't know where he took the other woman. It could have been her place or his. In this case, he thinks he is going to mine using a route that takes him along the perimeter preserve road."

She tapped the target on the map. "Here. I'll have him worked up enough that he will stop. You two get out. We take him down. Benny, you'll drive the car into the swamp here while Andre and Ace haul Grainger to the chopper.

Chances are, since it's Florida, there are alligators. From the look of this water, there is enough depth to partially submerge the car. Leave the door open as though he got out. Even if someone reports him missing, there isn't a body and he has a sheet."

"So, no one will look very hard to find him," Andre finished.

"Exactly. Once we have him restrained, you and Ace get to do the heavy lifting. I change shoes and we head for the helo. Taranda flies us out using a different route with an extra fuel stop. More open water under us. I don't want a straight back flight."

"Cautious."

"Always," Ace agreed answering Andre's observation.

"I have a contact that I will call to arrange his return to California to stand trial."

"What if he explains about his capture?"

Felicity shrugged. "My contact will cover when she takes him in. She ran him to ground when he returned to California. She caught a break because he got high on something and was hallucinating when she arrested him. Mumbling about some pool game and a woman called Kitty Kane of all names. Guy was really on something weird. Added alligators and a swamp to the mix."

Andre stared then shook his head. He grinned faintly. "Who is going to believe his story after that report?"

"We try to cover all bases. Less chance of something coming back on us that way." Felicity sighed deeply. "One more thing. Once we land, masks for everyone but Taranda. Kitty is the only face that Grainger is going to be able to describe."

Benny mumbled a curse. He hated face coverings. The damn things itched. "How come she is exempt?"

"With the headphones and the way I am tucked into the cockpit here, all he is going to see, if he even bothers to look, is black skin and blacker hair. I'm only a faceless pilot to him."

"Then he is stupid as well as being a murderer," Benny commented.

Felicity waited until Taranda had the helo at cruising altitude. The last refuel was complete and the next touchdown was their destination.

"How are you doing?" she asked quietly. Taranda had been practically living the sky for the last few days.

Taranda grinned. "You know I live for this stuff. I'm good. Once we are on the ground, you're the one who is going to be carrying the load for the next couple of hours."

"By the time this trip is over, I think we all will have earned a rest." Aware of the activity behind her while the men geared up had ceased, Felicity eased out of the co-pilot's seat. Benny took her place.

It was time to turn herself into Kitty Kane. The chopper wasn't ideal for the detail work she needed on her face and nails but she had dealt with worse. She had little less than two hours to become another woman with nothing on her mind but living dangerously and having sex.

She stepped into the small curtained off alcove where her garment bag and makeup case waited. She stripped to the skin, bundling her black tee and cargos into the duffel at her feet. She temporarily shed her boots and the earbuds they all wore to make communication easier with the engine noise of the helo.

First, she slipped into lace top black stockings and an electric blue G-string to match the skirt. Then a sheer black bra to pair with the black semi sheer blouse provided the underpinnings for Kitty's night out.

She slipped on the blouse, what there was of it, but left the skirt off for the moment. The clasp that held the blouse together, rode low under her breasts. The tiny camera it contained provided a visual record for the team on the ground and in control.

She left the skirt for last. The damn thing felt five sizes too small. Standing was a lot more comfortable than sitting while she handled the various steps to become Kitty.

Makeup took forty minutes counting the appliances to change her face shape. Next the wig over the net for her own hair. Styling took a few minutes more to achieve that barely staying in place look that men seemed to find sexy. The style also hid the ear bud communicator she wore.

Then nails, fake and as red as her lips, with glitter to catch the light and the eye of any male in range. Finally, she slithered, wiggled and cursed her way into the skirt. The black lacing from hipbone to waist gave little room to move. The design also kept the male contingency focused on the slender strings in case they parted under the strain of holding the sides of the skirt together.

"I heard that," Ace said from the other side of the curtain.

"You are liable to hear more when I try to bend down to put these boots back on," she replied.

"Bring you and your boots out here and I'll help do

them for you."

Having seen her in the outfit when she had done a dry run at the house, he wondered how she was able to move in that skirt. The only way she could walk in it was the side closure created a gap big enough to allow her the room needed to take a step.

She laughed as she looked at the boots. It wasn't that she couldn't bend over. She just wanted to breathe through the process.

"You've got yourself a deal as long as it includes you getting the boots off the floor."

She shoved back the curtain and stepped into the aisle, leaving the boots behind.

Ace grinned at the sight she made. Pure unashamed sex on stockinged feet was a sight to raise any man's blood pressure. Benny's wolf whistle didn't mask Andre's shocked exclamation.

Andre barely heard Ace's comments. He couldn't stop staring at the woman he had been so sure he would recognize. Nothing about her looked like Felicity Ramsey. Not her lush body, not the hair curling seductively around a face that demanded attention. The clothes, brief and tight though they were, were just a frame for the woman. This woman understood sex in a way that made a man want to learn everything she knew.

Until he looked into her eyes. There was Felicity. Even the addition of vivid blue contacts didn't mask the intelligence and focus that made her so good at what she did. Only a fool would miss how dangerous she was.

"You're right about not recognizing you as long as I don't look at your eyes. I see Felicity in them," Andre managed finally.

Felicity heard the doubt in his voice. He thought he understood what this night would bring. He was wrong. His training hadn't prepared him for what would happen in the next few hours. Covert work wasn't as cut and dried as security and assault. Stealth and deception were more often than not better and more effective weapons than guns and knives.

Felicity turned and closed her lashes for a second and when she opened them Kitty focused on Andre. If looks could singe, Kitty's visual inspection from face to crotch was a fire that burned away civilization and left behind primitive male.

She knew men, what they needed, their fantasies, their dark desires. She glanced up at his face, lightly touched her tongue to her lips, her lashes dropping to partially cover her blue eyes.

"Who is Felicity?"

The husky demand was barely blunted by the muted whine of the helo's engines. A slightly deeper breath pushed her breasts against the already straining fabric.

Stunned at the look, the voice and the gestures, Andre stared back at Kitty. He loved his wife. He was grieving. His body ignored both deep emotions and focused only on the woman in front of him. She was close enough to touch. His hands itched with that need even as he fisted his fingers and mentally cursed his body.

Ace eased between Kitty and Andre. He doubted Andre would forget the demonstration that Felicity had just enacted. He could almost feel sorry for the way the man had learned his lesson. The hard-on he was packing had to be a shock he wouldn't forget.

Boots in hand, he returned to his seat. Felicity lifted her foot and used one hand on his shoulder for balance. With her body between him and Andre, he looked up and shook his head. Felicity answered with a slight shrug and a cocked brow.

"Touchdown in ten," Taranda advised. "Strap in everyone.

"The only heat signatures in the area are animal," Cam reported. "Some cloud cover moving in but no rain showing yet. It's a fast-moving front with some storm cells that could be a problem."

"No sign of Grainger yet," Mia said. "His car is still in the drive of where he is staying."

Felicity reached into the alcove and brought out the high heels she would need later. Ace took them and put a shoe in each pocket on his thighs.

"Don't lose them."

He grinned, giving her a male look that was all challenge. "You could walk in there in those boots and I can guarantee no man would notice your feet."

She laughed as she sat on the seat beside him. "You would."

He looked at that smile, that mouth. It was Felicity's smile and Kitty's mouth. He would notice, working or pleasure he would notice.

CHAPTER EIGHTEEN

"You're clear to go," Cam said quickly, his eyes focused on the satellite images of Another Round. The bar was a popular place, both indoors and out. In this case, a couple had had a quickie in the trees just where the team intended to await Grainger's arrival.

Ace led the way, Felicity behind him and Andre bringing up the rear. They made it to the trees undetected. Andre kept watch while Felicity changed from boots to heels.

"Grainger is on the way," Mia reported.

Ace nodded, knowing that Felicity's body camera would note the gesture. Sound carried and the parking lot was only a few feet away. The night was darkening with the cloud cover beginning to blot out the moonlight.

Felicity watched her target pull into the dirt lot and park. He got out and headed straight for the door without even bothering to look around.

"He's not on guard," Cam said as he zoomed in on Grainger's image. A tee shirt and jeans didn't give a man many places to hide a weapon. "He's not carrying either. The computer says two sixty not the two thirty on his license."

Felicity ignored the weight difference. Since she was not one of the men carrying him, she was more interested in the way he moved. Balanced with a bit of a swagger. His size, both height and weight, created a visual strength that he exploited. His violence on women said he liked using his fists.

Ace studied the man that Felicity would have to vamp. He knew she could handle herself, but this one was big enough to hurt her if he got the chance, armed or not.

The activity in the parking lot was still for the moment. Grainger had had time to get his first beer and scope out the competition at the pool table.

Felicity touched Ace's arm. He glanced at her then nodded. Kitty stepped out of the trees and strolled toward the door. Ace watched her move, the swing of hip, the lazy movement of her hands and the sway of her breasts that marked her every breath.

The way she opened the door and paused would draw the eyes of the males inside. He would bet most if not all the men were looking in her direction, assessing their chances. The bait was in the water and the troll had begun.

He settled down to wait and listen. He was aware of Andre's attention and alertness.

"I haven't seen you around here before. I know all the ladies who come in."

Not much of a line Ace decided. The man didn't have a good delivery either.

"That's because I haven't been here before, honey."

"Can I buy you a drink?"

Kitty laughed, a husky chuckle that invited the man closer. "Maybe you could do that little thing."

She paused as she looked him over as though she was seeing him naked. He reacted quite nicely. He would make a good entrée into the game that was being discussed. Grainger was sipping his beer and commenting on the match that was ending. His back was to the door so he hadn't seen her yet.

"I kinda want to play pool first." She moistened her lips lightly, very aware that his eyes were following every move she made. "Do you play pool?"

"Not if Mick is here, I don't."

Kitty leaned nearer. He was cute if a bit too thin for her taste. "Is Mick that good?"

He grimaced. "He beat my ass."

Kitty tucked her hand around his arm. "I really want to

play. Maybe one game then I would love that drink. Maybe you could find us a quiet booth."

"One game? Win or lose?"

Kitty rested her breasts against the arm she held. She felt his instant response. "Maybe two drinks. You can console me."

The man swallowed hard as she pressed lightly against him. He could all but feel his hands on her soft skin, those red lips working over his body. He moved toward the table. Grainger would make it a quick game. The man liked to win.

"I'm Dale."

Kitty leaned more heavily against him. "I'm Kitty."

"She's got her blind," Cam said quietly. He muted his vocal on Felicity's end so that his words only reached Ace and Andre. "Three steps in the door in a minute and twenty seconds."

When Dale stopped two feet from the table, the conversation slowly died. Grainger turned around and got his first look at Kitty.

Kitty looked up at Grainger as he towered over her. Even with six-inch heels, he had her by four inches. She smiled slowly, her eyes roaming over every inch of his chest and lower body.

"Dale tells me you're the man to beat if I want to play pool. Are you?" She purred the question with enough doubt to be challenging and provocative at the same time.

"I can be." He did a lot of looking of his own. "Winner buys drinks."

Kitty laughed softly as she slid her hand off Dale's arm. "I really like a good bourbon."

Grainger reached for a stick and handed it to her. He grinned as he moved close enough so that his arm touched hers. "You have to win first."

He loomed over her. She widened her eyes in appreciation. "How big are you?" she asked as she picked up the chalk for her stick. She took her time with the small operation of chalking the tip. Her eyes on his, she blew a tiny puff of extra dust off the end of the stick.

She slid her fingers slowly up and down the shaft as she looked him over. The quick lust in his eyes was just the reaction she wanted. Her guy for the evening was leaning against the wall, watching Grainger. From his perspective all he could see was what she allowed him to see and hear.

"Big enough to get the job done," Grainger said as he took the chalk from her to do his stick. "How about if I give you a handicap?"

She smiled as she put a challenge in her look and her posture. Too easy and she could lose him. She wasn't after a quickie in the trees. He had to want her enough to look for privacy for a long night.

"Maybe I should give you one?"

He studied her for along moment, his eyes drifting over the skimpy outfit, the laced-up skirt that was barely covering her crotch and butt. He wanted his hands on her a lot. He would bet she could go the whole night.

"Even start?"

Kitty smiled slowly and slid the butt of her stick slowly up the inside seam of his jeans. She stopped at his knee. No one but Grainger could see the move, certainly not her blind. The last thing she needed was a bar fight.

His harsh intake of air was exactly what she wanted. He was hooked. Win or lose, they would leave together.

"Even it is."

Andre listened to the scene unfold in the bar. Anhe's killer was being drawn into the trap they had set. He was glad he had a part in bringing the man to justice. What he hadn't expected was the way Felicity was working him.

In his ear, the contest for drinks was beginning. He barely heard the repartee between Kitty and Grainger. He was focused more what the way Felicity, the team and Ace worked together.

Knowing the plan was a very different perspective from seeing it in action. Everything Kitty said and did was so out of character for Felicity, but so believable for Kitty Kane he had difficulty in reconciling her metamorphosis. She was two very different women.

He glanced at Ace. He was listening to his lover use sex, verbal and physical to trick another man. Two men. The blind was waiting for Kitty to deliver on her promised drinks. And what he wanted after. He couldn't imagine having a woman who shared his bed, using her body in the way that Felicity was.

The game was ending. Kitty was setting up for the last shot, the winning shot. A tricky one.

"Want me to help you line it up?" Grainger asked as he crowded her just enough so that she could feel the hard-on she had provoked.

Kitty glanced over her shoulder. She was leaning over the table, her skirt split so wide with the position that little of her lower body was covered. She could smell the sexual arousal of the man rubbing up against her.

"I've got it, honey."

Grainger bumped her graphically then stepped back a foot. "You will, baby. You will."

Kitty lined up the shot and tapped the cue ball with enough speed and spin to sink the eight ball. She kept her sprawled position until the black orb flowed into the pocket.

When she stood, Grainger was there to take her stick.

"You won. What do you want?"

Kitty looked him over for long second. "Privacy so you can show me just how big you are."

"What about him?" He didn't bother to look over his shoulder to the man who had brought her to the table.

"Your problem. Not mine. I just met him at the door." She handed him her stick and walked past him. "I'll wait for you outside."

She strolled around the pool table, putting it between her and the man she had used to get to Grainger. She didn't look his way. He had served his purpose. The situation would be settled better with her out of the picture.

She left the noise and the smell of the bar behind. The minute the door closed, she leaned against a post while she waited on the little stoop of a porch. The easy part of the night was over. The next phase required perfect timing and execution.

"Ready?" she murmured, softly.

"We're in place," Ace answered quietly.

Squashed like mashed sardines in a can in the trunk of Grainger's car he could have added but didn't. It was a good thing Andre was slightly smaller in build than he was and Mickey believed in full sized, gas eating cars. Otherwise, they wouldn't have fit into the trunk if they had been drenched in grease.

Felicity heard the door open behind her. Grainger's arm snaked around her waist and he pulled her hard against him.

"I want some of what you have been waving in front of me tonight." He curled his free hand around her throat and used his thumb to rub roughly across her mouth.

On the second harsh scrape, Felicity took his thumb into her mouth with one suck, then bit hard enough to make him curse. Her eyes on his, she licked the tip then sucked again.

"That's all you get until I see something reasonably soft to lay on and a locked door. In fact, I have a better idea. My place."

She leaned into him, letting him feel her heat and the curve of her body. "My king size bed will fit you just fine, honey."

Grainger's hold tightened. He saw no fear in her blue eyes, felt none in the lack of tension in her body. He frowned slightly. He had never had a woman challenge him the way this one did.

"Which is where?" he demanded.

"Follow the preserve road until it dead ends. There's a road that runs down the back border. I'm staying at the house at the end of the drive. It's real private."

His thumb still rested against the edge of her mouth.

She used her tongue again. The quick flick got his attention centered firmly on his dick when she added a subtle pelvic thrust to remind him that he was wasting time if his goal was getting her naked.

His answering thrust was quick. "Your place. You better be as good as you are promising. I hate teases."

He released her enough to walk her to his car. He opened the locked door but didn't wait for her to get in.

The front seat was crowded when he settled behind the wheel. Kitty didn't bother with the seatbelt and neither did he. He wheeled out of the lot and swung onto the road to the preserve.

"What do you mean staying?"

Kitty shrugged then angled her body toward him. "I needed a place. My friend gave me the keys for a while." She slid a hand over his thigh, stopping only when she nudged the bulge in his pants. "Nobody is there but me."

He looked at her. "Unbutton the blouse. I want to see what I'm getting. Better yet, take it off."

Kitty slowly traced the deep vee of the neckline as she toyed with the clasp that was the only fastening. Losing the blouse, meant losing the camera. Not going to happen. She leaned into him. She could feel his muscles tensing beneath her weight. Angling her head up, she nibbled at his ear, using breath and tongue to tease him into forgetting the clasp.

"Drive faster," she demanded breathlessly. "We're almost there." The last words were for Ace. "I'm ready."

"So am I," Grainger muttered harshly as he made the final turn.

Felicity saw the clearing coming up on the left. The sluggish backwater just beyond it was perfect. She bit down on Grainger's ear, hard enough to make him jerk the steering wheel to the left as he pulled his head away from her sharp teeth.

"What the fuck…." He slammed on the brakes to avoid sending the car hood first into the swamp.

"Just what I was thinking," Kitty purred. She slid across the seat and out of the door. "Come and get me."

Felicity headed for the front of the car in order to keep Grainger's attention off the back. As she rounded the hood, she caught the slight movement of the trunk opening. Ace would be out first, Andre second as planned.

Grainger threw open his door and got out. She wanted to play. He would show her the kind of game he liked. The hood would handle their weight and more. He reached for her.

He heard someone behind him. Before he could turn, pain struck, a shock that sent him to his knees.

"Bitch," he groaned as he blacked out.

Felicity studied him for a second. "Nice shot, Andre. Just like we planned."

"I hope it hurt him," he said.

"He felt it."

"He'll have the mother of all headaches when he comes to," Ace commented as he passed Felicity her boots.

Benny stepped out of the bushes. "You played him perfectly, boss." He nudged the muscled shoulder with the toe of his boots. "Big son of a bitch. Glad I only have to ditch the car. I don't want part of hauling his happy ass back to the helo."

"He left the keys in the switch, Benny," Felicity told him as he moved to the driver's side.

Ace motioned to Andre. "Tie him up and let's get him out of Benny's way."

"Get a move on everyone. That weather front has been picking up speed for the last half hour. You might have twenty minutes before it starts pouring."

Andre hurried to secure Grainger's wrists. The tie barely fit the thick joints. He tested it to be sure it would hold. "I'm ready."

Ace grabbed an arm at the shoulder while Andre did the same. They dragged Grainger toward the path leading to the helo. Felicity stayed with Benny.

"Too bad there wasn't somewhere to take him down that was closer to the chopper," Andre panted."

"Be glad it wasn't farther," Ace advised as the tree line

gave way to another clearing, one minus any water feature.

The door was open. Ace got in first. He handled Grainger's shoulders while Andre managed the man's legs.

"You two are too slow," Benny announced as he and Felicity stepped out of the trees when Andre heaved Mickey's feet into the helo.

Felicity got into the chopper, stepping over Grainger's body to head for the small area at the back. The tight skirt and lace stockings had to go, for comfort's sake if for no other reason. She would remain as Kitty until they handed Grainger off to her contact.

She heard the door being closed and the men securing Grainger in place when she finally shoved her feet back in her boots.

She returned to the front to take the seat behind the co-pilot's chair. Taranda's soft curse got her attention. The spatter of rain drops on the windshield and the darkening sky was a complication but not a real problem. Yet.

"We are in the air in one. How's the wind, Cam?" Her instruments were giving her information, all good on her end but she preferred confirmation when possible.

"Still in the safe range. What's heading your way is marginal."

"I really love flying before a storm," she replied, a smile of anticipation on her face.

Felicity shook her head even as she appreciated Taranda's attitude. "You like living on the edge."

Taranda laughed. The voice was Felicity but the face was Kitty.

"This is just a baby storm. We'll be out of range in a few minutes."

Benny eyed the darkness and the swirling clouds in front of him. "Good because I want coffee."

"Make mine hot chocolate," Taranda said quickly. "Extra marshmallows, if I get us out of this in three minutes. Different route, boss. Water only until the next fuel touch down."

"Good." She glanced at Grainger. He was still out. She frowned slightly. He should be coming around.

"Andre?"

She nodded toward the unconscious man. Andre needed to stand guard over the person who killed his wife. He had given up his desire to kill Grainger but he had been determined to be the one to take him down.

Andre reached out to check the man's pulse. Slow and steady. If he was faking it, he was doing a good job.

"Still out."

The clouds cleared and the moon bathed the night in silver light as Taranda guided the chopper out of the bad weather. Below them, the Gulf was a dark reflective surface that showed small ripples in the moonlight. Their course took them north and west over water to the private strip where they would refuel.

Then it was a water view across the Gulf south of New Orleans. Taranda could have taken other routes, but this appealed. Nothing about the flight indicated a certain destination. If anyone was checking, she was ferrying clients around, showing off what her bird could do.

Benny got up to take care of drinks for everyone. The scent of coffee in the air was almost as good as a mug in hand. Felicity leaned back, relaxing now that they were on their way home.

When Ace sat beside her, he handed her a mug of hot chocolate. "You didn't order so I did it for you."

She smiled faintly. Everyone was masked but her and Taranda. "I am looking forward to getting back."

He rubbed a hand across his black covered jaw. "So am I. These things are not comfortable."

"Better than being recognized. Besides I can guarantee you are more comfortable than I am."

She had shed the black stockings and the waist killing leather skirt. From the waist down, she was Felicity. Black pants, boots and belt. She kept the excuse of a bra and blouse to go with the makeup she wouldn't remove until she finished with the meeting with her contact in California when she handed over Grainger.

She leaned against the wall of the chopper. She could feel the power of the engines through the vibration of the metal skin at her side. Even with the earphones she could hear the chop of the rotors and the machinery keeping them aloft. She missed the silence of her mountain.

CHAPTER NINETEEN

They had hours of flying time before she could get rid of Grainger. Felicity studied the man. He had yet to appear to awaken. She wondered idly how long he intended to pretend to be unconscious. He had to know that escape wasn't possible unless he was prepared to crash the helo with all of them onboard.

Felicity nudged Ace lightly in the side where no one but he would know she had moved. He glanced at her, making the look seem absent.

She cocked her head slightly. The way his eyes narrowed told her he understood. Her lashes half closed, Felicity was aware of Ace focusing on their prisoner. He waited a few seconds then eased to his feet, stretching as though he was tired of sitting.

Benny came out of the back, four mugs in hand. "Coffee black, Andre?"

As he handed over the mug, a heavy arm slammed into his chest, sending the remaining mugs flying, drenching Andre in hot liquid. Grainger's leg shot out in a kick that was meant to knock Benny on his ass. Quick reflexes saved him from going down but he lurched into Andre as he snatched off his mask and he jumped to his feet with a furious curse.

Ace dodged the two men in the limited space. He caught Grainger's left arm, evading a hammer swing from the man's right. He caught a clip on his jaw that snapped his head back. He returned the blow with one to Grainger's kidneys.

Grainger struggled to reach the door. He grabbed the handle, using it for balance as he kicked out at the two men behind him.

Benny freed himself from the tangle with Andre and threw his weight into the fight, managing to pry Grainger off the door frame. Legs scissoring, fists punching, he fought back.

Furious, a deep bellow of rage as a signal, Grainger heaved Benny across the narrow aisle and used his free arm to drag Andre around the neck.

"Back off," he warned Ace as he applied pressure to the chokehold he had on his captive. He nodded when Ace released him and stepped back a few inches.

"Put this thing on the ground now or I'll snap his neck." He flexed his arm muscles, grinning when Andre gagged and struggled.

Half blind by the mix of hot chocolate and coffee that he had gotten full in the face and his upper body, Andre was no match for the larger man holding him.

"You kill the Frenchie, honey and you lose your leverage," Kitty purred staying in character.

Right now, Grainger was focused on the male opposition. Ace partially blocked her on the right. She was armed. All she needed was a diversion and a chance. Grainger didn't see her as a physical threat. To him, she was just a piece of ass, arm candy with an attitude.

"Shut it, bitch. Don't know who you are. Don't care. Tell the pilot to set down."

"She is."

Taranda understood Felicity's two words as the order it was. She brought the helo around in a smooth turn heading to the shoreline. The instruments indicated no one was on this particular stretch of beach. Cam confirmed the landing place as empty through the earbud they all still wore.

"It will be a few minutes," Taranda told him. As fast as the chopper was, it couldn't cover fifteen miles in seconds.

"How few?" Grainger demanded.

"About five."

"No way, bitch. You've got two. I'll kill him if you don't make it."

He used his free hand to unlatch and shove open the door. The wind whistled through the interior as well as the heavy sounds of the chopper's engines. He leaned against the wall, holding Andre as a shield.

He nodded at Benny. "You get over there with the hero and the pussy. If I get out, you get off the ground. If I don't get out, you get a dead man for company."

Benny moved slowly to the front of the chopper. He made sure he didn't block Ace or Felicity. One of them would get Grainger. He wasn't escaping with or without Andre as a hostage.

Felicity touched Taranda's shoulder once. Taranda's faint nod of attention was hidden by her body and Ace. Felicity had a knife in her right thigh pocket. She eased it out. Using the side of her hand, she pushed strongly against Taranda as a signal to turn right.

"On two," she whispered into the mike on the headphones.

She caught Taranda's faint nod of understanding.

"Ease up, honey or that guy is going to pass out before you get on the ground."

"I told you to shut up."

Felicity kept talking, right over his words, focusing on Andre's face. "If he does, he is going to drop like a stone then you are going to be one hostage short."

Andre heard the drawled words that belonged to Kitty. The look in the eyes locked on his was pure Felicity. She had a plan and he had his orders.

Become dead weight now. He dropped to the floor as limply as possible and did his best to tangle with Grainger's legs on his way down. The more off-balance Grainger was the better.

"Two."

Felicity whispered as sent her blade slicing through the air straight at Grainger's left shoulder. At the same moment, precisely on cue, Taranda executed a sharp right turn. Ace tensed beside her, ready to spring the second the knife hit its target.

Felicity wasn't aiming to kill, just incapacitate Grainger enough so that he would release his hold on Andre. Grainger was too close to the door. He would grab for any hold to keep from sliding out, taking an unscheduled dive into the sea.

Off balance, one hand flailing for a hold on something solid, Grainger let Andre drop to the floor. As he reached for the knife buried in his shoulder, Grainger slid toward the door.

Ace dove for him and missed as Grainger rolled too

close to the edge. Ace caught one seat to keep from falling out the door himself.

In his struggle to stand and not tumble out of the helo, Grainger jammed the hilt of the knife against the wall. He screamed in rage and pain as he flopped back. The move carried him the final few inches to the edge of the opening.

This time he found nothing to grab but air. He fell out the door and into the night. His curse lasted only a few seconds and then there were only the sounds of the rotors and the engines.

Ace got to his feet to secure the hatch. The only sign that Grainger had been on board were the drops and smears of blood on the floor and the restraint that had bound him. He picked it up and found smears of blood there too.

He handed the unbroken restraint to Felicity.

She studied the stains for a moment. "All he needed was a little slack and some time to work the loop over his wrists. That had to have hurt. The blood would have helped."

Andre saw the circle that should have been tight enough to hold Grainger. "I should have checked he was secured when we dumped him in the seat."

"Yes." Felicity didn't bother to sugarcoat the truth. "That oversight almost cost you your life."

"It would have if you hadn't...."

"Mistakes happen," Felicity interrupted. "Once should

be enough to teach a good lesson. You won't forget again."

"No," he agreed grimly. "I won't forget."

Benny offered Andre a hand. "How bad did I burn you?"

Andre shook his head as he dropped onto one of the seats. "I have no idea. The mask and the shirt got most of it but my eyes hurt." He started to reach up to his face. Benny caught his wrist.

"No. Don't touch them. You've got some redness but I don't think even first degree. The mask did a good job there. The eyes got the worst of it. Let me get the first aid kit and see what I can do."

With Benny seeing to Andre, Felicity dropped into the copilot's seat. "Taranda, let's find out what happened to Grainger. Tell me you have a fix on where he went in."

"Close enough." Taranda made the swing to bring them back to the area where Grainger hit the water. "Light?"

"What do we have in the area, Cam?"

The helo was noisy and a light shining in the darkness over an open sea was attention getting if they had company.

"Nothing showing here, boss. Just the chopper and the Gulf. No ships, no aircraft. Nobody on the beach either. By my gauge, you are about nine miles out. Nobody to see the light."

"Light us up."

Taranda flipped the switch. It took two circles, the

second one wider than the first, to find Grainger. She didn't find a man but she did find activity, a lot of activity, the frenzied kind. Taranda hovered over the roiling water below. Shark fins sliced and darted in a mad tangle of motion. There was no sign of Grainger.

"It has to be him," Taranda said quietly.

Ace leaned in between Felicity and Taranda to get a look at the carnage below. "Blood in the water."

"You can't tell that from here." Taranda pointed out.

"I can't see it but I have seen sharks go after a body before. Felicity drew blood. Fresh blood in the water is all it takes. It would have been fast and painful. He didn't have a chance even without the knife in his shoulder."

Andre heard Ace. He pushed Benny's hand away as he started to treat his other eye.

"I want to see." He got to his feet and moved to the front. "He is dead?"

Ace surrendered his place to Andre. The man had a right to see where his wife's killer had died. And how.

"Very. Even if he was a strong swimmer, he couldn't have gotten away from that."

Andre looked down at the scene in the spotlight. So many fins and no man lay in the water, dead or dying. Grainger was gone. Not by his hand, not even by Felicity's. The sharks had meted out the justice he had craved for Anhe's death. Grainger had known pain too.

He couldn't look at the scene below and not realize how terrible Grainger's last moments had been. His Anhe had been spared the man's cruelty. The women he had brutalized had not. They too had their justice. For the first time since he had touched Anhe's still face, he felt the beginnings of peace.

Felicity watched Andre's expression, seeing the change in his eyes that even the damage the hot liquid caused couldn't disguise.

"Is it enough?"

He looked at her, the woman who had cared for his Anhe, who had brought her to him. She given him this night where justice had been served.

"Yes," he said harshly. "For my Anhe and for the women he raped. It is enough." He straightened and returned to Benny for treatment.

"Let's go home," Felicity said quietly.

Taranda shut down the light and swung the chopper in an arc to head for the next refueling stop. Only two more to go. She had time to make up. The fight had put them off schedule. At least, they would not have to add a stop in California to deliver Grainger before they got home.

Felicity stood at the open slider, watching the sun rise

over the trees. The Farm was secure and off 'blue'. Anhe's killer was dead and Andre had his justice for his wife. Two women would not have to face retelling their rape and assault to a judge and jury. She had some of the answers to whatever Andre had overheard but not all.

"Can't sleep anymore?"

She shook her head without turning around. "We still don't know what they are hiding."

Ace threw off the sheet and got out of bed to join her at the door. He slipped an arm around her waist and pulled her to him. He had felt her get out of bed. He had waited for her to return. Then he had heard the slider open. He left her to her thinking, watching the rising sun gild her long body with red gold.

His woman. The fighter. The searcher. The warrior. The leader. The planner.

"Have you got your plan lined up?"

She leaned her head against his shoulder because it was there and she could. "Yes. Everything we have so far says Marco has answers, some if not all."

"Good. I like a good B & E with you."

She laughed softly. The anticipation in his voice emphasized his truth. He did like it. No other man fit her so well.

"It's going to be tricky," she said as she turned in his

arms. "He really is a family man. His wife and children are there."

"You want to question him somewhere else?"

"I thought about it and that's even trickier. That's also assuming we can pin down his movements on short notice."

"So, it is an in-and-out on his estate." He frowned as he considered the problem. "That means putting the wife out while you question him."

"Yes. I'll also have to have something along for the children in case one of them gets up looking for mommy and daddy."

"Wouldn't they go for their nanny? Didn't I see one on the list of household servants?"

"You did. I don't know what they would do. Neither of us have any experience with kids. We have to be prepared for them. I don't like using a drug on children. I would need to be really careful on the dosage too."

His arms tightened around her. "I don't like it either. Is it safe?"

"No drug is completely safe. We both know that. I know there are medications that are kid safe. I may have a contact I can tap to find out what is the least risky. I hate having to do anything to anyone in his family."

"Then we will make sure we don't have to involve the kids. Maybe we'll get lucky and discover they sleep in separate beds. Some couples do. They've been married thirteen years."

"Their youngest is four. That doesn't say separate to me. Especially since nothing we found says he has any woman on the side."

He sighed. He didn't like the choices but they had to be made. "Planning session after breakfast?"

"Yes. We need answers and it looks like Marco is the only one who has them. Whatever he tells us will be a factor in what we do about Gordon. Right now, she isn't doing anything politically to cause a problem. But there is still her hand in Anhe's death. There is no legal way to make her pay for that but if she is involved in whatever political scheme is in the works, we can still get justice done there."

"She's a loose cannon as well as a loose end."

"She is. She knew she was selling herself politically. If not Marco then someone else. She needs to be stopped."

He pulled her closer. "We will stop her. None of us will quit until we do," he promised her.

Ace studied Felicity as he sipped his last cup of coffee. Her silence was a sure indicator that she was planning something.

"You have an idea."

Felicity looked at him, smiling faintly. "More than one

actually. I am really glad you can ride.”

“I take it you are talking about horses?”

“I may have a way to get us on Marco’s stud farm without the B&E and eliminate the wife and kids issue as well.”

“I am all for that idea no matter what it is.”

“I have to make a call. My contact is well known in the equine community. He will be our references.”

She glanced at the time on her wrist unit. “I can’t now because of the time zone difference. Richard should be able to help us. He knows almost everyone. If he doesn’t know Marco personally, he probably knows someone who does.”

“Heading for control?”

“Yes. We’ll outline both plans just in case. I am certain Richard will come through, but I would rather outline both possibilities just in case. We’re on a time clock and we don’t know when the alarm is going to sound.”

CHAPTER TWENTY

"The good news is, while he has top of the line security, Marco is handling it as a rich man's home rather than some kind of rural fortress."

Cam highlighted the information on the system that protected Marco's home. The alarms, including codes. The roving guards with dogs. Only three teams and they were on patrol around the house grounds, creating a narrow perimeter of security around the home.

"The biggest problem is the open area around the main house. There is a lot of it. No cover. the timing is critical. Although there is time between the patrols, those dogs could get your scent and alert."

Felicity studied the schematics of the building and the

security system. "I think I have a way around that issue."

Cam leaned back in his chair. "What?"

"Simple is always better than complicated. We use a couple of horse blankets."

He frowned. "What?" he asked in a different tone.

Ace chuckled. "The man breeds Pasos. The dogs are used to the scent of the horses and the humans working with them. They smell human and horse and no alert." A simple solution to a tricky problem.

Felicity pointed to the smaller building close to one of the barns. The kennels were clearly visible.

"He doesn't have the patrols around the horse barns or paddocks. They are strictly house patrols at night. The dog kennels are near the barn area, probably kept there so that the children don't come in contact with them. Those dogs are accustomed to that scent."

"So, all you have to do is lift a couple of blankets, wrap up in them, dodge patrols, circumvent the alarms and get upstairs without waking the wife, kiddos and the man himself. A piece of cake."

Felicity grinned as she shook her head at his sarcastic tone. "Yes, that's it in a nutshell as a last resort. However, I have a better idea. I am going to set up a stable of Pasos on the ranch.

I have developed a love affair with the breed and I am

very particular about the stock I want. In this case, three mares and a stud for breeding purposes. I have heard about Marco's stud.

I know someone who may be able to give me a reference to the man himself. Apparently, Marco is very selective in those he permits to purchase his horses. I will need that reference to get us on the property. There is a time difference so it will be another two hours before I can talk to my contact."

Cam leaned back in his chair and waited for the rest of the plan. Getting on the grounds was only half the problem.

"You still have to question Marco. There is still the problem of privacy, the wife and the kids."

"Naturally, Ace and I will want to ride, sample the merchandise so to speak. In our research, I found a few comments about Marco's behavior when someone buys one of his horses. He is obsessive about his horses and who he sells to. He is so obsessive that he always rides with the potential buyer. He is known for refusing to sell if he doesn't like what he sees."

Cam looked interested but not convinced. "So, you have him alone out in a field somewhere. He's awake and aware. He isn't just going to hold out his arm and say, 'stick a needle with a truth drug in my arm'."

"No, he isn't. Ace and I will arrange an accident that

knocks him out. No wife, no kids to worry about. No one will expect us back until later. We ask our questions, get the answers and skip the horse blanket scenario."

Felicity studied the trails beyond the house and grounds. There were plenty of trees to provide cover and privacy.

"We revive him. The drug creates a memory loss so he won't remember much before the 'accident'."

"What about the loss of time? He'll notice that," Cam pointed out, glancing at Felicity then Ace.

Ace shrugged. "There isn't going to be that much time involved. All we need is a name and the details of the plan. The risks are a lot less this way."

"How are you going to arrange the accident?" Mia asked.

"I drop back while Felicity distracts him. It will only take one blow and he slides off the horse. Felicity grabs the reins so his mount doesn't bolt."

Cam nodded slowly. "It could work. At least, it gets those kids and the wife out of the picture. How are you planning to handle the travel arrangements?"

"We'll take the new executive helo. The operation we are setting up is a rich woman indulging a whim with a horse savvy lover. I have the ship in the Gulf that was going to handle the cruise for the families when we were on 'blue'.

Now, it is going to ferry us and the jet to South America.

Odds are, hopefully, the name we get from Marco, assuming he does have a partner or partners, is living in that area, so I want a full team. Taranda, Benny, Jonah and Nelson, Ace and me. Andre may be coming as well. You and Mia are in control. I don't have a confirmation on the visit to Marco yet but we can start nailing down the details. We'll have a full briefing on Friday."

"Not Ricky?" Cam asked.

"Benny can handle anything we might run into. Jonah and Nelson are insurance. I don't expect any problems with Marco, not with the scenario we have planned. It's the second name, the unknown factor that is the problem."

"You're planning to question the person that Marco gives you while you are down there?" Mia asked slowly. "You plan everything in great detail. How can you do that in this case? Isn't that taking too much of a risk?"

Every day she was learning more about how the Farm operated. Felicity left nothing to chance. She protected her people with every resource at her disposal. There seemed to be so many variables in this operation.

Felicity didn't like explanations but, since the team was expanding, she had changed her stand slightly. Mia was invaluable in digging out information which gave Cam, Ace and her more time for other tasks.

"We don't know how much time we have to block whatever plan is in the works. Also, the faster we move, the safer it is for all of us. We are operating in a foreign country in which I don't have as many safety nets as I do in other places.

If Ace and I do our part correctly, we won't leave any questions or evidence behind when we return to the ship. The rich woman satisfies her whim and purchases some beautiful horses and is now cruising back home with her lover. In reality, if Marco's partner or partners are in the area, we will fine tune and execute our next mission while we are at sea. You and Cam will be involved on gathering whatever additional intel we need."

She glanced back to the screen and the faces of Marco's family. "Plus, keep in mind, since it looks as though Marco and whoever he is partnered with, if he is partnered, are buying U.S. politicians. They have to have a very lucrative reason to take the risks involved.

Marco is crossing our border in disguise, using an alias. Crimes right there. He put his family in the crosshairs. He may be a faithful husband and a good father but he is risking their lives with his choices."

Mia studied the dark eyed children and the beautiful woman who was their mother. For a moment, she hadn't considered that aspect.

Felicity turned her head to look at her. "He thinks he

has covered his ass. He hasn't considered his wife and children at all. He tells himself that his plan, whatever it is, doesn't have any connection to his family. No matter how this turns out, Marco's family is going to be hurt."

Felicity knew there was nothing more she could do until her contact had an answer on whether or not they would be traveling to South America to check on some horses.

She glanced at Ace. "I feel like a run."

"I pick the path."

She cocked a brow at him. "Since when?" she asked as they headed for the door.

"Since you stuck me on that goat track for nine point three miles. I felt every muscle in my body cursing on the way down." The door closed on the rest of the argument.

Cam leaned back in his chair and waited for Mia to digest what Felicity had said. He had been on the Farm for almost six years and he was well aware that there was a lot he still didn't know about the scope of what Felicity did.

It was rare for her to use the drug on any of their operations. He had asked her its name the first time he had been involved. For one split second, he had felt, though not seen, her surprise at the question. The reaction had barely registered before she had answered.

"Truth. I call it truth."

He had wondered for months about the name and her

small almost undetectable reaction. He had finally decided, she had either created the drug herself or had someone do it for her. He leaned more toward the first than the second reason. He doubted she would have trusted someone with the creation. Felicity was very good at keeping secrets, her own most of all.

"Satisfied?" he asked when Mia continued to look at the center screen on the wall.

She sighed deeply as she angled her chair to face him. "She always has a reason."

"She has to stay alive. To do what she does, we have to stay alive too."

"Why does she do this? She is not a vigilante. She isn't trying to police the world. Or is she?"

"I don't know why? I can make guesses but that's all they are. I doubt anyone knows the whole story on why she has created this network she commands."

Mia frowned, not sure she believed that completely. "Ace must know."

"I suspect he knows a lot of it, more than I do."

"You've known her longer. That doesn't bother you? Your life is on the line. You almost died working for her."

He shrugged. "I could have died in the war when I was overseas. I had a hell of a lot less information then about what I was being ordered to do and why. The military does not encourage questions. They also aren't as careful of innocents as Felicity is.

If I am going to risk my life, I would rather do it following Felicity than any man I have ever served under. When we go on an op, she is either in control giving the team every edge possible or she is sitting in that aircraft with me, geared up and armed with me. She hits the ground beside me or in front of me. She never leaves one of us behind. She has secrets. We all do. When I need to know, she answers."

He leaned forward and took her hand. The hand that one of her attackers had stomped into a broken mass of flesh and bone.

"Remember how she met Ace? Over a gun, hers aimed at him with you lying near death at her feet. Your four attackers dead around you. She barely knew you, only through the file that came with you when you were a trainee here and the two weeks you spent with us. That's who she is.

Someone who would protect the children of the father who put them in danger, who is planning something big using and buying people in our government. She and Ace are going in unarmed as she plays the eccentric wealthy woman with her lover.

Her second plan is more dangerous than the first. Everything depends on the two of them carrying off the disguises and getting Marco alone on the trail, getting the answers we need."

"I figured that out for myself."

Cam searched her face, seeing Mia's growing awareness of what those in the field often risked. What he didn't see was rejection or discomfort about the methods Felicity had outlined.

"I told you I wouldn't break. I'm learning. I'm glad Felicity may have found a way to avoid questioning Marco when the children might have become a factor, but I understand why it still might be a possibility. Like Felicity said, Marco put his family in the crosshairs. Not us, not her."

Cam nodded. "You trust her."

"How can I not? She saved my life. She protected my family. Any questions I've had have really been about the work more than her methods. The rest of you have been in battles of one kind or another. I'm a rookie."

He leaned over to kiss her lightly. "Not a rookie in here."

His compliment made her smile. "I bet Ace gets all the answers eventually."

"Maybe. Or maybe like me, he doesn't care. Trust doesn't always have to know everything."

She nodded. "You're right. It doesn't."

"I haven't come this way before." Felicity jogged lightly beside Ace. The dogs were ranging to the right, left and in front of them.

"You aren't the only one who can find a new trail. This one has a surprise at the end."

She raised a brow. "Is that why you are wearing a backpack?"

"It is. We need a break. Almost twenty-seven hours of flight time and listening to you vamp a man over a pool table wore me out."

She laughed. "You really felt worn out this morning in the shower."

He loved her laugh, the freedom of it and the emotion that lit her eyes because of it. Only in the forest away from any eyes but his or alone in the home they shared did she relax her guard enough to share this part of herself.

"I got my second wind."

"I could have sworn you got me."

He chuckled and caught her hand to slow her. He pulled her close when she stopped. An idea had been building in his head, something he wanted, something he had never thought to have. He looked at her, watched the amusement on her face slide into silent questioning.

"I love you."

The words were so easy now. He wondered why he had

taken so long to admit the feeling to himself, much less to her.

Felicity sighed deeply. She had been alone by choice for decades. She had never needed a man, not for security, for physical pleasure nor companionship. Moment by moment, she had built her life exactly the way she wanted it. There were no missing parts to be found or filled.

Then Ace appeared with no warning. A question, a problem, a complication. He stood with her, beside her, watching her back, sharing her bed, bringing questions and answers to her life.

"I love you too." Studying his face, she saw his pleasure at her words. "Something is bothering you."

"No."

He caught her hand and kissed her palm. Neither of them was comfortable with romantic gestures but he wanted to make this one. The surprise at the end of the trail was only a few yards away.

"I have something I want to show you and something I want to ask you. Will you look and listen before you answer?"

She searched his face, the hard lines and planes, the eyes that could turn killer cold or lover hot in a split second. She loved one facet and needed the other as she had needed no one before him.

"Yes."

"Walk with me." He slid his hand down to take hers.

He said nothing as he led her to a small patch of wildflowers. A carpet of pinks, golds, yellows, whites and reds. Trees rimmed the tiny unevenly shaped circle. He dropped the backpack at the edge then turned to face her, still holding her hand.

"We both know traditional marriage and kids; a dog and a house aren't ever going to work for either of us. I do know you are it for me."

"You are it for me too." If he needed the words, she would give them gladly.

"You said you would look and listen…"

"I said I wouldn't ask questions. I'm not." She raised her hand to his face again. "No other man for me, ever."

He copied her gesture. "No other woman for me, ever," he repeated. "No witnesses, no ceremony, no fancy clothes and no cake."

She hadn't sought love but she had found it. Or it had found her.

Either way, here they were. Her earliest memories were of the forest, the wildflowers in hidden meadows. The beauty and the safety of the solitude of nature had often been her center, her heart hidden from the world. She could be just herself, no disguises needed.

Ace fit into her world and he had made it his. He was strong enough to accept who she was, whatever disguise she wore. So different, so alike, he fit her as no one else had.

She laughed softly. An open field, the sunlight vividly outlining every flower, leaf and blade of grass. Together with no one but each other to hear, just the two of them making promises, the death do us part type promises.

"But look at the flowers you gave me."

"I am only interested in the promise we just gave each other. Forever, Felicity."

The intense look in his eyes demanded more from her than she had ever given. Not her current alias, not for this.

"Forever, Skye."

She saw the name change register on his face. The heat in his eyes told her that her choice of using the name her mother had given her only moments after her birth was right.

"Skye, only for you, only for here," she said slowly, using her name for the last time.

The gift of her real name, spoken so clearly in the quiet of the forest and the flowers was more important than the ring he couldn't give her. No distinctive jewelry that might someday become a clue that might mean her death.

"Forever, Skye," he repeated quietly.

"Yours?"

He smiled. "It really is Ace."

She laughed again even as she shook her head. "Forever, Ace."

He laughed with her, loving the way her eyes lit with happiness and acceptance of their very private, never to be shared with anyone, marriage.

These moments were theirs alone. Forever, regardless of what the future held.

"I brought a blanket, chocolate cake and champagne."

"I love a man who is always prepared for anything."

CHAPTER TWENTY-ONE

Ace leaned against the door of the secure room as Felicity manipulated a background for the virtual call she had planned. She was in her disguise as the eccentric Felicity Ramsey. Hollywood perfect face, tousled hair, vivid copper lips and enough cleavage to attract an army of males. Below the silk blouse, the same hue as her lips, she wore a thigh high slit skirt in virginal white and blazing copper peep toe heels with six-inch spikes.

The woman didn't do her disguises in halfway measures, even when she was arranging something as simple as a virtual call. As a male, he appreciated her look with every red blood cell he possessed. As her lover, he preferred her when she wore nothing but a challenging smile and a hot look in her eyes.

"Are you going to stand there while I talk to Richard?"

He shrugged lightly. "I'm out of camera range and I like watching you work. You're going to be lucky if he doesn't drown in his drool."

She flicked him a look out of smoldering eyes. "Are you getting hot?"

"No. You're a doll in this disguise but not mine."

He moved to her, slid a hand down her silk covered arm. Even her scent matched the persona she had applied like a second skin.

"I love you in black, shrouded in night shadows or your face lit with the glow of these screens. That's the real Felicity." He tugged one curl. "Not this. This is work. An act."

She nodded once then turned back to the job at hand. "Stay out of range."

He returned to his position at the door. He watched her connect the call. Richard Morgan came on line, his smile as practiced as any actor. The lineless face and lightly tanned skin were as carefully contrived as wealth could provide.

"Felice, how are you, beautiful? What has it been, a year since we spoke last? At the Cameron's chalet, I think?"

Felicity laughed softly, easing forward just enough to allow her decolletage to play hide and seek with the camera. "Your memory is one of my favorite things about you."

One perfect silvered brow rose. "Only one? I'm devastated."

She shook her head, adding a slight hair flirt to the expected sexual dance. "You are always the first one of our group with the latest gossip. You know I am with someone."

"I heard but I don't see him."

"He is very close by," she purred.

He made a point of sighing just loudly enough for her to hear. "My loss, his gain. If you aren't calling to accept my repeated invitation to join me on my island, what can I do for you, my dear? My memory reminds me that I owe you for that connection you gave me for my little charity. It is working out quite nicely."

"I am the one in need of connection now, Richard. You know I love my horses and I have my heart set on adding to my stables."

He frowned. "You have a trainer for that. Surely, he knows more than I do. I do not ride as you well know."

"He is very good but not with Paso Finos. I don't want homegrown no matter how good they may be. I want stock from a stud with championship breeding. I have heard of a man, Marco Blanco. It is said, his stud produces champions.

I am hoping you know him or if you don't, you know someone who does. I understand he is obsessive about his stud and who he sells to. A recommendation from you or one of your friends would open the door for me."

She let the silence hang with meaning then added with a tinge of frustration, "It sounds like he interviews potential buyers and if he doesn't like them, no sale. I want my stock from him."

Richard picked up the drink sitting on the desk in front of him. He watched her for a moment, then nodded. "I don't know him personally but I have met him twice. It took me a second to place the name.

Lovely wife. His stud isn't that many generations old. Only two. His father started it and the son has made it into a rising star in the equine world. You're right about his obsessive streak when it comes to sales. I assume price is no object?"

"Now, Richard, really. You would ask me that?" She allowed a little pique to show in her voice and expression.

Ace shook his head. The woman was lethal in her guise. Richard was eating out of her manicured hand.

"I am even interested in finding a proper trainer for my new horses. I want someone who understands them. I hope Marco can recommend someone. I am quite determined."

Richard chuckled as he set his glass aside. "I know you when you get your sights set on something or someone. You may look like sex on stilettos but you are truly a relentless woman. All right. I will contact him for you. No guarantees."

"Now, you're teasing me. When have you ever failed to deliver when I asked you for something?"

The admiration in Felicity's voice was the perfect blend of truth and ego stroking. Ace grinned as he watched the older man all but preen in pleasure.

"Give me a few hours. Time zones are such an annoyance. I'll call you as soon as I have an answer."

Ace watched as Felicity ended the call with a little more sexual innuendo that was more play for both than real intent.

"I like this plan a lot better than wrapping up in a horse blanket to fool security dogs."

Felicity laughed as she rose and strolled toward him. "Me too. I much prefer silk to rough textures." She lightly stroked his early morning scruff. "In some things."

He caught her hand. "I am volunteering to get you out of this disguise. We don't have much time for what I have in mind for when you are you again."

Felicity tapped a few keys and the wall screens brought up images of Marco's stud, the main house and the outbuildings.

"We are all familiar with the problems of this mission. One, there is no place close enough, secure enough with the length of runway needed for us to land the jet. So that makes this operation   a helo transport. Two, the eighteen hours of flight time for the chopper means fuel stops in areas where I don't have any reliable contacts.

Three, taking the jet to the closest landing available would mean chartering a chopper and that is simply too much of a trail for anyone to follow. Activity at any kind of airstrip makes it almost impossible for us to get the weapons on board undetected when we cross borders."

"I didn't think there was an area in the world where you didn't have a contact available," Benny murmured as he studied the lay of the land on the wall monitors. He got an elbow in the ribs from Taranda who was sitting beside him.

Felicity ignored the remark. "I have sent word to the ship that was originally anchored off the Louisiana coast to head south to wait for us just off the Texas coast. He will arrive early tomorrow morning. Taranda, our cover story is that you will be piloting the six of us in the executive helicopter to the ship for a tour of the coast between Texas and the northern part of South America.

Our cover is twofold. I am interested in purchasing some horses from Marco and I am considering an aquatic expedition in the region to study the effects of climate change and ocean pollution. We have flight plans cleared for landing in Venezuela. Ace and I are guests at Marco's stud. The entry there is straightforward.

Everything depends on what we find out from Marco about his partner if one exists. If the person is close geographically, we will do an insertion then rather than make another trip. Every trip leaves a trail, no matter how faint."

"That's fast work, even for you, boss," Taranda commented.

She wasn't a fan of ocean trips of any kind. The sky was her home. She had not been born with fins and she was definitely not a fan of fish with teeth. Grainger's fate was too fresh a memory.

"It's amazing how cooperative people can be when there is money on the table," Felicity returned mildly.

"Captain David has only a skeleton crew aboard at my request. Benny, you are our medic and Taranda's back-up if things get dicey. Andre, Jonah and Nelson are with us in case we need more back up for the insertion at the partner's home. Cam and Mia are in control."

"If everything goes as planned, the worst part of this mission is the question of the second name and what it is going to take to get you and Ace to the man involved. We are planning this on the fly," Cam said as he studied the virtual images he had committed to memory.

"Does anyone have any questions?"

When silence was her only answer, Felicity got to her feet. "Cam, you and Mia establish some sort of schedule for sleep rotation. No pushing it on the hours you are on alert. Easy ops are scarce as we all know. This one has a lot of questions with no answers yet."

Cam leaned back in his chair. "Mia and I have already talked about that. If you agree, we are going to set up in here until you are home. We'll do a four-hour rotation. That will keep us sharp. I also talked to Benny about food delivery here as well. It is already set."

Felicity nodded. "Agreed."

"The chopper is prepped and ready to go," Taranda added.

"I've ordered a few meals for the flight. Nineteen hours is a lot of time with no food," Benny contributed.

The food storage unit he and Taranda had brought back from Denver was already in place in the Farm kitchen and his people would be working on the extra menus he had left to keep them busy.

The crew that handled maintenance for the aircraft had done a great job of installing a small refrigerated unit in the new chopper. The set-up had enough storage room to hold up to twenty prepared meals."

"Hot chocolate too?" Taranda demanded.

He grinned and nodded. "I didn't forget. You'll have to make do with a packaged mix instead of the real deal. Not enough room for fresh milk storage."

"I don't care how I get it."

Felicity headed for the door with Ace beside her. "I think it was easier when those two were sniping at each other. Hot chocolate on a mission. The last time the subject came up someone took an unscheduled swim in a crowd of hungry sharks," she said once they were outside.

Ace ignored the reference to Grainger. "I could point out that you drink the stuff too."

She glanced at him then shook her head. "We're putting together an op in a country where I have next to no contacts, using one of my ships from an arm of Skye/Sca, with a captain who has never been exposed to this kind of situation and we are discussing chocolate and food."

"I seem to recall a well-known saying 'an army marches on its stomach'. Napoleon or possibly Frederick the Great supposedly said that."

"We are not an army. We are seven people trying to find critical answers about a foreign source punching some kind of hole in our federal legislature. We have already uncovered Everly's sleight of hand to line his own pockets with moneys from various missions and operations."

Her tone was mild, almost academic. The look in her eyes was as fierce as a top-of-the-line predator.

"There is nothing political or illegal in Marco's background. No underground money sources. Nothing we have found indicates he has any ties to drugs or any of the other high ticket illegal organizations. He's a billionaire with dual citizenship. He is pumping money into our political campaigns. If he is getting favors, my programs can't find them."

Felicity entered her home and shut the door behind her.

"Are you thinking you failed?" Ace asked as he followed her into the elevator.

"Not failed but I am definitely thinking that whatever we do find out will help me improve my programs. If he has gotten through the net I've set up, I want to plug the holes that I missed. He's in one of the hot areas of the world I habitually scan and screen. He didn't pop no matter what filters I used."

"We'll find the answers."

"Some of them." She stepped out of the elevator and into the bedroom. "The question then becomes what do we do with Marco and/or his partner? I sure can't turn them over to Everly."

"What are you going to do about him?" Ace asked as he followed her into the secure room.

"I have a contact that is positioned above Everly. I'll set up a meet with her, dump the data in her lap and sit back to see what she does with it. She hasn't failed me yet but Everly is part of the home team. If she nails him, that will go a long way toward proving I can risk leaking Marco's activities to her."

Ace sat beside her, watching as she keyed in information. "I assume you aren't going to her as Felicity."

"No. Ann James. A homely loner, geek with a record of tech crimes. Not my real name. One they gave me when I turned on some nasty friends who were going to wipe out quite a bit of the Eastern seaboard's communications. The government was very pleased to have what I could give them and they in turn gave me a new identity and a pass on my part in the set up."

Ace's brows rose. "Homely?"

"Mousey. Dull brown hair, freckles and pale skin. No figure and the worst taste in clothes. I always look like I sleep in my tee and pants. Never look anyone in the eye and I mumble when I talk. I look like I'm afraid of my own voice."

"This one I have to see."

She smiled faintly. "You will. The minute I'm sure we won't need Everly to stop Gordon and Marco, Ann will make another promotion possible for my contact."

"Everyone strapped in?" Taranda asked as she checked the last instrument in front of her. The question had become her standard greeting of late. She waited for the quick answers then eased power into the rotors. The sound of the engines revving for the leap into the blue was music she never tired of hearing. She smiled as the chopper lifted smoothly up.

The sky was clear seemed to stretch into infinity without even a hint of clouds. She climbed above the trees and swung east then south when they reached cruising altitude. No weather fronts were indicated between home and the Gulf of Mexico. Only the sounds of the engines and the earth flowing beneath them in a multi colored ribbon of land, rivers and lakes.

"The captain has sent us his co-ordinates," Cam announced through the headsets. "I'm transferring them now. As requested, he has a skeleton crew of six hands on board with him."

"Including refueling, we should be arriving around three this afternoon," Taranda said as she adjusted her course.

"I'll relay," Cam replied.

Benny got up and made his way to the back. "Anybody want anything? I'm getting coffee for Taranda and me."

"Cold caffeine for me," Felicity replied.

Ace doubled the order for a soda. Andre, Jonah and Nelson opted for coffee. The small chopper wasn't full but there wasn't a lot of free space either.

The bird carried six passengers so every seat was taken. The ground crew had managed to find room for all the equipment they might need, namely com units, weapons, ammo, field gear and a few extras.

Not wanting to draw attention to the extra baggage, the gear was stowed in designer luggage that was Felicity's and Ace's personal requirements when traveling.

The cases were locked. Her obsession with security fit well with Felicity's reputation as a woman who enjoyed her wealth, played hard and made sure her belongings were not prey for thieves or nosy journalists.

Felicity leaned back in her seat and watched the sky outside the window. Beside her, Ace was once more in character as her lover of the moment. The silver in his hair, the increase in the lines on his face, the elegantly carved cane and the slight limp were showcased in black slacks with a designer label, a light blue silk shirt beneath a hand tailored jacket. His watch, his shoes and the gold ring on his finger spoke quietly of wealth and power.

She had coordinated her look with his, slim royal blue silk slacks, a black blouse that slithered over her curves to a tight waist cinched with a silver belt. Her heels were a lethal six inches of black leather. Sapphires on her ears, a statement bracelet on her ankle and wrist and nails of silver tipped with blue completed the look.

"Benny, I need you and Taranda to keep an eye on the crew. None of them are new hires but neither have they been in this side of our work. I'll need a report when we get home. Using a ship this way gives us a new entry method and our own controlled base."

"It also saves on fueling stops and the risks involved," Taranda pointed out.

"As long as none of us gets seasick," Benny added as he settled into the copilot seat.

"Take a pill."

Benny looked at Taranda. "Honey, I haven't ever been seasick in my life and I have been in seas that make a hardened sailor blanch. How about you?"

Taranda laughed. "The boss stuck me on one of her ships when I was nineteen."

"It was supposed to be a graduation present," Felicity reminded her.

"It was a nice one but there was nothing to do but check out men, play silly games or sit around drinking weird drinks. The best part of the trip was when we ended up in a storm. I spent as much time as I could topside watching the show."

She chuckled, remembering being asked to return to her cabin every time she had managed to slip out of the room and onto the open deck. Being a protégé of Ms. Ramsey's had its uses. It had certainly meant she had been given the VIP treatment. For a girl with her history that had been heady stuff.

But it also had given her a good look at the power and the reach of the woman who had rescued her. Everyone, from the captain to the cook, had watched her like there was no other passenger on board but her. Their attention had effectively clipped her wings for the short vacation.

"I had a full report before the captain docked at the end of the trip. You gave him gray hair and scared quite a number of the crew especially when you managed to get to the bow when they were plowing through the waves," Felicity said with a faint smile.

"I don't care for ships much, but I do like storms at sea," Taranda admitted with an unrepentant grin.

"We are not having any damn storms on this trip," Ace decreed. "I don't care how much you like them."

"No bad weather in sight for the next three days," Cam reported through the headsets. "You're making good time, T."

"I've got a tail wind."

"Delighted to have you aboard, Ms. Ramsey."

Felicity shook the Captain's hand then introduced Ace and the rest of her party. Taranda and Benny, the flight crew and Andre, Jonah and Nelson, her security team.

"As soon as we secure the helicopter, we'll be underway," Captain David said as he signaled his men to begin the process of unloading the luggage and tying down the aircraft.

"Andre, Jonah and I will help," Nelson offered. Their equipment weighed more than the clothes that should have been in the suitcases.

"Benny and I will take care of securing Baby," Taranda offered without waiting to see if the captain agreed or not. Even if the ship's crew had been her best friends, she would have handled the task herself. Her helo, her responsibility.

CHAPTER TWENTY-TWO

"This is some kind of spread," Taranda said as she circled the field that was rimmed with a white fence that looked as though it had been painted recently.

The Blanco Stud was no small operation. The land was green and lush with vegetation. The house was a two-story structure that lay in an elegant sprawl of brick walls, white trim and diamond clear windows. Gardens were spread like lush carpets of color around the home and the pool oasis at the back.

"Architectural Digest, here we come," Taranda murmured as she eased the executive chopper onto the clearly marked landing pad. "We have a welcoming committee."

Felicity looked out the window, assessing the area

below. At another time, she would have admired the view. Now, she was interested only in the needs of her people and how to get the job done.

They were one short right now. Purposely. Three bodyguards in this setting were over kill so Andre had stayed behind on board the ship. He had not been happy with the decision but he had understood the reason for it.

"Show time, everyone," Felicity announced as the engines shut down and the rotors slowed overhead. "Don't forget to talk, Jonah. Even bodyguards speak."

He grunted once then sighed. He knew the drill. He hated missions that involved him talking to people. He spoke five languages fluently. He even liked the sound of them. What he didn't like was the way people used their language. Most of the time, they talked just to make noise.

He and Nelson exited first, flanking each side of the door in a businesslike manner. Eyes and bodies alert they scanned the area, giving Cam a comprehensive visual with their hidden body cams. Two men stood as a welcoming committee, Marco and his bodyguard.

Ace stepped out next then reached up a hand to Felicity as she began her descent. She slid her arm through his as they moved toward Marco.

Analytically, Marco was even more handsome close up than his pictures. Coal black hair and sun golden skin. Sleek muscles and a smile that lit his eyes. His voice was rich and deep. Authority sat lightly on his shoulders, or so he wanted it to seem.

His stride flowed rather than stepped. The balance and fluidity spoke of martial arts training. This fact had not been confirmed in his file. His guard too moved with the same silent grace that Felicity had seen on the security camera footage of the two in disguise as they entered Gordon's office.

"Senorita Ramsey, welcome to my home."

Felicity smiled slowly, a little hint of a flirt with the angle of her chin and a flicker of female interest in her eyes. She watched him register both with charm but not with a return flirt. First blush, the file got the monogamous aspect right. Appreciating him was acceptable, vamping him wasn't on the table.

Marco greeted Ace with the same smile and words of welcome. "I have arranged for quarters while you are with us...,"

He paused to wave a hand to a small building about fifty yards from the landing pad. "... for your flight crew. If that is satisfactory? My own people are quite territorial of my aircraft. Perhaps, yours are as well. There is a private kitchen but they are welcome to have their meals with my crew if they wish."

"You are very kind. I will leave that up to them. My

guards stay with us?" She added the smallest suggestion of a question to her words.

He inclined his head. "Of course. One cannot be too careful in these troubled times. They will have connecting rooms on your floor. But come, the heat at this time of the day is quite intense."

He gestured to a cream SUV parked a few feet away. "I am a great fan of air conditioning."

Felicity smiled. "So am I."

Felicity stepped into the bedroom suite that they had been assigned. Ace shut the door behind them. They each palmed a scanner to detect any listening devices. They had found no cameras when they had searched the room before dinner. It didn't necessarily follow that something hadn't been added since.

"A delightful family," Felicity said as she worked one side of the room while Ace did the other.

"Pilar enjoyed her last trip to Paris almost as much as you did."

Felicity laughed. "We share the same opinion of that new designer that everyone is so sure is so creatively inventive."

"I think you two bonded over that judgement," Ace

replied absently as he scanned the last piece of furniture. "I agree with Marco. Neither of you should attend another one of his shows. Someone might overhear your scathing comments."

"I didn't say he draped fabric on his models like he was wrapping a mummy in the dark."

Felicity tucked her scanner back in her pocket. Although the room appeared clean, it was safer to stay in character. Transferring information to Cam and Mia was still possible.

Ace removed his dinner jackct and draped it over the back of a chair. The tie had to go. Three shirt buttons undone and he felt more like himself. He watched Felicity slip out of her heels.

The gown she wore was sex wrapped in velvet elegance. The slender column of fabric embraced every curve with a light skim of turquoise. The neckline was deep enough to give a hint of cleavage and the bare back design stopped an inch above being blatantly sexy. In short, it was the kind of dress to showcase a woman's assets without angering or intimidating another woman.

"I enjoyed the tour of the barns. The horses are exactly what I am looking for. I especially liked the black mare." Felicity moved to the vanity to remove the diamond necklace she had worn for dinner. Then she slipped the ear bud into her left ear.

"I noticed you eyeing the black stud."

Ace fitted his bud into place and deactivated his body cam while Felicity did the same. "I was looking at him but I don't think Marco is interested in selling him. The bay he showed us is a nice possibility. He would go well with the bay mare we earmarked. I like the little gray mare too."

"I'm really eager to try them out tomorrow."

She came to him and slid into his lap. Even if the room was clean there were all sorts of devices that could eavesdrop from a distance. Taking unnecessary chances was never smart. She wrapped her arms around his neck and leaned in until her lips brushed his.

"I really want that black stud."

"You're getting to ride the gray mare. Remember this country has certain ideas about what a woman can do. I am riding the bay."

Felicity nipped at his bottom lip as she whispered Cam's name.

"No outside listening devices detected. We're clear. Jonah and Nelson are on with us. I checked out the route that you got Marco to explain at dinner," Cam advised.

"There is a good place about a mile from the house. Enough vegetation to screen the 'accident' from view. At least we don't have to contend with Marco's bodyguard along for the ride.”

“I told you that Ace could handle that end if necessary. His little comment about Marco’s tight security and the fact we wouldn’t be far from the house stroked his ego just right. The only rub might be if we take a little too much time getting the information that we need.”

“We have you covered,” Nelson added. “Jonah talked Marco’s bodyguard into a little competition while the three of you are riding.”

“What kind of competition?” Ace asked, not sure he wanted to know the answer but damn sure he needed to know it.

“The man made the mistake of commenting on Jonah’s age being a factor for a bodyguard. Age slowing reflexes and such. He was a little too blatant with his arrogance.”

Felicity rolled her eyes. “Jonah, you are not going to wipe the floor with that man. I don’t care what he said.”

“What Jonah baited him into saying when Jonah pointed out that youth was not as good in defense as strategy and experience,” Nelson corrected with a laugh that carried clearly through the listening devices. “Marco’s man has a slight ego problem.”

Ace grinned. He had gone toe to toe with Jonah on more than one occasion and, so far, Jonah won two out of three of every bout. The man was lethal. Age was not a factor.

"If I have to, I'll let him connect a couple of times," Jonah offered. "You wanted him out of the way. This will do it."

"If his boss agrees."

"Marco has an ego too. Soft American versus tough Venezuelan? Besides, you're his guest and, in a way, so are we. *Mi casa es su casa* and all that," Nelson explained.

Ace rose with Felicity in his arms. "It gets the job done," he agreed as he walked to the bed and dumped Felicity in the middle of the turned down linen.

"We plan on leaving late tomorrow afternoon since Felicity supposedly got a call from the ship. A business situation that needs her personal approval ahead of schedule. Marco was quite sympathetic. A morning ride then we will finalize the horse sales before lunch. Lift off for us should be around four."

"A tight time schedule."

"Less risk."

"Also, no chance of a scheduled rematch between the guards," Cam commented.

Ace helped Felicity wiggle out of her dress then went to work on his shirt and slacks. "We'll have our audio contact on. Nelson, you can keep all of us posted on the competition so you can signal Jonah when to end it if that becomes necessary."

"Why does he get to have all the fun?"

"I'm older," Jonah grunted.

"By two lousy months."

Felicity heard the faint click of the disconnects of everyone but her and Ace. She reached up and took his bud as he reached for hers.

She smiled when she set it next to hers on the table beside the bed. "I like it when we travel together like this."

"So do I. I never liked working with a partner but I like working with you. I don't even have to pretend to enjoy myself."

"Nor do I," she agreed as she reached for him.

Felicity stroked the cheek of the pretty gray mare, saddled and waiting for her inspection. Ace held the reins to the bay stallion that Marco was willing to sell. Marco was mounted on an elegant gelding with a coat like tarnished copper. The distinctive Paso Fino build was smaller than the ranch horses, more the size of a good cow pony.

Their gentleness, willingness to please and their smooth gaits were what made them special. Felicity swung into the saddle, aware that Marco was watching her every move.

All to the good. Her task was to distract the man just

enough when they reached the interrogation point so that Ace could knock him out. His tumble to the ground, the damage to his clothes and person would lend credence to the accident explanation when Marco came to after she used the drug on him.

Marco rode between her and Ace. No one spoke for the first few minutes as they eased the horses gradually into a rocking canter that was as comfortable a ride as she had ever had. The trail took them out of sight of the house. Marco brought the pace to an easy walk. A light breeze muted the heat of the morning.

Finally, Marco spoke. "You both ride well. Light hands on the reins. Calm in the saddle. Some think pulling on a horse's mouth is necessary. I do not sell to those who would abuse my horses."

"My trainer holds the same opinion," Felicity told him. "He even tested me on five different mounts with very different personalities before he agreed to work for me."

Felicity infused indignation into her voice about a man who only existed for Marco's benefit. "If he hadn't been so highly recommended, I wouldn't have put up with his attitude."

She sighed deeply, playing to her audience as she watched Ace fall behind slightly. His stallion's head was now even with Marco's saddle.

"He is going to work with the four you are buying? He has experience with Pasos?"

"No, he is not personally experienced with the breed and I wanted someone who is."

She named the man who was well known in Paso quarters and who was currently reputed to be looking to relocate. Richard had been a fount of information.

"I am hoping he will consider my offer," Felicity explained.

"I know this name. He is very good."

Ace slowed his mount so that he was positioned properly for his part in the next phase of the ride. They were only a few yards from their goal. Felicity had all of Marco's attention as they talked horses and the methods of gentle training.

"Perhaps, I will reconsid…"

The soft thud of the padded small bat as it connected with the back of Marco's neck stopped the conversation. Marco dropped forward at an angle and slid out of the saddle between his horse and Felicity's mare.

Felicity grabbed the gelding's reins. Ace dismounted and pulled Marco to the shade of the trees a few feet away while Felicity tied the three horses to a couple of branches. She slid the drug case out of her pocket as she joined Ace.

Ace had Marco's arm exposed, with a tourniquet

around the upper muscles. Felicity positioned the needle for the injection. While she waited for it to take effect, she inserted her ear bud. Ace already had his in place.

"Are you ready, Cam?" Ace asked.

"We're set. Mia is monitoring the competition. And the heat signatures around your position. Nothing human showing but the three of you."

Felicity checked Marco's pulse. She broke open a small vial and waved it lightly under Marco's nose. In seconds, his lashes flickered as he regained consciousness. She asked a few test questions then nodded when he answered correctly.

"On the clock," Cam said quietly.

"Marco, do you have business with Senator Sharon Gordon?"

"Yes."

"You have invested millions through EnviroWorld into her campaign. Are you the only one involved with your plans with Senator Gordon?"

"No."

"Who is involved with you?"

"Ricardo Perez."

Ace stiffened at the mention of the name. Not good. Not good at all. His hissed curse was graphic.

Felicity was very aware of the seconds ticking away in her head. Perez was a complication that she didn't want.

Marco with his pristine background involved in buying government officials was bad enough. Adding a criminal like Perez to the mix increased the scope of corruption.

"Why did you choose Perez?"

"I did not. He chose me."

"Explain."

"He has Pasos that he bought from me. When we were riding the first time, he mentioned that he had heard of my first small project in your country. He wanted to participate."

"Why did you agree?"

"A man does not say no to someone like Perez. I had my family to protect."

"You are equal partners?"

"No. He provides seventy percent of our investment. I have thirty. The greater our capital the larger the deal we can achieve."

"Why when it was your idea?"

"His is the bigger risk if the politicos do not return our investment. I have my family's heritage to protect and increase."

"What is the plan that involves Senator Gordon?"

"We had placed three congressmen in positions of power. The U.S. has many resources which they are not using. Many bills are passed containing many unrelated projects. It is easy to add certain businesses we wish to develop."

"Examples."

Felicity listened as Marco detailed four projects that involved protected lands and resources, oil and natural gas. She inserted questions about the company names and those if any, besides Marco and his partner, who profited from the exploitation.

The two men that Skye/Sea had taken out had been carefully selected and placed in power. Ironically, the facts that Everly had given her for the eliminations had nothing to do with Marco's plans.

Gordon was the first of the replacements. Felicity got the name of the second replacement that had not yet been elected as well as the single Senator still in place, Senator Joseph Fulton.

Felicity asked about Gordon's involvement with Andre's wife's death.

"The Senator said she would handle the problem."

"You knew she killed the man's wife?"

"Yes. The fool she sent killed her."

"Does Perez know?"

"Yes. Perez was not happy when I told him that she had not handled the situation well."

"Do you have plans to meet again?"

"Yes."

"Where?"

Marco relayed the meeting place and Perez's security measures when asked.

"When?" Even as Felicity asked the question, she was aware of Ace setting the scene for Marco's awakening.

Ace brought the horses closer, retying all three quickly. He looked around for a branch that was old enough to have broken off a tree and big enough to knock a man out of the saddle.

He didn't have to look far. He grabbed the most likely and tossed it to the area where the horses had stopped and Marco had slid to the ground when he had hit him.

"Two days from today at eleven in the morning."

"Are you taking your bodyguard with you?"

"Yes."

"How many does Perez usually bring with him?"

"Two and his driver."

"Is that all?"

"All I have seen."

"Time is running out, boss," Cam reminded her.

Felicity completed her interrogation, questions about future plans, who was introducing the bills involved and what was being added in the wealth of legal jargon that few if any read.

The final question generated a list of the various deals that had been pushed through Congress. An offshore drilling operation, and a pipeline over protected land in two locations. All three were producing millions in revenue by legitimate means, creating jobs for Americans while lining foreign pockets with obscene amounts of money.

"Have you got it all, Cam?" Felicity asked quietly as she took her hand off Marco's wrist. Three large scale operations in such a short time. As bad as it was, it could have been worse.

"Yes."

Felicity tapped Marco's cheek lightly. "Marco, wake up. Ace, he should be opening his eyes now, shouldn't he? That branch didn't hit him that hard, did it?"

Marco heard the words in English, the worry in the woman's voice. He blinked, staring into the trees draped above him. His head hurt. He moaned as he reached up to touch the swelling at the back of his neck.

Felicity caught his hand seconds after his fingers barely outlined the lump. She added a good dose of concern and admiration to her voice.

"I swear your horses are wonderful. All three of them were so calm when that branch dropped on you. It scared me to death." She looked up as though she expected another limb to drop from the trees sheltering them from the heat and the sun.

"A branch hit me?" he demanded as he struggled to a sitting position. His looked to his horses, his first concern.

None of the three appeared hurt.

Ace pointed to the large limb on the trampled path.

Marco had to blink to focus on the branch and the roughed-up ground. "This is embarrassing. I don't remember the last time I fell off my horse."

"Any of us would have hit the ground with that thing dropping on our head. It looks like it might have been in the foliage, just hanging in the tree waiting for the faintest breeze to dislodge it. No one, no matter how good a rider, could have predicted the accident."

Ace reached down to help Marco to his feet. "I don't think it hit you dead on. More a glancing blow."

Marco eyed the thickness of the branch and grimaced. "As big as it is, I think I will be glad about that when my head stops hurting."

He moved carefully to his horse, checking him for injury. "At least, I am the only one harmed."

He gathered the reins and swung carefully into the saddle. He grimaced at the slight dizziness that accompanied the movement.

Felicity mounted as Ace did.

"I wish you had not had this accident but it certainly gave me a very good look at what your horses are like as well as their training. I am more than satisfied that your Pasos are exactly what I want if you will allow me the sale?"

She added a smile and just a hint of a question in her last words.

Marco managed a smile in return. "You honor my Stud. We will discuss the details for shipping and delivery after lunch."

CHAPTER TWENTY-THREE

Felicity sat at the head of the table in the ship's galley. Everyone focused on the screen that dominated the far wall which showed Cam and Mia in place in the control room. Nelson and Jonah were closest to the door. Ace was on her right hand and Taranda was on her left with Benny beside her. Andre leaned against the wall.

The entire system was heavily encrypted and feeding through her new satellite covering the Southern Hemisphere. Felicity had a laptop in front of her, as did Ace and Jonah. There were options for handling Marco and Perez. The question was which had the best chance of success and tied up all the loose ends of the situation.

Perez was the bigger problem. The man had a long

history of violence and too many brushes with all kinds of national and international laws where he had managed to slide through the law enforcement net no matter who threw it.

"Okay, Cam what do you have on Marco's partner, Ricardo Perez, in this scheme? Specifically, his home and its vulnerabilities."

Cam keyed up the aerials of the Perez compound first. "Vulnerabilities are few and far between. He lives in a fortress that is going to be hell to enter and even worse to leave. As you can see, there is no cover for a mile in all directions around the perimeter wall that surrounds the forty-acre main house and two other buildings."

He brought up another image. "The airfield, three hangars and a helo pad are also bare of cover."

Cam hovered the cursor over one of the buildings inside the wall. "Heat signatures on this structure tell me it is a bunkhouse. Fully loaded, there are forty men."

He moved the cursor to the right. "Haven't had much time and Mia is still researching. Equipment is state of the art on land. At least one missile launcher that she could trace and that was dodgy."

He indicated the four corners of the perimeter. "Guard towers. Twenty-four seven manned, six-hour rotations as far as we can tell from some of the documents we have accessed from outside sources and the limited surveillance we have in place since you talked to Marco."

"The last attempt to storm this location was five years ago and it was a massacre."

"Law enforcement?" Felicity asked the question but she didn't think the answer would be yes. She would have heard of that kind of operation especially if it had failed.

"No. A rival got cocky. He thought a hundred men with death wishes could do the job. Rumor has it each would have been paid a hundred thousand if they lived.

Perez had the leader cut into pieces and delivered in a stack of black wrapped boxes to the local church for burial. No one has attempted to storm the walls since. No one knows what happened to the hundred men with him. No bodies. No trace they existed after that night."

"How close did they get? Any record of that, even rumors?"

"Not much. Mia managed to pull up some satellite feeds around that time. The compound was definitely damaged. A hole in the north wall that took out a good portion of the bunkhouse then. The new one is farther away and the walls are thicker. One of the guard towers was missing as well. From the looks of the site, I would say planted explosives rather than a missile of some kind."

Felicity leaned back in her chair as she studied the images. "Any weaknesses at all?"

"None with the team and equipment you have right now. I could fly down enough explosives to level the whole compound. A precision drop to you wouldn't be difficult."

Most of the people inside Perez's compound were probably as dirty as he was but not all. A man like him would have women brought in for his private army. Less chance for infiltration that way. Plus, staff for the house and grounds.

"Hitting him there isn't an option right now. There might be innocents housed within the compound, staff who are afraid to leave if they even have the chance which I doubt. I am not taking them out with Perez."

"The only place he is vulnerable with what we have to work with is this meeting Marco says he has set up," Ace said quietly.

"Marco can't get away with what he is doing. If he loses Perez, he'll just find another partner. We certainly can't hand him over to Everly," Cam added.

Felicity nodded.

"Boss, I've been surveying that site for the meeting." Mia keyed in the commands to bring up the images she had gotten.

"There is a small clearing about four miles from the house. The house is empty.

Marco bought the property about five years ago. There is a road of sorts leading to it. No neighbors. Looks like it was once a small farm. The local records confirm that. Lots of cover between where Taranda could land the chopper and the meeting place."

"It would be a good way to take them both out at one time," Ace pointed out. "That isolated area will give us time to set the scene any way we want."

Felicity inclined her head. "The gossip will be hard on Marco's family but there is no help for that. At least they will be alive and out of danger. Six, assuming Marco is right about the number Perez usually brings, is a lot more easily managed than forty or so behind a fortress wall with unknown armament."

"A man like Perez won't stop with just two bodyguards and a driver, not in an open meeting place like this," Jonah said abruptly.

"No. He's smart and he has survived for decades by killing anyone who even looks like a threat. If I were he, I would send a team to scout the area. Then, I would set up a secure perimeter."

"Ten to fifteen men would do it," Ace commented as he studied the lay of the land and the small roughly cleared area around the tiny house. "The trees around the place are covering a lot of the footprint with foliage. Hard to make out by air."

"Five of you going in is a little over four to one counting

the Ace's estimate of the bodyguards. Doable," Cam added.

"The way you count, Cam, sucks," Nelson muttered as he looked over the leafy terrain. "You know damn well how easy it is to hide a man or an army in this kind of situation. I prefer to ride home without any holes in my hide."

"It's that or the fortress," Cam reminded him.

"Not much time to plan," Benny said. "We need to be on the ground and ready to move before the advance team arrives, assuming we are on the mark with Perez's thinking."

"This man doesn't take any chances. There will be a team. The only question is how many. Cam, I need you and Mia to watch Perez's compound.

The good news is the meeting place is easily sixty miles from his house."

"Sixty-one point three miles," Mia corrected quietly. "Forty point eight from Marco."

Felicity accepted the calculations with a nod. "Either of them can fly in by chopper. Each has more than one. Or either can do a motorcade."

"The ground approach is a lot quieter. I'm betting on that," Cam added, scanning the available routes, one longer than the other. He highlighted the longer. "I'd use this one. Less cover for any ambush which would be Perez's concern."

"I agree on both counts. I think Marco will choose a ground approach as well. The moment either moves, we'll know it. The number of men, the equipment with each. If it is more than is reasonable, we will abort. Neither of these men is going anywhere. We have time. Their plans are not on a short clock.

We are stopping them. They have killed and are prepared to kill again. They have infiltrated our government. With their first plan succeeding, how long before more legislation is corrupted. Where does it stop? So far the corruption is reasonably clean by Perez's standards but for how long?"

The grim look from each of her team members echoed her own feelings.

"If we can take them out together, their plan is destroyed. The only loose ends are Gordon and Everly. Both can be resolved without involving us directly at all."

Felicity shut down the satellite contact and looked at the men and Taranda.

"Taranda, you and Benny are with the chopper. You know the drill, Benny. As soon as Cam contacts us with any movement, we are in the air. The five of us will be in place before Perez's men arrive.

Most likely scenario with Marco is that he brings only his bodyguard as backup. Jonah, you, Andre and Nelson make us an escape hole in the perimeter. Ace and I are going to be inside."

"Where?" Jonah demanded, studying the small mud house with the ancient wood roof. At least it wasn't thatch like some in that part of the country.

She tapped the roof line and the small opening at one end. "I am thinking a tight attic. If we can get up there, cut a couple of holes in the floor, we can pick the men off before the bodyguards, who are probably going to be outside the main room, know there is a problem. Very few people look up first. They barge in, we take them out."

"It might work."

"It will work," she corrected him.

"We'll be sweating like pigs since they are going to be arriving midmorning," Ace pointed out. The chance of that attic having much space was next to nil. They would be sardines in a can.

"Better you than me." Jonah turned his head to grin at Ace. "Really glad you're on the team, man. Otherwise, she would have stuck me with that attic if there is one."

"If there isn't, Ace and I will play hide and seek with Perez's men."

"Maybe I like tight spaces a lot," Ace reconsidered.

"Think of the pool when we get home." Felicity closed down the computer. "That's all we can do until we know when Perez and Marco are on the move."

She got to her feet and headed for the deck. The sun

would be setting soon. She always enjoyed watching the ending of the day when she was at sea.

Ace stopped beside her and leaned a hip against the railing. The boat rocked gently with the roll of the sea. He watched Felicity's still face, the silent way she stood, her body motionless but alert.

"You're staring."

"You're worth staring at," he said quietly. "You're thinking about his family."

"They love him. And he loves them. He is risking more than many people ever have for money that he doesn't need."

"He probably tells himself that nobody is getting hurt. He is making jobs for others."

"Everything can be justified," she agreed. "I wish there was a way to clean up his death so that his family doesn't have to live with what he chose to do."

She turned to him. He drew her close. "At least they won't be in the direct line of fire." He gave her the only comfort he had. The heat of his body and his own reasoning.

She leaned into him and held on.

"I can't stop thinking about those beautiful kids. They and their mom are going to be devastated," Mia murmured as she leaned her head on Cam's shoulder.

They had eaten dinner while the scenes on the wall kept watch on Perez's compound and Marco's Stud. There was nothing to do until someone made a move on one of the screens. She had always thought she had patience to burn. She had been wrong. The longer she worked for Felicity the more she understood about planning and waiting for the exact moment to strike.

"I'm thinking about Andre's wife and Andre's grief when we brought her here to be buried. I think about our people risking their lives because some jackass wants more money when he already has more than he could possibly spend in his lifetime.

I am thinking how easily he and Perez dipped their fingers into our government under the noses of our congress. What else could they do if we don't stop them? Whether his wife knew it or not, the money Marco and Perez stole from us is paying for that family's luxuries."

Mia lifted her head to study his grim expression. The intensity of his words added weight to his opinion.

"I hadn't thought of that part," she admitted.

He cupped her cheek. "We aren't heroes, Mia. We are doing what we all were trained to do. We are doing the best we can to protect our country and anyone who needs our help. We aren't perfect and sometimes, the choices we make hurt someone. We can only do the best we can."

Mia felt the weight of his words. She understood the nightmare of trying to stop the infiltration of their government, the difficulty of trying to prosecute Marco and Perez for their roles in the situation. It would take years even if it could be done.

Then the nightmare of publicity, what it would do to the American public's trust in their government. That was already shaky. Gordon's role would come to light. Everly's financial sleight of hand, and his skewed view of his right to steal from the criminals his office existed to catch, that was another issue that might very well end up with a sweetheart deal just to cover up what he had been able to do.

The complications were endless and messy. Felicity's way wasn't without cost but it was, as far as she could see, the best way. No, they weren't perfect but neither was the world.

"This is the best we can do. I know that. Marco is the one who created this problem. He should have been thinking of his family instead of money which, like you said, he doesn't need to survive."

CHAPTER TWENTY-FOUR

Felicity checked the last of her equipment. Ace stood beside her equally armed and ready. She much preferred night work to day but Marco's meeting time was this morning.

Dawn had yet to break. The moonless night still surrounded them. The ship rode lightly on the dark waves and the silence was barely touched by the sounds of the water around them.

Everyone was in green camo and boots. The foliage around the deserted farm demanded the choice.

"Everyone set?" Five nods answered.

"Any questions?"

Five silent shakes replied.

"Let's get in the air."

Taranda headed for her bird, the first in and the last out with Benny right behind her. She did her preflight while the rest settled in their seats. The second she heard the door shut and lock, she was ready to lift off.

She would be flying low and fast, IFR since there was no moon nor any land marks lit to mark their route. Although her night vision was excellent, she took no chances with her aircraft unless a life was on the line.

"Coffee?" Benny asked when she reached her cruising speed. The lights from the instruments in front of them barely touched her face.

"No. When we land."

"I'll check the others." He eased out of his seat. Only Andre and Jonah accepted.

Felicity listened as Cam relayed the beginnings of activity at Perez's fortress.

"No one is leaving yet. Looks like business as usual so far. Guard change, same routine. No vehicles being brought out. No one moving at all on the Stud."

"Good. Our timing is holding."

"We will be on the ground before Perez's advance people can reach the meeting place," Ace said. "Wish we knew for sure if that shack has an attic, even if it has holes in it."

"I'm still digging through the deeds and stuff to see if I can confirm an attic," Mia assured him. "I am checking for a root cellar too or whatever they might call them down there. No luck on either so far."

"If you haven't found it by now, it isn't there. We'll make it work, Mia."

Felicity glanced out the window that was a dark slate with no light. "If Everly hadn't been as dirty as these two, we could have handed what we found over to him."

"Or his boss if we were sure he wasn't looking the other way on Everly's skimming. Everly's record is damn good as far as the work goes so the man above might just have let it go," Ace agreed.

"Politics is too often a dirty game that I really hate dealing with," Felicity said expressionlessly.

"I think most of us in the field would agree."

"We can see the dirt because we have to wade through a good bit of it just to survive," Nelson commented with rare bitterness.

"Politicians declare wars, send men they don't know and consider nothing more than tools out to fight, bleed and die. Politicians are damn good with body count statistics and winning. For the rest of it, they are all mouth and lies to get votes."

Ace grinned at Jonah's pithy summation. He was positive that was the longest comment he had ever heard Jonah make.

"Tell us how you really feel, Jonah."

"Shut up, Ace," Nelson said quickly. "You don't want to know any more."

"I'm getting some daylight, guys," Taranda announced. "We are going lower. Landing in about twenty."

Felicity glanced down. The trees weren't far below. They looked close enough to touch. The land was rugged but empty of habitation.

"T, you are dead on course," Cam announced. "No one is loading up at either place. P. does have some prep. Three vehicles, SUVs, light tan in color, are beginning to line up, two near the bunk house and one headed for the main."

"Twelve to fourteen men depending on whether the drivers stay with the vehicles," Ace calculated. "Two to one. It could have been worse."

"It could have been better," Andre voiced his opinion after he finished the last of his coffee.

His Anhe had died because of these two men. Felicity had granted him the opportunity to be involved with this last part of meting out justice to these men without honor or conscience. He would do whatever necessary to complete the mission. He would give his life and not count the cost if it came to that.

For Marco to risk his family this way was a betrayal of everything a husband and father should be. He would never know the joy of holding his child, a baby he and Anhe had created together. His hands clenched on his thighs. Felicity said vengeance was not the answer. Justice was.

He hoped he remembered that today.

"Everybody, we're landing in five."

Taranda eased the chopper in a gentle circle then slowly lowered the bird to touch down in the tiny opening in the density of green around them. The early morning sun barely filtered through the trees on the east side of the thick foliage.

No one spoke as Nelson opened the door and stepped down first. The team fanned out, taking the positions that Felicity had assigned.

"No human heat signatures but yours," Cam reported as he virtually scanned the area in all directions. "Two point four miles to the farm."

Felicity set the pace with Ace at her side when the greenery around them allowed. She could barely hear those behind her. Andre wasn't as silent as Jonah and Nelson but he was keeping up and holding his own.

"One mile perimeter coming up," Cam said as he called up aerials of the area. Their southern satellite was newly online. This was not the test run of its capabilities he would have chosen.

"Jonah, on your right, about fifty yards away, a little

hill. Looks like there is a small break in the tree cover."

"Nelson, your left. Really big tree. Monkey time. Two points of the perimeter triangle. Looking for the third."

Nelson's graphic curse answered clearly in the ear buds.

Cam ignored the comment and concentrated on his task. "Got it, Andre. About forty yards past the farm. A little rise with some big trees. Pick one."

In minutes, the men were in place. They had high ground lookouts. The plan was to take out the Perez's advance team as silently as possible. That meant hand to hand. Although suppressors could be used on their weapons, they were not really that silent especially in this kind of setting where any unnatural noise stood out.

Felicity wanted Marco and Perez unaware that their guards were down before she and Ace took the two men out. If possible, she hoped they discussed enough about the plan they had implemented that any players not known would be named.

She and Ace stopped at the door of the small house. The thick dust on the floor in front of it would easily betray their footprints if they entered that way.

"I'll check for an opening this side," Ace said.

Felicity moved to opposite side then met him at the back. "Locked tight."

"Mine too." He looked up at the roof. It was a low one. "I'll boost you up."

Felicity slipped her weapon over her shoulder before putting her right foot into the basket he had made with his hands. In seconds, she was on the sun heated metal and patched with old wood roof. Testing each step carefully, in case the old covering wouldn't bear her weight, she quartered the area.

"I found a hole," she said quietly as she went down on her knees to peer into the house.

Mia keyed a closer image of the satellite feed of Perez's bunkhouse area.

"Perez's men are loading. Head count, twelve in the two SUVs and two in the one at the house."

"We've got an attic."

"I'm coming up."

In seconds, Ace joined her to look through the plate size hole. "Looks like whoever had this place, made a loft on this end. If we can open the hole up, we can hide there, hear what being said below."

"It will work as long as we close up the opening once we are in. Too much sunlight overhead might make someone suspicious," Felicity agreed.

Ace and she went to work on the opening. Fortunately, the surrounding materials were pieces of wood haphazardly covering a larger entry underneath. It didn't take them long to drop into the small loft and drag the irregular scraps of wood over the hole so that only a few tiny streams of sunlight lit the warm gloom of the house.

Felicity could feel the moisture gathering on her skin as she and Ace chose their hiding places. With Cam giving them running updates on the men coming from opposite directions they didn't have to tuck themselves along the edges of the loft until The two parties started arriving.

"Everyone set?" Felicity asked quietly then listened to each person, including Taranda and Benny confirm his or her position.

"I am already fantasizing about a swim when we get home," Ace said as he swiped his arm at the sweat beading on his face.

"With this heat we are all going to be soaked before we get in the air again," Nelson replied before Felicity could. "Cam, the next damn time, don't stick me in a tree. I am not a monkey."

"I have not climbed a tree since my teens," Andre added. He knew he had drawn his own blood getting into position. He needed more practice, if he lived.

"Get used to it," Benny advised. "Falling will kill you as easily as a bullet."

Felicity listened to the banter without contributing.

She had never minded waiting. She had learned patience and stillness almost before she had learned to walk.

She leaned back against the rough ceiling and simply listened to the faint sounds the old house made as the occasional breeze stirred the humid heat. Bird calls, the rustles of foliage told anyone listening that nothing dangerous prowled the land around them.

At least, not yet.

"Advance men five miles and counting. Perez is stopped. Marco too. Holding for all clear. Best guess, Perez will want Marco to enter first."

Cam focused on Perez's convoy of SUVs as each stopped and men slipped out and melted into the forest. He had the capability of communicating with each of the team individually in order to minimize sound carrying.

The plan was to allow the men to believe they had secured the area. Only when Marco and Perez were inside the house, was their team outside to start taking out Perez's guards.

As soon as Cam gave the all clear, she and Ace would ease to the edge of the loft and use knives thrown to take out each man's bodyguard and then Perez and Marco. Guns were a noisy last resort.

They would have to be swift and accurate. There were no second chances in the small environment with no real cover for any of them.

After testing the floor of the loft for creaks and groans of old wood that would give them away at the crucial moment, they found none loud enough to be easily heard over conversation.

Felicity and Ace tucked themselves into position. The wood floor beneath them was littered with small holes, an easy way to watch the two-man team that checked the house's interior. Neither spoke as they efficiently completed their search.

Felicity listened to them discuss checking the loft. The Spanish they spoke was rough and crude. The older man of the two told the younger that there was no ladder and never had been since the place had been used for meetings. The only thing in the loft would be rats or birds. He could look if he wanted but he was going outside where there was at least a breeze that didn't smell of old wood and vermin.

In seconds, both left. Felicity could clearly hear him calling Perez to let him know the area was secure.

"Perez in ten. Marco in five."

"Benny, heads up. You've got two that are going to step on you." Cam zeroed in on the pair that was close to uncovering the chopper.

Benny glanced at Taranda as she flowed to her feet. It wasn't the first time they had hunted together.

"You are supposed to stay with the bird," he reminded her as they moved to the door.

"And let you have all the fun. I think not. Left or right."

"Right. Remember, no killing. Not yet."

She inclined her head before sliding out the door and heading left.

The two figures exiting the chopper made Cam curse silently. He didn't doubt Taranda's skill but she and Felicity were the only pilots for the chopper on the ground.

Taranda eased through the leaves and vines until she spotted the man searching the area. Young, agile but hardly silent. She shadowed him as he poked and looked, his path taking him farther from the chopper. Finally, he keyed his radio and reported all clear. Her close proximity allowed her to hear the Spanish reply.

"Hold position. No more communication for an hour unless trouble."

Cam's whispered 'Hold' told her he had heard the answer too. She settled down to wait. She had one target to secure her chopper and the team's way home.

Felicity watched the doorway below as the sound of a vehicle stopping outside alerted them to the arrival of the first of their targets. Two doors slammed and two men entered.

The first one was the bodyguard, Diego. Marco was second. Neither man spoke as both moved to the small table in the center of the room. There were only two chairs. Marco stood behind one as Diego took a position behind him with his back against the wall.

A moment later another car arrived and two more men entered.

Felicity knew that her team was ready to act. The timing was critical. Perez wouldn't expect constant check ins from his team now that the meeting was secure. That's when her team could start removing the advance guards.

Perez and his man entered. The older man sat and waited for Marco to do the same.

"This is the last time we will use this place," Perez decreed in harsh, heavily accented English.

Marco inclined his head. He had no liking for the rundown place but it had been useful.

"I am concerned about the Senator and her fumbling of the security breach. Nothing in our research indicated she was so good with computers. The information she found is disquieting since our experts have not discovered any connections between her predecessor's death and our other man in Congress.

There are such things as alerts and trips on computers. Her accidental discovery may cause us serious problems if her hacking came to the attention of the wrong people.

Fortunately, she found nothing in the report she discovered that made any reference to our most important and powerful link in place. We are the only ones who know of him."

"The fact that she knows this much is a serious concern and easily resolved with her death. I am more concerned with her fumbling attempt to handle the man who heard too much. If there was a murder, why is there no body? Why have our people been unable to discover the man she said she hired to handle this complication?"

Perez allowed his question to hang in the silence for a long moment.

"I do not like unknowns. You know this. You assured me that she was a perfect candidate for our purposes. From her actions, she has proven her unpredictability."

Marco more than shared his opinion. He wished he had never considered Gordon for their plan.

"I have my best expert on her background, rechecking. Also, he is searching for the file she said she found. I have been unable to discover anything more than I told you."

He hated making the admission but knew better than to attempt to withhold the information.

Perez stared at him, his dark eyes lethal slits of controlled rage. "Then she dies. Beyond our contributions to her campaign, we have no other link to her. If the man she hired surfaces, you will handle it. *Verdad?*"

Marco wanted badly to refuse but he knew the consequences of that decision. Perez did not accept no from anyone alive. And he certainly didn't accept failure.

"Yes. What about the natural gas line across the protected land? Do we continue with that with our reduced government support?"

Perez cursed in the guttural Spanish of his birth.

"I have invested millions in four politicians. Two have already died and now we know, thanks to that stupid woman, that the government had a hand in that removal. I am not pleased. Your scheme has worked well in the past and that is the only reason I am allowing you one more chance to make this deal.

I expect a return on my money from the only remaining one of our men in place. Senator Fulton has grown powerful on the Hill and fat at our expense. He can earn his pay or his bulging belly will make a good excuse for a heart attack."

Marco nodded. He hoped it would not come to murdering a politician with the national presence of Fulton. When he had created his plan, it had seemed so simple, so easy to make millions in the gray area of business known as politics.

The United States was not the only government to have

such an open access to funds if one knew the right people. He had never considered that anyone would die. Or that he would be the one to give the order.

Felicity looked at Ace. They had the conformation of the information that she wanted as well as a bonus of the new pipeline. He nodded.

They eased over the old boards as the men discussed the planned natural resource venture that they wanted Fulton to have passed while hidden in unrelated legislation. The voices below masked what little sound they made to reach the edge of the loft.

Together, mirror images of each other, they leaned over, each sending a knife slicing through the air to bury itself in a bodyguard's chest. Twin grunts and thuds barely preceded the second twin flashes of steel cutting through expensive jackets and hand stitched shirts of Marco and Perez. Blood flowed over white as Perez toppled from his chair and Marco slumped forward so that he draped over the table in front of him.

Felicity and Ace dropped to the floor and moved to check the pulses of the two targets. She found none. She glanced at Ace and got a head shake that confirmed his two kills.

They still had the four men ranged around the outside of the house to kill or disable. Each retrieved two knives before moving silently to the only door. Nothing was left behind to identify them as they sheathed the silent weapons. Stealth was no longer necessary.

CHAPTER TWENTY-FIVE

"Go team. On our way," Felicity said quietly, her gun in hand. "Cam?"

"One man on the cars watching the road, one patrolling the house perimeter. Coming around on your left. They aren't trying to hide."

There was no cover in the front. She and Ace would be silhouetted against the old house if they left through the door. The guard in front was mostly covered because he had stationed himself with the cars between him and the house.

"I've got a shot from here."

Felicity positioned herself in the only window in the house. Ace eased open the door beside it, his weapon ready.

Felicity took out the road guard with one round. Ace

handled his target with the same skill.

"Moving," Ace reported as he led the way across the small cleared area to the overgrowth beyond.

Taranda sighted the man she had been trailing. An easy shot since the fool was leaning against the tree like a rank amateur. She took her target with a single round to the head. A split second later she heard Benny dispatch his man.

"Pick up clear," Taranda announced the moment she saw Benny slip out of the dense foliage to her right.

"Lost one," Andre reported furiously in the com link as he moved quickly to catch the man he had missed. He had gotten a clear shot on his first target but the second had been moving away before the final shot from the farm house.

"Two down. Moving." Jonah's three words were whisper soft.

"Me too," Nelson added confirming his target hits.

Seconds later, everyone heard the sound of a shot through the earbuds.

"Got him. On my way," Andre reported.

"Move it. The engines are hot," Taranda said tersely. In seconds, she felt the team jump on board, one by one. She waited to lift off until Andre, the farthest out, finally boarded and secured the door.

"Any activity, control?"

"None. No one had a chance to get a communication

out. You're clear."

Taranda kept the chopper as low as possible. She held to the route that Felicity had scouted virtually which took them over uninhabited land. The thick foliage would help disguise the sound of the rotors and the direction of flight. Being so low minimized the chances of being seen.

"Anybody ready to hydrate?" Benny asked as he unstrapped and stood. "It was hotter than hell down there. I hate jungles."

"You hate deserts." Taranda shot him a smirk.

"And cities," Nelson added with a grin.

Jonah leaned back in his seat, his weapon on his lap. "Beer?"

"I wish." Benny glanced at Felicity. "You know the drill. Water, fruit juice, tea or coffee."

"Or hot chocolate," Taranda reminded him. "Not now. I'll have a soda."

The rest gave their orders and Benny passed out the bottles. The flight back to the ship wasn't long. The touchdown was light. Taranda and Benny took care of securing the chopper so that the ship could get underway. As soon as the captain got them within easy reach of American soil, they would be flying again.

"We'll debrief at the Farm," Felicity reminded the team before she headed for the cabin that she and Ace shared.

"I wish our shower was bigger than a postage stamp. I agree with Benny. I don't like jungles."

Felicity laughed quietly. "All of us have seen enough sweat and grime to last a lifetime. At least, this time, we only spent a few hours in the heat and the humidity."

Ace opened the door and followed her into the cramped space. "I have gotten spoiled with the pool and the mountains."

Felicity stripped where she stood. "At least we don't have to worry about running out of hot water. I don't think anyone is going to want even a warm shower."

Felicity leaned back in her chair and propped her feet on the desk. Ace lounged beside her, his legs stretched, his ankles crossed. They had landed less than an hour before, unloaded their gear and, with the exception of Jonah and Nelson, had dropped various duffels at home before gathering for debriefing.

Felicity nodded to Cam for him to open the session.

"We've been monitoring communications. Marco's wife contacted the local police when her husband didn't return. No one has mentioned Perez. There are search parties out. So far, the bodies haven't been found."

Cam glanced at Felicity. "Marco did arrange for the

Pasos you wanted to be shipped. The plane left his stud about the time he arrived at the house for the meeting with Perez."

"Jonah?" Jonah and Nelson would be on the receiving end of the equine delivery.

He nodded.

"We'll see to them, Boss," Nelson confirmed.

His contribution complete, Cam turned the meeting over to Felicity.

Felicity took a moment to make eye contact with every person in the room. "We have cut the head of the snake infiltrating our government. There are still some loose ends. Everly and his skimming. Senator Gordon and Senator Fulton."

"How do you deal with Gordon? As far as the world knows my Anhe was not murdered. The man who killed her is dead and only the sharks know where the pieces of his body, if there are any, can be found," Andre demanded.

Felicity looked at the man silently, aware that the rest of the team was waiting for not just an answer but her reaction to his questions. She understood his anger but here was not the place for it.

"As important as Anhe is to you and to us because of you, there is a greater issue here. Congressmen don't drop dead for whatever reason that often. Two have already died. Granted it was years ago but we don't want any chance of any more dots being connected between then and now.

Killing Gordon will not only create a scandal nationally but it will spawn an investigation I don't want. She is not old enough for believable medical or natural causes. That means we will have to create a scenario that will not reflect on her position in government."

Every word was a fact laid out in a cool, expressionless tone that sliced through Andre's anger and delivered a reprimand that was crystal clear.

"Fulton is the greater danger and we can't be sure of all that he did. He is a powerful figure and he has probably used a few key people to draft the wording on what he was trying to push through the Senate.

He's the big name and so is Gordon for different reasons but neither of them may be the only names involved. Fulton didn't vote alone. What favors did he call? What favors did he grant?

That has to be discovered to be mitigated. If it can be? What we did yesterday stopped future plans but it hasn't finished the job. We always finish the mission."

Felicity paused for a few seconds to let the complications and the ramifications set in Andre's mind. He was smart and savvy but he was working in an arena which was riddled with areas with which he had little familiarity.

"Phase two is complete. The finale is yet to come. I am

working on how to handle the loose ends without creating a governmental scandal we don't need with the kind of political climate we currently have. In the meantime, everyone stands down and enjoys a well-earned rest."

Taranda got to her feet and stretched the kinks from her body. The brief shorts and thin cream tank she had worn under her flight suit outlined every curve and lean muscle.

"I, for one, am on board with resting. Ben, babe, how do you feel about skinny dipping at the waterfall first?"

Benny rose with a grin. "We are out of here, Boss."

Jonah got silently to his feet, slung his weapon over his shoulder by its strap.

Nelson joined him. "You know where we will be."

Jonah grunted.

"Unloading horses," Nelson translated before following his partner out the door behind Benny and Taranda.

Andre stared at Felicity for a long moment. "I want to be involved with whatever you decide to do about Senator Gordon," he said quietly. "I need to finish this for Anhe and for myself."

Felicity didn't move from her relaxed position. She understood his feelings but nothing got between her and what had to be done.

"Andre, I have cut you some slack because of Anhe but you have no say in what or who is involved with any plan I make. My company is not ruled or run by a committee."

She held his gaze as she watched her words sink in. She read his surprise and resistance in his expression.

"She is my wife."

Felicity said nothing. She felt Ace focusing on the younger man, relaxed but ready to back her if she needed him. Andre's grief driven anger, frustration and a need to hit back were barely controlled. Each emotion was carved in the tight lines on his face and the flash of his eyes.

They had no place on the teams she had trained and placed in sensitive situations, dangerous missions for a man who couldn't set aside his own needs for the team, the mission or the final goal. His skills were good enough and, with time, would have gotten better. His emotions were another story. Loose cannons cost lives.

"I gave you a place on the team to find Grainger. You were also in South America when I could have left you here," she reminded him. "As terrible as Anhe's death was and is, there is too much at stake to concentrate on just Gordon's situation."

"I understand. I will accept whatever has to be done but I want a part of it. I need a part of it. How would you feel if it was Ace who died?"

He looked at Ace. "Or you if Felicity died?"

"Both of us know that is possible, even probable. We

live with that. We also know that losing one of us doesn't automatically mean that the one left will get the resolution that balances the scales. There is no balance even if everyone involves dies."

Ace angled his head to focus on Felicity's face. "What we do isn't just about one of us but all of us and those we protect or die for."

Felicity felt every word Ace spoke. She could not have said it better herself.

"You have only two choices. Be at peace knowing that Grainger died, even the way he died if necessary. Know that Gordon will be dealt with whether she dies or not in the final resolution.

If you can't accept your possible lack of participation in the plans going forward, if you can't follow orders, you don't belong here."

Felicity paused to let the ultimatum sink in.

"I will create a new identity for you. You can't go back to the life you had. Anhe is dead. The world you left behind doesn't know that and questions that you can't answer will be asked."

She saw the comprehension of the facts he had not fully accepted on his face. "Andre LaPlante might very well end up being a person of interest for years in the disappearance of his wife. If you contact her family and tell them what happened, how will you prove it?"

Felicity ignored his soft curse. "Your choice, Andre. Stay following orders or go. The Farm will finance setting you up in a new life, anywhere in the world. We will arrange for your move, set up employment and a place to live, a healthy bank account to open the door to your new future. The rest will be up to you."

Andre stared at her, hearing the finality in her words. He wanted to argue and knew, looking at her calm face and the battle-ready tension of Ace beside her, that he would be wasting his time. Of those in the room, only Mia showed any reaction or sympathy for his position. Cam was as still and as calm as Ace and Felicity.

"I understand. All or nothing here."

He had to make a choice now. He knew he didn't want to leave, to start over as though Anhe had never existed. He knew also that he needed to know that everyone involved in her death had to pay. He had to trust Felicity enough to allow her to make that happen without his interference.

He sighed deeply. She was right. Slowly, he inclined his head. "You are right. I will not forget again." He left quietly.

Ace got to his feet. "I'm ready for a little R&R."

"Me too," Felicity agreed.

Mia watched Felicity and Ace leave. Neither of them touched the other, yet she felt as though they were linked in ways that that couldn't be seen.

Cam set the computers on silent watch before he stood and went to her. He drew Mia to her feet. He touched her cheek.

"Problem?"

She leaned into his hand. "Not what I think you mean, anyway. I was just thinking how bonded Ace and Felicity look. They rarely touch each other in public but you can all but feel the connection. Ace and I have been friends for years, more than that for a while but we never had the closeness I see he has with Felicity."

"It bothers you?"

He hoped, for his sake, her answer was no. He didn't want her to think of the time she and Ace had been lovers.

She caught his face in her hands. "Absolutely not, if you think I am missing him or comparing the two of you. I love you. When you almost died, I realized how much.

I can understand how Andre feels about his wife because of what we have together. I could never have the acceptance of the life they lead, the risks, the possibility of death I see in Felicity for herself and for Ace. Ace has that same acceptance of the danger and the death."

"You have your own version. You know first-hand what happens when any of us steps beyond this compound. You didn't run when I was shot. I heard your voice, rock steady calling out positions of targets. I made it back because Ace came after me. Because you held control when Felicity left you alone here in that race to get the doctor to me. You didn't break."

"My hands were shaking." She had told no one that.

"None of us heard nerves or fear. Do you think we don't feel it too? We do. We would be robots if we didn't. Every one of us here chose this life, you included. Outside these gates, none of us exist anywhere. Many of the names you know us by aren't the names with which we lived before Felicity found us."

Mia stared at him, stunned. She knew Felicity had created a new identity for her, a different first and last name, a new background. She had kept Mia as a middle name.

"Even you?"

He nodded. "And no, I won't tell you who I used to be. That man is dead. He died in a desert decades ago. Facing death, accepting your own will either make you stronger or make you eat your own gun. Felicity gave each of us a purpose if we wanted to survive."

He framed her face with his hands. "One day I may not come back. I damn near bought it a few months ago. Even knowing that, especially knowing that, I suit up when Felicity calls. We all do. We make a difference. What we don't do is play vigilante. Andre is angry. He wants blood. Felicity deals in justice. Death is her last resort not her first choice."

"I know. Andre doesn't understand. I see him struggling to follow her reasoning."

"Yes. Answer me this. If Senator Gordon had been in this room today would Andre have killed her? She was the one who sent Grainger to kidnap Anhe."

Mia remembered Andre's rage and frustration, his grief. "Yes," she answered without hesitation.

"Would Felicity?"

"No." She didn't need to consider her answer. She had seen and learned a lot in the last few months. Not once, even when Cam had been shot, had she heard or seen Felicity react emotionally.

"Not unless she was defending someone and maybe not even then if keeping the culprit alive was more important."

"That is the difference between Andre and the rest of us. That is why she is offering him a new life that does not include work here. You had the same choice. Do you regret it?"

She searched his face, the amber eyes that had seen too much. "I miss my family some times," she admitted slowly then shook her head.

"I know they grieve for the woman I was. I understand why it is safer for them if I am dead. I hate that it was the only way to give Ace and me a life that doesn't include someone trying to use me to get to him."

She sighed deeply. "I am never going to be as aware of

the details that Felicity seems to have at her fingertips. I don't want her responsibilities and I sure don't have her skills."

"Your tech skills are your greatest contribution and Felicity knows that."

"She's better."

"Yes. But she can't be everywhere at once. You have given her some freedom."

Mia stared at him. "Have I really?"

He nodded. "You wouldn't be in control with me if you hadn't proven your worth."

"I'll never be as self-contained as Felicity."

"She would never ask you to be. Nelson will never be as sharp with a weapon as Jonah. I will never be as laser targeted as Taranda when she is in the air. Ace will never be as silent as Felicity on the hunt. None of that stops any of us from honing our skills or being on the line when we are called.

We are a team. It is who we are and what we do. Right now, Andre has chosen to be on the team. Most of that is because he wants the woman who is responsible for Grainger killing his wife and he believes Felicity is the only way he is going to get the resolution he thinks he needs."

"You don't think it will be enough for him, do you?"

Cam looked beyond her for a moment. "I don't know. He's a good man and he showed promise in training. Plus, he took a risk when he thought Skye/Sea was in the crosshairs."

"Felicity is giving him a chance."

"Yes. It will be interesting to see if it works out or not." He slipped an arm around her shoulders for a brief hug.

She leaned into him for a moment then drew back. "We have an assignment, I believe. Something about standing down and a well-earned rest," she reminded him.

He grinned as he lifted her into his arms. "You're turning into a nag but I like that about you."

CHAPTER TWENTY-SIX

Felicity entered the house a step ahead of Ace. She pulled her tee over her head as she heard the lock engage behind her. A sports bra was next as she strode across the bamboo floor toward the doors that opened to the pool patio.

"I really like the changing scenery," Ace said as she stripped to bare skin. He had to sit down to remove his boots before shedding his cargoes.

They stepped to the edge of the pool together.

"I have been fantasizing about this for hours," Felicity said before arrowing into the crystalline water.

The cool wash of moisture seemed to peel the layers of fatigue and responsibility from her body. She was aware of

Ace matching her stroke for stroke. Her muscles loosened, the tension of what still had to be done slid away.

For now, her world was only the glide of the water over her skin, the sound of Ace swimming beside her and the silence of the trees surrounding the house.

Death and betrayal, for the moment, were a world away.

When she slowed near the shallow end and the sun shelf, Ace was there.

"I needed that as much you did," he said as he slicked back his hair. He reached for her. "I did a little fantasizing of my own."

She wrapped her legs around his waist and took him in. "Did you?"

He was always ready for her, just as though he had been waiting for this moment of joining. It was so easy to need him when she felt his need for her to be just as strong, just as compelling.

"Oh, yeah. I see we were thinking the same thing."

He was a real fan of Felicity's limber body and muscle control. Her skilled hands were even better. She knew how to test his limits of his restraint. He loved the edge that she sometimes brought to their lovemaking, the edge that was so good at slicing away the bonds of civilization to leave on the primitive demands of his body.

She used her legs and her inner muscles to pleasure them, squeezing then relaxing as the water rippled around them. His hands on her breasts teased and demanded in turns.

"I'm hungry."

He grinned even as he felt his body harden to the point of pain when he denied his own release to prolong their foreplay.

"I can tell."

His voice harsh with the restraint he was exerting, he moved with her. Long, deep strokes that matched the rough sound of their breathing.

He was holding back, prolonging their pleasure. So was she. Her eyes on his, she leaned into him, brushing her sensitive breasts over the hair on his chest. She loved the friction the action created.

"I'll let go if you do," she dared and surrendered.

His mouth covering hers in a hard, deep kiss that answered and demanded her surrender and his.

Seconds or minutes. Time didn't matter as they sank, still joined in the water until she lay on top of him on the sun shelf with the ripples drifting around them.

Ace stroked her long back, enjoying the supple movement of her body against his. The sun filtered through the trees creating shadows while the birds flitted about the branches surrounding them. For the moment, no world existed beyond the peace and pleasure of the two of them together.

"The need keeps growing," he said quietly.

"For me too. I didn't expect it. I didn't expect you."

"Me either."

"I could stay here for a few hours, maybe even sleep here. But I really am hungry."

He laughed. "I could be cliché and say 'again'."

She lifted her head from his chest. "Steak or seafood?"

"Both. We were too busy to bother with more than basic food on the ship."

"I noticed. Everything was moving fast."

Ace kissed her grin then sat up with her on his lap. "I wonder how long it will take Benny and Taranda to clean up and head for the kitchen. Soon I hope."

"We could cook."

He shook his head. "You've been planning the next phase all the way home. That means we have to work tonight. Not cook." He traced the elegant line of her jaw.

Ace knew his woman. He had learned the way her mind worked. At least some of it. She had the information she needed for the next steps in cleaning out a nest of traitors.

She had the extent of Everly's side line skimming, Gordon's culpability in Anhe's death and her connection to

Marco and Perez. Fulton's complicity in betraying their country in a partnership with Marco and Perez was a big bow on an ugly package of lies, death and treason.

Felicity stood and offered Ace a hand. When he used it to pull himself erect to stand beside her, she took a moment to lean into him. He was more than her lover, her life partner, her teammate.

There was a time when anyone being able to read her as Ace had just proven he could would have meant her death or the reader's death. Now, she knew that while his depth of acuity surprised her sometimes, it didn't threaten the life she led or the work she did.

She liked it that he cared enough to notice her moods and concentration and to interpret them correctly.

"You order. I need to set up some stuff upstairs before I make my contact."

He inclined his head. "Eat before or after?"

"I'm thinking after if you can wait that long. We can watch the sunset and relax."

"How about an appetizer and a drink to tide us over?"

She laughed. His appetite was always a consideration. "I could be persuaded. Add a glass of wine for me."

Ace watched her detour to pick up her clothes and then head for the elevator as naked as the day she had been born. He had never met a woman so comfortable in her body. He loved every toned muscled inch of her. Her razor-sharp mind. Her skills in the field. Her disguises and her silences. The danger she wore like some women wore diamonds.

Felicity gathered the information she intended to give to her agency contact. Janet Witt had proven herself to be very able to sift through data and use her findings to burn more than one dirty agent regardless of his position or power base.

In the four years Felicity had used the woman, Janet had not failed yet. Best of all, as long as the information checked out, Janet managed to make it appear in all the right places so it couldn't be ignored or contested.

Felicity studied the computer trail she had set up that would convey the information to Janet's site, a location that only the two of them knew. One keystroke was all it would take to send the damaging data, including hidden accounts and assets in other locations. Then she would wait for the phone to ring.

"That is a satisfied cat with a canary filled belly smile if ever I saw one," Ace observed as he set the tray of antipasto on the desk beside the keyboard. He handed Felicity one of the two glasses of red he held.

She took a sip as she watched him settle in the chair next to hers.

"My contact is reading the data as we speak."

"We're waiting for her call?"

She inclined her head as she reached for a piece of pepperoni to wrap around a cube of cheese. The spicy bite sent her hunger to a sharper edge.

"Emmalina will answer. New Jersey twang intact."

Ace's brows rose at the name and description. He popped a pepperoncini in his mouth. Felicity was wrapped in a swath of silk that tied behind her neck. He knew for a fact one tug would have her naked. The combination of her alter ego, the skimpy silk, the food, the wine and the bed just a few feet away while she uncovered betrayal, lies and death was the complexity of Felicity.

The phone rang. The wall monitor displayed the number, caller and location. Felicity studied it then engaged her tracer to be sure the origin point was real not a fake. She wasn't the only one who took precautions. Janet hadn't attained her position without making sure her ass was covered. Satisfied, Felicity answered the call.

"Emmalina, you have dumped a fucking bomb in my lap. Everly is bad enough but two frigging Senators being paid and manipulated by two foreigners to get businesses set up in this country, businesses that are in plain sight? Operations on federally protected land. Offshore drilling where it shouldn't be. I can't do a hell of a lot about that woman's death when there is no damn body."

"Janet, we both know you can take out all three with the information I gave you."

Ace leaned back in his chair and closed his eyes. Felicity's voice carried the perfect pitch and delivery of a born and bred child of New Jersey. Even the pacing of her words was spot on.

"Yeah, I could handle it that way but that still leaves me with the problem of explaining the three deaths especially when two congressmen have already died."

The emphasis on the number was clear.

"The first two were years ago and no one but the two of us know the connection," she reminded Janet. "I can take care of Fulton for you. Senator Gordon should be easy enough. Have you read the sheet I sent you on her?"

Janet's fingers raced through the file Emmalina had enclosed. The single page covered Gordon's sexual habits. She had only given it a cursory glance the first time. Her brows rose as she studied the details her contact had provided. The senator apparently liked the kink, the rougher the better.

"I see where you are going with this," she admitted slowly. "It will cause a scandal."

"Yes. But there is absolutely nothing in a sexcapades episode gone wrong that will lead to a scandal about our government's legislature infiltrated by foreigners. That is critical.”

“Shit! It could work. Fulton is going to be more difficult. He’s a tight ass son of a bitch but he hasn’t got any vices I can exploit. Plus, his security is top notch since the current political climate has driven home the point that the public isn’t as passive political figures as everyone believed.”

Janet keyed in Everly’s information, looking for a weakness, any opening for a team to take him out.

“As for Everly, getting close enough to him to take him out is going to be damn near impossible. He’s got almost as much security as the president. The only place that he is alone and vulnerable is when he goes to his home in the Caymans.”

Her eyes narrowed as she focused on the pattern of dates that Emmalina had included. The woman didn’t miss a trick.

“He is due to leave this week. Ten whole days in the tropics. He likes to take his boat out alone. Accidents happen on the water all the time. Bad ventilation is always a favorite.”

Felicity could hear the determination in Janet’s voice. She smiled as she listened to Janet take the bait that she had dangled in front of her.

“I thought you might find that habit interesting.”

“I just bet you did. I’m taking the bait on both of them. Since I don’t see much in here on Fulton, I’m guessing you have a plan that doesn’t involve me.”

"He's an old man. Not particularly healthy. Heart attacks can happen very easily, especially at night when there is no one around to call for help."

Silence greeted Felicity's comment.

"When?" Janet asked quietly.

"Before Everly leaves would be best," Felicity said. "The timing is up to you."

"Need my help?"

"You are already giving it. Neither one of us wants to see another scandal in the government. Besides you get two to my one," she reminded Janet.

"I noticed," Janet returned bitterly. "I hate traitors and you have served me up two, even if one of them has barely gotten started." Janet cut the connection.

Satisfied with the first part of her plan, Felicity reached for her wine.

"When are we leaving?"

"Tomorrow."

"You didn't tell her exactly when?"

"I don't trust anyone outside these gates that much."

"Even though you have fed her intel for years?"

She inclined her head. "Even though."

Ace touched his glass to hers. "I like the way you think."

CHAPTER TWENTY-SEVEN

"Are you sure you don't want to watch us work out?" Cam asked. "I might just beat Ace's ass this time."

Felicity shook her head. "I want my trail and the dogs before we leave this afternoon."

Ace got to his feet. They had a few hours before he and Felicity had to head for Washington. As far as everyone knew, he and Felicity were going to the east coast to tie up some loose ends. Cam was going to be in the control room. Mia wasn't part of the team for this assignment.

"I'm in the mood to pound on something. You'll do just fine."

Cam grinned at him. He didn't like these off the books operations but he understood that, sometimes, there was no other alternative. What he really didn't like, although he understood the reason, was that he had to stay behind in control.

"My sentiments exactly."

Felicity watched the two men leave the operations room. The plan was in place. It was a simple in and out with two objectives. First, she had to know who Fulton had used to help him betray his country. She wanted every name. He had not worked alone. Assistants, legal aids, other congressmen who may or may not have known exactly what each was doing and for whom in the shadows.

Second, she had to make Fulton's death look natural after Fulton answered her questions.

Her dogs were waiting for her when she left the building, the door automatically locking behind her. She chose the trail that was the most difficult and started the climb. Ten minutes into the trek, Alpha alerted to another presence, not a threat. With Ace with Cam there was only one other person who would be on the path.

Felicity slowed her pace.

"I knew one of them would catch my scent. Damn wind is working against me," Taranda commented as she joined Felicity.

"Problem?" Felicity asked as she picked up her pace again. She knew Taranda could keep up.

"No. Just a couple of things I wanted to talk over with you."

The smooth delivery of her words was expressionless. Taranda's emotional control was one of the things that Felicity admired about her. She had learned her lessons in hell and turned them to her advantage. Skye/Sea was more than fortunate to have her working for them.

"They can't wait?"

"They have been waiting."

"There is a clearing up ahead."

Taranda nodded and said no more as she concentrated on the demanding trail. She was taking a big chance and she knew it. She also knew what she wanted for her future. Felicity had saved her life and her sanity. She never forgot that.

She had also educated her and shown her that the world was more than hell, greed, and cruelty. Felicity had shown her that there were heroes everywhere if one just looked and listened. She had a life filled with them and she wanted more.

Felicity entered the little meadow that had wildflowers dotted in patches of sunlight. She chose a rock in the shade of a towering tree. Her dogs spread out around her, alert, on guard.

Taranda sat in the sun. Her imprisonment for five years in a kiddie brothel that catered to the sexual depravity of mankind had left her with a need for sunlight and open spaces.

"I have spent years watching you, learning from you, Jonah, Nelson and Cam among others. I needed a home and you gave me one."

"This is old ground, Taranda," Felicity interrupted.

Taranda nodded. "I learned to see more than what most would notice. I had to so I could survive the brothel. You and Cam do work that the rest of us don't.

Then Ace came. He partners with you and now Cam sits in control. Sometimes, only Cam when you two go out. Mia isn't in that part of whatever the operation is. Once in a while, Jonah and Nelson are."

Felicity didn't move. "There isn't any secret about those operations. Mia isn't always needed."

"Maybe," Taranda agreed. "I think it may be more than that but I am not asking about Mia."

She paused for a moment. She was fighting for her future, for a chance to help Felicity.

"I want to be fully involved with your work, Felicity. Whether it is four of you or two, when you fly you have to leave the aircraft unguarded. I know all of the birds have all kinds of sensors and security. Who better? I know that leaving any of them alone is a vulnerability. I want in.

I can be back-up. A guard for the jet or the helo. I won't

break and there is nothing that you could do that would ever make me walk away or betray you. I would eat my own gun first. You have to know that."

Fierce determination burned through Taranda's usual control. Her eyes blazed with fire in the sunlight.

"What do you think we do?"

"Kill. I think you step up to the plate when whoever and whatever you've found can't be handled by the courts or the government. I think in those cases, you move outside the law."

"Do you think I would want you involved in that if what you say is true?"

Taranda shook her head. "No. I think you would do exactly what you have done for me and the rest of us. I want more. I stood over Roscoe wanting your knife in my hand. You stopped me from touching the handle, from leaving my prints on it, getting his blood on me. I thought I needed that with every cell in my body.

For you, I turned from that, to help you get us out of hell. I stopped then, don't stop me now. I'm not a traumatized kid anymore.

I have trained and learned everything you teach here. I'm not as good as Cam, Ace or you but I am damn good and I'll get better because I won't stop learning and practicing.

I can outfly Cam. In the helo, I can even give you a run for your money. You've got me beat in the jet but I am breathing down your neck. You know I am. You know what every one of us can do to our last breath."

She looked away from those too knowing eyes, that expressionless face that had killed in front of her without ever showing a single emotion. Gathering her last words, she faced the woman she admired more than any person she had ever met.

"Let me help, please," she said quietly. "There are Roscoes and worse everywhere. I don't have to kill them myself but I want a hand in finding them, in rescuing the victims and making the monsters pay."

Felicity felt Taranda's words as she had never felt any words before. There would never be a child of her body, a choice she had made consciously, willingly. A choice she didn't regret.

She did not see the woman standing before her as a surrogate child. She was more. A survivor. A new generation. A warrior. The scarred face was a face of fierce courage and terrifying determination.

No, Taranda wouldn't break. She would stand for the victims and against the hunters who preyed on them. She had the right, had earned it in a hell no child should ever have to face.

"Let's finish the trail."

Felicity got to her feet and returned to the path. She set

a hard pace as she considered Taranda's offer. She had made a good point, one that Felicity had considered. It would be helpful to have a pilot staying with the aircraft.

She knew very well that Taranda wouldn't turn from the simplest task or the most bloody that was needed. The younger woman had nerves of titanium. She wouldn't give up or run no matter what the odds. More, Taranda could fly like no other pilot she had ever known.

"What about Benny?"

With the question, Taranda felt the knots in her stomach loosen. She had a chance.

"I'll tell him nothing you don't want him to know."

She couldn't tell if she had given the right answer or not. There was no expression in Felicity's voice or on her face.

"If he pushes?"

"He won't. No questions. It's our rule too."

They reached the end of the trail. Felicity stopped.

"We leave at four this afternoon. I'll brief you on the way. The assignment is a short touch and go."

Taranda nodded. "I'll be ready."

If mental handsprings were possible, she would have been doing them now. She had gotten her chance. More importantly, Felicity had trusted her enough to let her into this part of her life.

"I had a feeling that this was coming," Ace said as he stepped out of his closet with a shirt in hand.

Felicity glanced at him, one brow cocked in a silent question.

"Taranda watches every one of us, but you most of all. There is one sharp mind behind those tiger eyes. If she has any nerves, I've haven't seen any signs of them in the months I've been here."

"You see a lot."

"I'm still alive. We both are. You expected it too."

"Not expected as much as suspected. She doesn't have much free time with the work she already does. She is rarely on the ground. It's a good thing she is salaried not hourly."

He chuckled as he pulled the shirt over his head. They were leaving within the hour.

"How did Cam take it when you told him that Taranda would be joining us?"

"After he got over his surprise, he decided it was a good idea."

Ace pulled on black cargoes while Felicity dressed the same. "He didn't realize she was looking for more work?"

"No. He's not pleased with himself."

Ace buckled his belt, his gaze on Felicity's smile and the

amusement in her eyes. "He told you that?"

"No. He showed me that. It will bug him that he missed what was going on right under his nose. These days he's the one most often in control. He works closely with all of us. He makes it his business to know what is going on with any of us. He considers it a major part of his job description."

"Figures he's perfect, does he?"

Felicity slid her feet into the soft soled custom-made shoes she preferred for the kind of work they would be doing. The soles were hand-made. Any stray prints would not pop on any manufacturer's list. Ace had a similar pair in his size.

She ignored the question that was more an observation. "It's good for him. Keeps him sharp."

"What about Benny?"

"Need to know and he doesn't."

No room for misunderstanding that answer. "Will that work for them?"

"It will have to."

Benny lay on the bed he had just shared with Taranda and watched her move about his room. The sunlight pouring through the windows stroked gold over her dark coffee toned skin. The long length of her sleekly muscled body appealed in ways no other woman ever had. Her face was elegantly shaped, beautiful lines and hollows. Dark lashes over feral eyes that made him itch with just one look.

"You're staring."

Taranda pulled on a dark brown tee, skipping the bra. She hated the things, and she was firm enough, neat enough shaped that she could afford to yield to her personal favorite in dressing for comfort.

"I like staring at you, woman. There isn't an inch of you that doesn't appeal to me."

He slid off the bed and moved to her. He caught her silk clad hips and pulled her to him. "I wish I was going with you. I'll be here when you get back."

He had asked no questions. Maybe he thought this was one of her usual flights. Maybe he knew it wasn't. She asked no questions either.

"I'll be back in the middle of the night," she reminded him. "I can just go to my place."

He slipped his hands under her shirt. "Is that what you really want? I don't like sleeping without you. In fact, I don't sleep without you when you're gone."

She searched his eyes. His voice held emotion she hadn't heard before. She enjoyed him. In fact, he was the first lover she had ever had who made her consider a relationship rather than a pleasurable encounter.

"You don't?"

"I don't. I would really like you to consider moving in with me. Or I with you although my place is bigger than yours."

"I never…"

His hand cupping her scarred cheek stopped her words. "Neither have I. This place is a tight community. We all know a lot about each other. I don't date here and neither do you. We also don't stay over outside. This is a big step for both of us. All I'm asking is for you to think about it."

She wrapped her fingers around his wrist. "I can't believe I'm saying this but I will."

He grinned at the shock in her voice. "You sound just like I felt when I thought of it."

She laughed then leaned in to kiss him. She knew how to do it right and they were both breathing heavily when she stepped back.

"I've got to get out of here. Work," she reminded both of them.

"Make sure you come back in one piece," he said.

He watched her hesitate then turn to look at him, a look of surprise he had never seen on her face.

He stood still as she returned to him, cupped his face in her hands.

"I have never had anyone to come back to, not like this."

Her eyes blazed with a fierce promise as she kissed him hard and fast, ripping a response from him even as her fire burned into him. Then she was gone, the door snapping shut behind her.

Ben sat on the edge of the bed, looking at the closed door but not really seeing it. How many times had he seen Taranda walk away from him, snarling and snapping as she left the dining hall to fly out on another assignment? He couldn't count them.

How many times had they worked together, in the air and on the ground, both armed, ready to do what had to be done? Those he could count. Every moment. He couldn't pinpoint when it had happened, but things had changed for him when she flew, when her eyes blazed with that wild light that called to the primitive in him.

The verbal sparring in the dining hall had started then. He shook his head at his own stubbornness. He should have recognized that verbal warfare for what it was. Their kind of foreplay. Two scarred people circling each other, each looking for an opening, a moment of surrender.

He chuckled. He couldn't think of another woman who could have gone toe to toe with him one second and guarded his back the next. That was Taranda.

Neither of them had surrendered. It wasn't in their nature. But they had found each other. He still felt his years, the age difference but only in the wish that he was younger so that he would have longer with her.

He stood and headed to the closet for clothes for the day. He could imagine her response to that.

"Hell, we could all die tomorrow. I'm having every moment I can get today. Worry all you want and it won't change a thing. Get used to it."

CHAPTER TWENTY-EIGHT

Taranda guided the jet low over the rocky and treed terrain below. No auto pilot now as it took human skill to skim the land so that no flight plan would leave behind a trail for some fool to follow back to the Farm.

Soon, they would reach a small private airfield where they would change the call numbers for the jet to match the flight plan that would take them into the more crowded airspace of the east coast. Any trail would begin and end there.

"I can fly and listen at the same time," Taranda said when Felicity settled in the seat beside her.

She could hear Ace moving around behind her. The smell of fresh coffee brewing was welcome.

"This run is simple. Cam has the coordinates

programmed into the navigation system. We land. There is a SUV waiting for us. If we don't run into any problems, we'll be back in three hours. We leave the SUV and you fly us home.

Cam is in control and you will be monitoring us every step of the way. If you have a problem here, get the jet in the air. There is an alternate pick-up point in navigation. You know the drill on keeping the communication to a minimum."

Felicity had given her all the information she needed for her part of the operation, whatever it might be. The fact that neither she nor Ace were heavily armed or armored indicated Felicity wasn't expecting any kind of confrontation. Stealth and speed seemed to be the name of the game.

Ace passed her mug of coffee then handed another to Felicity. He leaned against the co-pilot's seat with his own drink and looked at the black star-studded sky.

"At least we don't have any rain in the forecast. Getting wet when I'm working is not a favorite of mine."

Taranda laughed as she set her coffee aside to maneuver the jet over a patch of tricky terrain. "Me either. I like my creature comforts. Wearing wet clothes and tromping around in soggy boots doesn't qualify."

"There is no bad weather in the forecast for anywhere near your destinations," Cam reminded them, repeating information they all knew.

"Taranda, you've got about ten minutes to touch

down," he warned.

The jet had a maximum cruising speed of over seven hundred miles an hour but flying this low, the speed was less. In spite of that the aircraft covered miles quickly.

We'll be ready," Felicity replied.

"I've got you," Cam said quietly. "Roving patrols to the east and west also covering the back. Gate guard is covering the front just as we figured. All three have dogs. Timing now."

The upper windows of Fulton's house were dark. They couldn't see the first floor from their position in the backyard of a next-door neighbor. They were depending on Cam to be their eyes until they breached the solid wall surrounding Fulton's home.

"Waiting."

She and Ace stood in the shadows of the trees of the neighbor's mansion. Cam had discovered the man depended on high tech internal security rather than a full property set up.

Their ride was in a mall parking lot two miles away. They had covered the distance between the vehicle and their target on foot, keeping to the shadows, avoiding cameras, thanks to Cam's ever vigilant surveillance.

"Got it. The guy on the west side is either new or damn

bad at his job. He is barely bothering to check anything. Ten o'clock from your position. On his next pass, go over the wall on my call. About three feet away are some shrubs that curve toward the main building."

Felicity had the aerials of Fulton's house and grounds memorized. The arc Cam was describing was bisected by a stone path.

"Monitoring wind direction. Looks like it blowing away from you if you don't cross the path until the dog gets to the back. By my count you have ninety seconds to get in the house."

She and Ace knew that the home security alarm would sound if the system was down longer than fifteen seconds. The timing was critical on Cam jamming the system from control for their entry.

The dog would definitely catch their scent if they were still outside when the guard returned. He might even sense that strangers had entered his territory and alert. As long as the guard found no physical sign of encroachment, he would consider the alert to be a false signal.

She glanced at Ace and got a sharp nod. On Cam's call they moved. Held while the dog and guard passed then slipped through the shadows to the door. The quiet snick of the lock signaled entry. They moved silently through the rooms, counting on Cam to lock the door behind them.

"One heat signature upstairs in the master suite. Three in the servants' wing. No other life forms showing."

"Moving," Felicity whispered.

They entered the bedroom, Ace in the lead. He stepped silently to the bed and depressed the carotid artery and subdued the faint struggle that Fulton made before slumping into unconsciousness.

Ace set the tourniquet so that Felicity could inject the drug in Fulton's vein. Cam called the time until it was safe to awaken him. Felicity engaged her voice distorter.

"Recording," Cam murmured.

Felicity asked the basic questions that she used to make sure the drug was in effect. When Fulton answered clearly, she got down business. She named the first project Fulton had slipped through the voting process.

"Did you work alone?"

"No."

"Who helped you draft the bill that got passed."

He named five people, one his most senior aide and the other four were Senators. Two who owed him favors and two who needed funds for reelection.

"You are sure there was no one else?"

"Yes, only needed four more votes to get the bill passed," Fulton answered mechanically.

Felicity took him through the second project. This one

only added another two names, two in the House who needed favors and money. They had cost him two hundred thousand and two future favors.

Ace's graphic curse barely registered although she agreed completely with the reaction. Betrayal had a small price tag.

Felicity finished with questions about the moneys he had taken and hidden, account numbers, properties accumulated and stocks traded.

Over twenty million in under the table cash to a man who knowingly betrayed his country, the people who had voted for him and the oath of office he had taken. Those were facts not idealism in action.

"Time, boss."

"We're done here."

Ace turned the covers back carefully. The original injection site on the Senator's right arm was barely visible but a second mark would be suspicious. The drug they used left no traces in the system after three hours. A small scratch on the man's skin would disguise the first site if anyone cared to look beyond the obvious heart attack.

He pulled down the Senator's pajama bottom to expose the femoral artery area. Felicity quickly found the place she wanted. His pubic hair would mask the site of the second injection. The drug administered here would go straight to his heart. The heart attack would be swift and fatal.

After Ace straightened his night clothes and the bed covers, they stayed just long enough to be sure Fulton was gone. They left the room together, leaving no trace of their presence. Their exit from the grounds was smooth, the guards undisturbed by their passage.

"Twenty million dollars," Ace said bitterly the moment he eased the SUV into traffic. "That's all it took."

"He had more than that in his bank account before Marco bought him," Cam reported. His fury and bitterness were as clear as Ace's.

"Too bad the bastard couldn't be brought to trial," Cam continued.

"With the country as divisive as it is, we would be lucky if we didn't end up with a war in the streets. He was very popular with his party and his voters."

Felicity shortened her comment to the basic facts. She could have added that the men and women who had voted on the bills on both sides of the aisle would be called into question. How had they missed what had been right in front of their faces if they had bothered to do their job and read what they were voting to approve?

Felicity glanced at the roadside and the sign on the

edge. "T, we will be there in ten."

"I'll be ready."

Felicity leaned back in the seat and contemplated the situation they had revealed with a few questions.

Ace glanced at her. "You're planning something again."

"Money always leaves a trail. If Janet plays it right, the money Fulton paid can easily be traced to his 'friends'. If any of them knew about the foreign influence, they would be fools to admit it. That can be considered treason. They all benefitted materially, aided foreign interests and used our resources for foreign nationals.

With the mood this country is in you can bet that word is going to come up, not just in the media but in every hot-blooded American who thinks he or she is being cheated. There are a lot of them out there and there are a lot of weapons in angry hands.

The sitting government can't afford this kind of open scandal. The only solution is a cover up and with this many high profiles involved, I'm glad it won't be me dealing with the clean-up.

Janet and company will have to round up the Senator's friends and his aide, offer them deals and a quiet retirement with no benefits, fines or light sentences and this mess might get washed clean."

"They would have to move fast and shut it down even

faster. What are the odds?"

Felicity sighed deeply as Ace returned the SUV to the shadows where they had found it. She left a thick envelop in the glove compartment before she got out. She walked quickly to the jet and strapped in still contemplating the situation.

Taranda had heard everything that had gone down in Fulton's bedroom. The smooth operation showed that Felicity, Ace and Cam had done this kind of scene before.

Fulton's answers had disgusted her. He knew what he had been doing when he sold out his country. How much money was enough? He had so much already. And the others? So many willing to look the other way.

She headed home without retracing their route. Ace and Felicity stayed in the seats behind her, neither speaking. Cam was as silent, only reporting any nearby aircraft she could avoid. They stopped once at another field to exchange the jet's call letters. It was early morning when Taranda finally landed.

It was impossible not to think of everything she had heard tonight. The complications. The stealth. The interrogation and the death of the Senator and the need for the steps that Felicity had taken. She couldn't see a way out. She wondered if Cam or Ace did. What about the others?

Felicity's comments had painted a picture she didn't want to consider but knew there was more than a grain of truth in what the boss had predicted.

No one spoke as they exited the plane. Benny was awake and waiting for her when she opened his door. She walked into his arms, very glad he was there. For the first time in her life, she didn't mind someone knowing she desperately needed to be held.

CHAPTER TWENTY-NINE

"I don't like it at all," Ace said flatly when Felicity explained her plan.

"Those bastards are going to get no jail time, nothing but a few slaps on the wrist fines, loss of the moneys they were paid and retirement from public life with no benefits. We are at mid-term elections. Political figures and judges are being targeted with threats, media attacks and there have been deaths already."

Felicity was tired right to the bone. She didn't like her solution either but it was the only way she could see that would prevent an open scandal that wouldn't be resolved for years, if at all, and would, most likely, create enough public outcry that people would die.

"Even if they went to trial, we both have lived long enough to know that the chances of convictions are next to nil. There are enough loopholes in the legal system in this kind of situation to resemble a sieve."

Ace stalked to the window to look out into the night that was almost over. "It's not right."

"No. It isn't right. What is right now? We have politicians playing to the media like they are actors in a play. There is a huge gulf between the voters and the people they elect. There is a media war between the two parties of our government. No one is winning that.

I, for one, don't want to throw gasoline on that bonfire. That doesn't count the lies and misrepresentations of facts that are flying around like gunfire in a madman's hands courtesy of the social media."

He swung around to glare at her. "Everything you say is true but I still don't like it. But I damn well don't see a better solution. Your idea is the best shot we have of cleaning up this mess."

He sat down beside her, facing the computer that would connect her to her contact. "Make your call."

"You're sure?" She didn't need his answer but she wanted it.

"Yes."

He laid his hand on her jean clad thigh, joining them

while Emmalina connected with Janet and filled her in on the situation. The recorded transfer of the information Fulton had given them confirmed everything that Felicity had told her.

"That tight assed son of a bitch," Janet swore when she finished listening to Fulton's own words answering Felicity's voice distorted questions.

"There is no damn quiet way out of this fucking mess. Shit! Shit! Shit!"

Felicity appreciated the woman's temper, frustration and disgust but she really wanted the night to be over. She desperately wanted a hot shower to scrub away the layers of the filth through which she had waded to get the information that Janet was cursing.

For the moment of Andre's call to warn her about a file that should never have been created, she and her people had done nothing but wade through political filth. She had never felt so dirty in her life.

"I may have a solution," Felicity said when Janet finally ran out of curses and words.

"You have got to be kidding. There is no way out of this. Three deaths this close together is bad enough even though there is no visible common thread between them. Now you are dumping seven more traitors on the list, all but one of them high profile government officials in the House and the Senate. The only way it can get any worse is if the President himself was involved."

"There may be an answer if you will listen."

Janet found a new curse for what could have been. "Go. Just don't tell me it is wholesale murder."

"It isn't."

Felicity outlined her plan carefully, step by step. Janet stayed silent as the complicated idea unfolded.

"Holy shit!" Janet breathed when Felicity finished. "Every one of them deserves prison time but you're right. The chances of them getting it is the first cousin to zero. The scandal and the possible civilian insurrection resulting from that factor is worse than having all seven of them dead on the steps of the Capitol."

"Can you sell the idea to your superiors?"

"At least four of these names are dirty words in my circles. On principle, I don't like the idea at all. On the reality side, it is the only thing that might work. I like the irony of using the midterms and the mood of the country as a selling point on the plan." She laughed without humor.

"Remember, keep my name out of this. Your idea. And no ill-considered file detailing one second of tonight hanging out in cyber space for some hacker to find."

Silently, she added, *I don't want to correct that kind of mistake again.*

"I am not that damn stupid. If it works, I may end up

running this department."

Janet sighed roughly. "I am going to wake some people up early. Since I'm up before dawn, they should be too. Give me a contact so I can update you."

"I'll see it in the media."

"You know I will protect you."

"Tech is always going to be vulnerable, easily hacked. I don't take chances."

"I know. I shouldn't have asked. It seems crazy to say thanks for this fubar you have dumped in my lap but I do thank you. Six wrong politicians and one smug assistant won't be so safe and smug in the next few days because of you. So, thanks."

Felicity disengaged the call. Ace reached for her hand and pulled her to her feet. When she leaned against him, he held her close. Once he had been alone and, now he wasn't. Neither of them would be again.

Whatever had been or would come, he was with her for the long haul. Brutality had brought them together. She understood him as no one else had or ever could. It was a gift that he would never take for granted.

"Tonight, truth wins," he said roughly.

Her head against his beating heart, she sighed deeply. "We're wrapping it in lies."

"To serve the greater good."

Felicity looked at him. He looked as tired as she felt. He stood with her, in the dark and the light, the blood and the triumph. Because he did, she could wade through the filth and the lies to find answers. He was with her even when only dark gray solutions filled with more lies were the best answers.

"You can live with that?"

The fact that she could see that he did accept her solution was a truth she had never thought to have in her life.

"We both can. We are in a war. Sometimes, lies are the best weapons to find the truth, to protect the truth so that the battle can be won."

He kissed her, not with passion but with acceptance of who and what she was.

"Right now, my truth is I am tired to the bone and I want a hot shower and you naked in our bed."

She laughed when she hadn't thought she had any humor in her. "Now that you mention it, that sounds perfect. It has been one helluva day."

EPILOGUE

Ace rolled over in the bed and found only empty space where there should have been a warm woman. He sat up, very aware that the bedroom held no one but him. There was only one other place Felicity could be at this predawn hour. Four whole days to decompress after dumping Fulton's mess into Felicity's contact's lap.

Without bothering with a robe, he walked naked to the secure room. He heard the sound of female voices, one with a New Jersey accent.

Felicity didn't pause in her comments to her contact as she turned her head to smile at him.

Janet's voice filled the room.

"Fulton's aide was the most difficult to handle. She kept

holding to her story that she'd had no idea what the Senator was doing. She was adamant that the fifty thousand that had appeared in her bank account was a bonus for her work," Janet reported, her disgust evident.

"Nice work if you can get it," Felicity drawled in a best New Jersey style. "So, did the senators and the representatives take the deal?"

"All of them jumped at the retirement offer when they were confronted with the evidence you had gathered. The first two of them got so green around the gills that I wasn't sure we weren't going to need the janitorial service to mop the floor of the interrogation room after they threw up everything but their toenails. They were the youngest of the four and the least experienced."

The idea of them being that scared was a very small down payment on what they deserved as far as Felicity was concerned.

"Then I hit them with the charges we would be filing. Fortunately, Allen, my partner in the interviews, shoved a waste basket under the nose of one or we would have needed the mop. Despite the smell, I enjoyed the reaction more than I can tell you."

"Better you than me."

"Yeah, I would have liked having you sit through those minutes. Anyway, all four eagerly grabbed the alternative to doing time in prison until they realized that their funds had been frozen. Anything they had acquired with the money Fulton had given them was confiscated.

Equally, any ventures in which any of them had a part, involving any of the favors Fulton had offered had to be forfeited. By the time we finished, no one profited from anything involving Fulton and his dirty political games."

She laughed bitterly. "I wish you could have heard them object. They squealed like I had hold of their balls and was twisting them tighter with every word.

It was music to my ears and even more music when they realized they wouldn't receive any benefits for retiring either, including medical insurance. They didn't see that one coming."

"Welcome to the real world," Felicity, in the guise of Emmaline, commented.

"Oh yeah. In spades. Three of them are going to discover the joys of a very tight budget. That trio, according to our forensic accountants, enjoys living above their income. Next to no savings and mortgages on everything but their too perfect teeth."

"What about book deals and speaking engagements? Those possibilities are almost a given."

"Not going to happen. I thought of that too and so did my bosses. There is a big, very legally outlined gag order in the deal for every one of them. One word to the media in any form will result in a trial with the kind of details that will ruin whatever is left of their lives."

"Did they believe you?"

"Oh, yeah especially when our lawyers laid a confession in front of each of them. No signature. No deal. We had them by the short hairs and they knew it. Treason is not a petty crime no matter what side of the aisle you are on."

Janet sighed audibly. "I owe you Emmaline. We all do. If there is ever anything I can do, you have my number."

"I'll remember. I take it your bosses are pleased."

"I would say relieved that there was any kind of solution to this fubar."

"How are you handling the resignations? One at a time?" Felicity hoped that wasn't the choice. There were too many pitfalls.

"No. My bosses don't want these people in office one second longer than they have already had. Three of them are old men as you know. They are going to be resigning this morning because they have gotten so many threatening emails and letters, so much negative social media feedback that they want out of public life completely. They fear for their families as well as themselves.

They will be appearing in a joint televised announcement later this morning eastern time. It was decided by those above me, to take advantage of the current mood of the public and give it a meaning that I personally think is very ironic.

The fourth will make a surprise announcement this afternoon because, she, too, has been inundated with hate mail. Seeing the old guard walking away prompted her to withdraw as well. She still has children at home and a husband trying to hold a regular job.

The assistant isn't going to make any kind of announcement beyond her sadness about Fulton's death and her need for personal time before she decides what to do with the rest of her life."

"That is definitely going to cause an avalanche of media coverage."

"It gets even better. Gordon is out of the picture although no one knows that yet," Janet said quietly.

"We set the scene just as we discussed. There will be an internal cover-up when the details of her death are confirmed. Her party won't want the salacious aspects of her sex life to reach the media especially with the frenzy of the two-party resignations in play.

With luck and the right spin her death will be little more than a footnote, maybe a home invasion gone wrong or a stalker. My bosses intend to let that play out through party channels. Let them clean up the mess."

Ace moved to the mini frig to extract two sodas. He really wanted something to drink. Justice was being done but not in the courts and not with truth.

It was too early for liquor. A nice bourbon might have washed the bad taste out of his mouth. Cold caffeine would have to do. He popped both tops and set one on the desk beside Felicity.

She reached for it with a look of gratitude. After a sip, she asked, "What about Everly?"

"He was picked up by his regular driver two days ago. Two hours later after hearing his own voice detailing his activities for years, he faced my boss with no defense.

Our accountants had found every one of his properties, his accounts, his stocks, his cars, his boats, his island. We locked down everything thanks to the information you provided.

When he realized what he was losing, how deeply we had dug into his life, he tried pushing the patriot doing his job angle. He needed the moneys he confiscated for his people. That didn't fly for obvious reasons."

"He must have been really shaken to try that reasoning."

"I wish I had been there even as a second chair. The lawyer got that position. Again, a signed confession, a massive gag order then retirement with no benefits.

Late yesterday, he informed his boss that he had a family emergency that necessitated him leaving immediately. His request for retirement was granted. Because of the importance of his position, an interim replacement has already been appointed to handle his job.

The good news is that his department is low key enough that the media frenzy probably won't extend in his direction. Special elections will have to be held for the departing congressmen so that will help keep his leaving low profile.

Who knows? The group resignations may be a much-needed wake up call to the public haters and to the politicians who think they are beyond accountability to those who vote for them. Party lines have over taken the people's choices."

"Maybe you ought to run for office," Felicity suggested.

"I'm not that stupid. Politics right now is more dangerous than the work I do," Janet said flatly. "You run."

"What have I ever done to make you think I'm interested in politics. I can't think of a worse life."

Janet sighed audibly. "Considering the filth that I have just waded through, I agree completely. Don't forget to tune in to the show this morning at nine. I want you to see the results of your work even though you won't ever get public credit for it."

"I'll make it a point," Felicity replied before she disengaged the call.

She leaned back in her chair and took a second sip of her soda. "What do you think?"

"I think we do damn good work, publicly acknowledged or not." He tapped his can to hers in a toast.

"Our team does damn good work thanks to Andre's tip. Let's get dressed and head to the dining hall for a really early breakfast. I'll contact everyone involved and let them know that their presence is required in control at nine. All except Jonah and Nelson since they are back at the Ranch. They can watch virtually. We'll bring everyone up to speed and watch the media circus perform. Not necessarily in that order, depending on the commercials and the talking heads' face time."

Ace laughed as he got to his feet. "Sounds like a plan."

Felicity grinned as she keyed her systems to background mode. Today would start with a web of cleverly disguised lies fed as truths to the media. She didn't regret one of them.

ABOUT THE AUTHOR

Why would a traditionally published author, published internationally with over thirty books in more than twenty languages and two lifetime achievement awards just to name few accolades, choose to self-publish?

If your first answer is that she has lost her mind, my answer is NO!

You'll notice the capital letters. Film stars regularly finance and produce their movies and movies of other stars. Why can't authors choose to produce their books, leaving behind the traditional format for the freedom of writing what the author wants and when the author wants to write?

I haven't lost my mind. I've gained by creative freedom. Writing is more than a career for me. It always has been from the moment I ran out of books and decided, for my sanity's sake, to write a story while I waited for more books to arrive. A fluke involving another writer who had just started a writing club was my first brush with the machinery that is traditional publishing.

It was supposed to be hard to get an agent. That writer thought I had talent, although she didn't tell me that at the time, and she sent my story to her agent. I sold four books that year.

I discovered that interesting word genre. Darn it. I had to write a certain way. Because I had a 'male' name and only women wrote romances at that time, I had to have a pen name. Because I wrote faster than my home house would publish a single writer, my agent sent my extra stories to other houses. Each wanted a different pen name. Hence, I have multiple pen names.

Lacey Dancer was and is my favorite. It represents a moment

in my life when I called a halt to the process of traditional publishing. I was worn out by the rules and requirements. I understood their business model and it does work for publishing in general. It didn't work for me the writer. I wanted to create real people characters, dealing with real problems. Life is too interesting to be reduced to a fairy tale.

After a discussion with my agent, I decided to quit. It wasn't the first time I made that decision. She had four of my books at the time, another series that I knew none of houses for which I worked would even consider because one of the main characters was too old to fit the profile of what they believed sold.

Unknown to me, she sent those books to a new house, one which didn't have a profile or requirements. The house bought all four books. I loved working for Meteor and Kismet Publishing. The character that no one would have considered was very popular. Her name was Pippa and her author is Lacey Dancer.

When Meteor was sold to its biggest competitor, I decided for family reasons to retire from writing. I missed writing too much to stay retired. Computers, the internet and social media arrived and opened doors to new ideas and ways to publish.

I love a challenge and I really like breaking new ground. Is it easy? Absolutely not. There are more questions than answers some days.

For me, this new world of publishing is tailor made. I make my own rules, write my way, stories I like with characters that drive me nuts on a good day and make me crazy on a busy day. I love what I do. I especially love the freedom of doing what I do my way.

CONTACT THE AUTHOR

International, Award-Winning Romance and Suspense author, Sydney Clary a.k.a. Lacey Dancer, has written and published over 36 books over her lifetime that have been published in 20 different languages in over 100 countries. She is working on adding 20 or 30 more to the count as well as bringing her backlist into the 21st century. During her writing career she has garnered 2 Lifetime Achievement awards from the Romance Writers of America.

Email: laceydancerauthor@gmail.com

Website: https://laceydancer.com

Twitter: https://twitter.com/LaceyTheAuthor

Instagram: https://www.instagram.com/laceydancerauthor/

Facebook: https://www.facebook.com/BooksByLaceyDancer/

LinkedIn: https://www.linkedin.com/in/Lacey-Dancer-Author

YouTube:
https://www.youtube.com/channel/UC_WljciDF3CCXtGLic11M9w

Pinterest: https://www.pinterest.com/laceydancerauthor/

Goodreads:
https://www.goodreads.com/author/show/362798.Lacey_Dancer

OTHER BOOKS BY THIS AUTHOR

The Live Oak Series

Live Oak is a real place. Small towns all over the country are struggling to keep their way of life and heritage intact and still survive in the 21st century. That is the background for the Live Oak Series, but the characters are the heart of the stories, their struggles, triumphs, and solutions to the twists and turns in life. Live Oak in my fictional world is filled with challenges and triumphs.

Every character in this series is fictional. Except two. Those two are Jennifer and Tina who appear in books three and four. These two friends of mine talked me into putting them in the story. We made a deal. Each had to create her own physical description. Each will have her own book. I am working on Jennifer's now.

A stalker sneaks into town to kill. Country justice comes in the form of an irate donkey named Jay.

A city woman who needs her lattes and shoe stores discovers the misadventures of tractors and barnyard animals that have no idea when to shut up in the morning. Normal people do not wake up at dawn.

The construction crew arrives to build a vision of the future for Live Oak. Mother Nature has other ideas with a hurricane on the east coast and a bomb on the west coast.

Add in a child escaping terrible abuse and neglect, a cranky judge, a sheriff who heads the local country band, and a wounded veteran who is not going to give up and the plot thickens with every book.

That doesn't count the three weddings to date and two more in the future.

Chase the Fire - Book 1

Playing with Fire - Book 2

Strike the Fire - Book 3

Catch the Fire - Book 4

Light the Fire - Book 5

The Pippa Series

Pippa, an aunt, a friend, a writer. Following rules, unless they are her own, is so not on her agenda. She writes and values her solitude. Birthdays, specifically hers, are not to be celebrated. Have a permanent man in her life is a complication she can happily forgo. However, her relatives and friends might just need a little help in finding a life partner. And she loves a challenge.

Tragically injured, hiding from the world, her niece. Lorelei is the first to discover how ingenious a loving, determined woman can be. Pippa issues a challenge. The doctors are positive Lorelei will never walk again. Pippa dares Lorelei to prove them wrong. *"Come live with me and rebuild your life. Needing a place to recover, Lorelei accepts the challenge."*

When a workaholic male appears in the neighborhood, Pippa takes his measure and makes her plans. The impossible becomes very possible.

Pippa decides that her plans worked so well with Lorelei, she really must do something about her nephew, Jason. The Iceman faces the frozen wasteland of his life as Pippa adroitly maneuvers him into meeting Diana Diamond. Diana shuns the spotlight and Jason lives for it. Opposites are so much fun to match, especially as the sparks fly. Yes, she definitely has her hands full with these two but she is up for the challenge.

With two successes to her personal credit, Pippa decides on a trip, a thirteen-day cruise. Wow, Lilah is like a wounded creature, hiding from the media, shrinking from the least contact. Pippa reaches out even as she is discovering her own match in Joshua Luck.

Joshua is stunned at the woman who challenges and entices with every word, every move. Following her thought processes is like chasing a rabbit on steroids. Pippa is like no woman he has ever met. She makes her own rules, delves into lives, meddling, and arranging with such heart it is impossible not to admire her tactics even as he deals with his reaction to her.

She makes the rules, breaks the rules, and dares everyone with whom she comes in contact to reach for their every wish and dream. The bigger the challenge, the happier Pippa is. Impossible is a word she doesn't recognize, and no is a word she ignores.

What's a man to do with a woman like that? Marry her? Spend his life wondering what she will do next? Who will she decide needs her special matchmaking touch?

Choices – Book 1

Diamonds and Ice – Book 2

The Truth Series

Felicity Ramsey could be anyone. Your best friend? Your worst enemy? She moved through the shadows without making a sound, no warning given. She was a hunter. She had been taught from the cradle how to seek her prey and make the kill. She hated killing but she killed. Her prey was the monster who could escape the law, could hide in plain sight from justice.

Evidence and alibis could be manufactured. Governmental lines could become borders over which the law could not pass. The monsters were many. She was just one. But there were more. The human weapons trained and formed by governments to fight wars with no real winners. Men and women who could not forget the lethal skills they had learned and reenter the world that they had fought to protect.

Skye Farm and Skye/Sea were born, created on her own private mountain. The Farm was home and haven to those lost warriors who no longer had a place in civilization. Their skills and training were sought and valued by the government and the private sector.

Secure on her mountain, Felicity sought the monsters the law could not catch or exact retribution. She worked alone until one man; Ace Faulkner faced her in a room with a friend beaten to near death lying on the floor between them.

Ace had a choice. Shoot to kill? Or holster his gun?

Felicity had a choice. Trust the man? Or save the woman at her feet?

One choice made. Two guns laid aside to save a life.

Two loners, working together.

An expected phone call on a line that no one should have, creates a threat to everything that Felicity has built, the Farm, the Ranch and all those who work and live on her three mountains. A code 'blue' thrown over all of Skye/Sea. An infiltration by foreign interests in Washington, an accidental death of a loved one of one of their own has created more questions rather than answers.

In the air, on the sea and on the land, the teams gear up to protect their home and find the traitors in their government who profited from their acts of treason.

Truth Kills – Book 1

Truth Tells – Book 2

Truth Wins – Book 3

BOOK BY SYDNEY CLARY

Are you facing the task of care for an aging relative, a child or loved one through a serious illness? This book is a real-life approach to handling the multitude of problems that crop up each day.

In your home, in a care facility and all the variations of caregiving locations, there are ways to help those who matter to you and help yourself survive the stress and strain of caregiving.

- How to wait in waiting rooms.
- How to find a new location for your loved one when the present situation no longer meets the needs of your relative or friend.
- How to handle medical insurance.
- How to handle home care.
- How to resolve problems with medical staff.
- How to get bills paid.

There are answers to these issues and many others, real-life answers that work. Need an idea or new avenue for that dead-end you are facing as a caregiver.

The goal of this book is to provide those answers, those suggestions. Examples of use are in every chapter, real people dealing with problems and solutions. Some will make you smile; some will make you cry but each will show what can be done as you face this demanding and rewarding task in your own life.

Caregiving: Real Life Answers

BACK BOOK LISTING FOR LACEY DANCER

Only available at used paperback book outlets*(enhanced and revised)

Single novel

Sunlight on Shadows (1991)

Baby Makes Five (1992)

Starke-McGuire

Silent Enchantment (1990) – Re-released and enhanced titled – Choices*

Diamond On Ice (1991) – Re-released and enhanced titled – Diamond and Ice*

13 Days of Luck (1991)

Flight of the Swan (1992)

Forever Joy (1993)

Lightning Strikes Twice (1993)

His Woman's Gift (1993)

Many Faces of Love (2003)

St. James Series

Silke (1996)

Caprice (1996)

Leora (1996)

Noelle (1996)